T0353366

THE SHADOWS
OF GOD

Greg Keyes was born in Meridian, Mississippi, to a large, diverse storytelling family. He received degrees in anthropology from Mississippi State University and the University of Georgia before becoming a full-time writer. He is the author of the 'Age of Unreason' tetralogy, as well as *The Waterborn*, *The Blackgod*, the *Star Wars* 'New Jedi Order' novels, *The Briar King*, *The Charnel Prince* and *The Blood Knight* – Books One, Two and Three of 'The Kingdoms of Thorn and Bone'. He lives in Savannah, Georgia.

Novels by Greg Keyes

The Chosen of The Changeling

The Waterborn

The Blackgod

The Age of Unreason

Newton's Cannon

A Calculus of Angels

Empire of Unreason

The Shadows of God

The Psi Corps Trilogy

Babylon 5: Dark Genesis

Babylon 5: Deadly Relations

Babylon 5: Final Reckoning

Star Wars®: The New Jedi Order

Edge of Victory: Conquest

Edge of Victory: Rebirth

The Kingdoms of Thorn and Bone

The Briar King

The Charnel Prince

The Blood Knight

GREG KEYES

THE SHADOWS
OF GOD

BOOK FOUR OF

THE AGE OF UNREASON

TOR

For Steve Saffel,
Del Rey Books

First published 2001 by Del Rey,
an imprint of The Ballantine Publishing Group, New York

This edition published 2013 by Tor Books
an imprint of Pan Macmillan, a division of Macmillan Publishers Limited
Pan Macmillan, 20 New Wharf Road, London N1 9RR
Basingstoke and Oxford
Associated companies throughout the world
www.panmacmillan.com
www.toruk.com

ISBN 978 0 230 77227 4

Copyright ● Greg Keyes 2001

Introduction 'What Has Gone Before' copyright ● J. Gregory Keyes 2002
Excerpt from *The Briar King* by Greg Keyes copyright ● J. Gregory Keyes 2002

The right of Greg Keyes to be identified as the
author of this work has been asserted by him in accordance
with the Copyright, Designs and Patents Act 1988.

All rights reserved. No part of this publication may be
reproduced, stored in or introduced into a retrieval system, or
transmitted, in any form, or by any means (electronic, mechanical,
photocopying, recording or otherwise) without the prior written
permission of the publisher. Any person who does any unauthorized
act in relation to this publication may be liable to criminal
prosecution and civil claims for damages.

The Macmillan Group has no responsibility for the information provided by any author websites
whose address you obtain from this book ('author websites'). The inclusion of author website
addresses in this book does not constitute an endorsement by or association with us of such sites or
the content, products, advertising or other materials presented on such sites

A CIP catalogue record for this book is available from
the British Library.

This book is sold subject to the condition that it shall not,
by way of trade or otherwise, be lent, re-sold, hired out,
or otherwise circulated without the publisher's prior consent
in any form of binding or cover other than that in which
it is published and without a similar condition including this
condition being imposed on the subsequent purchaser.

All Pan Macmillan titles are available from www.panmacmillan.com
or from Bookpost by telephoning +44 (0) 1624 677237

Contents

CONTENTS

Acknowledgments

Thanks to the editing team—Veronica Chapman, Martha Schwartz, Betty Harris, Melanie Gold, and Alix Krijgsman, who managed things. As usual, Terese Nielsen provided a wonderful painting, which Min Choi and art director Dave Stevenson transformed into a terrific cover. Thanks to Nell Keyes, Kris Boldis, and Ken Carleton for giving me their impressions of the manuscript.

What Has Gone Before

In 1681, in his laboratory at Trinity College, Isaac Newton discovered Philosopher's Mercury, the key to matter and energy, and from this discovery came a flood of inventions.

Heatless alchemical lights brightened the night streets of London and Paris. Aetherschreibers sent messages instantaneously around the globe. Kings and princes commissioned terrible new weapons with which to fight their wars.

And in Boston, a young man named Benjamin Franklin sought his destiny. Not happy as his brother's printing apprentice, Ben longed to study the scientific. He read and dreamed in his spare time, and through his studies, he found a way to modify an aetherschreiber to receive not only the messages intended for it, but also to eavesdrop on any that might be floating in the aether. He fell into correspondence with an unknown mathematician, one striving to complete a complex calculus equation. Blinded by his love for science, when Franklin saw the solution to the problem, he shared it immediately.

A continent away, Adrienne de Mornay de Montchevreuil was also searching for her path in life. Not content with the roles available to her gender, her forbidden love for mathematics found a release when she became secretary to the philosopher Fatio de Duillier. De Duillier was employed by Louis XIV, the absolute monarch of France, and his work was of an urgent and secret nature.

Though Adrienne never understood—or much cared about—the purpose of the research she was participating in, when a mysterious correspondent on the aetherschreiber offered her part of the solution, she immediately saw the implications and made practice from theory.

Thus together, Benjamin Franklin and Adrienne de Montchevreuil solved a mathematical problem and changed the world as profoundly as Newton had.

Each independently concluded that they had given Louis the XIV the weapon he needed to end his war with England. Each raced desperately to stave off disaster. Ben sailed to England, in hopes Sir Isaac could help. Adrienne turned to the dangerous intrigues of the French court.

Both failed.

Using their calculations, the philosophers of the Sun King pulled a comet from the heavens and obliterated London. But they hadn't foreseen the full consequences of their actions. Much of Europe was also devastated, plunging western civilization into a new dark age.

Ben was in London, apprenticed to Sir Isaac, when the comet began its fall. Seduced and kidnapped by Vasilisa Karevna, an agent of the Russian tsar Peter I, he watched in helpless horror as the center of the English Empire was destroyed. He lost a brother, many friends, and his innocence.

Adrienne—whose quest brought her to the very bed of the insane King Louis—lost much more; her true love, Nicolas, her virginity, and her hand. Then, in the aftermath of the comet, she made yet another discovery—she was with child, the child of Louis XIV.

Moving behind the bright world of matter, other forces were at work. In the spaces between atoms, certain beings who did not want humanity to possess the secrets of alchemy—beings who had subtly guided the course of human history—now began to be less subtle. However, unable to work directly in the world of matter, they used human agents to achieve their ends, posing as angels, demons, or djinni. The cataclysm precipitated by Ben and Adrienne was ultimately of their design, and they planned more damage to humanity.

Newton called these beings the malakim, naming them for the angels of the Old Testament.

The malakim moved carefully, offering their aid to certain philosophers, plotting the deaths of others.

Rescued from Karevna by Newton, Franklin continued his apprenticeship with the great philosopher, whose work had turned entirely to a science of the malakim. Adrienne, too, was seduced by their power. Her missing hand was mysteriously replaced with the hand of an angel, enabling her to see the very structure of the aether and of matter—and to alter it as she saw fit. Gradually, she became more sorceress than mathematician and learned that the malakim, too, were torn by strife. One of their factions desired to suppress humanity's search for knowledge. The other sought the absolute extinction of the race.

Meanwhile, the world plunged further into turmoil. Driven by ever-harder winters, Tsar Peter built a fleet of airships and embarked on a quest to conquer the weakened nations of Europe. Across the Atlantic, a Choctaw shaman named Red Shoes joined with the Sieur de Bienville, the pirate Edward Teach, and the Puritan minister Cotton Mather in an expedition to discover what had become of the Old World.

All were drawn together in a battle for the city of Venice. In that battle, Ben watched as Adrienne was forced to kill Isaac Newton. And for Adrienne there was another tragedy—her infant son, Nicolas, was kidnapped by the malakim.

Adrienne found a new home in Russia, as a philosopher in the court of Peter the Great, and Benjamin returned to the American colonies to settle in the city of Charles Town, South Carolina.

For ten years, an illusory calm prevailed. The Russian Empire, foiled at Venice, instead pushed eastward, across Siberia to the western shores of America. In Saint Petersburg, Adrienne attracted students and sycophants and built ever-more terrible weapons for the Tsar. Benjamin created a secret society to keep the Americas free of the influence of the malakim.

But this calm was not to last. Red Shoes, the Choctaw shaman, followed signs into the great western plains and found an army on the march, an army composed of Russian, Mongol, and Native American troops, led by the mysterious and powerful Sun Boy. In Charles Town, Ben confronted the sudden appearance of James Stuart, the Pretender to the English throne, come to claim the American colonies as his rightful kingdom. Ben quickly discovered that Stuart was backed by Russian submersibles and troops. After making the knowledge public, Ben fled Charles Town to a wilderness fort, where he and other leaders of the English colonies met with James Oglethorpe, the Margrave of the renegade colony of Azilia, with various Native American leaders, and with a band of free Africans known as Maroons. They determined to resist the Pretender and any other continental power that threatened to extend its influence in the New World.

Ben then set off for New France, through the territory of the powerful Coweta tribe, in hopes of winning both the French and the Coweta to his cause. On reaching the Coweta, he discovered that the Pretender's men had already arrived by air under the leadership of a malakim warlock named Alexander Sterne. Captured by the Coweta, Ben faced torture and death until rescued by his ally Don Pedro of Apalachee.

In Russia, the tsar mysteriously vanished, and Adrienne found herself facing a hostile new leadership and an even more hostile church. Assembling her students and soldiers loyal to the tsar, she set forth to discover Peter's whereabouts. In doing so, she discovered the secret invasion of North America, and worse, that its leader—the Sun Boy—was her own lost child, Nicolas. She also found that the philosopher Swedenborg had invented dark engines capable of allowing the most powerful of the malakim to wreak havoc in the world of matter. Facing one of these engines, she could do nothing more than flee, for no science or spell in her possession could affect it.

Tsar Peter, meanwhile, a captive of his own lieutenants, escaped them with the aid of Red Shoes. He vowed to regain control of his nation and end the war. Guided by Red Shoes, a Wichita man named Flint Shouting, and a former pirate named Tug, the Tsar set off for New Paris.

On the journey, however, Red Shoes was forced to fight a powerful malakus, and in defeating it became corrupted by its power. His companions watched in horror as he murdered the people of Flint Shouting's village. They escaped Red Shoes, continuing alone.

This did not concern Red Shoes, for in his power-driven madness he had conceived a new agenda—the destruction of the world and the making of a new one.

From the aether, the malakim guide their army and marshal their dark engines, bent on destroying the last bastion of resistance to their plans—New Paris.

Prologue

Dimitry Golitsyn watched the eye of hell slowly shut.

"Why? Why send it back?" he asked, though the sight of the thing, even as it diminished, made him tremble. It was now half the size it had been, a great black cyclone with a heart of crackling white fire. His airship, the *Elisha*, was poised high above that terrible eye. Around and beyond, the plains of America stretched away, rolling and bare as the steppes of his native Russia.

"Because it is not yet time," Swedenborg's detached voice answered.

"No. That makes no sense," Golitsyn snapped, fingering his mustache nervously, watching the storm shrink further. "The dark engines work. You've proved it. We should send them ahead of us, lay waste our enemies from a distance."

"It is not yet time," Swedenborg repeated, turning his face toward Golitsyn. The prince shivered again. The sorcerer's face was framed by wild, unbound hair; and he wore a pair of oculars that made him look like some sort of a blind insect.

"Professor Swedenborg, with all due respect, I am the commander of this expedition in matters military. I need a better explanation than that. Why should I waste the lives of my men or trust our untested Indian and Mongol troops when we have *that*?"

The eye was nearly closed. Where it had passed nothing remained but white ash. Tens of miles of ash. No tree, no living thing, not even bones were left to tell that once there had been life where Swedenborg's dark engine had churned.

For answer, the sorcerer merely turned away, lost in whatever he saw behind those thick lenses.

Golitsyn leveled a frustrated gaze on the third person clutching the bow rail, the metropolitan of Saint Petersburg.

"Your Grace, speak to him. Get some sense from him."

The priest pursed his lips and stroked his long gray beard. "What is there to say?" he asked. "Swedenborg has the angels. The blessed saints speak to him, not to me. It is as God wills it. But he has shown me glimpses—" The metropolitan shook his head. "It is too much for mortal man, even for the patriarch. That is why Swedenborg is mad. But it is a holy madness."

"Everyone is mad," Golitsyn exclaimed. "I am mad. I've betrayed my tsar and led an army into the wilds of America, for what? It's all lunacy."

The metropolitan raised an eyebrow. "Neither I nor Professor Swedenborg had anything to do with that. You did what you did from lust for power, not from any desire to serve God. Swedenborg's motives are pure. My motives are pure. Yours have never been, and so it is not your place to question us."

"But how can you be sure? How can you be sure this—this *boy* we bow to is really the child of God and not the devil? What is our purpose in this limitless desert? What care we for the American colonies, when we could have the empire of the Turk at our feet, the riches of China?"

"How can—" He broke off, for Swedenborg was looking at him again. The professor was a soft-spoken, polite, gentle man, and yet the words that now issued from his mouth were clipped and grim, almost another voice altogether.

"Prince Golitsyn, you do not, cannot, comprehend what lies ahead. I can. The American colonies are the last refuge of the godless science. It is where the devil has dug his cave and built his watchtower. It is where he crafts his hideous strength into knives and guns. We are the chosen, the servants of the prophet, the champions of godly science. What more do you need to know?"

"And yet we consort with the ungodly," Golitsyn argued. "What is godly in the gibbering idolatry of the Mongols or the pagan superstitions of the Indians?" He turned to appeal to the metropolitan. "Surely, Your Eminence—"

"All will come to God," the metropolitan said. "Though they be pagan, still they have eyes to see. They recognize the prophet for what he is. Indeed, it seems that everyone but *you* sees that truth."

"I—" Golitsyn's mouth went dry. Behind Swedenborg, something had appeared. It was the shape of a nude man, a silvery, translucent cloud. It had no face as such, but it had eyes everywhere. They winked and blinked on its palms, arms, belly, thighs. Pale blue and green eyes, all watching him, all seeing the darkness in his heart.

The thing leveled an accusing finger at him, but it was Swedenborg who spoke. "Stay on the path, Prince Golitysn. The apocalypse is done, and the world is ended. Now is only the sorting of things. All souls that do not follow me are damned. The prophet is my servant. Swedenborg is my mouth. The metropolitan is my text. I thought you were my sword. If you are not, I must forge another."

Golitsyn dropped to his knees. "No. No! I am yours. I just don't understand why we can't use our best weapons, why we must keep them in reserve."

"Because something remains," Swedenborg replied huskily. "Something needs to be found. When we have it, there will be no need of the engines at all."

"Then why—why—"

"You are a sword, Prince Golitsyn. Be content with that."

It was a command, not a suggestion.

"Yes, my lord," Golitsyn replied, and bowed again.

Tsar Peter the Great dipped his paddle in the water and gave an exclamation of pleasure as the canoe slid into the stream.

"It's good to be on the water again," he said. "I've always loved ships, great and small."

Behind him, the broken-nosed giant named Tug grunted vague disapproval.

"You don't share my love, sir?" Peter asked. "I thought you had been a sailor."

"Damn sure I was, Peter." He grunted. "It may be a fine life if y'r lord o' the ship 'n' all, but f'r a common sailor, 's more 'n half misery. An' rickets, and scurvy, and the black belly-ache. An' when you finally come ashore, they sell you watered rum and poxy whores. No, sir tsar, it's no life."

"To each his own. I love the swell of the sea, the feel of a boat. When I was building my navy, I myself went in disguise to the shipyards in Holland and learned the shipwright's art, working as a common laborer."

"Well, we clean fergot t' christen this'n when we stole 'er from the Tonicas. Y' got a name f'r our lady?"

Peter thought for a moment. *"The Catherine,"* he said softly, "for my late wife."

The third man in the boat, an Indian named Flint Shouting, said nothing but sullenly dipped his paddle in the water, propelling them along.

They camped that night on a sandy natural levee, and Peter and Flint Shouting built a fire with the sticks at hand while Tug searched for more wood. The Indian went about his task with quiet efficiency. He was a changed man. When first the tsar had met him, he had been a boisterous, talkative fellow, always quick with a laugh and a joke. Now, he might go days without speaking.

"Why are you still with us?" Peter asked him, poking at the fire. "I know you care little for us."

Flint Shouting didn't answer at first, and after a time Peter didn't think he would.

"I did not always like the people of my village," he finally said in a surprisingly weary voice. Peter thought there ought to be anger there, or hatred, but it seemed to be mostly just exhaustion. "But they were *my* people. They did not deserve to be rooted up and burned like weeds. And I brought their killer to them. I smiled, and I told them Red Shoes was a fine fellow, and they let him into the village. And he killed them all."

"I understand that," Peter said. "I understand the need for revenge. I thirst for it myself. I have many debts of my own to settle."

Flint Shouting nodded. "I will kill Red Shoes," he said softly. "To kill him I must find him. Red Shoes is a Dream Walking, and I am not a magician. I cannot see him. He leaves no tracks, breaks no branches, bends no grass. I cannot find him." He looked up at the tsar and met his eyes squarely. "But one day Red Shoes will find *you*. And Tug. And then I will kill him."

Peter didn't flinch at the icy promise. After all, he, Peter Alexeyevich, had sent the heads of his rebellious Strelitzi guard rolling in the snow. He had ordered his own son knouted to death. However many men Flint Shouting promised to kill and then made good on, it was unlikely he could match Peter's own record.

He clasped his hands together. "I already knew you wanted to kill him. I already knew why. I just wanted to know why you hadn't left Tug and me to do so. So tell me—you say Red Shoes is a Dream Walking. What does that mean? What happened to him? He was once our friend, I would swear it. He saved my life. But your village . . ."

What had happened at Wichita village was no worse than other things Peter had seen. But he had never seen a whole town murdered by a single man.

Peter was no stranger to the scientific beasts that fools called angels, devils, and spirits—many had pretended to serve him, and his philosophers often showed him their experiments with them. But none had ever made him feel as he had when he saw Red Shoes stride through the huts, leaving flame and death behind him, twisting the necks of children and dogs. Something had prickled at Peter, beyond sight, sound, and smell, some sense that knew a kind of fear that the tsar himself did not.

"I don't know what happened to him," Flint Shouting said. "I said I am no magician. Maybe a spirit ate him and walks in his skin. Maybe he was always a monster in human disguise, and fooled us for a time. I don't care."

"But you saw what he did. If you are no magician, how will you kill him?"

For a moment, Flint Shouting's devilish old smile raced

across his face again, and years fell from his features. "Carefully, Tsar. Carefully." Then the frown returned, and he poked at the fire.

That seems to be the end of that, thought Peter. "How much longer before we reach New Paris?"

"That depends. I don't know. A few more days, a month. I don't know this river or its people very well."

A crash in the underbrush was Tug returning.

"I reckon that'll be enough," the big man said, dumping an armload of wood near them.

"As warm as it is, we hardly need a fire," Peter commented.

" 'Squitos. Wolves. Snake birds. Fire'll keep the bad things back. Well, some of 'em."

"I was just asking Flint Shouting how far New Paris was."

"Y' got me. I wish we'd get there, though. It's been too damn long since I had me a drink an' a woman."

"Watery rum and poxy whores?"

"Now I'd settle for a piss beer an' a one-eyed grandma." Tug grunted. "I reckon we'll get there in a couple o' weeks, if we get no trouble from the Natchez. Last time me an' Red Shoes went there, we were pretty welcome. Without Red Shoes . . ." He shrugged and looked sorrowful. Peter knew that Tug and Red Shoes had been friends for a long time. But Tug had seen the same things he and Flint Shouting had. "An' what'll you do?"

"Me? Petition the French king. Raise an army. Take back Russia."

"That same song?"

"It's what I have to do."

"Why?"

"Because I am the son of Alexey. Because I am tsar. Because I took a nation that was nothing and made it the greatest in the world, and I will not be denied my place in it by warlock usurpers." He paused for an instant. "Because they killed my Catherine. Because they took my ships."

"Well," Tug said after a moment, "New Paris ought t' be fun, then. Me trying to find a lay that hain't a bowlegged crone, you tryin' to raise an army—I don't know which of us dreams the bigger."

Peter chuckled, and they began to talk about what they might find to eat.

Part One

THE DESIGNE OF
THE APOCALYPSE

Consider also the designe of the Apocalypse. Was it not given for the use of the Church to guide and direct her in the right way, And is this not the end of all prophetick Scripture? If there is no need of it, or if it cannot be understood, then why did God give it? Does he trifle?
—Isaac Newton,
Introduction to a Treatise on Revelation

1.

New Paris

Benjamin Franklin crouched low on hands and knees, pressing his face toward the ash gray soil. The forest surrounding him chirped, clicked, and hummed lazily in the soggy noontime heat.

A sudden rattling in the branches made him look up, for the forest had proven deceptive, these last few months. Sleepy it might be, but it dreamed of panther, Indian ambush, rattlesnake, and the corpse of Benjamin Franklin.

But it was only a flight of green parakeets, settling into a live oak. For the moment, the forest was not trying to kill Franklin. A Spaniard, this forest: disdaining to do much of anything between noon and three o'clock. So this was a good time to pry at the land's secrets. Franklin knelt a little lower, wishing the Coweta hadn't taken his hand lens when they tried to torture him to death. He needed it now. He continued his work with squinting eyes, sat up briefly, scribbled in his book, then peered back at the dirt.

When he heard the footsteps behind him, it was too late. Or would have been, if it hadn't been a friend.

"Reading our futures there, Sir Wizard?"

Franklin didn't turn. "Hello, Voltaire," he said, the belated tingle of alarm fading. "They fascinate me. Look at them."

The Frenchman crouched beside him, his long arms folded on narrow knees, a merry grin on a face that was mostly pointed chin. "I take it you mean the ants?" he said.

"Of course. See here, how they form a train to supply their city? I followed this one back—it goes to the corpse of an opossum, some twenty yards in that direction. For ants, that

11

would be a distance of leagues, I should think. And here—
these that so fiercely guard the citadel when I threaten it. Like
guards or warriors."

"By 'citadel' I assume you mean this little mound of
earth."

"Yes. But, again, if you give an ant the stature of a man,
how impressive does his mound become?"

"Modestly so if size is the only quality you note. Even so, it
would be only a very *large*, uneven, unlovely mound of earth.
Nothing to be compared to, say, the Louvre or the Sistine
Chapel."

"The ants do not build to impress you, my friend. Given
our relative proportions, which would have more space for
living and working? This mound, with its tight-packed tun-
nels, or the Sistine Chapel, with its vaulted ceilings—space
mostly wasted in vain grandeur? The ant's eye is all toward
efficiency."

"Ah. They are perhaps German, then, or English. There are
no French ants, I suppose?"

"Butterflies I suppose to be French," Franklin replied
good-naturedly. "Fireflies and lacewings."

"Would that you were right." The philosopher sighed. "But
it was no horde of butterflies that laid waste Europe, no
lacewing that left that hole where once London was."

"No, I suppose not," Franklin said absently. He bent to
watch two ants meet. They seemed to exchange information
of some sort, then scurried off purposefully.

"No empty greetings or pleasantries, I'll wager," Franklin
murmured, "no small comments. It's all business with them.
The food is *there*, danger is *here*, the south tunnel needs
repair."

"You admire them, then?"

Franklin looked up at last, his brow furrowed slightly.
"They interest me. Each time we stop, I try to find one of their
cities, and indeed they are everywhere. It is not so much to
say, I think, that below our feet, scarcely noticed, is an empire
we are all but unaware of. Seen from the right prospect, the
world could be said to be ruled by ants."

"Yes? And yet now that you have brought them to my notice, I could destroy their great city there. I could bring this outpost of empire to naught."

Franklin dusted his hands on his breeches and stood. "Four days ago we passed over ground still smoking. Everything green was burned, and all four-footed things had either fled or succumbed. I found ant cities there scorched black by what must have been terrific heat—and yet they were there. Knock down a mound, and it will be refurbished in the space of a day or two. And then there are the million cities elsewhere, scattered over all the world. For all our greater size and knowledge, I can think of no way we could destroy the race of ants, not utterly."

"Now I see your studies have a more than theoretical bent," Voltaire said. "Who do you liken to the ants—mankind or the malakim?"

The very word still sent a tremor through Franklin. He wished his old mentor, Sir Isaac, had named them differently— from the Latin or Greek rather than from the Hebrew. The latter held too much of the fear and fire of the Old Testament.

But then, the malakim *were* fear and fire.

"We are their ants, I think," Franklin replied, "living beneath their heels, usually unnoticed. Occasionally *we* notice *them*—and worship them as gods, angels, or devils. And occasionally they notice us in turn and grind us beneath their heels."

"But never all of us, no more than we could grind out all the ants. Is that what you're saying?"

"They've failed until now. But we haven't learned the trick of setting the ants against each other, to pit one city against another and send warriors to the deepest chambers of their catacombs. But the malakim seem to have perfected the science of turning man against man. There are men happily inventing more ways for those aetheric devils to kill us every day."

Voltaire nodded. "The malakim seem quite determined to exterminate us. More determined than I should be to destroy the kingdom of ants."

"Perhaps if you had been stung enough, you would have a different opinion. I've heard that in the Amazon, there are ants that march as an army and can strip clean a living man in a few heartbeats."

"The ants turning the tables and destroying the man? Would that *we* could be such ants, then, so we might pick clean the bones of our unseen enemy," Voltaire commented. "For—"

"God's sake, are you two at it again?"

Franklin and Voltaire turned to face the new speaker, a handsome fellow with flowing auburn hair, dressed in buckskin breeches and the shabby remains of a burgundy justaucorps.

"Hello, Robin."

Robert Nairne leaned against a tree, folding his arms. "The world is all at war, with the angels themselves against us. We wander starvin' in the wilderness, blood-lusty Indians at our heels, and you fellows are talkin' philosophy t' worms an' such."

Franklin shrugged and grinned. "The mind is an insatiate master—it demands substance even when the belly has none."

"My poor brain has enough to chew on, trying to figure ways to help us come through this alive," Robert commented dryly.

"And right well you do at it," Franklin said cheerfully. "But between you, Captain McPherson and his rangers, and Don Pedro's braves, that's all well covered, I trust. I don't know how to follow a trail or find fresh water, and you've seen me hunt! I'm best used thinking of our higher problems."

"So, have the crawlies told you how to defeat all the armies arrayed against us, with our thirty-odd stout fellows?"

"They certainly give me ideas," Franklin replied, feeling a bit defensive despite his oddly buoyant mood. After all, Robert was right: any sober and sincere thought proved their situation to be a few leagues south of hopeless. And yet . . . yes, Franklin was hopeful. There was no problem that human ingenuity could not resolve. How could dwelling on the negative help them?

Or worrying—say, about his wife, Lenka.

That thought must have changed his expression.

"What?" Robert asked.

"I was just wondering how the war is going. How Lenka is."

"She was well, when I left her," Voltaire said.

"I thought I charged you with keeping an eye on her," Franklin said.

"She's quite a woman, your wife. She can look after herself. *You* were the one who needed rescuing—we were all agreed on that." He paused. "She did feel you neglected her by leaving her behind."

"I nearly got her killed once. I thought it was safer for her to stay back there. I hope I wasn't wrong."

"If I had a woman like that, I would let her make her own decisions."

That stung a little, and Franklin felt a sharp reply in his throat, but he swallowed it down. He wouldn't let his worry and shame speak for him.

"What's done is done. When we reach New Paris, God willing, we will find an aetherschreiber to replace the one the Coweta took from us, and I shall discover how she fares. Until then, I try not to worry. Hope is better tonic than despair."

Robert nodded agreement. Then his gaze went past Franklin, and he suddenly drew the pistol at his belt, perhaps forgetting he had neither powder nor shot.

Franklin turned to follow his friend's determined and worried stare, and saw that the forest was a lighter sleeper than he had hoped.

Franklin, Robert, and Voltaire stood on a small, grassy field, surrounded by mixed cane, brush, and a few lone oaks fringing a forest of enormous pine. Franklin saw the sun glint off steel, and his vision adjusted. In the tall cane crouched men, at least six of them, possibly many more. Indians, the long barrels of their muskets level to the ground, aimed at Franklin and his companions. And these fellows, Franklin was willing to bet, were well supplied with powder.

"What do we do?" he whispered.

"Nothing, if they want us dead," Robert replied. "They have us fair."

"Are they Cowetas? Would they follow us this far?"

"They might. But there is no lack of Indians in this country. They come out of the earth, like this damned cane."

"Or your ants," Voltaire added.

"Perhaps we should call for our companions," Franklin said.

"You wandered some distance from them in your scientific curiosity," Robert said grimly.

"What then?"

"You're the ambassador," Voltaire suggested. "Parley with them."

"Ah. Yes." Franklin licked his dry lips. "Well, I suppose they know we're here already. Robert, put away your weapon. It's useless anyway."

"They don't know that."

"They know you can kill no more than one of them, and probably not that at this range with that popper. Put it away."

Robert did so reluctantly.

Ben stood a little straighter, showing his empty hands.

"Hello there!" he called. "Who do I have the pleasure of addressing? I am Benjamin Franklin, appointed representative of South Carolina, and I am on a mission of peace and diplomacy."

There followed a nerve-racking pause but finally a shout came back from the thicket.

"Parlez-vous français? Je ne parle pas anglais."

"Oui, un petit peu," Franklin replied. *"Je m'appelle Benjamin Franklin, de Carolina Sud—"*

"You are in Louisiana," the fellow replied, still in French. "That is very far from Carolina."

"I've come to treat with the French king," Franklin replied. "I have the papers to prove it."

Another hesitation, and then the voice said, "Come forward, you." Franklin could see the man now, gesturing with his hand. He wore a blue French coat, but his features looked Indian.

"I'm coming," Franklin replied.

"Hold there, Señor Franklin!"

Another man had emerged from behind them—also an Indian—a silver crucifix bobbing at his throat, a rapier hanging jauntily at his side, and barbaric tattoos decorating his exposed flesh.

"Don Pedro!" Franklin exclaimed gladly.

"The same," the Apalachee chieftain replied. He jerked his head toward the Indians in the brush. "What do those skulking scoundrels want?"

"I'm not sure," Franklin admitted. "They speak French."

"Yes?" The Apalachee cleared his throat and called out in that language. "I am Don Pedro Salazar de Ivitachuca, prince and Nikowatka of Apalachee. Stop hiding, you rascals, and face me like a man."

"There are but four of you," the man in the woods replied. "Lay your arms on the ground or suffer the consequences."

"You should take your own advice," Don Pedro replied, and snapped his fingers.

Suddenly, on all sides, the forest began to move as Apalachee warriors seemed to appear magically from behind every tree.

"Much as we despise it," Don Pedro called, "the Apalachee, too, can skulk. And now, my friend, it is you who are surrounded and outnumbered."

Another long pause, and then the French-speaker stood. "The French king will mislike this behavior on his own lands."

"Take us to him, then," Franklin called back. "That is all we ever desired. Won't you come shake my hand and let us have peace between us? What sense for this warlike behavior, when we are not at war?"

"In these days, everyone is at war," the man replied. "But I am coming."

He emerged from the forest a moment later. Seeing him more closely, Franklin guessed he was half Indian, for his features owed strongly to the European. He wore a silver gorget at his throat and carried an officer's smallsword.

Beneath his blue coat, his flesh was bare, save for the flap of a loincloth.

"I am Henri Koy Penigault," he said, when he drew near, "captain of the king's march guard and war captain of the Mobila. Stand your men down, and I will escort you to New Paris."

Franklin clasped his hand. "Captain Penigault, it is a great pleasure. We feared you were Coweta, for they have been trying to murder us since before the last new moon."

"Well, we have that in common at least." Penigault grinned. "An enemy of the Coweta might be a friend of mine. Shall we meet and smoke together?"

Franklin remembered the last time he had smoked the pipe of peace, how near he had come to losing the meal in his belly. But at the moment, his belly was quite empty.

"I would be delighted," he lied.

After the smoke, however, there was brandy and freshly slain venison, and most fingers came off triggers and sword hilts. Franklin and Voltaire sat around a fire, along with Don Pedro and James McPherson, the rugged captain of the Southern Rangers, regarding Penigault and his chief men across the wavering flames. They were a mixed bunch, French and Indian and one Negro.

"My father was French," Penigault said. "My mother was Alibamon. I was schooled in New Paris, but I prefer to live here on the frontier, with my mother's people. We keep the borders, as I told you."

"Thank you for the brandy. I've never tasted the like."

"Good, yes? We make it from persimmons and wild plums. Now, tell me of your adventures with the Cowetas. We are eager for news of them, and of the Carolinas. We hear little these days, what with the war."

"I'll want to know what you know of the war," Franklin said. *Is my wife alive? But they couldn't know that.*

"Not much," Penigault said. "The English king has taken both Carolinas. The margravate of Azilia still stands, but word is for not much longer."

Franklin nodded. "The English king, as you call him, is a pretender to the throne, James Stuart. He took the seaboard colonies by trickery and with the aid of Moscovado troops."

"Moscovado?"

"Russians," Voltaire clarified.

"Ah, yes. Tsar Peter. We have heard of him." There was something in the man's voice, as if he had a secret.

"Yes, well. You may know that years ago the English colonies signed a treaty of mutual protection with Louisiana, with the Cowetas, and with the Spanish in Florida. I've been trying to unite those signatories to fight together against the Pretender and his allies. I went first to the Coweta, and from there was to continue on to New Paris, to treat there with King Philippe."

"The Cowetas are snakes. They attacked you?"

"They had already been approached by emissaries from the Pretender. They outstripped us, you see, for they came on a flying craft—"

"Shaped something like a great leaf and gliding like a buzzard?"

"Yes. You've seen it?"

"We have. We thought it was a lightning hawk—a creature of legend, a sort of demon that eats children."

"You were not far wrong in that. Their craft is engined with a demon of sorts. In any event, they had already struck a bargain with the Coweta king, and he determined that we should die by torture. But my good friend Don Pedro prevented that."

"Praise God, not me," the Apalachee said, sounding nevertheless quite pleased. "It was our Lord gave me the strength and the foresight to rescue you from the heathens." He hunched forward. "I assume, my friend, that you are a baptized man?"

"I am," Penigault acknowledged.

"Then God has delivered us back to Christian lands, as I knew he would."

Penigault acknowledged that with a tilt of his head. "And so you escaped the Coweta," he pressed. "Did you take many scalps?"

"I do not brag," Don Pedro said, "For He-Who-Sits-Above saw it all and knows I tell the truth. I took four scalps myself, and would have taken many more, but it was not for me to risk glorious death that day but to make certain I survived, to deliver Mr. Franklin to his destiny. I see that clearly. We are engaged not merely against the English king or the Russian tsar but against the very forces of hell, and those deceived monarchs merely twitch like puppets for them. Our true enemies are not flesh and blood, but are the damned spirits that ride the wind at night and by day stay hidden in black clouds that crawl in the spaces beneath the world, shunning light."

Penigault, whom Franklin had reckoned a pragmatic sort, suddenly shivered and crossed himself. "The dark things stir," he said. "It is well known. The accursed beings walk amongst us. Old men have died, eaten from within. Strange warnings and signs come from the west, where demons dwell. They say the house of the dead has opened up and the damned come to take all our souls. Is this true, Mr. Franklin?"

Franklin drew his brows together, wondering how to explain. The malakim were indeed both the angels and devils of superstition, but they were more than that. Moreover, science had proved them real, and it rankled him to hear them spoken of in these medieval terms, just as Newton's biblical appellation rankled.

A soft voice spoke from beyond the circle of light.

"It is true."

Franklin peered out and saw faintly red-glinting eyes. Penigault gasped. "A sorcerer."

"Please join us, Mr. Euler," Franklin said.

A young man stepped into the light. His mild eyes, now blue, surveyed them all. "I am Leonhard Euler, gentlemen, and I am at your service."

"You are accursed," Penigault said. "I saw your eyes!"

"I was once accursed," Euler said. "I was a warlock of the malakim, a pair of human hands to work their mischief. But I am no longer their tool."

Penigault looked to Franklin for confirmation.

"So he claims," Franklin told the Louisianan. "I once doubted him, but he has been a friend to us. Without Mr. Euler, we would all be dead or captive back in Charles Town." *Which does not mean I trust him,* Ben finished silently. His brother had been killed by a creature like Euler, and that sort of thing was hard to turn his back on.

"Thank you, Mr. Franklin. Those are kind words."

Penigault switched his regard back to Franklin.

"And you—you are a wizard, they say. The wizard of Charles Town."

"I've been called that. I am a man of science, which is the most useful form of wizardry."

"And can you stop these night-goers?"

"Not alone. But with allies, and the spirit of many peoples—yes. I believe I can."

Penigault nodded. "I hope you can convince the king, then. I do hope you can."

"You don't sound optimistic," Voltaire noticed.

"There are reasons I prefer the marches," Penigault said glumly.

"There she is, fellows," McPherson said, "France in America—New Paris." The ranger's voice held a note of good-natured contempt that Franklin hoped Penigault and his fellows didn't catch. After all, Penigault had not only guided them through the silty maze of the lower Mobile River but had obtained the canoes they now traveled in.

Franklin mopped his brow, grimacing at the slimy sweat that seemed to somehow ooze up from the river itself. He peered ahead to see what the ranger found worthy of his disdain. Not that he was expecting much. The last several leagues had taken them past villages—Indian, European, and Negro—more squalid and impoverished than any he had seen in the interior. While some of the *habitants* halfheartedly tilled wilted fields of corn, more came wading into the river, begging for food and brandy—especially brandy.

But even thus introduced, even with expectations lowered,

to call the town he saw ahead "New Paris" required a breath-taking amount of wishful thinking.

The muddy shores sloped up from the bay, and houses, scarcely distinguishable from the Indian habitations he had grown accustomed to, spilled down to the water and even walked on stilts to mingle with dilapidated docks. At one long stone quay were moored a sloop, a frigate, two brigan-tines, and a ragged collection of canoes and pirogues—which, for all he knew, was the sum of the modern French navy. Beyond, south, he could see the squat form of Fort Condé commanding the mouth of the bay. It, at least, looked sturdy, though Franklin knew his eye for such things was questionable.

As for the city itself, the mud huts did give way to larger, more impressive dwellings as the eye tracked farther from the shore. And surmounting all of this was a truly ... if not grand, at least bizarre structure. It looked like some idiot madman's attempt to construct a chateau. Never in London, Prague, Venice, or anyplace between had Franklin ever seen such a rambling monstrosity, half built of timbers, half of stone, decked in places with a mishmash of columns and tow-ers that even to his untrained eye seemed completely wrong.

But, by God, it was *big*.

"Mon dieu!" Voltaire exclaimed. "It is a parody of Ver-sailles itself!"

"I hope the real one looks a bit better," Ben said.

"The real Versailles was in questionable taste, I'll grant you, though doing such questioning aloud once was a faux pas of the Bastille sort. Next to that—that thing—however, it was sublime." He cocked his head. "Who rules here? Do you know?"

"The last I heard it was Philippe VII. Does that explain anything to you?"

"The former duke of Orléans? No, it doesn't explain much to me. He was a strange little man, flighty, not given much to serious matters, but not known for such dramatic bad taste ei-ther. He was a lover of science, though."

"Perhaps that would explain why the upper tier of the

palace is crusted with those glowing gargoyles," Ben said. It was almost dusk, and the pale pink glow of alchemical light was clearly visible, both in the castle and outside.

"Here come the gunboats," McPherson said.

"Let me talk to them," Penigault said. "I'll explain who you are."

Franklin turned a wary eye on the approaching craft. "Sterne and his cronies have been here for almost a month. He's had plenty of time to poison the well, as he did at Coweta. I hope we fare better here."

"It does feel a bit stupid just walking in," Robert added by way of agreement. "Sterne is a persuasive warlock."

"And a murdering one," Franklin said. "But what else are we to do? Skulk about? That will never get us a meeting with these French. The only way to do it is to be bold. Still, it's been nice knowing you fellows, should anything go wrong."

"And if it don't?" McPherson asked.

"Then you are the smelliest bunch of blockheads I've had the poor fortune to share a canoe with," Franklin replied. That got a few nervous laughs.

He glanced back. Don Pedro and his Apalachee warriors filled two more boats, which was comforting, though Franklin doubted that their increased numbers would matter much here.

"Voltaire, you say you know this duke somewhat."

"I've met him."

"How do y' suppose he would take to Sterne and Sterne's King James?"

Voltaire offered a Gallic shrug. The journey had taken pounds from him that he could ill afford, and he looked almost like a scarecrow in his muddy justaucorps. "Louis XIV, his uncle, was always kindly disposed toward the pretenders to the English throne, as they were thorns in the British backside. He supported both James' conquest of Scotland, and was supporting it still when the comet fell. Orléans and James used to sport a bit, though I seem to remember they also had some argument over a certain mistress. As I said, Philippe never had much of a political head on his shoulders—what with the way things have gone, I'm very much surprised he has *any* sort of a head on his shoulders, much less any fraction of a kingdom to rule." He repeated the shrug. "I'm sorry. I cannot say."

"Will he remember you?"

"If he does, I'm not sure it would be with favor. I was exiled from France for writing a satire of the court at Versailles—which he seems to have satired here quite a bit better than I ever did."

"Ah. Well, you should be able to help us with our manners, at the very least."

"Always count on me for the very least."

The gunboats drew up, and French marines in blue justau-corps called a challenge. They were armed with what looked like Fahrenheit guns.

Penigault spoke rapid-fire French, and tired as he was, Franklin had trouble following it.

He saw the result though. The marines snapped up their guns and fired.

2.

Faith

With a thought and a motion of her hand, Adrienne de Mornay de Montchevreuil warmed the water in the tub to almost boiling, then drew the screen that separated it from the rest of her cabin. She started working at the fastenings of her gown, absently gazing out the window. Her ship flew on, level with the clouds, and through one of those clouds, half obscured, she saw the *Dobrynya*, another vessel in her aerial flotilla. It looked like a large, flat-bottomed man-of-war, save that instead of mast and sails it was borne aloft by eight glowing red globes, prisons for the ifrit who pushed against the pull of gravity. She stopped at the fifth button and raised her right hand, the one given her by the angel Uriel. For an instant the ships and clouds vanished, replaced by lines of force and attraction, the aetheric patterns behind the mask of matter.

The ifrit were well, her people on the other ship safe. That was good.

She pressed her face against the glass, extending her sense farther into the aether. *Where are you, my son?*

She felt him, like a slender strand unraveled from her dress, being pulled from far away. Wherever he was, he did not hear her now.

Someone scratched at her door.

"Who is it?"

"It's me—Crecy."

"Come in."

Crecy was a tall, slim redhead. Her hair was drawn back into a long queue with a black ribbon, and she was outfitted in the blue-and-silver justaucorps, waistcoat, and breeches of Adrienne's personal guard. She was, in fact, the captain of it.

"Have I come at a bad time?"

"I was going to take a bath," Adrienne replied. She reached up and took the comb from her hair, so her black locks tumbled to her shoulders. "Is it important?"

Crecy shrugged. "I came only to wish you a happy birthday."

Adrienne blinked in surprise, then smiled. "It is, isn't it? I had forgotten. I'm—what?—I'm thirty-two today."

"Not that you look a day of it."

"How courteous of you. I feel it, though."

"Youngster," Crecy muttered. "Here. Do something with this." She held out a small package.

"Crecy! What's this nonsense?"

"Just take it, please, and no hysterical protestations."

Adrienne took the small, linen-wrapped package and unwrapped it, then stared at the contents with a surprise that left her speechless. Her throat tightened.

"This—this is the first treatise I ever wrote, when I was eighteen."

"Indeed, 'Monsieur La Monte.' "

"They would not publish it under a woman's name," Adrienne murmured. "Where on earth did you find this?"

"In the library in Saint Petersburg, of course."

"But why?"

Crecy stepped near and looked at her earnestly. "To remind you, Adrienne, of who you are."

A shiver went through Adrienne, head to foot, and a tear threatened in the corner of her eye. "Veronique!" She sighed. "I needed that more than any present I could imagine. How do you always know?"

"I don't. I wish I knew more often. I was lucky, this time."

"Well, thank you." She opened the book and thumbed through the pages, smiling at sentences she had forgotten even writing. "Thank you," she repeated.

"It is nothing."

"How is everything?" Adrienne asked, gently closing the volume.

"No mishaps, if that's what you mean. Your students are eager to see you but understand the ordeal you are recovering from."

"Hercule?"

"Hercule is as well as can be expected, considering he lost his mistress and his wife all in the same month. But he is still able, still capable. Still Hercule."

"I should never have let our affair continue for so long," Adrienne said softly. "He should not have been the one to have to break it off."

Crecy didn't say anything. It was not a comfortable topic, the affair with Hercule.

"And Irena?" Adrienne went on. "How goes the search for her killer?"

"I believe it was her secret lover, but I can find no evidence of who that was, none at all." She paused. "Many still think *I* did it."

"What nonsense."

"Even Hercule thinks it," Crecy said.

"Well, I do not. I never did," Adrienne replied. "But it would be best if we could find the real killer, to set such talk to rest."

"Of course." Crecy looked down at her feet and cleared her throat. "Well. I shall leave you to your bath, Adrienne. And happy birthday."

Adrienne caught her by the arm, leaned up, and planted a kiss on the redhead's cheek. "Thank you, Veronique. It is no wonder I love you so."

Crecy smiled and then reached to steady Adrienne as the ship tilted.

"We're descending," Adrienne said. "I wonder why."

"I shall discover it," Crecy promised.

"Wait," Adrienne replied, fastening her buttons again. "I'll go with you."

* * *

Elizavet Tsarevna squealed in delight as the musket in her arms kicked and belched black smoke. She staggered, but she did not close her eyes at the flash of powder, and her aim was steady. She was Tsar Peter's daughter, that much was clear. A piece of his fierce heart beat in her chest.

What effect her shot had was more difficult to tell. One of the great beasts fell, but a hundred other bullets whizzed into the mass of flesh and hair beneath them, and any one of them might have knocked it down.

Elizavet, however, was certain. "I killed it!" the dark-haired young beauty shouted jubilantly.

Adrienne congratulated the tsarevna absently, transfixed by the scene below. The airships were cruising only a few tens of feet from the ground, and the massive humps of the *buffle* seemed almost within arm's reach. Once beyond the western mountains, America was flat as a board, with no hills to run aground on or in which to hide enemy artillery, but still it seemed unsafe to be so close to such a herd.

Adrienne had seen a buffalo before, in Louis XIV's menagerie, when she was his mistress. She had been impressed by the size and savagery of that first bison. But she could never have imagined so many thousands, never extrapolate the din of their hooves pounding the earth like an immense drum, the furious bellowing that turned birds in the sky. The crack of one rifle or a hundred meant little to such a living earthquake.

Elizavet, whooping, took a fresh musket from a servant and fired again.

"God makes strange, powerful things, doesn't he?" said a man on her left, his own dark eyes also wondering at the spectacle. He nearly had to shout, even from a few feet away, to be heard.

"Good day, Father Castillion. Indeed he does," Adrienne shouted back.

The Jesuit flashed a bright-toothed smile and shook a lock of his gray-streaked chestnut hair from his eyes. "Look at you!" he exclaimed. "You look just like that little girl in my mathematics tutorial, when I presented a new problem. Never daunted or puzzled—just quietly excited."

She couldn't deny it, though his observation made her feel suddenly frivolous.

"Ah, I said something wrong. Look how your face transfigures. Surely you are allowed to enjoy yourself now and then."

"I do not know that I am. I have little time for distraction."

"Time enough, surely, to remind yourself of what you fight for? That the world is a beautiful place, worth saving?"

Surprised, she studied his lean face for signs of irony. "Are you serious?" she asked. "That does not sound like a Jesuit talking. Shouldn't you be preparing me for God's kingdom to come, rather than urging me to love this one?"

"This *is* God's kingdom, or one of them. I cannot believe He made it beautiful merely to tempt us."

"Again, quite unjesuitical."

He grinned wryly. "I'm fairly certain that if I were to return to Rome now—and open my mouth—I would be a Jesuit for no longer than the tick of a watch."

"You've lost your faith?"

He scratched his chin thoughtfully. "When I was in Peking, my order was embroiled in a debate with the emperor. In fact, it wasn't much of a debate—the Chinese emperor is absolute, and when he says his final word on something, it *is* final. My order, however, had difficulty accepting this, and so brought the matter up again and again. The argument had to do with conversions and pagan rituals. The emperor, you see, cared not in the least if we made Buddhists into Christians— but he insisted that the rituals of obeisance to the throne continue, even for Christians. He said they were secular, despite their clear religious content. He was inflexible, but we argued it with him every few years. I think the emperor saw more clearly than we, for, despite their pagan origins, the purpose of those rites *was* secular—to bind his subjects to him. We Jesuits could not admit it because that might be to allow that we Christians have the reverse problem: we pretend that secular ceremonies—the crowning of a king, for instance—spring from religion. It made me wonder: How much of religion arises from social necessity?

"The thought festered in me until it produced a more terrifying one. I wondered how much religious ritual arises not from faith but to disguise the *lack* of faith? Like a child repeating, 'It *is* true, it *is* true' to convince himself."

"An uncomfortable thought."

He nodded. "And they aren't new thoughts, of course—indeed, in theology they are sophomoric. And yet the sophomoric is often true, yes? To me, the things I saw and heard in China proved to me that I had never had faith but only a *desire* for it and a fear of being without it. The very strange thing—another of those powerful and strange things, you see—is that I did not lose my faith—I *achieved* it. Abandoning my pose of knowing God, I came to truly know Him. So I believe, anyway."

"Then perhaps you can tell me where He is in all of this?" Adrienne asked. "His angels are loose in the world without any governor, and it is impossible to distinguish between those angels fallen and those still in grace—if there ever was a distinction. Monstrous things tear at His creation, destroy His beauty, and war is everywhere. I cannot see God. Where is He?"

For an angry instant she thought Castillion's answering gaze contained pity, and so she nearly told him to go to hell, if he still believed in it. But then she realized that his eyes reflected something more complex, with no hint of condescension in them. He tapped his chest and then, carefully, hers. "He is there," he said. "You cannot see Him—that would defeat His purposes, I think. Spectacles make Him no more visible than the naked eye, nor telescopes nor microscopes nor that fabulous hand of yours. It is the mistake that Newton and other philosophers in his vein made—to think that in dissecting the universe they would at last find God. God is not to be seen; He is to be felt."

She drew back from him a step, staring at him with new suspicion. Not long ago, in a dream, she had heard nearly those same words, spoken by a creature who claimed to be Sophia, the mother of angels. Was this really the priest who had taught her so many years ago? Or was he more than he seemed?

And so she raised her right hand and *looked*, peeling away the gauze of matter that covered Father Castillion, dissecting him in just the way he had just been complaining about, revealing the ghostly etching of the vortices and secret knots that bind the world. She saw nothing unusual there, no hidden ifrit or angel.

But she no longer had faith in her power. What she saw with her hand came from Uriel, an angel she did not trust— who might not even be alive, for she had not heard from him since the battle of New Moscow.

Castillion hadn't noticed her reaction or her deep glance. He was still preaching, looking not at her but at the distant skyline. "Some things we see may reveal God, however, by opening our hearts. You feel nothing when you see that?" He gestured at the vast herd. "No joy, terror, awe, worship? I do, and I think you do, too. I said you looked like a little girl just now. Is it not said that only coming as a little child shall we find the Lord? That is what I mean. Mademoiselle, when I lived as a Jesuit, I never once felt like a child."

Something in that lodged in her throat and pressed behind her eyes. With that foolish suddenness she had avoided for many, many years, her eyes filled with tears. She looked away, to hide it from him, but he would not be fooled. He took one of her hands and squeezed it. His hand was warm and rough, and it felt good. She felt foul for having doubted his humanity.

"Do you still hear confession?" she murmured.

"I do not," he replied, "though I am willing to talk of anything you wish. Your confessions do not need me for God to hear them and forgive."

"It is not forgiveness I need. It is advice."

"I offer whatever I have, but I will not pretend to perfect wisdom."

"You know by now we are searching for the tsar."

"I know you follow the prophet and his army," Castillion said cautiously. "I know you think the tsar may be a prisoner." His brow wrinkled. "But there is more to it. You want to talk about the boy, the prophet."

She nodded. "When I met you, you said you believed that this 'prophet' was the Antichrist, come to destroy the world. All of that is written in the Bible, yes? If we are to believe the Bible, this time was bound to come—God ordained that it should. And yet just now you exhort me to save God's beautiful world. But if God Himself desires that it be destroyed, what point in striving against Him?"

"Ah. I was unclear. I spoke in the language of the Bible, but I did not mean it literally. Revelations is a much disputed book, and for good reason. I do not trust it. Even if I did, I must trust all of it, yes, including that proviso that no one can predict when the end will come. No one. And, in terms of the signs, I am not aware that most of them have been fulfilled. What I meant was, this prophet *supposes* he is the Antichrist and *intends* to destroy the world."

"Then you think he should be stopped."

"That thing at New Moscow—*Angelos keres,* you called it, after the Greek spirits of death? It was an abomination. If the prophet was responsible for that, he must be stopped, yes. We are God's instruments in that."

"Why does God need 'instruments'?"

"I don't know. Why do the devils need armies and sorcerous engines? I do not deny that God is mysterious, Adrienne. It is His nature." He cocked his head. "What is this about? Ostensibly, your expedition hunts for Tsar Peter, who vanished while visiting his wayward American province. But I've heard many on these fabulous flying ships whisper that you will join battle with the prophet and his army."

"It is my intention to confront him, yes. I do not know if I can fight him."

"Why?"

"Because he is my son."

Castillion blinked, pursed his lips, but nothing came out.

"You see my dilemma?"

"How can this be?" He slipped his hand from hers, clasping it with his other, as if he were washing them.

"He was my son by King Louis, and he was stolen from me when he was but two years old. For ten years he has been lost, and at times I thought him dead. Instead, I find that they have *made* something of him. Something dangerous, as you say. We approach him—I can feel him more strongly each moment. The pictures in the chapel in New Moscow showed the prophet—I know it is Nicolas. I know it is my son. If I must kill him to save the world—I cannot."

"Then there must be another way."

"I don't share your optimism, Father."

"You ask for my opinion. I do not think God would ask that of you. I think it is a clue that there must be another path."

She shrugged. "Do you know what a certain angel told me about God, Father Castillion?"

"I would be very interested to hear it."

"He told me that to create the world, God had to remove Himself from it—that to form the finite, the limited, He must in that sense limit Himself."

Castillion's brow furrowed in fascination. "A very old heresy," he murmured. "The gnostic heresy. It claims that the God of the Old Testament is really Satan, in disguise."

"Exactly. Not being able to enter the world, God sent angels to do His bidding. Once free of His immediate command, they began doing as they pleased."

"And an angel told you this?"

"One of the aetheric beings who style themselves angels, at least."

"Are they, in your experience, always truthful?"

Adrienne laughed bitterly. "In my experience, they are rarely so."

Castillion considered for a moment. "I see no contradiction," he said at last. "God may be outside the world and yet present in our hearts. There must be some spark of Him in us, that we live at all."

"But if this world is—and has always been—the kingdom of the fallen angels, we can hardly expect fairness or justice. It may be that destroying my son *is* the only way."

"I won't believe it," Castillion replied evenly. "But I will think on all of this, if you wish."

"I would appreciate that, Father." She looked down again, as the ship began turning.

"We're going back?" he asked.

"For the beasts they shot. We can use the meat and skins."

"How long before we reach your son?"

"Less than a month, I think."

After loading the meat, they flew on until near nightfall and then, on a narrow river copsed about with a few trees, they landed all the ships for the first time since crossing the mountains. The soldiers found, by some miracle, enough wood for a score of fires, and soon the scent of roasted meat filled the air. Adrienne had a table and high-backed chairs lowered to earth and a pavilion erected, so that she and her officers might dine in some civility. Wine and vodka were poured.

Hercule d'Argenson, the overall commander of Adrienne's forces, lifted a glass. "To this fine beast," he toasted, gesturing at the meat before him. "In America, even the cows are bigger, it seems."

"A little gamy for my taste," Crecy remarked, raising her glass, "but a good fellow to die for our bellies all the same." Her eyes glimmered darkly, and in the firelight her copper hair and the glass of wine were the same ruby shade.

"And to the other wonders that may cross our path!" Hercule said, taking another swallow.

It was good to see Hercule in a happy mood. He smiled, and that small difference in his face pulled away the years, and she remembered when they met, twelve years before, in the ravaged countryside of Lorraine. He had always been cheerful then, full of life and swagger, a rascal and a good heart. She scarcely connected him with the brooding character he had become. And she knew that she was in large part responsible for the change.

Could she amend that? So many of her works needed mending.

She lifted her glass. "To you, Monsieur d'Argenson. For being the soul of this expedition, for seeing it through dangers none of us could have imagined. And for being my loyal friend."

That brought a strange, almost shocked silence to the entire table. Had it been so long since she had said such a thing?

Apparently. And Hercule was blushing.

Well. She could mend nothing with a single toast, but it was a beginning.

Glasses clinked, and Hercule downed all his wine. He would be drunk within the hour.

"Vodka!" Crecy called to one of the servers.

Across the table, Mikhail Sergeivich, a middle-aged artillery captain, laughed. "That's a Russian drink—not made for your French blood."

"Oh?" Crecy said. "Or is it that I'm a woman?"

"No offense, please," Sergeivich told the redhead. "You're a man in my book. You dress like one, you fight like one, you ride like one. But even a Russian woman could drink you down the river with vodka. It's what they bathe us in when we're born."

"How would this be, then, sir?" Crecy asked. "I will match you, drink for drink. If I meet Morpheus first, you will have the opportunity to learn that in no book whatsoever am I a man. If you go under first, you give me that Hungarian saber you're so proud of."

"Done, by the saints!"

"I'll go at that, too," Elizavet put in, "to show what damage a Russian woman might do."

"Then we need a fourth," Adrienne heard herself say.

"Are you volunteering, Mademoiselle?" Elizavet made no attempt to hide her astonishment.

"Indeed." She raised her voice. "More vodka for the table. Two—no, three more bottles!"

Crecy leaned so her lips were touching Adrienne's ear. "What strange wind is blowing between *your* ears?" she whispered.

"Don't discourage me," Adrienne pleaded, just as softly. "Please."

"No secrets!" Elizavet said. "And no scientific trickery!"

"Never fear," Crecy said. "We need no science against the likes of you. Have at it." And she drained her newly filled glass.

The contest quickly involved the whole table, and within the hour was essentially forgotten. Crecy and Sergeivich were arm in arm, singing some off-key song in the Russian that Sergeivich had been trying to teach them. Hercule's head was tilted back, and gentle snores escaped him.

Feeling quite unsteady but not unhappy, Adrienne decided it was time to return to her cabin before she did anything even more foolish than she had already.

On the way she bumped into three of her students, who were swaying a bit themselves.

"Mademoiselle!" said the first, a tall young fellow named Lomonosov. "It is good to see you up and about."

"It is good to be so," she replied. Or hoped she did. Her voice was a strange roar in her own ears.

"We have much to discuss with you, Mademoiselle," a young woman said. Even in the dark, Adrienne imagined she could make out the young woman's green eyes and infectious smile. She also saw that the third fellow, Carl von Linné, was standing quite near her. Had they been holding hands when she arrived? She suspected that they were lovers.

"Well, we shall begin our meetings again," Adrienne said.

"Oh, we have kept up with them. We have found something quite astonishing."

"We could even speak of it now!" Lomonosov said.

"Well . . ."

"*There* you are." Elizavet's voice came, from behind. "Monsieur Linné, I disht—dishk—*distinctly* remember that we had an appointment this evening. How can you dish—*disappoint* a tsarevna?"

"I—but I—"

"Not because of this fat little thing?" She poked a finger at Émilie.

"What?" Émilie choked out. "What did you say?"

Elizavet paid no attention to Émilie but stepped forward

and gave Linné a sharp slap on the face. Then, laughing, she stumbled back the way she had come. "No matter," she said. "There are *men* somewhere in this camp."

Linné cleared his throat. "I—"

Émilie slapped him, too, and without a word she turned and ran, sobbing.

"Oh, dear," said Lomonosov.

"Well," Adrienne said, "I think we will delay our discussion until a more appropriate time, yes?"

"Yes, Mademoiselle," Lomonosov said.

Feeling suddenly mischievous, Adrienne turned back to him. "By the way, since you seem to have lost your companions, perhaps you could ask Mademoiselle de Crecy for another fencing lesson."

She wished it were light enough to see him blush. Lomonosov was cute when he blushed.

"Good night," she said, and continued on.

Feeling a little dizzy, and fearing to lie down in such a state, she walked to the little river, hoping to clear her head. She paused to stare at the moon, huge and orange on the eastern horizon.

La loooon! she thought she heard, in the voice of a child, *her* child. She remembered showing Nicolas the moon and teaching him what to call it.

Nicolas? she asked, into the silence of the night.

I said never to call me that. You said you would call me Apollo.

"Of course," she murmured aloud, her heart skipping. "Are you watching the moon, Apollo?"

Yes. So are you.

"Beautiful, isn't it?"

Yes. Then, almost shyly, *I haven't told anyone about you. Are you still my secret friend?*

"I always shall be. What—how are you?"

A face seemed to form on the moon, features between boy and man, Adrienne's own dark eyes and the prominent Bourbon nose.

I have enemies, he replied. *Evil creatures who resist me and my heroes. But it doesn't matter. My teachers say it doesn't matter.*

"You are very strong," Adrienne said cautiously. "I saw the keres you made."

That was nothing. But he sounded proud. *I have a secret. The keres, my heroes, the great cleansing—it is all just the beginning. My great purpose is above all of that.*

"It is?"

Yes. But—but something is missing. I don't know what. I can't do it yet.

"What is missing?"

This time a sort of panic crept into the voice. *I don't know. What if—* He stopped.

"What, Apollo? You sound distressed."

What if I can't do it? They say I am the one, the prophet, the Sun Boy, but sometimes—sometimes I think they must be wrong. They know there is something missing. And I have enemies who want to kill me. And sometimes I don't think I have any friends. Not really. They say they are, but—

"I am your friend," Adrienne said. "I ask nothing of you except that you talk to me."

Yes. But you could be my enemy, nonetheless. You could be tricking me. You said you were my mother before.

The vodka wanted her to cry out that she was, that what he thought he knew was a lie. But she knew deep down that that would be the end of it, that he would break the fragile bond, as he almost had when first they spoke.

"I cannot tell you what to believe," she said softly. "If you think I am your enemy, I cannot dissuade you. I can only assure you that I care for you."

Why? Because I am the Sun Boy? Because I hold life and death in my arms?

"No."

Then why?

"Because you sing to the moon."

He didn't reply.

"Apollo?" But after a space of five minutes, he still hadn't replied.

I shouldn't have been drunk, she thought. *I shouldn't have let my guard down. I said the wrong thing.*

Her eyes clouded with tears, and she turned to go onto her ship. But suddenly a shadow sprang at her, and something hit her in the chest, very, very hard.

"Die, bitch," a man said.

Adrienne's hand went to her breast, and with dull shock she felt warmth spurting between her fingers, and her legs wobbled.

Her attacker yanked her hair back, turning her throat up to the moon.

3.

Return of the Margrave

James Edward Oglethorpe stood as still as the knobbed cypress trees that drew their dark outlines against the starry sky. He took in the thick, hot night air in small sips so the grating of his lungs wouldn't deafen him to the faint voices in the distance. His eyes strained against the moonless night, until he saw, at last, through the trees and Spanish moss beyond, the flicker of firelight.

"There," he breathed.

"I hear," whispered Unoka, the little African, captain of the Maroons under Oglethorpe's command. "I see."

"Come along, then," Oglethorpe said, "but quiet as mice, all of you."

"Listen to 'em," said Tully MacKay, his head in silhouette nodding toward the faint laughter. "They wouldna' hear Gabriel comin' wi' his trumpet blawin'."

"They have devils with them," Oglethorpe reminded him, "black-souled warlocks who can see like an owl and hear like a cat."

That sobered them all. They started off again slowly, wading through water that came up to their waists. The water was the temperature of blood, and Oglethorpe knew for a fact it teemed with leeches and snakes. But it quieted their progress, and he doubted that their foe would imagine anyone wading through half a league of flooded rice fields at night.

But he wasn't anyone. He was James Oglethorpe, and he had already taught his red-coated former countrymen some bitter lessons about warfare in the New World. And this wasn't just any rice field—it was his own property, and he knew it like he knew the lines of his hands.

He meant to have it back, and his country with it. The lightless memory of trees and Spanish moss swallowed up the firelight again, but he had them placed now, at the bend where Megger's Creek came around the little spit he had used to call Italia, for its shape.

He wondered how many foemen waited. In his band were only six—the rest of his forces were back with Captain Parmenter, across the Altamaha. Six, but six good men for night work: Unoka, with his pitchy skin and years in wilderness both African and American; three Indians—two Yamacraw and one Yuchi, ghosts in these their native lands day or night; MacKay, a margravate regular, born in the hollow of a tree during Queen Anne's war, as surefooted as a fox; and finally himself, who, though born to privilege in England, had been well educated these past twelve years.

They proceeded with less noise than the alligators they doubtless shared the waters with, came around the bend, and saw their enemy.

Ten men caroused on a sandy bank: six English, by their knee breeches and pale skin, and four Indians Oglethorpe figured to be Westo, judging by their hair. The men were reeling about a small bonfire, drinking rum or brandy from a clay bottle. With them were three women, all Indian or half Indian in look. These three bore expressions ranging from terror to fury. All were young and passing attractive, and it was clear what the men's intentions toward them were.

"Here, darlin'," one of the English grunted, thrusting the bottle toward one of the women, a pretty thing in a worn checked dress. " 'l make you more sociable." Oglethorpe recognized her suddenly—Jenny Musgrove, the daughter of an Indian trader. She had been working for Oglethorpe at his own trading station when last he saw her, and taking tutoring from his valet. His brows bent further. The Musgroves had trusted him with their daughter, and this was what had become of her: a plaything for the occupying army.

Another man was not drunk and he was not drinking, and Oglethorpe did not even think him a true man. He wore a dark green coat, black waistcoat, black riding boots, and a narrow tricorn. A basket-hilted broadsword sat propped against a tree, within his easy reach.

And his eyes glinted red in the firelight, like the eyes of a wolf.

He looked bored.

"That one," Oglethorpe said, with barest breath. "A Moscovado by his dress. But see his eyes? He'll be hellish."

"Got t'at one." Unoka grunted. The bow he had been carrying above the water creaked as he slipped an arrow in place. The three Indians bent their staves as well.

"A little closer."

The water was lower, here, only to their knees, but still enough to stop a good charge.

The Russian's eyes flashed and pointed at Oglethorpe, and he bounced to his feet as if he had a steel coil in each thigh.

"Murderer!" the warlock shouted, his English heavily accented. "In the water!"

An arrow took the Russian in the throat before his drunken companions even reacted. Then, cursing and swearing, the others went for their muskets. Two sprawled with arrows in their flesh before Oglethorpe managed to splash onto the sandy spit, but another was turning with his weapon, firing the musket point-blank at Oglethorpe's midsection. He saw the flint spark, but there was no answering flash of powder from the pan—the weapon had lost its prime. Oglethorpe hacked with his heavy military broadsword, cleaving through shoulder bone to sternum, then wrenching his weapon out. The man spewed blood and rum on Oglethorpe's shirt as he went down. The only sound he made was a gasp, but several wretched screams from his companions cut the night's peace.

Oglethorpe felt as much as heard the rush behind him, and leapt aside as a broadsword took chips from the cypress next to him. He looked up to see the Russian, arrow still in his throat, mouth set grimly. Above each shoulder stood a floating eye of flame and mist.

"God of mercy," Oglethorpe swore.

Came the warlock's broadsword again, too fast, quicker than a man ought to be able to wield one. Oglethorpe hurled himself back, and the wind from the blade parted his hair. Then he fetched into a tree, yanking his own blade up for defense.

Two more arrows appeared in the hellish creature, spun him halfway around. Oglethorpe took the moment to cut at his foe's elbow like a butcher separating a soup bone.

The arm came half off, hanging by a few tendons, and the Russian's broadsword dropped to the ground.

The warlock turned and ran like a deer.

"Damn it all!" Oglethorpe growled.

A quick look around showed the rest of the enemy already dead or captured, and no shots fired. Their screams hadn't been loud enough to carry to the house to whoever was garrisoned there. But if the hell man made it to them, the rest of Oglethorpe's foes would have warning.

So he mustn't make it. Swearing, Oglethorpe followed the warlock into the inky woods.

Following was not easy. The warlock's glowing familiars had vanished and the night had swallowed him. Oglethorpe could hear him, though, a wounded beast crashing through the brush. Inhuman he might be, but nothing injured as this creature could run a straight course. Oglethorpe followed the noise, knowing from memory that the path would soon come to the old fields near the plantation house itself. There, in the open, he must catch the villain.

Oglethorpe emerged from the forest panting heavily. A sickle moon was just reaping on the horizon, and in the pale light the sea of broom spread out before him. Farther, on higher ground, he made out the lights of the house.

But of the warlock, he saw nothing. Was he bedded down in the grass, like a wounded panther?

Sweeping his hanger before him, Oglethorpe worked frantically forward.

But the warlock was behind, still in the trees, uttering a ragged gasp of pain as he lunged from the woods, striking

Oglethorpe with enough force to send his sword spinning into the tall brush. Fear jabbed Oglethorpe hard beneath the ribs, and turned there into fury. It was an old friend, that harsh lightning that came from nowhere. It took away all concern except that he should strike and strike, until what he hit was broken or he himself cut down.

The warlock staggered away, but Oglethorpe flung himself forward again, his fingers locking around the monster's throat. In turn, the Russian closed his remaining hand around Oglethorpe's Adam's apple. Despite his wounds, the fiend was still hideously strong.

"Die," Oglethorpe gasped. "Die." Then he had no air, and could only squeeze harder. For a long moment, the only movement the two men made was a faint trembling.

And then the eyes appeared again, just in front of Oglethorpe's nose, and he knew sergeant death had come for him.

Then more blood spattered in his face, and the vise around his neck slackened and fell away. The red eyes, so near his own, still stared at him with preternatural fury as the warlock stepped back. Oglethorpe could see that an ax was buried in his skull, just above his right ear.

The Russian sank to his knees. He shook a finger at Oglethorpe, as if in accusation.

"Damn!" Unoka, darker than a shadow, stepped up and wrenched his throwing ax from the warlock's head, and the man finally fell prone. The ax chopped a half-dozen more times as Unoka cursed in his own tongue and then finally straightened, holding something vaguely pumpkin shaped.

"I t'ink he dead, now," the Maroon observed.

"Very good," Oglethorpe managed, massaging his throat. "Let's rejoin the rest, see if they managed to leave any of the Tories alive that we might question them."

They hadn't, but the women were all right. Jenny Musgrove leapt right into Oglethorpe's bloody arms.

"Margrave!" she gasped.

"There, miss," he soothed. "Are you well?"

"Well enough."

"Did they ... ?" He didn't know how to complete the sentence.

She looked down, her eyes a little dull, and he took that for an affirmative.

"Poor Jenny," Oglethorpe said, stroking her hair. "I've betrayed you." By leading the doomed Continental Army. He should have been here, with his people, not off on Franklin's errands.

"You're here now," Jenny murmured. "You'll set things to rights, won't you?"

"By God, yes," he said. "Can you tell me how many more men there are on the plantation? In the house?"

"A few more in the house, but most of 'em went to Fort Montgomery. They say to fight Mr. Nairne, who brought the army down from Fort Moore."

"How many is a few, Jenny?"

"Ten, I think."

"Ten." He almost laughed. Who was this general who had taken his house for a command center? Not the best or the brightest the Pretender had to field, Oglethorpe guessed. He turned to MacKay. "Go. Tell Captain Parmenter to cross the river by the hour before dawn and join us at my house. I'll have it back, I think."

"We took most in their beds, sir," Captain Parmenter told Oglethorpe a few hours later. "Van der Mann was wounded, but he'll live. Otherwise, no casualties."

"Good. And who did we catch napping in my bed?"

"I think you'll like this, sir."

"Will I?"

"Yes, sir."

Oglethorpe followed him into the house. It was a two-story building, not logs, by damn, but good split timbers over a stone foundation. It would never compare with his family's estates in England, but then those were destroyed, and this still stood, and he had built it from nothing. There was something good in that.

"Sir!"

He turned at the familiar voice and saw Joseph, his valet.

"Good God, man, are you well?" Oglethorpe asked.

"Well enough, sir, now that you've returned."

"You remained here? I expected you should have fled."

The old black man shrugged. "Where to, sir?"

"Well, I'm glad you stayed. And I'm glad you're well. Do you have any complaints I should take up with our guest?"

"Not so much for me, sir, but the women had some rough treatment."

"I'm aware of that. Did this general, whoever he is, take part in that obscene business?"

"No, sir. I don't think he knew."

"We will sort out who did what—and who knew what. You will help me with that, Joseph?"

"Quite right, sir."

"Good. Well—show me to my guest, will you?"

"With pleasure, sir."

He followed Joseph to the library, where the leader of the occupying force awaited. When Oglethorpe saw who it was, he uttered a sharp laugh.

"Well, I'll be damned. Bobbing John."

The ruddy-faced old man in the armchair blushed a darker shade of crimson. "Young Oglethorpe," the Earl of Mar muttered.

"Not so young anymore, my good Mar, but I'm flattered that you place me."

"You disgust me. You're a traitor to the cause and a warrior without honor. You studied with Eugène of Savoy, man! How is it you conduct yourself this way, attacking a gentleman in his headquarters, in the wee hours of dawn. It isn't right!"

Oglethorpe grinned coldly. "My lord, this is *my* home you are squatting in. Those are my friends and servants your men have been abusing and raping. This is *my* country you and your hellborn allies have invaded, and I will conduct the defense of it any damn way I please. And you, sir, will be damned lucky if I don't let my Indian friends practice their tortures on you."

"You wouldn't dare!"

"Sir, you should not try me there." He cocked his head. "By any chance, is the siege of Montgomery your command?"

"Of course it is."

"Well, that's grand, very grand." He looked up at Joseph. "Did he leave me any brandy?"

"I hid the best bottle, sir."

"Bring it here, if you don't mind, and pour yourself a dram."

"Yes, sir."

"What do you intend to do with me?" the Earl of Mar asked.

Oglethorpe didn't answer until the brandy was in his hand and he had taken a sip. "I'm usually a temperate man, you know," he said. "I had some unfortunate occasions in my youth involving this stuff. Just now, however, I need to steady myself for what may soon come."

"What, sir? What do you mean?"

Mar's bluster was nearly gone, leaving only a shrunken, pitiful old man. Why in heaven's name had James kept this fool as a general?

Oglethorpe set his drink down. "Sir, how you are treated very much depends upon you. If you give me the details of your campaign against Nairne—true and accurate details, including the number and placement of all your diabolic engines—and if you tell me everything else you know concerning the Pretender's troops, designs, and intentions, then I will treat you as a gentleman. But if you vex me in the slightest, I fear I will be forced to demonstrate just how we treat your sort on this continent, if we take a mind to."

The earl tried to glare, and the veins pulsed on his forehead.

"James is your rightful king," he said weakly.

"I once would have agreed with you," Oglethorpe said mildly, "as well you know. But that was before he forsook God and took Lucifer and the damned Russians as his bosom companions. Now only two sorts of men serve him—the evil and the foolish. Which are you, Mar? Evil I will not tolerate. I have the head of your pet witch in a bag. My Indian friends wish to burn the evil from you, slowly, with all the craft of their kind. But if you are merely foolish, you can make amends. You can set things right."

"May I have some brandy?"

Oglethorpe laughed. "Yes, and you may have some brandy."

"No—I meant—now, I meant . . ."

"I know you did. You may have it. Will it be one cordial of many to come or your last drink before dying?"

"You are no gentleman, sir, and your father would be ashamed."

"My father is dead, and his estates are ash. Answer my question."

The earl dropped his head. "Curse me for an old man," he muttered, "but do not give me to the savages. I'm tired of this place, weary of this war. I will tell you what you wish to know. Only do not give me over to them."

And Oglethorpe smiled as he might at a wayward child.

"You have my word. Serve me as I wish, and you will be quite safe. Joseph, bring him some brandy, will you?"

"Yes, sir."

Mar gulped at it when it was in his hands. "I heard you were dead, you know," Mar said, after a moment. "We had reports that your army had been crushed."

"I don't doubt it. I put those reports out myself."

"Eh? But General Simmon's command—"

"Quite destroyed. But I found one of his field aether-schreibers, and thus sent word back to Charles Town and your false king of a . . . different outcome. I'm sure they're onto the trick by now, but now they don't know where I am. Even with their flying corvettes, they must have some idea where to look, and they have none." He raised his glass. "But they will. Nairne is at Fort Montgomery."

"Yes."

"And you have laid siege to it."

"I have."

"And how does that proceed?"

"Not well, thus far, but—" Mar stopped quite quickly.

"I did say everything," Oglethorpe reminded him gently. "Vex me in the slightest, I said."

"I sent for reinforcements," Mar admitted.

"Are they coming on foot or in the flying ships?"

"Neither."

"Boats, then, up the Altamaha? Come, sir, do not make me guess."

"Boats, yes. The underwater boats the Moscovados brought."

"Oh, yes. Franklin told me about those. I have not seen one with my own eyes. But I think I shall. How many men do you have at the siege?"

"Five hundred men and fifty taloi."

"Fifty taloi." Five hundred men was a lot, considering he had only fifty-four. The taloi were automatons, made of alchemical stuff and inhabited by demons. At close range they could be dealt with, for the wizard Franklin had supplied him with a depneumifier—his men called it a devil gun—that could strip the demons from their artificial bodies. But the redcoats had learned that much and used the taloi as mobile artillery; and in that capacity they were still very much a danger.

"How many men do you suppose Nairne has?"

"I have guessed two hundred. But the women and even the children have been seen firing muskets."

So Nairne probably had fewer actual soldiers than Mar thought.

"When will the amphibian boats arrive?"

Mar took a long, deep breath. "By morning," he murmured.

"How many?"

"Four, each with fifty troops."

"Two hundred more men. Seven hundred men, four gunboats, fifty taloi. Anything else?"

"No. Fort Marlborough would spare me no more."

"Ah. So they hold the Altamaha sound. Thank you for that, too, Mar."

I have fifty-four men, Oglethorpe thought. Then he smiled. Fifty-four men and an idea. He had won with less.

4.

Big Mile

Red Shoes brushed his fingers along the drying stalks of the corn hedging the trail. He let his gaze wander up the breadth of the fields that dotted the small prairie to the forested hills beyond, where plumes of smoke coiled cloudward.

"I feel like the ghost of myself," he told the woman by his side.

"Why?" she asked, her dark eyes turning this way and that, perhaps trying to see what he saw.

"Because I'm home. Home is the only place that can put flesh on the bones of memory. The smell is different, somehow, the light. It reminds me of who I was when I was five, and twelve. And before I left the last time. All my old selves, all dead men, following me as ghosts."

She didn't comment on his recitation but focused on the pragmatic. "This is your village?"

"It is. Kowi Chito."

" 'Big Panther'?" she translated. Choctaw was still a new language for her, this beautiful and formidable woman of the high plains who called herself Grief.

He shook his head. "*Kowi* also means 'a distance.' What the French call a league. We named the village that because it is a league to walk around it. At least, that's what they say now. My great-granduncle once told me it was a lie."

"Why lie about the name of a town?"

"There is a place a few days nearer the rising sun. It is a town of the dead now, almost forgotten, covered in trees. I went there once to seek visions. But once, in the Ancient Times, it was the most powerful town in all the land. Larger

51

than even the cities of the Europeans, perhaps. A place of great warriors and magic makers. The people bred their children to the spirits, and grew stronger still. Finally they became so proud that they neglected the sacred fire, the eye of Hashtali, whose other eye is the Sun. Some say they even tried to kill Hashtali. I don't know how much is true. I only know that most of them are dead now. What my uncle told me is that some of them didn't die but settled here, and these were the people of the Panther god. He said people are too timid to talk about that now."

"Why?"

"The Panther people were sorcerers, powerful, terrible—wicked. That sort of thing runs in the blood. Our town is the chiefest in the Choctaw nation. Some might claim we made ourselves so with witchcraft." He smiled sardonically.

"That story must be true," Grief said softly, "for surely you must be the greatest sorcerer there ever was."

"*Hopaye,* in my language," he said. "Grief, my people can't know how great my power has become. Not right away. Maybe never. They remember me as a formidable shaman; and many were suspicious of me even then, because power can always be used for good or ill. If they knew I had the might of the Antler Serpent in my blood, they might try to kill me. If they kill me, I can't save them."

"Are they worth saving?"

"They are my people. That question isn't worth asking, as you ought to know."

"I suppose." Her voice grew chilly. Her own people had been slain by the army of the Sun Boy, whose scouts they had managed to escape only because of Red Shoes' newfound power. Soon, the Choctaw would face the same foe.

"Though it's different," Grief continued, "I lost my own kin—my mother, my brothers and sisters, my uncles. It's them *I* mourn."

"It *is* different," he admitted. "The Choctaw are not all kin. They aren't even all one people, not really. But they *could* be. They must be."

"And what will I do?"

He stopped and touched her cheek, felt the blood beneath it, smelled it; and for a moment he saw her only with the cold eyes of the serpent, a *thing* like any other, another hated human being to be destroyed.

But then he saw her with eyes of Red Shoes, who loved her.

"You are with me," he said. "You are part of me. As long as you want a place by my side, it is yours."

She touched his face in turn. "You used to frighten me," she said. "I can see the spirit you swallowed. It is still there, a poison in you. But I do not fear it any longer."

"You should. I do. But I will not let it harm you, Grief."

"I know. You may destroy the world—"

"Only to rebuild it as it should be. And I have not decided to do that."

"Yes. I was saying you may destroy the world, but I truly believe I am safe with you. A strange thing."

"Everything is strange. And I—"

An arrow thunked into Red Shoes' back. He heard the nearby twang of the bow, this hiss of the shaft on a corn leaf, and was already dodging. Not quickly enough. He didn't feel any pain, just impact, but that was the way it was with arrows. A dull shock, like someone thumping you. He yanked his ax from his belt as he whirled, gathering his shadowchildren around him. He shouldn't have relaxed, not even here, not with the Sun Boy and his scalped men searching for him.

"I got him!" someone whooped, and a chorus of shrieks went up in the corn. Grief had drawn her *kraftpistole*— though it was empty of charges.

Someone in the corn started singing the war song. Red Shoes looked down. The arrow was a blunt piece of cane, lying harmless on the black earth.

A boy leapt out onto the path, his face smeared with red and black clay. He held a toy war club carved from a branch.

"Got you, Uncle!" the boy shouted. "Now your scalp is mine! My name shall be He-Killed-a-Wizard!"

"Chula?"

"Welcome home, Uncle."

Red Shoes sighed and placed his ax back in his belt. "That was foolish, Chula. I might have killed you."

"You never even heard me!"

"That's true. That—" He broke off, remembering himself as a boy. He smiled. "That was good, actually. I always said you would be a great warrior. Now I see some proof of it."

"They said you were coming!" Chula said. "The old men foretold it. They said you were coming to lead us to war! Is it true?"

Red Shoes looked at the boy. No boy, really, but a lithe young man of fifteen, eager for war. But for the Choctaw, war usually meant a raid, two or three deaths, a scalp for a trophy and then months of bragging.

It did not mean facing an army as large as a plague of locusts, an army with artillery and airships, whose numbers were so great that the whole Choctaw nation could disappear into them like a drop of water into a sea.

And so it was with some pain he saw the joy on Chula's face when he said, "Yes, that is so."

The boy whooped and shook his toy war club, and out in the corn, his friends answered.

"Are you coming to Mother's house?" Chula asked, when he had started the war song again, forgotten the last part, and broken it off.

"If I'm welcome there."

"Mother said you were."

"Then come along," he said, mussing his nephew's hair.

"Who is she?" Chula asked, gesturing at Grief.

"My wife," Red Shoes replied.

"Your wife," his sister said, voice flat. "You never took a Choctaw woman, and yet now you bring this—what *is* she?"

"Awahi, a tribe far out on the high plains."

His sister scowled, ruining what was usually a pretty face. "And where will you live? In her house on the plains? Has she any property? Do you expect to move in with me, or take a Choctaw wife, one with a house?"

Red Shoes smiled. "It's good to see you, Speckled Corn, little sister."

She hesitated. She had probably sworn not to forgive him this time, for leaving for so long. She had done it before, in front of witnesses.

As before, she broke it. She threw herself into his arms, weeping. "Where have you been? Why do you do this? My boys need their uncle. Since our brother died, and mother, who is there?"

"I'm sorry, little sister. You know how it is. I must do what Hashtali has allotted me."

"You should do what a man is supposed to do. Hunt. Teach his nephews to hunt. Why did you have to be born this way?"

"Someone must. Without a few like me, what defense would we have against the accursed beings? Especially now."

"Yes." She stepped back and wiped at her eyes. "I've heard the talk. So has Chula." Her voice softened. "What are you going to tell the old men, Red Shoes? What will you tell Minko Chito?"

"They already know what I'm going to say."

"If they do, they don't like it. There was some talk of killing you before you reached town. Did you know that? They tried to keep it from me, but if a flea speaks in this town, I hear it."

"Who wants me dead?"

"Bloody Child and his friends, of course. But the Holata Red agreed, and the Mortar. Why, Brother? What do you have to say that could make them so fearful?"

"That which comes is very bad. Worse than the smallpox, the black cough, worse than a five-year drought. It is the worst thing we have ever faced, and I imagine there are those trying not to face it."

"Don't go with them when they come for you. They may kill you yet. They may try to lull you into relaxing."

"Don't worry about me, little sister."

"Who else will?"

"I have a wife for that now."

Speckled Corn glanced out the low, narrow doorway of her

house to where Grief stood on the bare ground before it. A number of people had stopped to stare at the stranger, some merely curious, others with undisguised hostility.

"She doesn't look right," Speckled Corn complained.

"Nevertheless, she is my wife."

His sister nodded, then set her jaw and walked outside. "Why are all of you staring at my house and my guests?" she shouted. "This is my brother's wife, and she is welcome here, and it is no one's business until I say it is. Now go, all of you!"

They went, some grumbling, most averting their eyes, knowing they had been rude.

But all of them had something to gossip about now. By nightfall, every Choctaw house and village within walking distance would know that the sorcerer had returned with a foreign witch wife.

"Home." He sighed to himself.

"Corncrib," Red Shoes repeated.

Grief actually giggled. "We have them, too, but ours aren't big enough for *this*."

He lowered himself down on her again, and the ears of dry, shucked corn beneath Grief shifted as the weight of his body came down. Back and forth, she rolled, as he continued.

"That feels good," she said.

"Thank you."

"I meant the corn rolling under my back."

Later, they lay panting in the smoky comfort of the place. The corncrib was like a little house, raised well above the ground on stilts, with a narrow ladder leading up to it. It was one of the few places two people could actually get privacy. Red Shoes' first taste of a woman had been in a corncrib, and he had led Grief here, once the sun was down and Chula was asleep.

"Lots of corn in here," Grief observed. "Your people are rich. No two houses had this much corn amongst my people."

"We are rich," Red Shoes acknowledged. "And while that is good, it also means others will want what we have. Especially our corn."

"You mean the army of the Sun Boy. The iron people."

"Yes. Even they need to eat."

"You will defeat them."

"I hope so."

"No. You will. Because you promised me you would."

"So I did," he said, and kissed her.

"Strange, this white man custom, kissing," she said, "but nice."

They slept there, and in the morning Red Shoes heard voices, lots of them. He peered down from the corncrib.

"Ah," he said. "They've come."

"Who?"

He pointed to the gathering outside his sister's house. "The old man, with the wreath of swan feathers on his head. That's Minko Chito."

"That means 'great chief'?"

"Yes. Chief of all the Choctaw, though that doesn't mean much, really. He can't tell the district or village chiefs to do anything they don't really want to. But he's a great persuader. That thin fellow with the broken nose next to him, that's Tishu Minko, the assistant to the chief. The big warrior behind him is Bloody Child, a man who doesn't like me very much. The thin man with the snake tattoo is Paint Red. Red is a war title, a sort of captain."

"Like Red Shoes?"

"Yes. 'Red Shoes' is usually a title for the war chief. Red Shoes walk the warpath."

"Are you a war chief?"

"Of a sort. I took the title when my uncle was killed, because I was the only one to carry it. Everyone still calls me that—they say I'm the war leader against the spirit world. The Red Shoes of the nation is him, there, with the sun tattooed on his arm."

"What was your name when you were a boy? Before the war name?"

"Why do you want to know?"

"I never knew the boy you were. At least I could know his name."

Red Shoes shook his head. "As I said, the boy I was is dead. We don't speak the names of the dead."

She rolled her eyes. "Who are all those other men?"

"Village and district chiefs. Shamans. Taken together, they are the leaders of the Choctaw."

"Who are those four? With the black streaks around their eyes?"

"Ah, you notice them. They are rarely seen. Those are the Onkala priests from the House of Warriors, where the bones are kept. We also call them the Bone Men." He reached for his loincloth and matchcoat. "They are the men I came to see."

"Some of those men are from far off, yes? How did they know you were coming?"

"I made shadowchildren, each with the name of a chief or priest beneath its wings. Each carrying a vision of the Sun Boy and his army." He fastened the breechcloth and shrugged the deerskin matchcoat over his shoulders. "Stay here with my sister."

"I'm going with you."

"You can't. Stay here."

"And if you don't return?"

"Then I don't."

She looked at him silently for a moment. "Return," she said.

"Very well." He kissed her, then went down to where the leaders of his people awaited.

They watched him descend in silence. When he stood facing them, Minko Chito clasped his hand.

"You've come. It's good."

"I hope that it is," Red Shoes replied, flicking his gaze across Bloody Child and Paint Red. The two brothers seemed to think his return was anything *but* good.

But no one had tried to kill him yet.

"Is it true?" the chief asked. "The dreams we've had? Did you send them?"

"I sent them, and they are true. With my own eyes I've seen the army. With my own hands I've fought against them."

"He is a brother to the owls," Bloody Child snarled. "Any dream he sends is a lie."

"We've heard other things," Tishu Minko said. "The Shawano trader who stayed with the Yellow Canes told of strange things beyond the Water Road. And what would it profit Red Shoes to make such a lie?"

"To lead us away from our villages, perhaps," Bloody Child said. "To leave our women and old men defenseless against his English friends."

The chief cleared his throat. "Red Shoes, why does he come, this Sun Boy? Why is he our enemy and not our friend? Many have joined him."

"Yes. Those who join him become his warriors. Those who do not, die."

"Why not join them, then," Paint Red asked, "if they are so strong? We've fought for the French, when it was in our interest, and with the English as well. If he offers us glory and scalps, why spurn him, this child of the Sun?"

"He shines, but he is no child of the Sun," Red Shoes said. "He is the black man, who lives in the West, the chief of the night-goers, the god of ruin. He is the serpent with wings of blood."

"Perhaps *you* are the serpent with wings of blood," Paint Red said. "Perhaps you are not who you say you are."

"It is the danger of being a *hopaye*," one of the Onkala priests said quite suddenly. "Sometimes they walk out into the woods human and return as—something else." He turned to Minko Chito. "We cannot hold this council here, great chief. We must go where the truth lives, to the navel of the world."

The chief nodded. "To Nanih Waiyah. Yes. We will go there now."

An involuntary chill crept up Red Shoes' back, the snake in him moving. For an instant, the winter rage came on him, and he knew he could kill them all, that perhaps he should. His sister's warning came back to him.

But if he killed them, he failed. And the Bone Men might

surprise him. They remembered things no one else did. They might destroy him.

Besides, the rage wasn't his. The anger wasn't his. It was in him, but he did not have to accept it. Each time he used the snake's venom it became easier to swallow, and it tasted better.

He remembered the Wichita village, where he had killed everyone, from the smallest child to the oldest man. That could not happen here, even if it meant his own life.

"To Nanih Waiyah," he said. "Let us go, then."

5.

King Philippe's Reception

It was several seconds after the crackle and thunder of weapons faded that Franklin understood that he was alive and well and that the volley had merely been a welcome, a sort of friendly handshake.

"Silly," he muttered. "And wasteful. Why not drums and fifes, or bugles or shofars or what have you, if a noisy greeting is needed? That volley could have been spent more wisely. I, for one, will be quite cross if this war is lost by one volley."

"Will that be the opening speech of your parley?" Robert asked.

The French captain on shore shouted something. For all the ringing in his ears, Franklin could scarcely hear it.

"He says we are welcome, and to follow him in to dock," Penigault translated.

"Said the spider to the fly," Robert muttered.

Franklin got his wish, albeit belatedly, as they marched up the muddy street to the sound of trumpets and drums. Negro page boys in filthy stockings scattered flower petals before them, but that did nothing to keep the earth from sucking their shoes half off. Throwing down a good layer of gravel or sand, Franklin reflected, would have been an infinitely more practical use of time and labor.

Once inside the gate, the same page boys scrupulously cleaned the Carolinians' shoes. Embarrassed, Franklin shooed his away, taking the rag to do the cleaning himself. A bit later, they were offered some sour but drinkable wine. Franklin took it in moderation, worried about poison but very much in need of something to drink, as sweet water had become scarce near the salty Mobile Bay. They were at the mercy of the French now, and if he was to die, poison was probably as pleasant a way as any.

The grand hall was dimly lit by alchemical lanthorns in motley shapes. Indeed, the lack of theme—here an angel, there a sort of pumpkin, there a naked woman—suggested that the lamps had been salvaged from various places rather than made to suit the particular architecture of the place. The inconstant glow of some of them suggested the same—most had probably been made more than twelve years ago, before the comet fell, and were nearing the end of their usefulness.

But for those uneven lights, the hall might have been a troglodyte's cave, so little could he see of it.

They were ushered into an anteroom, this one better lit and decorated with fleurs-de-lys wallpaper. There they waited for half an hour, if the sun-faced pendulum clock on one wall kept proper time. At last a thin fellow with a ridiculous periwig and vivid green frock coat came out and had a look at them, though he didn't say anything and ignored Voltaire's overtures. He vanished, and a few moments later, the pages reappeared with fresh clothing for all of them.

"It seems they have their standards here," Franklin remarked, "and we are not up to them."

"It's a good sign," Voltaire said, "in a way. It means that they will see you even if you aren't up to snuff."

"Hmm."

The outfit he was given was all of bright red watered silk, reminding him of his one-time master, Sir Isaac Newton, who had favored rich, scarlet garb. It fit him loosely and had an unpleasant odor. Franklin wondered, unhappily, if its last wearer had died in it.

Then more waiting, and finally the thin man appeared again.

"The king will see Mr. Benjamin Franklin now."

"And my companions?"

"He will see Don Pedro of the Apalachee at another time. All others are invited to dine this evening."

Franklin looked to his friends apologetically. "I suppose this means I'll see you later, fellows."

He followed the thin man through a warren of corridors and chambers, which he supposed were meant to be grand. Actually, they seemed somewhat askew, with corners not quite square and tilting floors. Each step felt like a league separating him from his companions.

"How do you find the royal palace?" the thin fellow asked.

"Large," Franklin said truthfully.

The man smiled indulgently. "Yes. Large."

"Your pardon, Monsieur—"

The fellow stopped. "My deep apologies. I am d'Artaguiette, the minister of New France." He paused in the darkened hall. "I wonder what you must think of us."

"Monsieur d'Artaguiette, I have little basis on which to think anything."

"You will find this court rather—despondent. I would not hope for much."

"Well, we all must hope. I think I have things of great importance to say to His Majesty."

"His Majesty is not often disposed to hear important things. I wish you luck."

Franklin thought the minister could have sounded more sincere.

They continued on, eventually reaching two large doors that admitted him into not a throne room, salon, or council chamber, but a bedroom with a huge, canopied bed. The walls were light and papered, and the room cheerfully lit by a rather large, misted window beyond the bed. Seven men in florid clothing watched him enter with varying degrees of disapproval. The room reeked of perfume. In the bed lay the man Franklin supposed to be the king.

At first he thought the king might be dead, for he seemed motionless, glassy-eyed, dressed in a high wig and silk gown, covers drawn to his waist. He sat propped against pillows in such a way that did not require life to maintain the position.

But then the royal head nodded, almost imperceptibly.

"Monsieur Benjamin Franklin," the thin man announced, "I present you to the most glorious king of France and her colonies, Philippe VII."

"Your Majesty," Franklin said, bowing in the complex fashion that he had learned at court in Prague.

Everyone in the room took in a sharp breath, followed by titters of laughter.

"I was not told Mr. Franklin was a grandee of the Spanish court," the king remarked, a little smile on his plump, red face.

There was louder giggling at the king's remark. It occurred to Franklin that he should have had Voltaire instruct him in the French style of bowing, but it had been a long time since court etiquette had concerned him, and the steaming forests of America had not encouraged thoughts of such.

"Your pardon, Majesty, but as I understand it, you are also Philippe VI of Spain, are you not, and thus due the Spanish genuflection?"

"A good point," the king replied, a certain weariness entering his tone, "and one not to be giggled at."

The courtiers fell immediately silent.

"Well, Mr. Franklin. You have come here for some purpose other than entertaining my courtiers, I suppose? It has been long since we heard from the English colonies. We thought our friendship with you quite abandoned."

"Far from it, Your Majesty. I have tried without pause to communicate with you by aetherschreiber. I fear, from your remarks, that some agency intercepted all."

"Indeed?" Did his gaze flicker suspiciously about the room? Franklin could not tell for certain.

"Is Your Majesty aware that our colonies are under attack by foreign powers?"

"As I understand it, you are in most indecent and unlawful rebellion against my beloved cousin James."

"Your Majesty, then, received the embassy of Mr. Sterne and his fellows?"

"Well, of course. How could I not? And *they* came well dressed, without need of hand-me-downs. They even gave me a ride in their flying carriage, which much amused me. Did you bring any contrivance as entertaining?"

"No, Majesty, I fear not. We came in through your back door, a charming but strenuous path."

"I should think that the wizard of America should have his own flying machines. Did not your old master, Sir Isaac, invent them?"

"Indeed, Highness, but together we discovered that the cost of using them is too high, to body but especially to the soul."

"Ah, yes." The king raised his hand, and a Negro servant appeared from behind a curtain to place a glass of wine in it. He took a sip. "Mr. Sterne suggested I arrest you, you know. My ministers like the suggestion very well."

"I must say, I hope Your Majesty was not swayed by that opinion."

The king rested the glass on his belly and smiled at it. "Mr. Sterne is a most forceful man. So forceful, in fact, that his suggestion sounded much like a command. I did not like the tone."

The stale air in the room suddenly felt cleaner to Franklin. "I am most grateful, Sire."

"Yes. You may take this matter up with Mr. Sterne at dinner, I think."

"He is still here?"

"Yes, of course, and still eager for my aid in pacifying my cousin's enemies. I suppose you are here to make the opposite case."

"Yes, Sire, that is so. And to remind you of the treaty we hold with Louisiana."

"Ah, yes. The Sieur de Bienville was signatory to that, and had not the power of the throne behind him. You are aware of that?"

"Yes, Sire, I am. But Bienville made that agreement in good faith and without knowledge that a king still lived."

"May I make a suggestion, Sire?" This was one of the courtiers, an oily-sounding fellow with an undoubtedly false mole on his alabaster-powdered face.

"I am always happy for advice from my court, Monsieur."

"Wouldn't it be amusing if Mr. Franklin and Mr. Sterne were to engage in a contest—perhaps a game of tennis—over the right to further petition you for your aid in this little conflict of theirs?"

"Oh, *très amusant,*" another courtier echoed.

"You have to understand my court, Mr. Franklin," the king said. "We are short of the best amusements here. Few of our dwarves survived the last winter, and Indian jugglers have lost much of their power to entertain. What do you think? Shall we decide the future of your country with a tennis match?"

"Sire, I regret that I cannot fully convey to you the gravity of this situation—"

"Gravity! How droll from a student of Newton!" the oily fellow said. They all laughed.

"Did Mr. Sterne explain to you how deeply indebted James is to the tsar of Russia?" Franklin pressed, ignoring the jibe.

"He forecast you would make much of it."

"Perhaps a fortune-telling contest," another of the courtiers quipped, "would be more suited to the talents of our English friends."

Franklin felt a warmth flush his face. "Very well, sir," he said to the man who had spoken. "I forecast that if you continue in these posturing games of wit instead of paying serious attention to matters at hand, you will find this castle of yours has crumbled about your ears, that devils you cannot even imagine will perch on your bones, and that your wit will be of very little use when you find yourselves extinguished, excised, extinct."

"Oh, dear," the oily fellow said. "That isn't entertaining in the least, I find. Have you another soliloquy, perhaps more suited to the occasion?"

The king sighed loudly. "Out, all of you. All of you except Mr. Franklin, begone."

D'Artaguiette bridled. "Sire—"

"You, too."

They hesitated, but not for long. More than one gave

Franklin a glance that promised their dislike of him was gaining proportion.

"That's better," the king said, once the last of them had closed the door. He rose from his bed and went to a cabinet, from which he drew a worn blue justaucorps to throw over his dressing gown. He went to the blurred window and gazed out at the muddy mess of New Paris.

"I never wanted to be king," he said. "Never. I was perfectly content as the duke of Orléans. I could do what I wanted to, then. I could do *nothing* if I chose." He turned back to Franklin. "You see what I am surrounded by now? Idiots, all of them. They insisted I greet you as I did, impress you with our indifference. Well, you are suitably impressed, I hope? As impressed as you are by my great city, my wonderful palace? You must think me mad."

"Sire—"

"*Where* have you been, you English?" he exploded. "You left us alone here with Indians. New Orleans is a moldering ruin. The Natchez slaughtered our concessionaires on the great river. Hundreds have starved and died from the pox, and all my court can do is to shrink from it, imagine we still have a kingdom, lose themselves in dreams. Now you come to me and ask for help—against my royal cousin? What care I if he has Russians at his back? What care I, if he might help restore the world I once knew?"

"Sire, he will not do that."

The king was silent for a moment. "I love science, did you know? I was a great admirer of Newton, and have admired your own papers in the last few years. I have a laboratory here, where I perform experiments when I have time. That perfume you smell—I made it myself, would you believe? I was the head of the Academy of Sciences, which—which—" He suddenly broke off, and Franklin understood that the sovereign was weeping. "Which *did this thing*." He groaned. "And I did not know, did I? I, who thought myself in command—I never knew what my damned uncle—" He broke off again. "I was nothing. I am nothing. What do you imagine you will find here, Mr. Franklin? My five hundred pitiful soldiers? My four ships? Do you think I really have anything you need?"

Franklin's heart sank. The French were weaker than he had suspected. No wonder Bienville had signed the protection treaty—the Atlantic colonies outnumbered and outgunned them thirty to one.

But— He ordered his thoughts. "Yes, Sire, I do," he said at last, and found that he meant it. "The battle we wage is not just for ourselves but for our very race. And it is not merely a battle of arms over territory but a fight for our very souls. If you have any men at all who will fight—we need them. If you have any ships that can sail, or cannon that will yet fire—we need them. But most of all, we need your heart and your courage and your conviction. I, too, played a role in the tragedy that is upon us, that fist of heaven that smote the Earth and spoiled it. A greater role, Sire, than ever you did, I swear. I may be damned for it. But I will be twice damned if I do nothing to correct what I have done, if I do not find the courage to face the children of my mistake and tell them that they will inherit no more evil from me. That is what I hope to find here, a spirit of that kind."

The king turned back toward the window. "Go," he said. "Go away from me."

"Majesty—"

"Go. I will see you at dinner tonight. Perhaps I will ask you to play tennis after all."

Franklin bowed before leaving, but the monarch did not turn to look at him again. He spoke, still facing away.

"There is someone recently come to my court, Mr. Franklin, who would like a word with you. I will grant it to her, I think. She may say much that shall enlighten you. Then again, perhaps not— She has said much to me, and I remained most unenlightened, though her company is pleasant enough."

"Thank you for hearing me out, Sire."

"Do not thank me yet. My page shall escort you."

As promised, one of the pages was waiting outside.

"Suivez-moi, je vous en prie, Monsieur," the boy said.

Franklin could only follow the boy farther into the maze of the chateau, up stairs and down yet another dark corridor.

The room he was admitted to was illumined by a new, untarnished lanthorn. It was like opening a door in hell and finding the sun.

And his breath caught, for in that light, more beautiful than ever, on a small tabouret, sat the first woman he had ever loved.

"Vasilisa?" he croaked.

"Hello, Benjamin, my dear," she said in that low voice he remembered so well, that he still heard in guilty dreams now and then. "My, but how you've grown."

6.

Geneaologies

Time eased by like a summer breeze, unhurried. Adrienne blinked at the stars, felt the tendons of her neck tightening in anticipation of the keen-edged knife that came to part them.

Maybe it was best that she die.

It was a brief thought, a coward's thought. The stars dissolved from patterns of light into spidery matrices of gravity and affinity, and her servant angels, her djinni crowded around.

Mistress?

Her attacker's body was a complicated minuet of matter and spirit, but its dancers were mostly one compound, water, which was in turn made of phlegm, aer, and lux. At her silent command, the djinn split each ferment of water into constituent atoms. The dance became a riot.

The fellow never even managed a scream but fell away from her, a tongue of flame licking from his gaping mouth, twin jets from his nostrils, his eyes popping like fireworks.

Without him to support her, she fell ungracefully. She barely felt the cold earth, but the stars were still there, untroubled.

Fever slashes came after that. People around her, then someone lifting her, Crecy's face. Father Castillion, another bloody knife, a castle of pain that built higher and higher and finally collapsed. And then, at last, darkness.

But not silence. She felt she was in a great mausoleum, for the voice echoed many times.

I'm sorry. My enemies must have found you. They are everywhere. But I will help. I will help to heal you.

Apollo—
Do not exert yourself. Sleep.
So she did.

Adrienne woke, her hands resting on the quilts mounded upon her. She was nine years old, in her father's house, the chateau at Montchevreuil. She had the fever, she remembered, and she was cold. But where was Grandpapa? He had been here with her, and, despite what the doctor said, he made her know she would be safe, that the black angels had not come for her yet.

"Grandpapa?"

"Ah. You wake. How do you feel?"

The voice wrapped her more securely and warmly than any blanket—for an instant only, and then that security turned to sudden fright. The gentle words had the same rustic accent her grandfather had spoken with, but it was not the same voice.

She turned toward the sound and saw Father Castillion, and it all came back. She was not nine, she was thirty-two. Where could twenty-three years go, even for a moment? What was wrong with her?

He must have seen the confusion and the terror, and he put a hand on hers. He was in a chair; and beyond him, in another, sat Crecy, chin dropped down to her breast. "All is well," the priest said. "Your wound was grave, but God has given you the strength to survive it."

She remembered Father Castillion standing over her, and pain. "God gave you the skill to heal, it seems."

"He blessed me with knowledge, yes. I studied the healing arts and learned many peculiar things in China. Yet I know my measure. If my hands had been the only ones at work, you would no longer be among us. You lost a grievous amount of blood." He gripped her hand. "Do you see Him now, among us? Can't you see He is here?"

"He is here," she repeated. But she did not mean God. She knew from whom the miracle had come.

Nicolas, her son. She had given him life, and now he had done the same for her.

"Who did this to me?" she asked.

Crecy started awake then, with a sudden gasp, her fingers flying to the hilt of her sword. Then she understood and relaxed somewhat.

"I told you to wake me," she said to the priest, an angry edge in her voice.

"She only now woke," he said.

"It's true, Crecy. We've only spoken a few words. I was just asking who tried to kill me, and why."

"It was Karoly Dimitrov, the Orthodox priest we brought along with us. I have asked questions, and believe he must have been a spy for the metropolitan."

"I see." She frowned. "He was going to cut my throat, as Irena's throat was cut. Do you suppose he killed her, too?"

Crecy hesitated. "Perhaps we should discuss these matters when you are stronger."

"Discuss them now, please."

"Very well. I've believed Irena was going to meet her lover when she was killed. And, as you say, her throat was cut ear to ear. But I have a reliable report that at that time Father Dimitrov was on board the *Dobrynya,* which never landed that day. Irena was killed in the woods. What's more, Dimitrov was never far out of sight of our men."

"Maybe your sources are not as reliable as you believe."

"I think they are."

"Where is Hercule?"

"Questioning everyone who knew Dimitrov, and not too gently. He thinks, as you do, that the attempt on your life is connected to his wife's death. Dimitrov is dead—and in a singularly unlovely way, I must say—but the other killer is still free. We guess that both work for the metropolitan or perhaps the Golitsyns."

"Why Irena? What did killing her accomplish?"

"It divided your people. It gave Menshikov the wedge he needed to steal some of your supporters."

"Because they thought I killed Irena. But why not kill me in the first place?"

"You are too well protected, generally. Your guardians are not usually all drunk."

"This was not your fault, Veronique."

"Tell me no such nonsense. I should have been at your side, and so should have Hercule. We both failed you."

"I failed myself. If I had been sober, the man would never have touched me and, further, would still be alive for our questioning. Enough of this. Our people have lost their priest and I have killed him. How was that taken?"

"We gave it out that he was killed trying to save you."

"That was good thinking."

"That was a lie," Father Castillion said disapprovingly.

"Yes, it was," Crecy said. "Would you have told the truth?"

Castillion shrugged. "I don't know. But to lie is to slap God. Best, perhaps, to say nothing."

"But now our Orthodox soldiers have no priest. That will not go well, especially if we must go into battle," Adrienne noted.

Castillion raised his hands. "I will minister to them."

"Father, no offense, but you may remember an incident or two in France involving religion? My Russians will not accept the Roman liturgy."

"Then I will learn theirs. The two have more in common than you think."

"You would do that?" Adrienne asked.

"I told you China changed me. As strange as the religion of China is, at its base it is the same as ours. If that is the case, then the differences between Orthodox and Roman are truly minute. I will do what I can to minister to your people. I will do my best, and if you can find me advisers on the matter, I think you will be surprised at how quickly I can learn."

Adrienne regarded him silently for a moment. "God bless you, Father. You are an exceptional priest. And an exceptional man."

"All men are exceptional, and women, too. *He* made us, after all."

Adrienne nodded. "I tire now. Crecy, you must calm Hercule. We cannot have more strife, more hard feelings. If we find this killer, we must find him quietly. Very soon I shall have to ask things of my people that should be asked of no one. I must be confident that they will obey me."

"They love you."

"Love is fickle. It is not so strong as an empty belly or the fear of a bullet. If my people think I have betrayed them, they will not hesitate to betray me. Even Saint Joan was burned at the stake, after all."

"Politics, that was."

"Politics are all around us. Stop Hercule."

"I will not leave your bedside."

"Crecy, only you can do this. Set as many guards as you wish. Send for my students to keep me company. But speak to Hercule, and now."

Crecy's eyes were as hard as gemstones, but after a moment she nodded. "Very well."

"Thank you," Adrienne replied.

Miracle or not, her wound did not heal quickly, nor did it stop hurting. Fever came and went, but it was mild. Father Castillion stayed by her side.

The next day, Émilie came to see her. Like Adrienne, Émilie was French by birth, spirited away from the collapse of that nation by the mathematician Maupertuis, who had brought her to Saint Petersburg, where it was well known that Tsar Peter would enthusiastically welcome anyone with scientific talent, male or female. Maupertuis joined the Saint Petersburg Academy of Sciences, where Adrienne already had a position. When Maupertuis went to Amsterdam to help with the reconstruction there, Émilie stayed as Adrienne's student.

Émilie was not exactly beautiful. Despite her family's class, she had a peasant's big bones. Her personality was forceful, however, and it made her attractive in a way her pleasant but unremarkable features could not.

"I so fear for you, Mademoiselle," she said.

"No need to fear for me, Émilie. I'm very hard to kill."

"God protects you."

"He may or may not, but I do not count on it," Adrienne responded, with a glance at the priest. "Have you continued your research with Linné?"

Émilie flushed a bit at that. "A little. He has been—distracted."

"Ah. Elizavet."

"What can be done? She is very beautiful, and a tsarevna."

Adrienne smiled. "I love Elizavet like a daughter, but she does things by whimsy. Her interest in Linné will wane as soon as she is certain she has him."

"*I* know that," Émilie said. "And yet if he rejects me for her, I shall not take him back. How can I? I may be no beauty, but I am no fool. I have my pride."

"But you love him."

She hesitated. "Yes."

"Then do not let her take him. Tell him what you just told me, and make him believe it. If that fails, you were better off without him."

Émilie nodded. "Thank you, Mademoiselle."

"And, Émilie, you are far from ugly."

She nodded again.

"Well. Now tell me of your research."

"Oh. Yes. The classification of the malakim proceeds—"

"What's this?" Father Castillion asked.

"Explain to the good father, Émilie."

"By the malakim you mean the angels?" Castillion asked.

"We mean the aetheric beings science deals with," Émilie said cautiously. "Some may call them angels."

Castillion frowned but nodded.

"Carl—Monsieur Linné—and I have been trying to classify them into kinds, as we might animals. A bird is a sort of animal, a raptor a sort of bird, a hawk a sort of raptor—"

"I'm familiar with the idea," Castillion said.

"The trouble is that animals and plants may be classified by outward structure—wings, feathers, beaks, and so forth. The malakim, not being composed of matter—or of very much matter, anyway—have no outward structure to observe."

Castillion scratched his chin. "And yet I have seen some of them, as wisps of fire, and, by our Lord, the keres—that was indeed a thing of matter, was it not?"

"In part," Adrienne said. "There is, among the malakim, a hierarchy."

"As the Bible states, and rabbinical sources, and even the Chinese scripts. The seraphim, the cherubim, the ophanim, and so forth," said Father Castillion.

"They are masters who have servants, and their servants are in turn masters over yet weaker servants," Adrienne said. "But it is the weakest among them, those of lowest rank, which have the most material substance. Some of my servants, for instance, are able to manipulate the substance of phlegm, others lux. Some can mediate between any two substances that I point out to them. But the great ones—call them the seraphim, if you wish—are creatures entirely of spirit. They cannot touch us or we them, save in spirit."

"Those nearest God are more of spirit; those nearest men are more of matter. But these seraphim can touch us, yes, by sending their more earthly servants," Father Castillion said.

"Yes. That is the old order of things. But it is changing, due to science. The keres, for instance, is a new thing. Generally, though, the malakim ignore mankind, until we achieve the sciences that let us affect the aether where they live. When that happens, they act, either killing the philosopher who made the discovery—as they did the man the Egyptians called Thoth and we call Hermes—or by offering their services to him."

"Why that last?" asked the priest.

"With magical djinni to serve your every whim, why continue the difficult and often disappointing business of the philosophical experiment? And after a generation, all science is forgotten, magic prevails, and then the malakim vanish back into the aether, leaving only mumbling fools behind them."

Father Castillion shook his head excitedly. "It would explain much," he said. "It would explain much of the ritual of

China, for instance, or the worship of pagan gods. It is a short step from having a djinn who serves you to having a god you must beg for favors."

"Precisely."

Castillion looked to Émilie. "And so we have digressed. If there are these sorts of malakim, each with a throne higher than the other, why not keep them in their natural categories?"

"Because they are more various than their rank. And we did find a way! One of our colleagues—Monsieur Lomonosov—has proposed a startling hypothesis. In his view, there is no matter in the world. Newton himself approached saying this, but shied."

"I should say he did," Castillion said. "The Church teaches that matter and spirit are separate. How can there be no matter?"

"It is all spirit. Or rather, it is all affinity—attractions and repulsions. Like gravity, which is not made of matter, or magnetism."

"But both are created by matter. Gravity by atoms, magnetism by iron."

"Lomonosov does not think so. He believes there are various sorts of affinities, some nearly perfect—nearer God, if you will—some less perfect. The most perfect affinities do not diminish with distance. The middle ones, like gravity, weaken in a proportion relative to the distance from the source. The least perfect affinities are those things we mistake for matter. But since all of these things are spirit existing at different levels, one may become another, and all are connected," Émilie explained.

"This is making my head spin."

"Think of a musical scale. All notes on the scale are different, and have different qualities, but all can be reached by lengthening or shortening a string."

"So if we 'shorten' matter, we get gravity? Or the holy spirit?"

"Yes, very like that."

"And your malakim—those with the most masters between them and God and those nearest man—are the most imperfect, the most material. And the archangels, the thrones, and great powers, are farthest. But can one, then, become the other?" He sounded skeptical.

"We are matter, and imperfect," Adrienne said. "But aren't we taught that we can become spirit, and perfect?"

"I must hear more of this," Castillion said. "Much more. The implications—this has been borne out by experiment?"

"It has been suggested by reasoning, and by some experiment. We have yet to devise satisfactory tests, though young Lomonosov is trying."

"And now—my head spins on—how does this apply to the classification of the malakim?"

"They are made of patterns of affinities, each unique like the ridges on our fingers. We can observe the pattern, using certain instruments. The weaker, less perfect malakim are simpler and more specialized than their masters. What we have discovered is that these masters make their servants from their own substance—not by natural reproduction, but by excising some part of themselves, then changing its 'musical pitch' so to speak."

"All this we knew," Adrienne said. "I thought you had made progress."

"We have. As a man's child carries resemblance to him, these malakim made from other malakim resemble one another, but much more strongly. Their patterns tell their parentage, as it were. And our calculations—based, Mademoiselle, largely upon your own papers and observations—suggest something interesting."

"And that is?"

"That in all the world, Mademoiselle, there are really only two true malakim. Two, from which all the others are descended."

7.

Guns on the Altamaha

At midday, the sun scarcely touched the sluggish waters of the mighty Altamaha River. Not here, at least where it was narrow enough that the gallery of oaks it flowed through could nearly twine their branches in an arch, the Spanish moss hanging like stalactites from the roof of a cave. Somewhere the sun was shining; here the waters flowed dark and quiet. Cormorants perched on snags, and a great blue heron came flapping by on heavy wings.

Oglethorpe glanced at Tomochichi, the aging chief of the Yamacraw. Even at his advanced years, he was arresting, his still-muscular chest tattooed with black wings, his earlobes slit and dangling with jewelry. His intelligent face, painted red and black now, expressed something Oglethorpe rarely saw on it: concern. He was staring at the water.

"What's wrong, old friend?"

"Things live down there. Snakes that once were men. Pale cannibals. An entire world we cannot see, should not see."

"That isn't who we fight."

Tomochichi met his gaze, something the Indians did only to express disbelief or emphasize a point. "Yes, it is," he murmured. His certainty put ice in Oglethorpe's veins.

The water rippled, and the forest moved. Yamacraws, Yuchi, Maroons, and rangers, shadows one moment, men the next, now shadows again. Oglethorpe kept his eyes focused on the bobs, little bits of light wood floating on the surface of the river with cords going down to weights on the bottom.

An instant later, one went under, and then the next. And the next. A faint V appeared on the surface of the river.

79

"Catfish large enough to swallow men," Tomochichi murmured. "Panthers with rattlesnake tails."

Oglethorpe's heart was hammering. "Not yet," he pleaded. "Not yet."

The next bob went down, then the next two.

And there, where the deep channel came against a dry, clear bank, something poked its head from the water. It looked, at first, like the head of a giant turtle, a flat-topped cylinder a yard across, sticking two or three feet above the river. It was the color of black iron.

Though he could not see them, Oglethorpe knew there were windows in the thing, and intelligent eyes behind the windows. He prayed they would see nothing besides trees and birds.

He was still praying when the water rose up in a mound the shape of a lozenge, and then the water poured away, and there lay something that looked like a giant manatee, the cylinder that had first appeared standing up near its front.

"Steady, boys," he said under his breath.

And they were. Oglethorpe's men had fought demons of steel, flying men-of-war, and spirits of mist and flame. This was just a boat. A boat that went underwater, a boat made of metal, a boat with an engine sent to Earth by Satan himself perhaps, but still a boat filled with men.

Oglethorpe examined the thing more closely. Now that it floated free, he saw that it was, in fact, shaped like two war galleys placed one upon the other, one flattened keel facing the sky and the other toward the bottom of the river. He wondered suddenly, not at its strangeness but at why no one had ever built such a thing before.

And the watchtower was also a hatch—a giant screw, for as he watched, it began to untwist. Near the hatch, one on each side, were mounted two swiveling guns of unknown design. He suspected they could be worked from inside the turret, as well as from outside.

After a long moment, the screw came off, fastened still by a cable from the inside, and a man stuck his head out. He wore a grenadier's red, floppy hat. After a moment, Oglethorpe heard him shout.

" 'Tis clear! *Eto khorosho!*"

Two men skittered out of the thing like ants from a hole and manned the swivel guns.

Another of the ships surfaced, as fifteen men trooped off the first, throwing down a gangplank so they could cross to shore. Then yet two more ships breached the river's skin. By the time the fourth had fully surfaced, there were upward of thirty men on shore, and that was too many.

Oglethorpe raised his hand and chopped it down, and the river sucked in blood and lead.

First to go were the gunners, though one managed to get a wild tear off into the forest, a lance of blue-white flame that charred what it touched but left no fire behind. A huge oak fell, cut in half. The gunner's right eye blew out the back of his head, along with some of his brains, as a ranger's bullet put an end to him.

Maroons shinnied into the overhanging trees and dropped grenades into the open hatches, and oily black smoke puffed up. The Russians and Tories on land returned fire as best they could, but mostly they died. Two of the ships sank again from sight, one with its hatch still open. Air boiled up furiously, and men with it. One ship had never opened its hatch, and it went down more smoothly.

After a volley or two, Oglethorpe gave the command to cease fire, and the sound of muskets trailed off raggedly and finally stopped. A few men were still clambering from the remaining amphibian, and about half of those on shore were dead. The others were trying to form a square, frantically loading and priming their weapons.

Oglethorpe could see only one officer.

"Surrender, sir," Oglethorpe called. "Surrender, and no more of you shall die. Resist, and every man of you will be cut down."

The officer, a Russian, stared hopelessly for another moment or two, then motioned for his men to lower their

weapons. Instantly, Oglethorpe's regulars moved in to confis-
cate them.

Oglethorpe confronted the officer.

"Do you speak English, sir?"

"Some."

"You have ships down there. I want them up and open."

"I have no more ships."

"I just *saw* them. Man, how do you think we knew to be
right here, at the very moment when you came to surface?
Mar told us all. Not only that, he ordered his troops here to
move elsewhere, so you would have no cover. Downstream,
my men have already stretched chains, but they won't be
needed. At this range, we can use the same device we've used
against your airships to render your amphibians powerless.
I'd rather have them working, naturally, but I have one already, and that will do."

The man hesitated a long moment. "I shall have to use the
aquaphore in my ship. By the time the wretched smoke you
filled it with clears enough, the others will either surface to
fight or try to run. There is nothing I can do until the smoke
clears."

"That is if they surface."

In the end, they ran. A detachment followed them down the
river a safe distance from the captured ship, then used the
devil gun. An hour later, two ships surfaced and floated until
they fetched against the chains. The stuff of their hulls was
too hard to break through with the weapons Oglethorpe's
men had, but they unmounted one of the blue-fire guns, took
it downstream, and tried that. It cut the ships open quite
nicely, and they sank. As they took on water, the hatches
came open then, damn fast, and after the first three men on
each had fallen dead from musket shot, the rest came out with
hands raised high.

They marched the prisoners back to Oglethorpe's mansion
and added them to those chained in the servants' quarters.
Meanwhile, Oglethorpe set the more scientifically minded of
his men to finding out who the pilots of the ships were.

"I want us to be able to use that ship by morning," he said. "And I'll need volunteers to learn its operation."

"Sir, I'd like to do that!" MacKay said.

"You've experience in this line?"

"I ran a steam galliot against the Spanish, Margrave."

"Good. You'll be our chief pilot, then."

"Thank you, Margrave."

Oglethorpe nodded briskly. "Meanwhile, I want an order to go down for half of those redcoats laying siege to Nairne and his people to march south, away from here. Have Mar sign it, as he did the last."

"Sir, this can't last forever," Parmenter said. "Sooner or later they will realize they've been tricked."

"Indeed, and I will not count on this succeeding. But it is certainly worth trying."

"And now what, General?"

"We move by morning, using the amphibian boat. We'll attack from the river side, coming out of their own ship. They'll never know what hit 'em. The real trick is to get Nairne to start something at the same moment, so we can have the confusion as great as possible."

"I can do that, sir," Parmenter replied.

"How?"

"I know that fort, sir. I can get near enough to put a message over the wall."

"Without getting caught? Because if you're caught, they'll be onto us."

"I can do it, sir. I swear it."

Oglethorpe regarded the ranger for a moment, thinking that he had never known a man with a more level head.

"Very well, Captain. How many men will you need?"

"Two will do, sir. If they'll do it, I prefer Unoka and Jehpath."

"Both Maroons?"

"Best for this sort of work."

"And damned hard to see at night, eh?"

"Yes, sir."

"Go to it then."

Two months ago, Oglethorpe mused as he watched Parmenter go, *no white man or Indian I knew trusted those
Africans as far as they could spit. Now we can hardly do without them, no more than we could do without the Indians.*

Because this was their sort of war, which by European
standards was merely murder. But then, all war was murder.
Why put an uglier face on this, or a pretty one on what he had
seen at Vienna? He blinked away the memory of the Turks,
practically swimming up siege trenches full of their own
blood, falling under the ruthless rain of lead the Holy Roman
army had loosed on them. For his own part, Oglethorpe had
never even known if one of his own bullets killed or not. It
was impossible to tell.

Here, he knew what he did, what he was responsible for.
What he fought for. He could look in his heart and feel no
shame, despite it all. He did what he must.

They landed the ship without being seen. Fort Montgomery
commanded a high bluff, and the land around it for nearly a
league was pretty clear. An outer wall surrounding the town
of Montgomery—a town of some two thousand souls—had
already fallen, and now trenches zigzagged very near the fort
itself. The fort had been built sturdily, the lower wall of
dressed stone quarried far up the Oconee River and ferried
arduously down at great cost. It was worth it—a wooden fort
would have fallen long ago. This one would have, too, if the
invading army had sent its best artillery, or even the blue-fire
weapons that he had captured yesterday. Or who knew? From
what he had gathered, Mar had bungled the siege very badly,
losing three aerial ships to Nairne's devil gun. Perhaps he had
lost his firedrakes and seeking cannon as well. Nairne, after
all, had Indian fighters aplenty.

Whatever the case, this was old-style warfare. Trenches
snaked up the hill, the angle mostly protecting the diggers. Of
course the diggers were taloi, and in fact the ground near the
fort was littered with the broken forms of the automatons.
Mar had tried at least one straight assault.

The battle would have ended today, however, with the weapons the amphibian boats carried.

A few redcoats came down to water, curious, as Oglethorpe's men set up their artillery, but at that moment the fort loosed what was probably most of its remaining firepower, and there was even a sally from the gate. Oglethorpe's men, dressed in Russian and English uniforms, quietly killed those who came to investigate. When they had their guns set up, they started to fire into the enemy's rear.

At first things went well, and the new weapons did their work with awful efficiency. But then some enterprising English captain managed to get a charge together, and they came crashing through the withering fire.

Oglethorpe admired them, of course; but if they made it, he and all his men were doomed. If their line fell, there was nowhere to go but the river.

He wheeled around, shouting encouragement, firing his pistol. He found himself staring into the mouth of a musket less than ten feet away, and he took careful aim at the man, not flinching when the weapon belched and something hotter than fire seared along his cheek. Oglethorpe's *kraftpistole* crackled, and the redcoat died. But the enemy surged forward in good order, reloading and firing even as they died.

His own men were turning skittish. They were good at what they did, but this was not what they did. He had made a mistake, and now his men and everyone from Azilia—everyone in the *world*, if Franklin was right—would pay.

And then, like the sun parting a cloud, the attack fell apart. The blue fire of the swivel guns from the amphibian ship blazed through one too many of them, the stench of their burning comrades snapped their courage, and they ran or threw down their arms or dropped to their knees in prayer.

And it was over. By three o'clock that afternoon, James Edward Oglethorpe and Thomas Nairne, governor of South Carolina in exile, clasped each other like long-lost brothers and began to discuss what to do with a captured army twice the size of their own combined forces.

*   *   *

They did not spend long in celebrating. Mar still had men in the area, tricked into relocating by Oglethorpe's false communiqués. The two commanders dispatched troops to deal with them, and Oglethorpe sent for Mar to be brought to the more secure Fort Montgomery.

"You did well by me, Governor Nairne," Oglethorpe said that evening, as they sat in a half-darkened room, poring over maps and papers taken from Mar's things.

Nairne, a square-faced fellow with salt-and-pepper hair, nodded wearily. "Thank you, Margrave. I most sincerely tried to. For commanding the Continental Army, we all owe you immeasurably. I could not see your capital taken while you were elsewhere." He leaned back and took a deep puff on his clay pipe, and the pungent scent of tobacco bloomed into the air. "Besides, where else to go?"

"Another few days' march would have had you in Apalachee territory, which has more easily defended forts," Oglethorpe pointed out.

"And abandon good Englishmen?"

"I have taken to calling us Americans," Oglethorpe said quietly. "After all, many who fight with us owe little to England. Our own colonies were enemies not long ago."

"Aye. And I want that well mended," Nairne said.

"I believe you do. Those in your Parliament who hate Azilia are with the Pretender now, as I see it. Out here, we are all brothers. Azilians, Carolinians, Maroons, Yamacraws, Apalachees."

"Now you sound like our Mr. Franklin."

"Mr. Franklin is wiser than I first gave him credit for." Oglethorpe lifted his sherry. "I got this from the Apalachee. It was a gift from Don Sancho of San Luis. It is my last bottle." He sipped it carefully. "Have we heard from Mr. Franklin?"

"That he was in danger. We got word that the Pretender's ambassador, Sterne, had gone ahead to the Coweta. Don Pedro—speaking of Apalachee bravos—followed after Franklin, to warn him."

"What about his aetherschreiber?"

"As you must know, we've been having trouble with those. It's my guess that the Russian warlocks have some method of intercepting their messages. We've stopped using them."

Oglethorpe frowned, then turned to MacKay, who sat, half drowsing, at the end of the table.

"Captain MacKay, go invite the Earl of Mar to join us, please."

"Yes, sir."

"And, MacKay, by 'invite,' I mean ask civilly, but if he gives you any back talk, haul him here by his ears."

MacKay winked. "Yes, sir."

Mar was nearly apoplectic when MacKay brought him in.

"Good evening, my good earl," Oglethorpe said. "Captain MacKay, you may release the gentleman now."

"Very good, sir," MacKay replied, letting the blustering lord's very red ears go.

"What is the meaning of this?"

"Have a seat, Mar, if you please."

"I do *not* please. What more can you ask of me? I betrayed my entire army to you."

"Indeed, and so you are several times a traitor. Do you think I'm grateful to you? You are a worm, sir, and so act like one. If you do not, I shall expend whatever energy is required to bring you 'round to your wormdom, though I doubt it shall need very much. I may not even need my Indians."

"What do you want?"

"You've met Governor Nairne?"

"I have not."

"The pleasure is all mine," Nairne said. "I am very well pleased to see you here. I hope you and your murderous friends have treated my city of Charles Town well, or I may be more pleased to have you with me than you can imagine."

"Charles Town is quite well, and under proper English rule."

"Oh, indeed? And how can English rule be proper without English law, which I have seen none of? Never mind, sir, we are not met here to debate."

"What then?"

"Governor Nairne has learned that you have been intercepting our aetherschreiber communiqués. Where are they?"

"I don't know what you're talking about."

Oglethorpe drew his pistol, took careful aim, and shot Mar in the foot.

That set off a bit of scurrying among the guards, but it was just as well. Mar wasn't able to talk properly for a few moments, but he drew a packet of letters from the inside pocket of his coat.

"That's all of them," he said feebly.

"Sir," Oglethorpe said, "I have let you keep as much dignity as possible, but you are trying me. I did not have your person searched, and see how you repay me. If I suspect you are hiding a single thing from me, I will have you publicly stripped and searched. Do you understand me?"

Mar hesitated another second, then pulled two final letters from his pocket, weeping.

"There's nothing you can do anyway," he murmured.

Oglethorpe read one while Nairne read the other, then they switched, neither uttering a sound. Then the two leaders looked at each other for a long moment.

"MacKay, find the officers. We need to parley, now, this moment."

Captain Parmenter had come in during the commotion, and he now cleared his throat. "What is it, sir? Another attack?"

"Hmm? Yes, General Henderson is at Fort Moore, and he has sent six hundred troops to reinforce Mar. They will be here in a week's time."

"Six hundred? You can whip 'em, sir."

"No doubt. But there is a problem. The other communiqué is from Charles XII, the Swedish king exiled in Venice. He sailed more than a month ago from Venice with four men-of-war and four thousand men."

"Jesus, sir. I mean, pardon me, sir, but four thousand men would be better than gold to us right now."

"That is true. But Charles doesn't know his message was

intercepted by the Pretender. In fact, he doesn't know a thing about what's going on here, because he's been sent a pack of lies that he thinks comes from Mr. Nairne. In eight days time, he will rendezvous with what he thinks are our forces in the Altamaha Sound, and there he and all his men will be cut to pieces. The Russians, you see, have a deep hatred of Charles, and they have been trying to end his life since seventeen hundred. Unless we take a hand, they will have their way."

"And we lose four thousand allies before they can be of any use to us," Nairne added.

"What's it mean, sir?"

Oglethorpe scowled, then rubbed his forehead wearily. "With our new amphibian boat, we might have a slim chance of reaching the sound and breaking the teeth of this trap, or at least warning Charles and his flotilla. But it will mean abandoning Montgomery to the redcoats. We can't do both."

"Abandon Azilia, sir? Again?"

"That's the choice, Captain. That's the choice."

8.

In the Navel of the World

There were two Nanih Waiyahs. One, the smaller, was a modest mound of earth, flat on top. Once, the Choctaw had a fire temple on Nanih Waiyah there, but the fire had gone out, and no one could build it again. The building had long rotted away, but the hill still stood, abandoned save when the chiefs met to discuss matters of law or other great affairs. Red Shoes hoped they would stop there, at the lesser mound.

They didn't. They continued past it, across a damp bottom that eventually became a marsh, and finally *lunsa*, the darkening, the swamp at the navel of the world.

And from *lunsa* rose Nanih Waiyah the greater, a much larger, round hill. The smaller mound had been built by human hands, carrying basketloads of dirt. The greater Nanih Waiyah had been built by no human hand.

"Hashtali, whose eye is the Sun," one of the Bone Men intoned. "When the world was all quagmire, when all of the world was the water of the darkening, Hashtali reached down, and with his hand he pulled up the mud and spread it out. He spread it over the realm of the snakes, and the White People of the Water, over the fish and worms. He pulled it up here, and Nanih Waiyah is the mark of his hand. It was open like a crawfish hole; and, like crawfish, he found creatures of mud inside. Some saw the light and climbed up, curious to see it. Some of those could not bear it and went back down, but some continued up, and their skins dried and split, and they crawled out into the sun as human beings.

"More came, and more, and with them, hidden among them, the evil ones, the accursed. So Hashtali put down his hand again and pressed the earth shut, here, at Nanih Waiyah. That is all I have to say."

And he fell silent, without finishing the story. The silence stretched until Red Shoes guessed it was expected for him to say something.

"They are our ancestors, down there, those things that are not men. They are our cousins and our aunts."

"And at times," the Bone Man said, "one must be chosen to consult with them. Are you that one, Red Shoes?"

"You say that you are," Bloody Child mocked. "If you are, you can go in and return. The guardians of this place will not harm you. But if you lie—"

"You know nothing of the mysteries," the Onkala priest snapped suddenly, cutting Bloody Child off. "Only *we* know what will happen if Red Shoes fails."

Bloody Child bowed his head and fell silent, but his face remained unrepentant.

"Must I do this?" Red Shoes asked. "War is coming. You cannot avoid it, whatever happens to me."

"But we must decide what to do," Minko Chito said. "I must know whether to join the Sun Boy or fight him. I must counsel my people one way or the other. You claim to be our war prophet, our seer. You claim to speak the truth. Go into Nanih Waiyah. Return. We will know what to do, or so the Bone Men tell me."

Don't do this, Red Shoes wanted to say, remembering again the burning village of the Wichita, the people the angry power in him had caused him to slay. *I am a snake trying to remember he is a man,* he wanted to tell them. *I am an accursed being trying to do good before his soul unravels and has no choice. This will hasten my end, if not end me. And then there will be no war, for what I will become will devour you and scorch your nation from the Earth.*

But he could not speak. They might try to kill him on the spot if they knew what he was thinking, what he could do. Instead, he faced the great mound, bounded on the right by the still water of the Darkening, by cypress that made a cave of the sky; on the left by the shadowed forest. And there, at the point where the mound met the earth, waited a small, dark opening, just large enough for a single man.

He squared his shoulders and stooped into it.

It went down, a tunnel cut not through stone but through a hard, slippery clay. It descended into water—first to his ankles but quickly to his waist, his shoulders; and then only his head was out. The gray light behind him faded, and then the roof of the cave came down into the water.

He held his breath and ducked under. After an arms-breadth, the roof went up again, and he had air once more.

But no light, no light at all.

Should he make a shadowchild for light? No. He must not attract attention here. He must not. He must keep his shadow-children close, and quiet.

The tunnel continued, narrower and narrower. Though the roof in this section seemed very high, now Red Shoes had to turn sideways to squeeze forward.

He stopped to catch his breath, and above in the dark-ness he heard something like the legs of a very large spider brushing.

And music. The soft, distant *pung pung pung* of a water drum. The faint chanting of voices.

Inside him, the coiled snake stretched, and Red Shoes felt his bones, rods of lightning ready to burn out of his skin. He trembled there for a long moment in the dark, trying to re-member who he was.

I am Red Shoes. Choctaw. I am not accursed. I am not the feathered snake.

He remembered his friend Tug, the sailor who had saved his life in Venice, who had become his companion these last ten years. Tug, his friend.

Tug, who ran from me. Who still runs from me.

But Tug had reason.

He remembered Grief, her quiet anguish, her fierce lovemaking.

He remembered the old man he had known as a child, who had battled the spirits and lost. His eyes as vacant as pumpkin seeds, his drooling mouth, not even able to feed himself.

I am Red Shoes. Not accursed. Not yet.

The trembling stopped, and he went on.

The roof drooped again, and once more he had to hold his breath and swim in the dark. But this time the tunnel slope did not rise again. It continued, until his lungs ached, and he suddenly realized he was swimming down, toward the bottom of the Earth, to the place where his people had come from. To where some still lived.

But then he found the skin of the water and cut through it, and was born again into darkness.

Or near darkness. But there was singing, and a small glimmering light, and a vast cave that could never fit into the hill of Nanih Waiyah. Song echoed about him, and the tapping of the water drum was like thunder.

From the darkness walked a woman. She appeared neither young nor old, though her hair had streaks of silver. She looked Choctaw, but her skin was pale, as if she had been in this place for a very long time. Her face was tattooed in the old fashion, around the mouth and her arms were strung with the twisting forms of serpents, and water panthers, eels, and garfish. She wore a breechcloth and a white feather mantle upon her shoulders. She stopped singing and regarded him.

"You swam very deep," she said.

"I swam until I found air," Red Shoes replied.

"Most never find it. Others find it quickly, far short of this place. Only a few can come this far."

She stepped closer, and he felt the snake in him again—a sudden anger, a flare of vicious hatred that was in no way human.

"Ah, I see," she said. "You have the scent of one of my children about you. I did not know mortals could do that. Be careful with him; he sleeps in you, but is not dead."

"Your children? Who are you?"

"Give me a name. I am a mother to many things. I bear them in darkness. Some even say I bore you, you human beings, down here in my dark womb. I think perhaps I did, before Hashtali took you from us, dressed you in that clay. Mother Dead. That is what I have been called."

"You summoned me here."

"Perhaps I did. I felt you coming, and was curious. These are strange times, even for me, who has been here for so long I no longer remember what is real and what isn't."

"What are you?"

"What do you mean?"

"I have kept company with many shamans from other tribes. I have spoken with the philosophers of Europe. All of us, when we come here, to this place behind the world, we see something different. We see what our eyes are accustomed to seeing."

"Yes. Your eyes are clay, and can see only clay, or the image of clay. But there is the spark in you that is more, that came from us, else you could never come here at all. What am I? What I said: a mother. Not a thing made of flesh and blood— no more than my son, whom you swallowed, was a snake. We are the eldest, those Hashtali sent into the world to create it. And once here, we took it from him. He made you to get it back. That is why we really fear you, you know—my brother, my children and nieces and grandnieces—he clothed you in clay to take you from us, to let you work where we could not, after he turned the world inside out and made us ghosts."

"Must we fight, then, as I fought your son?"

"No. Let Hashtali have the world back. I wish to be free of it. I wish—there is a human word, *redemption*. That is what I wish. But what you must understand, Red Shoes, is that I am nearly alone in that. My brother is my enemy, and all of his children. And most of my own have turned against me as well. Things go badly for me."

"The Sun Boy?"

"Yes. He is the key, though even I cannot say exactly how. He is doom or salvation."

"But is he my enemy? And are you my friend?"

She shrugged. "I cannot answer that. I want the Choctaw to live and multiply. I want to preserve humanity in all its varied forms."

"How can that be done?"

"The sky must be broken and mended. The world must be turned upside down again."

"But that is what the Sun Boy wants. It is what your son, the Antler Snake inside me, wishes."

"Yes. And no. I do not know the final answer, Red Shoes, only the vague shape of hope. You creatures of clay are the ones made to find it."

"I will find it then. But you—are you in danger, Mother Dead?"

"I am hidden where they cannot find me. I wait. Only you and one other have found me, and both of you are mortal. Given time, my enemies will find my spoor, follow my trail, and then I will die. I stay quiet here, waiting, hoping, watching. Giving what help I can. Some of my children are still loyal, but they fall even as we speak. They plunge from the heavens like burning stars, and I can only weep."

She turned her back on him. "Go. Leave no trail."

"Can you tell me nothing more?"

"Only that I will be there if I can, when the time comes. That is all. Now go."

Red Shoes reluctantly returned to the water; the trip back seemed longer. When finally he reemerged in the dark tunnel, he was bone weary, shivering, as weak as if he had just run for seven days and nights.

Painfully, he went forward to where the others were waiting. The passage narrowed, as before, then dipped underwater again.

When he emerged, there was no light, and there ought to be. The entrance should be only a short distance away.

Perhaps night had fallen while he spoke with Mother Dead.

But then his groping hands encountered fresh dirt and clay, and he understood the truth. While he had been beneath, his companions had been busy. They had entombed him in the mound.

9.

Old Acquaintance

"Have the years struck you dumb, Benjamin?" Vasilisa asked, a laugh somehow threaded through the sentence.

She was more beautiful than he remembered. There was silver in her otherwise onyx hair—a streak of it, pulled fetchingly down one side of a face which did not otherwise seem to have aged. It still looked like polished ivory, her eyes gently slanting jewels, her nose small and upturned, like that of a girl in the earliest year of womanhood.

But he knew very well that the slight frame beneath her jade dress was that of a full-grown woman. He had tasted it, loved it, reveled in it, when he himself was barely more than a child.

"What shall I say?" he managed. "Shall I say I am happy to know you are alive? I suppose I am. Shall I say I am pleased to see you? I cannot say that with the same surety. You betrayed me, Vasilisa."

"Benjamin! I saved your life. Are you so quick to forget that?" She reached for his hand with both of hers, and so paralyzed was he that she managed to catch it. Her skin was warm, her fingers smooth, uncalloused. "I know that it is difficult for you to forgive me. But it was best for you—you must admit it."

He withdrew his hand. "What are you doing here, Mrs. Karevna? You still serve the Russian tsar, I presume, and so once again, I think we are enemies. Are you with Sterne?"

She smiled somewhat unconvincingly and stood. He realized with a shock how short she was, for when last he had seen her, he had been only fourteen. She looked suddenly vulnerable in a way he had never imagined she could. "Sterne—I never met him until I arrived here. Who I serve has become rather . . . complicated. Russia is no longer ruled by the tsar, as such. I find myself . . . confused."

"You, confused? It is difficult to believe, Mrs. Karevna."

"Once you called me Vasilisa. You did when we met just now."

"Once I was a boy with a tender heart. Thanks much to your influence, I am no longer that boy."

"I never meant to hurt you, Benjamin, that much is true. I think you know it is." She cocked her head. "Your hand calls you married."

He touched his wedding band. "Indeed. Some ten years now."

"I congratulate the woman. She is American?"

"She is Czech, actually."

Vasilisa smiled broadly. "You seem to have acquired a taste for Slavic women, my dear."

That brought a blush he didn't think he had left in him. "It is good to know you are alive," he said, a bit of the bluster leaving his voice. "I thought, once, that I saw you on a Russian ship—"

"When you fell from the sky with the Swedish king and laid waste to the Russian fleet over Venice? Yes, I was there. It was a glad moment for me, to know *you* were alive—but, as you remember, there was not much time or opportunity for a reunion. But seeing you then is, in part, why I am here in America. I assumed you would gather importance and therefore be easy to find."

"Not in *this* colony."

"My duty brought me to this colony, from quite a different direction as your Pretender and the Russian traitors with him. My heart would have brought me, eventually, to seek you out, to offer my apologies."

"That, I cannot believe," Franklin replied, forcing some of the hardness back into his voice. "You were never in love with me."

"No, but I did *love* you. And I wronged you. There comes a time when one wants to set things right, to make life over."

"Is that so?"

"Yes, and there is more. I need your help."

"Which makes more sense to me."

Now her smile grew even wider. "Benjamin, you have indeed grown up. You are more cynical than ever I was. I'm not sure I like it on you, this rough and prickly suit."

"You helped pick it out."

She laughed, and it was the laugh he remembered, pure and musical. "In that case, let me be plain and businesslike, yes, Benjamin? I can help you against Sterne and his Pretender. But I need your help as well—help of a scientifical nature."

"Really?"

"Yes. Our *real* enemies—you know who I mean, I think—gather themselves. Certain philosophers in the Russian empire have given them new muscles, which soon we shall see flexed. We must stop them, Benjamin, or all the world will burn."

"You wish me to think you traitor to the tsar?"

"The tsar is probably dead, but I serve him yet," she said heatedly, her voice actually quavering. "Did I ever tell you how I came to meet the tsar?"

"You never did. Why should I care?"

"He saved my life. More than that, he gave me a new one, a better one. No man—no person—has ever done such a thing for me. You must believe me when I say I loved the tsar and despise those who have taken his country. And the masters they serve—those creatures Sir Isaac once called the malakim—they will be done with all of us. We *are* on the same side, Benjamin. Do not let your bitterness toward me obscure that. It will not serve either of us well."

"You've always been a great talker, Vasilisa, but you were never shy of turning the truth front to back, and for all I know have made practice perfect these twelve years gone. Can you offer any proof of what you say?"

"You called me Vasilisa again," she said softly.

"Can you prove what you say?" he repeated insistently.

"I think so. We will speak again."

"I would rather have it now."

"All I have to offer you now is my word and myself," she said simply. "If either will do, take them. If not, then you must wait a bit."

"I cannot wait too long," he cautioned. "But I will give you time to prove your case."

"You will not regret it."

He left, and the page showed him to a small, damp, drafty apartment. It made him almost yearn for their camps on the forest trails, which at least gave one a view of who might be coming.

He had scarcely seated himself on a hard stool when a rap came at the door.

"And how is the ambassador?"

"Evening, Robin. I'm afraid I can't really say. The afternoon has left me somewhat . . . bewildered."

"Well, we ain't under arrest as I can tell, so things seem better here than at our Coweta congress."

"Or perhaps just strung out longer. Sterne is here, as we suspected, pressing his case. The king says it does not please him, but I seem to make him no happier." He wondered if he should tell Robert about Vasilisa, but he needed to know what he himself thought about that little matter before taking another's counsel.

"To tell you the honest truth, Robin, I think this was all a tragic mistake. This diplomacy is proving a dry well, and now I think it was water we never even needed. If we had won the Coweta and the French, what would we have? A thousand more soldiers—maybe. I've been preaching that our real foe are those in the aether, and yet what have I done to attack them? Not a thing."

"Yet wasn't that what brought you here? The need for such supplies as the French might have?" Robert asked.

"Who knows what they have? Or whether I'll ever be able to use it?"

"Y' couldn't have known."

"Couldn't I? Where was our intelligence? How could we have known so near nothing about this place?" Franklin asked, exasperation touching his voice.

"Well, there I may be able to help you. I've met up with one of our French brothers."

"A secret Junto member?"

"Indeed."

"He is about?"

"No, he's bein' high cautious. Actually, Penigault introduced us. It's the Du Pratz fellow, who wrote the history of the Natchez. He paid a call whilst you were in chambers. According to him, the king here has plentiful scientific stuff."

"He did claim to love things scientific," Franklin mused. "Maybe there is something to bait the hook with. Maybe. And it may be I have some hope of a defense against the malakim as well, or at least some intelligence about these dark engines of theirs that Euler told us about. And we have Euler himself."

"There, see? God may well have provided you what you need."

"This from you, who never once has thought God a reasonable fellow? What, has some Quaker girl worked conversion on you?"

"Hardly. But I figure if God is responsible for all of this, there's no hope for us at all. If he isn't, then he may well be against it, so maybe I ought to curry some favor."

"The cautious Robin," Franklin said.

"But what hope have you found, specific? You didn't say."

"Nor will I just now. An old foe, maybe a friend now."

"Hmm. Wasn't it you who said, 'Beware twice-boiled meat, and an old foe reconciled'?"

"That *was* me, wasn't it? It must be sound advice then. Are you ready for dinner?"

"I could eat a bear."

Which was fortunate, as bear was the main course. It was tolerably good, well roasted and exceedingly greasy. Robert was as good as his word, vanishing great hunks of it down his throat. Voltaire, Franklin noticed, was somewhat more cautious.

Franklin didn't want to look at Sterne, for when he did, he saw the bloody ghost of his brother James Franklin. For more than twelve years he had lived with that last sight of James, his death-dimmed eyes and confused expression lit by his burning print shop. For twelve years, Franklin had thought James' murderer dead.

But in Coweta territory, Sterne had claimed the killing as his own. Was it a lie?

It didn't matter—that he would claim it was enough. That he was a warlock was enough. That he had worked against Franklin was enough. He would pay the toll for his evil words and deeds, and Franklin would see to it.

So he forced himself into a seeming of good humor and smiled at Sterne, and took comfort that the dinner seemed to disagree entirely with the periwigged fellow. After the first round of toasts to the king, Franklin couldn't help himself. He raised his cup and said, "To good Mr. Sterne, who was so lately my host in the wild—may I have the chance to host you in as good a fashion—or, I hope before God, better!"

Franklin's friends—the rangers and the Apalachee drank to that with great enthusiasm—the French with some puzzlement. Sterne, of course, did not drink to himself. The smile he managed looked uncomfortable. Franklin took all this as a good sign—a sign that the court had not thrown its weight behind the Englishman.

The king seemed to have recovered a certain amount of good cheer. In fact, he raised his own cup in toast.

"To Sir Isaac Newton," he exclaimed. "He brought us the benefits of a new science to help us through these dark days. And to his greatest apprentice, whom they call the Wizard of America, Benjamin Franklin. I do hope I can convince Mr. Franklin to demonstrate an experiment or two for us."

Franklin couldn't have asked for a better opportunity. He began to think Robert might be right about God, after all.

"I would be most delighted to do so, Your Majesty. Indeed, as you have told me you are a scientific man, I greatly desire that we might collaborate on something. Perhaps we can speak of this later?"

He guessed nothing he could have said would have had a more profound effect on the king. His eyes positively gleamed. "That sounds most delightful, Mr. Franklin. Most delightful indeed."

Sterne couldn't sit still for that, and he didn't. "Your Majesty," he said, "I must remind you that your cousin James has been kept waiting for too long. You promised an answer when Mr. Franklin arrived; as you see, he is here now. Will you delay longer? Consorting with him in matters scientific can only add to the insult my sovereign already perceives. I—"

The king slammed his cup onto the table, bringing an end to Sterne's speech and to every other sound at the table.

"Mr. Sterne, I do not wish to discuss politics while taking my pleasure. It is disgusting—and with ladies present! Mr. Franklin has the good grace and manners to understand that. Your own behavior baffles me. As for my cousin, he was always an overbearing, self-important little shit, and I will hear no more of his indirect pomposity here. If he truly wished to make an impression, he would have come to see me himself, yes?"

"Sire," Sterne began again, in a more humble voice, "my sovereign has the pressing matter of the rebellion to occupy him, else he most assuredly would be here."

"Of course he would—eating my food and drinking my wine as he and his father did for decades at my uncle's court. Yet when has he invited me to dine at his?"

"Sire—"

"Hush, Mr. Sterne. This will be a pleasant evening, even if *you* must spend it in irons."

"Your Majesty would not dare."

Another dead silence, and this one stretched long, until the king lifted a single finger. Immediately, from the wings, two guards appeared and grabbed Sterne by the shoulders.

"See here!" he shouted.

"Gag him and put him in irons," the king said, "but leave

him at the table. I would not have my cousin say I did not receive his envoy as honorably as I could."

And it was done.

"Now, Mr. Franklin. I have often wondered on the nature of colors and what their origins might be. I recall in his *Optics*, Sir Isaac did some experiments using thin films . . ."

And they talked, as they say, of quinces, bears, and cabbages, but not of politics. Franklin found it immensely cheering and stimulating to his conversation to glance—every now and then—at Sterne's flushed face, and wink.

That night he dreamed of Vasilisa, of their first dinner together, in which she proffered cup after cup of Portuguese wine, and with each sip her face grew more beautiful. He dreamed of her naked limbs, wrapped about him, of her sleeping face the next morning.

He dreamed of the nightmare sky, after she had kidnapped him, of her grip on his hand as the horizon vomited toward heaven.

He dreamed of a magnetism that connected them, that had never let him think she was dead. And in his dream, he loved her as only a boy in love for the first time can love, a love as full of fear as of hope, brittle and beautiful as a snowflake—and as impermanent.

Or was it? he thought, on waking. It was still in him, wasn't it? Not really gone, just buried.

He lay in the dark and forced thoughts of his wife, Lenka, instead, of how he had felt when he thought she was dying, of the joys he had known in her embrace. Solid joys, dependable ones.

Of course, Lenka had as much as threatened divorce last time he had seen her . . .

This was stupid. He would go back to sleep and wake with no thoughts of women at all. That was the very last thing he needed on his mind right now. Or on any other part of him, for that matter.

But when he finally did sleep again, it was to dream of bodies in motion, and not those of the celestial sort.

*   *   *

Franklin came out of his restless sleep almost instantly when Robert tapped him. In light of the lanthorn his friend's face looked drawn.

"What is it?"

"There's news of Carolina."

"How's that?"

"I don't know. I got word from the Junto fellows here. They want a meeting."

Franklin sat up, rubbing grit out of his eyes. "Show me to 'em," he said.

Penigault was waiting outside. "It's this way," he told them.

Once again, Franklin found himself twisting through the maze of the palace until at last a ladder was climbed, a trapdoor lifted, and they were outside. The air stank of swamp, decay, and salt.

They followed Penigault out, into the muddy streets of the town, twisting through narrow alleys paved with night soil and offal, until at last they came to the door of a largish house. The fellow rapped thrice, then again, paused, and rapped twice more.

Bolts slid, locks ticked, and someone opened the door a crack and peeked through.

"Mr. Franklin?"

"At your service."

The door opened fully, and the man stepped back into the lighted room. He wore a plain cotton shirt and knee breeches. He wore no hat or wig, but his dark curly hair was pulled in a queue. A second man stood in the room, his eyes distant, unfocused. He was a little older, with little more than a fringe of iron around his mostly bald head.

"Sir, I am Antoine Simon le Page Du Pratz, and this is my friend André Penigault, whose son consented to guide you here. We are both much pleased to meet you."

"I can speak for myself," Penigault replied dryly, sticking out his hand. Franklin suddenly understood that he was blind. He clasped the outstretched fingers and gave them a brisk shake. "Good to meet you both. Monsieur Du Pratz, I much enjoyed your volume on the habits of the Natchez Indians. I hope I can expect a longer work from you in the future?"

Du Pratz smiled. "When our present troubles are resolved, God willing," he replied.

"Come, come," André Penigault muttered. "Enough time for back patting later. We have business now. And speaking of which, Mr. Franklin—no offense intended, of course—but what would you say if I did this?" He put his hand over his heart.

Franklin smiled. "I should say a few things," he replied. "I should ask you some questions. For instance, do you sincerely declare that you love mankind in general, of any profession or religion soever?"

"I do," Penigault and Du Pratz said in unison.

"Do you think any person ought to be harmed in his body, name, or goods, for his mere speculative opinions or his external way of worship?"

"No," they answered, again together.

"And do you love truth for truth's sake, and will you endeavor to find and receive it yourself and communicate it to others?"

"Yes."

"Fine," Franklin said. "Then I propose we call this meeting of the Junto to order and waive the other standing questions, as I gather you have urgent things to tell me."

Penigault nodded, seeming satisfied.

"Have a seat," Du Pratz said. "Can I offer you wine?"

"Something a little more stimulating, perhaps? Tea or coffee?" Franklin suggested.

"I am supplied with neither, though I can offer you a certain Indian tea which has much the same effect."

"Cassina?"

"Yes."

"We drank that often enough in Carolina when trade ran thin. That would be wonderful."

"Angelique?" Du Pratz called.

"Sir." A young Indian woman entered the room with

several cups and a steaming pot. It seemed Du Pratz had anticipated the request.

A few moments later they all sipped at the strong, black tea. This had a more roasted taste than what Franklin was used to, with a certain burnt bitterness that was unusual but good. He felt its effect almost immediately, jostling the sluggish parts of his brain.

"First," Du Pratz said, "I must tell you I received a message by way of aetherschreiber from the Junto."

"Sir?"

He handed over the letter. It was in Thomas Nairne's hand, written in the coded language they had last agreed upon.

"Have you translated it?" Franklin asked.

"Yes. It's a general communiqué to all of the Junto officers. Its contents—" He grimaced, then went on. "Oglethorpe's forces were routed. All of the Carolinas have fallen into the Pretender's hands. Nairne still holds Fort Montgomery, but he expects it to fall very soon."

The worst thing Franklin could imagine hearing, and there it was. He put his head down in his hands.

"So quickly," he murmured into his palms. A great hole had opened in the world, and he and all he loved had fallen into it. Tears stung the corners of his eyes as he remembered the soldiers at Fort Moore, cheering for him, all confident that a few weeks of Indian fighting and the magic of their wizard Franklin would save them and make the world as it had been. How many of them now lay dead, crippled, prisoners without arms and legs, cursing him now?

Good God, what had become of Lenka? He'd left her with Nairne. She would try to fight, knowing her.

"How bad. How bad was it?"

"Of Oglethorpe and his part of the Continental Army, we know nothing. Nairne thinks him dead. Governor Nairne plans a sally from Fort Montgomery and a march through Apalachee land to here, and he expresses the hope—"

"That I have done my job and brought the French to our side," Franklin finished grimly. "Does King Philippe know of this? Anything of it?"

"I do not think so, no."

"About that," Robert said. "How is it you receive messages when neither the Coweta nor the king have received any in months?"

Du Pratz raised an eyebrow. "I cannot say about the Coweta. But Nairne expresses the worry that many of his aetherschreiber messages are not being received, and perhaps even intercepted. Oddly enough, this latest one ends in mid-stride, so to speak. Add to that the fact that the king is often . . . protected . . . from such things by one of his ministers. We are not certain which one, though we have a good idea."

"A traitor?"

"A plotter for the throne, more likely. Several of the officers and noblemen here believe they could govern more efficiently than His Majesty."

"I'm sure. And just to keep things up front," Franklin said, "could you tell me where you stand? Are you backing someone other than the king?"

André Penigault coughed roughly. "Don't think we haven't considered it—rule by Junto even, though we don't have anyone highly placed enough to do the job. D'Artaguiette would probably do a better job than the king—he was here when Bienville was our governor, and commanded this city when it was still named Mobile. But no, at least as it stands we support Philippe."

"Is this d'Artaguiette the chief plotter for the throne?"

"Chief? He's the most likely to succeed at it, if that's what you mean. The others are all posturing fools, and I doubt they could snatch the king's messages from under his nose. D'Artaguiette could."

"Then he might well know that what's left of our army is marching here, even if the king does not. How will he use that?"

"We think he has made overtures to Sterne; and after last night, my guess is that Sterne will solicit him more carefully. The king, after all, seems to be leaning your way. So d'Artaguiette will use that to bargain with Sterne. If Sterne backs his move against the king with enough force, we may see trouble."

"Damn." Franklin sighed. "Can't anything in this diplomat business go easy?"

"How many troops remain?" That was Robert, ever practical.

"They don't say," Du Pratz told him. "I think they fear even the coded messages might find interception here."

"And that's well thought, too." Franklin gulped down the rest of his cassina and waited for the girl to refill his cup. "May I use your aetherschreiber?"

"It is at your command, sir," Du Pratz assured him.

"I must contact Governor Nairne and Oglethorpe, if I can."

"Then what?" Robert asked.

"Then do what we can here. Monsieur Du Pratz, what if d'Artaguiette attempts a coup? What then?"

"The Junto has some resources, but we are mostly outnumbered. Your men added may be enough—provided they don't start at the top, with regicide. All we can do is keep our eyes and ears open."

"No," Franklin said. "We can't wait for anything, watchful or sleeping. We have to act."

"You have a plan?"

"No." He was having trouble breathing. "You got the memoir on the submersible ships?"

"Yes. No sign of them in our harbors, though I expect if the eastern coasts are now secure—"

Franklin saw it. "Yes, damn it. They'll send them south around Florida. That's probably why Nairne doesn't say he will try to hold Apalachee—they have no sea fortress. How long will it take them to get here, I wonder?"

"What was your plan, before all of this?"

"To take my time, play on the king's love of science as I did at the banquet. But I have undermined that already, haven't I? I surely convinced Sterne that he cannot deal with the king. He will move in other ways. With our luck, the coup is already over, the king dead in his bed."

"Don't be so excitable," André Penigault said gruffly.

"Didn't we say we have *some* sense of what's going on? No such a thing happened tonight."

"Well," Franklin said. "Something will happen tomorrow night."

"Is that a prophecy?"

"No. A promise."

"Ah. Then you *do* have a plan."

Franklin uttered a noise enough like a laugh to sound painful. "No. But I will. It may be no better than my last three ill-conceived designs, but I will not sit on my hands."

"Bravo," Robert said. To Franklin's surprise, he did not sound altogether sarcastic.

10.

Hercule

Her third day in bed, the angel Uriel came to Adrienne.

"I thought you were dead," she said.

The seraph folded and unfolded its six wings, the eyes that covered them winking slowly. "Almost, I was. The battle does not go well. The Sun Boy is strong. I have hidden myself again, slipped their notice, but I fear the next time I meet our foes will be my last. The great ones are all in motion now, and the time is approaching."

"The time for what? What are they planning?"

Uriel was silent for a time. "You've seen the dark engines. They are ready now, and with them they will kill your race."

"There is more to this. Why should your kind wage civil war over our fate? There is something else, something some of you fear and some of you desire."

"God's wrath. God's forgiveness."

"You lie. What are they doing with my son?"

"I've told you what I know. Like you, he has the power to bridge our worlds, to connect spirit and matter. Through him, the great ones of my kind can put their hands into the world."

"As they could at creation, before God changed the world."

The seraph hesitated.

"Come. You told me yourself that to make the world God had to withdraw from it. He created your kind to work where he could not, and you rebelled. But the universe is made of natural law, and even from outside it God was able to change that law, wasn't he? Just a little, just enough to rob you of your communication with matter. You, but not *us*."

"That is essentially true but unimportant," Uriel replied. "What is important right now is that we stop your son from unleashing the engines again."

"Is it? I wonder."

"You've been hurt," Uriel said.

"Why, yes. You aren't the only one who has been in danger. Uriel, why didn't you tell me that all of you are only descended from two archangels?"

Another hesitation. "Does that matter?"

"It might. You cripple me when you do not tell me everything."

"I don't have time to tell you everything. I tell you the things I think you most need to know."

"And withhold those you most fear my knowing. Yes, I understand."

"That is well."

"Have you anything more to tell me? Anything about my son?"

"No."

"Then leave me."

Uriel vanished, at least from her sight.

Crecy entered about an hour later.

"Good. Help me up, Veronique. I need to walk."

"You are not fit for that yet."

"My wound is healing quickly."

"That *is* true," Crecy admitted. "You heal almost as quickly as I once did."

"Is that an accusation?"

"An observation."

"I have had help," Adrienne replied.

Crecy nodded and didn't press any further.

"Now come, I need to find Hercule."

"I will bring him here."

"No, you won't. He's avoided me since the attack. Since Irena's death, really—"

"Not so. He comes when you sleep, when he is certain you will not awake. If you feign sleep—"

"Enough. Let us find him. You lend me your shoulder."

Crecy sighed and offered her arm.

Far from tiring her, the act of walking seemed to give Adrienne strength. The terrain below was still mostly open plains, but here and there, along rivers especially, trees huddled together as if for comfort against the vast space.

"There he is," Crecy said.

"Stop," Adrienne whispered. "Wait."

Hercule had a boy on his shoulders, a lad of about five, a little Hercule. The two of them were chasing a girl, younger—three? All were laughing.

"Come here, little girl, or we'll eat you up!" the boy shouted. "I am the giant with two heads, sent by Koshchey the Deathless to capture you!"

The girl squealed as Hercule's arms closed about her. "Save me!" she cried.

Adrienne's throat tightened. "Another time," she murmured. "I shall speak to him another time."

"Too late," Crecy said.

Hercule was staring at them and lifting his son down.

"But, Papa!" the boy said. "You said we could play!"

Hercule kissed the boy on the forehead. "We will, Stephen. But a little later, yes? I must speak to the Lady Adrienne right now."

The children turned to stare at her. Adrienne expected resentment, but instead their eyes grew round.

"Saint Adrienne!" the boy said.

"I'm not a saint, dear," Adrienne replied. "I'm just a woman."

"They call you a saint," the boy responded.

"Do you know what happened to my mama?" the little girl asked. "You can talk to the angels. Can you tell her I miss her?"

"I will t-try—" Adrienne stammered.

"She will try, Ivana," Crecy finished for her. "I will see she does."

"Thank you, Aunt Nikki."

"Run along, children. Stephen, you keep your sister's hand until you get back to your nurse, yes? Go, now," Hercule said.

When they were gone, he turned to her. "You shouldn't be up yet."

"How else was I to see you, Hercule?"

"You might have summoned me," he said stiffly. "I am your servant and cannot refuse your commands."

"You are my friend. I do not wish to command you. I want you to talk to me."

Crecy cleared her throat. "I'm past due to inspect the guard. Hercule, can you take my place here?"

Hercule blinked for a moment, then nodded.

"I will sit, for a space," Adrienne said, and lowered herself onto a bench.

Hercule dithered for a moment while she caught her suddenly rare breath.

"I have reduced speed," he offered. "If I hadn't, we would have caught them by now, and I feared with you unwell . . ."

"That was a good thought, Hercule. You were right, and I shall need all of the strength I can find." She looked at him significantly. "All of it."

He compressed his lips. "I'm sorry," he murmured.

"Why must you avoid me? Why can't we be friends the way we once were?"

"Because nothing is as it was, Adrienne. Irena was a good wife to me, yet I never loved her. Now she is dead, and I am left with the pain of knowing that at the moment she died, I was probably thinking of you. And now my children—my children whom I adore—are without a mother. And still I love you, and still you will never love me, and I am ashamed, ashamed to think that even when Irena is dead—"

"I do love you, Hercule," Adrienne said quietly. "I do. I should have married you, all those years ago. I know that now."

His face twisted curiously into anguish. "That's not true. Don't torture me like this. I may deserve it, but please do not."

"You deserve no cruelty, Hercule, no blame. It was all me.

I lost my first love to bullets. I lost my only child to the malakim. I could not—I could not let myself feel what I should have, when I needed you to *live*. Those I love die."

"You love Crecy."

"Crecy is different."

Hercule could hardly argue with that. But after a moment he said, "It is too late for all this, isn't it? It doesn't matter. It's *too* late."

He turned, but she grasped his hand and held it tightly. "Not too late," she said. "Not too late, but too soon. But in some tomorrow to come, when all of this is behind us . . ."

"Yes. Of course," Hercule said, and he gave her hand a squeeze.

This time the silence that lay between them was almost comfortable, an old friend.

"Speaking of 'all this,' " Hercule said after a moment, "we are now following the wake of the army itself. Our trackers believe that this Sun Boy has several thousand troops, most mounted, and a number of airships. We will be outgunned *and* outnumbered."

"And you wonder how we will fight them?"

"Well—yes. Not that I am afraid, of course," he went on, some of his old bluster coming back. "After all, I have led few against many on more than one occasion and snatched victory from the jaws of death. We *will* succeed. But—it will require, I think, a miracle such as only a saint can provide."

"You know better than anyone, old friend, that I am no saint," she said, "but I do have power. And this battle, I think, will not be won with armies. That isn't the part you will play. Get me near, keep me alive—that is all I ask of you and our men, though I cannot promise victory." *Near. So I can convince my son of who I am, so he will remember me at last.*

Hercule shrugged and brushed his oversized nose with his thumb. "We will do what must be done. I am a simple man, and have been much distracted of late, but I think I understand that this is a battle we must not lose. Not if my children are to grow old. Not if that tomorrow you mention has any hope of arriving for anyone." He sagged a little. "The weight of that has nearly broken my back, I think, as much as anything else. And yet you, how must you feel? For you bear more of this on your shoulders than any of us."

"That is the problem, I think," Adrienne said. "We used to share our burdens—you, Crecy, me. Lately we've each been trying to carry it all. I'll take some of yours if you'll take some of mine."

"I will carry anything you ask," Hercule replied.

She regarded him for a moment; and as she had done, long ago, just after they met, she stretched up and kissed him lightly on his crooked nose. In his smile she thought she saw the memory come to him as well.

"Would you escort me to my students?" Adrienne asked. "I wish to speak with them, too."

"But of course, Mademoiselle, of course."

11.

Downstream

Oglethorpe, determined not to weep, watched the flames take his home.

"Why, sir?" Parmenter asked quietly, the red light playing across the hard planes of his face. "Spiking the cannons, yes, and poisoning the wells, perhaps. But this?"

"They'll get nothing from us," Oglethorpe replied. "Nothing. If in the end we lose this war, and Azilia goes down to dust, then I will not have our enemy sitting in this house again, benefiting from my work."

"And the assembly?"

"Yes, I should see them now. But this had to be done first."

"To set the example."

"Aye."

And to set me free, Oglethorpe finished silently. To sever him from the idea of defending Azilia, which couldn't—shouldn't—be done. He had built it up once, and he could do it again. But for now, he had a bigger war to win and precious little to win it with. His attachment to the margravate would only hinder him.

The assembly hall of Fort Montgomery was less than three years old, for the old one had burned down and nearly taken the town with it. Oglethorpe would never forget that night, the soot-blackened faces, the men and women straining on the bucket line. And then the rebuilding and the celebration. They always took time to celebrate when they could in Azilia.

The assembly was thin, for many who had sat in it had

died, and there had been no time for elections. Oglethorpe stood up and cleared his throat. But before he could say anything, Robert Taft stood to be recognized.

"Mr. Taft?"

"I only wish to express, Margrave, how happy we are to see you. We had thought ourselves lost, but now you have returned to us. I speak for all of us here, I think, when I say we are at your service."

"You most certainly do not speak for all of us, Mr. Taft," another man shouted, his long face a furious red beneath his bedraggled periwig. "For this war was not voted on by us! We should be *with* the Pretender, not against him. He is our king, by God, and all of our tragedies may be laid on *that* man." He thrust his finger at Oglethorpe.

Oglethorpe sighed. He set his shoulders back and clasped his hands; then, removing his hat and setting it on the table, gazed across at men who had once trusted him. "How many of you are with Mr. Prescotte and feel I have embroiled you in the wrong sort of war?"

It came, he reckoned, from the confusion of yeas and nays, to be about half. He smiled grimly. "More of you will agree with him soon, for I am come here to give you some hard truths. The first is this: We are at war with the Pretender and his diabolic allies. If you think you can make peace with them and live as free men—or live at all—you are naïve and do not know what I know, and I will take no further steps to convince you. Stay here and wait for them if you please. But I am margrave, and, further, I command the army of the continent."

"That army you destroyed?" Prescotte roared.

"If my strength is all gone, then come for me. Depose me. Try to pry my men from me, Mr. Prescotte." He aimed a finger at Prescotte. "During all this, while good men have died, where have you been? You and all the other naysayers in the assembly, all those craving to crawl on their bellies to the Pretender and give them all we've fought for. You were on your plantation, eating corn and pork!"

"I could not leave my family alone with my slaves, not in times like these! You know that well."

"Oh? Many planters fought with me. I myself abandoned my own plantation."

"But you have no slaves."

"True. But Williams did, God rest him. And Mr. Thomas Gerald." He frowned at the memory of their deaths, then shook his head. "No matter. I am freeing the slaves. Slaves weaken free men. They've weakened the margravate, and you men are proof of it."

That brought an explosion all right.

"You can't do that!" Josiah Marner shrilled. "They are our property!"

"Stop me," Oglethorpe said, and he said it so coldly and quietly that it actually brought the furor to an end. They sat or stood, mouths agape, as he continued. "We need the slaves free so they will fight for us, not against us. Freemen will fight in their own best interests, and that interest is in defeating the Pretender."

"Errant nonsense!"

"Right now my men are collecting a levy of slaves to put under arms. They are being informed of their freedom and the freedom of their families."

"They'll run away!"

"Some will, some won't. The smart ones won't, because there's no place to go, really. But they won't stay here. When the redcoats come to burn you out of your plantations, they won't find slaves here to conscript."

"But you just said we're going to fight."

"Not here, not at Fort Montgomery." He paused significantly. "Not in Azilia. This very day, we start a retreat through Apalachee territory, where we will find lodging for the women and children. Soldiers under Governor Nairne will march on to New Paris. I have another mission."

"But what of Montgomery?"

"I'm going to burn it. And each of you, in turn, should burn your plantations. I've already destroyed mine."

"Burn Montgomery?" Prescotte shrieked. "This exceeds your authority, Oglethorpe, all of it. All of it!"

"Authority? These are martial times. My authority is in my scabbard. Will you test that, sir?"

Prescotte withered beneath the stare. "But—burn our homes, free our slaves—I'll be ruined!"

"You are already ruined, you babbling fool," Oglethorpe snapped. "You were ruined the day that army of devils set foot on this shore. We're going to fight them until they are gone or until there is no breath left in us. And what I cannot save, I will burn, for they will not have it. Now, gentlemen—I do not ask you to love me, or even to believe that God does. But you must follow me. You must follow me or perish. Your childhood is past. Be men. Be men, or God damn you."

And with that he rose and left the shadowy hall.

Parmenter found Oglethorpe on the bluff, looking down at the river.

"They're with you, sir. You won."

"All of them?"

"It don't matter about Prescotte and his like, does it? Some vowed to stay. But the whole commons was with you, sir. Few of them hold slaves, and the rest resent them that do. And the army is behind you, and 'most all of the folk. They love you, sir."

Oglethorpe looked at him in genuine surprise. "They do?"

"Of course they do. You hardly seem human to 'em. How many times have you stood up for them—against Howe, the bloody Spanish, Carolina? Each time you come out with a victory for them. If it weren't for you, there wouldn't be no margravate, and only a fat-assed fool wouldn't know that."

"After today, there won't be a margravate."

"Sir, wherever you go, there the margravate will be."

Oglethorpe nodded, then exclaimed in surprise.

"Sir?"

"The first good news we've had in a long while, Captain Parmenter. Look there."

Across the river, just becoming visible from the forest, stood an army.

And they did not wear red coats.

"I'll be damned," Parmenter swore. "It's Martin, from North Carolina. And, if I make no mistake, those are Cherokee with him."

"No mistake, Mr. Parmenter. No mistake."

"How did they know to come here, with the aetherschreiber messages taken and all?"

"I do not know, but I am grateful for it." He frowned. "And cautious. Find me a boat, so we can go talk to him."

"Sir, that's hardly cautious."

"A boat."

Martin, it seemed, had been a few days behind him for almost a month.

"I pressed ahead faster than I thought possible, and hoped to meet you on the upper Oconee, where our Cherokee friends heard tell of a battle. We got there late and found a lot of red-coated corpses and fallen demon ships. The last we'd heard on the aetherschreibers was that we would fall back to Azilia if things got tough north, and that looked liked where you were going. We thought you could use the help."

"Damned if we couldn't." Oglethorpe grinned. "And you nearly missed us again."

"Oh?"

Oglethorpe outlined the plan.

"Margrave, I've got nigh two thousand men behind me—stragglers from Virginia and both Carolinas, a good number of Cherokees, and even some Oconees who have broken with the Coweta empire. Are you sure you wouldn't just rather hold this fort?"

"I'm sure. Mar was a fool. A real general, with all the alchemical weapons the Russians have on hand, could reduce Montgomery in seconds. We can't sit in one place—we have to move, strike, and retreat. We have to worry them like a pack of wolves worries a buffalo herd. The only reason Nairne held up here was because of his civilian charges, and he was preparing to march again when Mar caught him." Oglethorpe wondered if he could have made that decision a few days ago. With his plantation drifting smoke, it was easy.

Things were looking better, but they had to have the Swedish king, his ships, and his men. Which meant they needed to go, fast.

"Come on across," Oglethorpe told Martin. "We've plans to make."

Oglethorpe left the next morning, boarding a hundred men into his amphibian ship. The great exodus was already beginning, Nairne and Martin at the head of four thousand troops and five thousand invalids, women, and children. Of course, of that four thousand, nearly half were Negroes, many of whom had never held a gun before, most of whom still did not. Despite his confident talk, Oglethorpe did not think the freedmen could be trusted with arms. But they could dig trenches, build redoubts, and cook meals. A few could be armed.

Montgomery was a column of flame and smoke.

"General, it's time y' came on board, ain't it?"

Oglethorpe glanced over at MacKay, whose head stuck up out of the amphibian they had named *Azilia's Hammer*.

"I shall," he said, trying to think of a reason to put it off. But he needed to do this. Even mounted, they could never follow the marsh-edged Altamaha as fast as the ship could sail down it. And speed was their chiefest need. "Make way."

Oglethorpe stepped tentatively onto the metal back of the artifice, then, determined to appear bold and unconcerned, went down the small wooden ladder.

Inside, the amphibian positively reeked of men and oil. Mostly it smelled like the sulfur his men had used to clean the Russians out. And it was close inside, terribly so. The bridge was the size of a rowboat, and four people were already crowded into it. A wooden bulkhead cut them off from the rest of the ship, so the effect was that Oglethorpe felt he had been stuffed into a small box.

Panic squeezed his lungs, but he forced himself to breathe. He had never liked small spaces. Never. He'd been trapped in a pantry once by one of his cousins, and had not been discovered for hours. When they found him, he had beaten his hands bloody.

He concentrated on other things. The most obvious were the windows. Plates of alchemical glass—really a sort of transparent metal—were bolted into the ship's frame, so he could see the yellowish blue murk of the Altamaha's water, though such was the nature of the stuff that no one outside could see in. The occasional silver glimmer of fish flashed there, but otherwise there wasn't much to see. In fact, the obfuscating water did nothing to lessen his discomfort. No, rather, it heightened it, for he was a poor swimmer, and the thought of water pressing in on him from all directions was unpleasant.

"How does it work?" he asked MacKay.

MacKay indicated a wheel, smaller but not otherwise vastly different from any other ship's wheel. "This goes back to the rudder," he said. "And this makes her go." He indicated a long lever with several notched settings.

"How? How does it go?"

"There are wheels on the side, as you've seen, with paddles attached."

"Yes. What turns the wheels?"

"A demon, sir."

"Yes, yes, but how?"

"I do not know. I only know she works, sir."

"Where is the demon?"

"This way, if you want to see."

"I do."

They passed the bulkhead that separated the bridge from the rest of the ship. Behind, there were two decks: an upper, where supplies were stored, and a lower, where the rest of the men were packed in tight—an awful, windowless place.

"Hello, lads," he said, as he went among them. "Cozy down here."

"Yes, sir!" they answered.

Near the center of the ship, the lower hold was interrupted by a metal cylinder, a bit too large for Oglethorpe to put his arms around. From that, two heavy shafts stretched out to the sides of the ship, where they slipped through gaskets to turn the wheels outside. On the large cylinder was a small door. MacKay produced a key and opened it.

From inside the cylinder, a giant red eye stared back at him.

"Good God," he swore. He looked quickly away, but his gaze came inevitably back.

It wasn't an eye, exactly, but a large sphere of some translucent material, inside of which was a red glow with a black center that looked very much like a pupil. He had seen globes very like this powering the Russian airships.

"This turns the shafts, somehow. And keeps us down?"

"No, sir. We use ballast, just as any ship would, except we want to sink, of course, so we have a lot of it. The boat has big bilges, too, and clever pumps the lads work to clear them. They don't work if we go too deep, though—if we do that, we have to drop the solid ballast and replace it later."

Oglethorpe shook his head. "Clever indeed, except for the reliance on the devil to power it. Why didn't they use steam, I wonder?"

"I reckon you'd see bubbles rising, and then not be so invisible."

"I'd think the water would take the steam back to its bosom, as a liquid," Oglethorpe argued. "I think instead these Russians have become as reliant on their pet demons as our planters on their slaves. And so it makes them weak, don't you think?"

"In a way, I suppose. But this ship ain't weak, sir. Far from it."

"You mean those flame cannons?"

"Oh, there's more," MacKay said, eyes twinkling. "We've a magazine of bombs that float up if we release them."

"Why? Oh. You would swim the ship under a man-of-war—"

"And let 'em float up. Yes, sir, and I'll wager blow a great huge hole right in the bottom."

"Delightful. And if we encounter another amphibian?"

"The Russian pilots said they had nothing for that. They

reckoned they would never meet an amphibian that was an enemy."

"And yet we will. We certainly will, and we must think of some countermeasure."

"Well—we could always drop them bombs from above, onto amphibians below."

"I thought they floated, these bombs?"

"We could take off the air bladders. They'd sure sink then."

"And drop them how? Through the deck?"

"Ah!" MacKay shook his finger, grinning. "I haven't shown you the *other* hatch. Here."

He walked a few feet farther on, knelt at a round, metal screw, much like the one on the top of the ship; and began turning it.

"MacKay!" Oglethorpe protested. "You'll let the water in."

"No, sir. Not as long as the upper hatch is closed."

"What on earth do you mean?"

"Here."

The screw lifted out, and beneath was water. It bobbed there, coming no higher.

"How?"

MacKay shrugged again.

"Don't know, sir, but it works."

Oglethorpe considered that. "Yes, it does," he said finally. "But can we trust it? And in any event, if we are positioned to drop mines on them, won't they be positioned to let theirs float up to us?"

"Aye. But they won't know we're the enemy, at least not the first time we do it."

"Not the first time," Oglethorpe agreed. "We shall need another weapon or stratagem after that."

"Well, there are the guns. We've fired 'em underwater. They work tolerable well, though they churn the water fierce and makes cones instead of clean lines. At short range they ought to work."

"They can be fired from inside the hatch, then?"

"Aye, though not aimed. We have to point the ship to orient 'em."

"Well. That's better than I feared. I wish Franklin could see this. He would invent something, no doubt, that would do us good."

"No doubt," MacKay replied. "But he's not here."

"Aye," Oglethorpe replied, clapping him on the back. "We poor soldiers will have to make do. So let's set sail, or start swimming, or whatever term we should use for this unnatural business."

"Aye, sir."

And a few moments later, still gritting his teeth, Oglethorpe stood near the helm and watched the mud of the Altamaha flow by.

12.

To Slay the Sun

Red Shoes stood in the dark water, wondering. Had he come the wrong way? Was this a different entrance?

But no, this earth was freshly turned, and he could smell human hands on it.

They must have all agreed, he thought. *But whose idea was it?*

Bloody Child and Paint Red had influence, but not that much influence. Minko Chito would not have begun the idea.

It must have been the Onkala priests, the Bone Men. Only they might have seen what was in him and recognized the danger. Or perhaps the Bone Men had been seduced themselves by the minions of the Sun Boy. The Sun Boy attracted followers by sending dreams of glory and purification. Perhaps he had sent such visions to the keepers of the dead.

Well. But the Onkala priests did not know how powerful Red Shoes was. They did not know he could easily rip his way through this inconsequential barrier of earth. Eagerly, he gathered his strength. His rattles hissed in the darkness.

No. That was the snake, whispering in his ear. To the others, it would only prove he was the monster they thought he was.

And so he sat in the darkness for a time, and thought, and remembered something Mother Dead had told him. About the hole that led down to where she was.

He squeezed and ducked his way back down the tunnel, until he came again to the place where the roof went beneath. He took a few deep breaths, then dove, trying to ignore the hornets in his skull, the lizards on his arms, the scorpions between his toes, the voice that said to dig through the earth and kill, to make shadowchildren of blood and poison to burrow into frail human minds.

He swam down, feeling for different turns, earlier ways than the one he had taken down to the heart of the underworld. After a moment, he found one, one that led vaguely up.

As he swam, the tunnel straightened to a vertical, and his body became heavier, his arms lethargic. It was as if something had taken hold of his feet and was pulling him down. He kicked, but his feet were pinned together. He braced his arms on the walls to pull, but they would not, could not, and then he was sinking.

His legs knit together, and one of his arms was stuck to his side, then the other. And still something was dragging him down, naming him a name that was not his own but which was familiar.

Father, he thought, and his head was suddenly full of the wide reaches between stars, of the boundless nothing that was behind the place behind the world; and a terrible joy mingled with his terror.

Down. It was over. He had lost. Too long, in the underneath.

No. I am the water spider, sevenfold walker. I am the kingfisher, who dives beneath and always returns. I am the words beneath the black paint, the earth above the grave. I am Red Shoes, a house with many rooms but RED SHOES!

And he broke from the water into thick, hot, moist air, but air, and the light riddling through the tall cypress, in the headwaters of the river of the Choctaw, the River of Pearls. He stared up through the trees for a long while at the yellow eye of Hashtali winking through at him.

"Thank you, Hashtali," he murmured. "Keep my spirit strong. Keep the Sacred Fire in me unpolluted, at least until I save your people."

Nearby, someone chuckled. Red Shoes knew the voice, and whirled.

"Hello, chieftain of the snakes," the scalped man said. He crouched on the rotting carcass of a cypress tree, his eyes gleaming. He was painted and tattooed like a warrior, but his head was a mass of puckered scars, all in a neat circle, where the skin of his head had been cut off.

"Not yet," Red Shoes told him.

"But near, so near," the scalped man rasped. "You will join us, soon."

"I will not."

"You prayed to Hashtali, the creator, the sun eyed. Do you remember why you were made?"

"I was not made. I was born to human parents."

"The Antler Snake was made from a man, to kill the sun, to strike the creator dead. Did you know that?"

"It's one of the stories, yes."

"It is *your* story, Red Shoes. Let it tell itself, brother."

"I think I shall kill you."

"Your friends are watching," he said, pointing.

Red Shoes turned to look. When he looked back, the scalped man was gone.

But his words remained. *Slay the Sun.* Was that what he was to do? He had been made to slay something. But an arrow could slay its maker. It could.

"Thank you, Hashtali," he said again. "I will send you tobacco, when I have some that is dry."

Minko Chito, the Bone Men, and the rest were still watching the sealed cave entrance when he found them. Red Shoes drew on *hoshonti*, the cloud, and walked up behind them without sound.

"How's he ever going to get out of there?" he asked, dispelling *hoshonti*.

They turned almost as a man, all astonished except for the two Bone Men. They just nodded. "You are the one," the elder of the two said. Then, to Minko Chito. "He *is* the one."

The old chief nodded, and though Bloody Child and Paint Red scowled, they said nothing.

Indeed, Red Shoes thought, *I am the one. But perhaps not the one you think I am.*

They returned to the village and began making plans for war.

13.

Demonstrations Quaint and Curious

Franklin found Euler the next morning, playing cards with several courtiers and seeming to enjoy himself.

"A word with you, Mr. Euler?"

"But of course, Mr. Franklin, if the ladies will forgive me."

One of the ladies looked cross. "We will forgive *you*, Monsieur, but perhaps not your wizard friend." Then her frown became a smile. "Unless his demonstration this evening is exceptionally amusing."

"You will find it so, I hope," Franklin replied. "And I will have Mr. Euler only for a hand or two. He has a condition, you see, that requires fresh air now and then, and one of its complications is a forgetfulness of that fact—so I must see to it."

"Not contagious, I hope?"

"The only contagious thing in this room is admiration for you, milady," Franklin replied.

"You make a good courtier," Euler remarked when they were out upon the terrace in front of the palace. "But then you were one once, weren't you?"

"I had the training," Franklin admitted, "and remember some of the lessons."

"Well, you've taken me out of my little box to ask me some question again, haven't you? Something so important you must ignore the fact that you do not trust me."

"You're a perceptive judge of character," Franklin said. "That is exactly what I've come for."

"Let's hear it, then."

"Tell me, did you know Sterne was a warlock?"

"I did when I saw him last night. I never knew the name before."

"He knew yours."

"Well, he is more in the know than I, surely. Is that your question?"

"No. It is this: How can I make him reveal himself?"

"You have no device for that?"

"I have a device that detects warlocks, but it proves nothing to the uninitiated—a needle pointing like a compass makes no good demonstration. I need for his malakus to appear, for all to see him revealed for what he is."

"Ah. Try to kill him, then."

"At dinner? In front of everyone?"

"That's what you want, yes?"

"Not exactly. What if I draw a pistol and nothing happens? Then I merely jeopardize what goodwill I have earned here."

"If he is in serious danger of his life, his malakus will appear, with or without his consent. It is the only thing I can suggest."

"But if, for instance, the guards notice my motion before he does—no. I cannot risk it."

"I'm sorry I couldn't be of more help."

Franklin nodded thoughtfully. "It will have to do, I suppose. There must be some way to make use of this. Thank you, Mr. Euler—you may return to your card game."

"Back into my box, eh?"

"For now."

When Euler was gone from sight, doubts returned. What if this were some sabotage, finally, on Euler's part? An agreement with Sterne to make Franklin look not only idiotic but idiotic and murderous?

But there was one way. A dangerous way, but not as dangerous as standing up during the toasts with a gun. Not to him, anyway.

He had only an hour before his appointment with the king. With any luck, he could arrange it in that time, if he could bring himself to ask it.

*   *   *

Franklin gazed around him in almost stupefied delight at the laboratory. It was almost wonderful enough to push aside his other worries. Entirely at odds with the rest of the makeshift chateau, located in a separate building surrounded by withered botanical gardens, it was almost as light and airy as a pavilion. Its shelves were cluttered, not with the rubbish Franklin feared, but with every sort of scientific apparatus imaginable. Cabinets burst to overflowing with vials and jars of chemicals.

A fine layer of dust covered everything.

"Will it do?" the king asked.

"Will it do? Your Majesty, I have never in my life seen a better-equipped laboratory, even when I was with Sir Isaac. Did you supervise its outfitting yourself?"

"As a matter of fact, I did," he said proudly. "Before Paris fell I loaded almost the entire contents of the Academy of Sciences on wagons and sent them to the fleet I was gathering. I don't have to tell you how many miracles it took to see it all here safe and sound." His face fell a bit. "Now I know it would have been better to load the ship with provisions and other necessities of life. I did not know, then, how poorly our New World colonies had fared. It is an act of vanity for which I have not forgiven myself."

"But, Sire, the answers to many of your troubles are here! I can build you a manna machine, for instance, to feed your hungry. In fact, I'm puzzled. I sent the Sieur de Bienville a manna machine years ago, as a token of friendship."

"We had one, but it failed eventually. No one here had the skill to repair it. I was too proud to admit it to you English. Can you really make another?"

"In a few days, if you give me an assistant or two."

"I would be most grateful." He looked thoughtful for a moment. Franklin could almost see the scales in the king's mind, weighing this against that. "I give you and your men the freedom of the palace and grounds. I give you the freedom of the laboratory, as well. I pray you do not abuse my hospitality."

"I will not, I assure you, Majesty. But may I ask, does this mean—"

"I have not yet decided to join your rebellion, Mr. Franklin. My reservations are still deep. Moreover, I hear things do not go well for the English colonies."

"What have you heard, sir? My aetherschreiber was lost when the Coweta captured us."

"I will make one available to you—one of our own Frank-linned ones, if that will help. As to the other, Sterne tells me that your forces have been defeated, with only a few remaining outlaws in Indian country."

Franklin waited for the rest of it, but the king seemed to have finished. He did not know, then, that that remainder was marching to New Paris, in hopes of a friendly reception. Or did he?

Either way, if he did not bring it up, Franklin certainly would not. This wasn't the time to make explanations about the Junto, which could be seen pretty easily as a spy organization.

After a moment, the king did go on, however, in a slightly different vein.

"It may be that in the end you may realize that you must take refuge here—refuge I would willingly give you, I might add, whatever my cousin should request. That, if nothing else, I will promise you."

That was a sort of opening, Franklin figured. "Sir, if that be the case—and I hope it is not, I will tell you, for if the struggle against James goes badly, it is bad for us all—and my welfare lies with Your Highness, I wonder if I might make a few suggestions?"

"Certainly."

"Your defenses, Sire. I fear they are not strong enough should your cousin force the issue. You have heard, no doubt, of the submersible ships he brought to Carolina. I wonder, can you be assured that no such ships lie in your own harbor?"

"Oh, dear."

"And the flying ships. You have no defense against them either, nor against the other demonic things they have contrived in Russia this past decade. I can help you with that."

"You would do this?"

"Yes, Your Majesty. I believe what I say, you see. This is no small struggle between countries. It is a fight for the liberty and life of everyone. If the English colonies are defeated, it is a tragedy. But the fight must go on."

The king frowned in irritation. "I have told you—"

"I understand, Your Majesty, that you do not yet consider this your fight. I know also that you do not have all the facts and that you are used to deception in those you treat with. I am willing to gamble that when the time comes—and it will come, Majesty—that this *will* become your fight. I want you to have the means to do it, that is all. If I'm wrong, you will still have gained, for there are foes aplenty around you. I understand you have had your differences with Cuba, Mexico, and Florida."

The king nodded thoughtfully, but his eyes soon narrowed with suspicion. "And if you find your own weapons turned against you? If I join my cousin in his conquest of the New World?"

"Sire, I have not known you long, but I will be impertinent enough to judge your character. When you see what it actually is that we are fighting, you will understand. You will agree with me. But—they will be your weapons, your defenses. Clearly you can do anything with them that you please."

"Sterne has promised me mechanical men and airships. Will what you build me be better than that?"

"Remember always this, Sire. I was with Sir Isaac when he invented the talos, the template for those mechanical men you speak of. Surely you have heard the tale? By now it is famous."

"How it turned on him?"

"Yes. The aid Sterne offers you is of a very powerful sort— and it cannot be trusted. The creatures that locomote his airships and automatons will not be loyal to you. They are not loyal to Sterne, or to King James, or even to the tsar of Russia. They are loyal to distant creatures in the aether, invisible masters who wish for nothing less than the extinction of humanity. If you would invite such into your very home, I can do nothing to stop you. But it would be foolish."

Philippe paced across the laboratory. "They say," he murmured, "that my uncle Louis XIV was possessed by a demon in his last years. He was blind, you know—and yet he could *see*. And he brought that *thing* down from heaven." He looked up. "I am not unaware of the creatures you speak of. The priests argue over the matter, but most of the Jesuits believe them to be demons. Is that your belief?"

"Yes. Or to be more precise, they are beings of great power who wish us harm. I will leave it to theologians to decide where they are placed in God's plan. For my part, I believe in a God who is not nearly so devious and fickle in His designs."

The king fidgeted. "I don't like this sort of talk. I don't like it at all. But I must face it, I suppose. Still, though Sterne is somewhat boorish—and, forgive me, what Englishman is not?—I see no evidence that he leagues himself with the devil. Indeed, since he makes the same claim of you, I don't know what to believe." He rested his hand on a table, looking very old and very tired. Franklin knew exactly how he felt.

"Well," he said, "if Your Majesty will bear a change in subject, here is the demonstration I had in mind for the dinner crowd tonight. It is to do with the composition of the atmosphere. I think you will find it both instructive and amusing."

The king brightened immediately, and his spirits continued to improve as they worked out the particulars. He became less like a king and more like a young boy, fascinated by the world. A little of it rubbed off on Franklin, and he found he was, at times, enjoying himself.

It was after the king was gone, and he straightening up, that he felt more than heard someone else enter the room.

Vasilisa stood in the doorway, wearing a gown of deepest violet.

"Hello, Benjamin. I understand you are making quite the impression around here."

"Really? I was surprised, I admit, not to see you at dinner. You seem to have insinuated yourself into the machinery here as well. I've only yet to figure out just where—which treachery you're involved in."

"I was invited to dinner. I thought it best not to go. I will attend tonight, however. The king wishes me to see his demonstration."

"You are friendly with the king?"

"Why not be blunt, Ben, as you seem bent on hurting me? I am not his mistress. He has two of those, both quite vicious. I have enemies enough here as it is."

"Yes, and I have enough without acquiring yours."

Finally, a small, vexed frown disturbed her composure. "I thought you wanted me to speak," she said. "You said as much."

"Speak, then."

"It has to do with the dark engines."

That caught his attention. It was the same phrase Euler had used. Of course, she might well have met with Euler in the last day, but either way, it was worth hearing more about this.

"Go on," he said.

She smiled faintly. "Science has taken something of a different direction in Russia," she explained. "An angelic direction, if you understand me. Almost all advances there have hinged on improving Sir Isaac's use of the animal spirit, on giving the malakim material bodies."

"So far you aren't telling me anything I don't know."

"Now I will, I think. We have gone beyond Newton, Ben. We have invented a way for the malakim to become manifest— more than manifest, near omnipotent—in the world of matter. No more taloi made of metal and alchemical muscle, no more clumsy airships, no more fighting battles through human allies. They will take a hand directly, themselves. Do you see?"

His mouth felt dry. "Then why all this?" he asked quietly. "Why the underwater ships, the Pretender, Sterne—why all this farce?"

"Because we didn't know we could do it, and because the malakim are divided. Some forbid the use of the dark engines; some don't even know about them. Battles can be fought in the aether, too. Those who wish to exterminate our race must pick their moment. They must pretend to have the matter in hand with their armies and cannon and intrigues in human kingdoms. But, Ben, it will all be for naught if we can't defeat the engines. All of it, I swear."

And suddenly, in a cold light, he saw something on her face he understood perfectly. It was the face that looked out of the mirror at him when he remembered what he had done to the world, the face that knew itself responsible for millions of deaths.

And—the unfair part—she was weeping.

A weeping woman has a magnetism that few men even think to resist. Franklin was no better, and he found himself with a hand on her shoulder, gruffly trying to soothe.

The next moment, he found her in his arms.

It was a shock, how familiar it was. The scent of her hair was the same, the bones of her body, so delicate.

But he did not recognize this grip, this feeling of helplessness emanating from her. She had always been the confident one, the one in control. It had always been he who needed her. It felt good, this change in roles. It felt like such good revenge that he didn't even want revenge anymore. No, he wanted . . .

Despite what he wanted, he gently pushed her back.

"Come, Vasilisa. If what you say is true, I will help you. Of course I must. But if it is distraction—"

"It is not, I swear."

"You said you had proof."

"I have some of Swedenborg's notes on their making. From them we can create a countermeasure. We must! Together, I am certain we can."

"Notes are not proof."

"You look at them. You judge. I leave them with you."

Where she produced them from—the folds of her skirt?— he wasn't sure, but she lay several bound sheaves of paper into his hand. Then she was gone.

He opened the first up. Latin, at least, and not Russian. He would be able to get through it passing well.

He sat down and began to read, scratching every now and then with pen and paper to check an equation.

The sun changed its slant through the windows and worked toward the red end of the spectrum until it settled on a brutish sort of brick orange.

A cool breeze swept in from seaward, easing through the open windows to replace the ferocious heat of the day. Despite that, Franklin kept sweating, for by that time he believed.

He became so lost in the notes that it took Robert and Voltaire to rouse him from them and remind him that the dinner hour was fast approaching.

"Every part of your plan is in place—except you, you dunderhead, and the scientifical apparatus."

"Yes, thanks, fellows. Could you carry these things—or find some servant to carry them—while I put on fresh clothing? The king, I fear, has already seen me in this."

"Your court habits are coming back awful fast, despite y'r protestations that you have no use for 'em," Robert observed.

"It's necessity, Robert. To win this French king over, I must play the game by his rules."

"Really?" Voltaire asked. "I wonder about that. Sterne, I think, knows those rules better than you, and this d'Artaguiette surely does."

"A lecture on rules from the man who talked himself into the Bastille?" Franklin replied. But something about Voltaire's comment rang true. "Well, perhaps I shall do some bending, then, and see how that works."

His outfit was greeted at first with titters and stage-whispered comments. He smiled and nodded politely as if to the highest praise, kept his back straight and his step even, and presented himself to the king. As he bowed, he doffed his raccoon-skin hat and kept it off.

"Some new scientifical garb?" the king asked mildly, surveying him. Franklin wore a deerskin matchcoat borrowed from one of the Apalachee and beneath it a very plain waistcoat of linsey-woolsey with cloth-covered buttons. His breeches matched.

"No, Your Majesty—American garb. It is quite the rage in Charles Town." That last was something of a lie—men of means dressed exactly as these French did, in habitual imitation of the lost European courts. But he did look rather like a deerskin trader or ranger, down to the hat.

"Really? How quaint. Perhaps I should have such an outfit made. We are, after all, Americans in a sense."

"In the highest sense," Franklin agreed. "Indeed, I am told that this habit was borrowed by our English traders from the French in the Natchez concessions. In any event, I find it comfortable."

"I find it rather crude," d'Artaguiette said, a brittle smile on his thin face.

"I prefer natural, sir. Survival in this New World, you will admit, requires a certain vitality. All of us here at this table have it—evident by our survival. We have been tried by our environment and found adequate, much as the natives have. I feel this dress is a badge of honor, a mark of distinction, and an important step in admitting—*embracing*—that our nations are unlike any ever to exist in Europe or anywhere in the world. Despite our creeds, languages, and governments, Your Majesty, I offer that we are all Americans." He strode to the table and lifted a glass of wine. "To his majesty, Philippe I— the king of France in America—an American king."

"Here!" Voltaire seconded, standing to raise his own. All Franklin's companions followed suit, as did a scattering of Frenchmen he strongly suspected were Junto members. He noticed Vasilisa, too, seated a few chairs from the king, repressing a smile.

When the king nodded in acceptance of the toast, all of his court joined—even d'Artaguiette.

Sterne—unshackled this time and dressed in finest silk— did not drink.

"You do not drink the king's health, sir?" Don Pedro asked loudly.

"I will gladly drink the king's health," Sterne replied. "I

did not hear a toast offered to his health, only some maudlin, common sentiment that the noble blood of France has somehow become polluted by the savagery of this continent and its peoples."

"Peoples like my own, sir? You understand that I am a prince of Apalachee."

"I understand that—*prince*—and if I have given offense where none was intended, I do apologize."

"And will you say that none was intended?" Don Pedro asked. "Or must I assume you meant to insult me?"

"I do not know you well enough, don, to say. Why don't you tell us whether I have insulted you or not?"

A faint grin appeared on Don Pedro's face. "I do feel insulted, and, moreover, my people have been insulted. Your Majesty, I require satisfaction from this man, but I will not pursue it unless you give me leave."

A murmur of excitement swept through the room.

The king frowned. "I had already planned a diversion for the court, with Mr. Franklin's help."

"Begging Your Majesty's pardon. I am fully satisfied to await Your Majesty's pleasure. I am eager to see this demonstration and see no reason why I cannot send Mr. Sterne to our Lord for judgment *after* the meal and its entertainments."

"Like you, Mr. Sterne is our guest. I cannot ask him to fight a duel."

"If he must be compelled, the question of honor is already settled," Don Pedro said, "and the court will know where to find it."

"By God, enough of this, you babbling monkey!" Sterne snapped. "I will meet you at any time convenient to His Majesty."

Philippe looked a bit swept away by things, but the sounds from his court were approving. It must have been a long time since they had blood sport. If they were so keen for a tennis match, this ought to *really* please them.

"Very well," Philippe concluded. "After the demonstration, if you gentlemen must conduct your argument, you shall. Take the opportunity during the meal to appoint your seconds. Now, Mr. Franklin, if you would be so kind as to help me with these devices, we shall provide less bloody and more illuminating amusement."

The experiments went well and drew polite—sometimes even enthusiastic—applause. Using a pair of graduated cylinders, the first demonstration proved that air had weight and pressure. Then, by means of a burning candle in one of the cylinders, they demonstrated that, though its pressure remained, some substance in the air necessary for combustion was used up quite quickly. Finally, they engaged a device Franklin had invented, quite by accident, in Prague. It repelled the substance in the open atmosphere, extinguishing a nearby candle. Courtiers were then invited to approach and discover that the same chemical which fed combustion was also the sustaining fuel for human beings, drawing laughs as they stumbled away, light-headed.

"What we must conclude," Philippe said, when all was done, "is that we have something like a slow fire burning in each of us. Note that your flesh is warm, and that fever, which increases the ferocity of that fire, can consume and waste us away. Indeed, it might be that such a device as you have just seen might be of use, somehow, in treating fever. Certainly it could be of use in extinguishing the blazes that take too much of our property when necessity—" He smiled. "—*American* necessity—demands we build our homes of wood."

More applause, and then the meal. As soon as it was done, Sterne stood. "Your Majesty—"

"Your pardon, Sire," Don Pedro interrupted. "I notice that people are still discussing your experiments. I don't wish to interrupt the discussion until it is quite done. It would please me if you would judge when our duel should be fought."

"Very good," Philippe replied, obviously pleased not to be so quickly upstaged. He then leaned close to Franklin. "Is this some scheme of yours, Mr. Franklin, to rid yourself of an adversary?"

"No, sir," Franklin lied. "Don Pedro, as you must know, is rather impulsive."

"Too impulsive, perhaps. I have seen Mr. Sterne at practice. Rarely have I ever seen such skill with the sword. For all of his bravado, I somehow doubt that our Apalachee friend could have received such training in his own kingdom."

"He is his own man, Sire." He felt a certain emptiness, though. It hadn't occurred to him that Sterne might be an accomplished swordsman. That would complicate his plan considerably, especially if Don Pedro's own boasts were inflated. Still, the Apalachee claimed to be a master of the Spanish rapier, and Robert—who used the same weapon—tended to agree.

After another hour or so, Philippe raised his hand for attention. "An insult has been given and replied to with a challenge. The matter may be settled now. Gentlemen, have you chosen your seconds?"

"Yes, Your Majesty," Sterne said, indicating one of his men. Don Pedro, on the other hand, chose Robert. The Apalachee removed his coat, unsheathed his weapon, and made a few passes with it.

Sterne watched him for a moment, then whispered to his second.

"Your Majesty," Sterne's second said, "my master is in need of a rapier, of the older sort. Is one to be found?"

"Indeed," the king replied. He signed, and a few moments later a servant returned with several. Sterne tried them, one by one, finally settling on one somewhat longer and heavier than the Apalachee's weapon.

A murmur went up at the unusual choice. Though some still wore such old-style rapiers, few still fought with them, preferring the lighter, nimbler smallsword, for good reason: while a man with a rapier made one thrust, the bearer of a smallsword could parry and riposte twice, despite the difference in length. Don Pedro's Spanish weapon was almost as light as a smallsword, and so could be fenced with in the usual manner. The weapon Sterne had chosen must weigh three pounds.

"Will you use a *main gauche*, sir?" Don Pedro asked.

"I suppose," Sterne replied.

It was then that Franklin remembered something about warlocks. They were very, very strong.

"Uh-oh," Franklin heard Robert mumble.

Franklin's belly clenched again, and he quickly made his way to Don Pedro's side just as Robert was handing him the dagger he would use in his left hand.

"He is not a normal man, Don Pedro," Franklin whispered. "He can wield that rapier like a smallsword."

"An interesting thing to learn, now," Don Pedro said solemnly. Then he laughed, and slapped Franklin on the back.

"I regret our bargain, Don Pedro. Call this off."

"Nonsense. It isn't the sword that wins or loses, or even the strength of the arm—it is the man and the God he worships. That man is an agent of Lucifer. God will give me the victory. If he does not, I am not worthy to live anyway." He held out his hand for Franklin to shake, then took his place in the cleared space on the floor.

Part Two

ON THE SHOULDERS
OF GIANTS

If I have seen further it is by standing on the shoulders of giants.

—Isaac Newton

1.

Abomination

Minko Chito stared off at the West, straining to see what no mere mortal eyes could discern.

"It is out there, this army?"

"It is," Red Shoes assured him.

Minko Chito nodded absently. "I have killed many men," he said. "I once went amongst the Chickasaw, into Long Town itself, and came out with two scalps. I ran for half a month to fight the Big Hill people, and half a month back, chased by them the whole way, and I laughed. But this—this is different. These enemies come from the West, from the Nightland, where the accursed live."

"Some say *we* came from there," Red Shoes reminded him. "Do not fear them. They have accursed beings, yes. But you have me, and I have never failed you."

"I failed *you*," Minko Chito remarked contritely.

"No. The Bone Men were right. You had to know. You can't be trusting when you deal with the other world. What seems helpful can easily become terrible." He clapped the chief on the back. "Tell your warriors to strike with their arrows and muskets, with their ball-headed war clubs and their steel-toothed axes. Leave the accursed beings for me to fight."

"Else we perish, as I saw in my visions," Minko Chito muttered. "Our bones gnawed by dogs, never picked smooth and bundled into the House of Warriors. Yes, I know we must fight. I know the vision was true. But I am not too proud to say I fear the spirits, as I fear no man. No one can fault me for it."

"No one does," Red Shoes told him. "But as you fear no

man, I fear no spirit. I have defeated the Long Black Being. I have defeated the Snake Crawfish, the Antler Serpent. I will defeat this child of the witches."

Minko Chito nodded. "When?"

"Soon they will try to cross the river. We must stop them."

"How, if they have ships that fly? What will the river mean to them?"

"They have too many men and horses, too few ships. I think they will try to build a bridge. If they use the flying ships, I shall deal with them."

"I'm going to shoot a *lot* of them," a young voice said. It was Chula.

"Hello, younger cousin," Red Shoes said.

"Hello, elder cousin," the boy replied. "In a few days, you will never call me Chula again. I will have a war name."

"Or we may call you nothing at all," Red Shoes answered. "You might be dead, and we do not speak the names of the dead."

"I can't die!" Chula said. "Not when we have Red Shoes, the greatest *hopaye* of all to make our war magic." Then his face twisted in fear, as he thought of something. "Do you *see* it?" He gasped. "Do you see my death?"

"I see you growing old and honored," Red Shoes said, "so long as you are as cautious as you are brave. Always use your head. Never use your bow until all of your powder is gone, and never use your war club until all of your arrows are gone. And when your war club breaks, throw yourself into the forest, hide, and fight another time."

"Now you sound like one of the old men."

"They are old for a reason, Chula. Stupid men die young. Maybe very young."

"I'm not stupid."

"Good."

Red Shoes saw the Sun Boy long before he saw the ships. He saw him as the old Wichita priest might have, a giant with legs like long, thin stilts, striding with his head almost as high as the Sun. Then again, when he blinked, he saw instead a tree of a thousand branches, and on each branch a hundred birds. Each bird was a spirit. In some places a branch was swollen, like the pustules on trees from which certain kinds of beetles were born. Again, when he blinked, they were more like wombs, with tadpole things curled inside.

He wondered how the Sun Boy would perceive him. Just now, he saw nothing, Red Shoes was certain. All of Red Shoes' strength went to hide himself, to hide his fellow Choctaw, and to watch.

When the first airships appeared, a few warriors had to be restrained from giving the war cry and shooting at them—but not as many as he feared. Terror of witchcraft made them sober, even the berserk *Hacho* warriors. They kept to the cover of the trees, where Red Shoes could draw *hoshonti*, the concealing cloud, over them.

As Red Shoes suspected, the Sun Boy and his army did not plan to ferry all the horsemen across in the flying ships—with all those skittish horses, that would take a long time. And why should they, when the flying ships made building a bridge so easy?

It was interesting to watch. First they used airships to draw long, heavy cables across to the eastern side of the river. Seeing this, once again, some warriors began edging toward the enemy.

"Restraint," Red Shoes cautioned Minko Chito. "We might kill a few if we attack their airship when they land to attach the cables. But think how many more we shall kill if we let them start across the bridge and destroy it."

"Surely they will notice us before that," Minko Chito said. "Surely they will establish themselves on this side, with the airships to protect both ends of their bridge."

"Surely. But it will do them no good. Tell the warriors to go back into the swamps. Convince them to wait."

"It will be difficult. Now that they have seen the enemy, they want to blood themselves."

"They will spill more blood and take more scalps if they do what I say," Red Shoes assured him.

* * *

Now the Sun Boy was a spider, spinning a great web, weaving lines of attractions and repulsions and threading spirits on the strands like beads, wheels within delicate wheels. Like a black sunrise, his web spread in the West, lazily spinning about the effulgent hole in the sky that was the Sun Boy.

Red Shoes fasted and chanted, let the snake grow sharp inside him, let the wings spread out on his back, took on the scent of the enemy; and when he was ready, he drifted up into the web and slipped in, to the heart of the Sun Boy's strength, to his right hand. Unnoticed, unnamed. And there he began to steal and murder, to weaken strands, to prepare to slip the knife into the Sun Boy's back.

Red Shoes was a weapon, yes—a thing made to kill. Not to kill the sun itself, but this false child of the Sun, this mockery of Hashtali.

All this he did with his shadow, and so powerful was he that he could slip back into his crawfish-clay human skin and instruct his people. He met with the Bone Men and with the shamans from the nearest and farthest corners of the Choctaw country. He learned their secret names and the scent of their shadowchildren so he would know them when the battle came. Some were legends. Bullet Arrives, who had killed more than thirty men in his days as a warrior, now in his seventieth year, slowly sinking into the underworld that would take him one day, but for the time being still commanding shadowchildren of great power. Hopaye Minko, who some said might be a witch, but no one wanted to question. Night Painted, who, though young, was once nearly as powerful as Red Shoes.

Now Red Shoes dwarfed all of them, of course. Now even Bullet Arrives must learn from him.

He also had to be careful, to continue to hide his true nature from them. After this was over, he might well have to kill them. Once the Sun Boy was dead, it would be Red Shoes who decided what the world would be.

He made love to Grief, and he walked with her, showing her the sorts of food and medicines that grew in his country, some the same and some very different from those she knew.

"I want to fight," she told him one day.

"The warriors won't like that," he told her. "Men must separate themselves from the power of women before battle. Women are stronger, but different. They can weaken a warrior."

"I have no womanly things in me," she said. "I only want to kill them that killed my family."

"You felt womanly to me, just now."

"Not in my spirit. You must know what is in my spirit. Besides, your women talk of battles they have joined in."

He shrugged. "It *has* happened. Most often they yell and urge us on, but some have taken up arms in times past. Still, I would rather you guard me. My body will be vulnerable, when I battle the Sun Boy. I need someone to protect it."

"You do not fear I will weaken you?"

He laughed. "Power can come from purity—from maintaining separation of things that ought to be separate. Male and female, underearth and sky, fire and water. A warrior's power flows from purity, from being clean. Mine comes from abomination, from mixing what ought not to be mixed. Like the boys who mixed squirrel brains and bird eggs and turtle eggs and ate them."

"What became of them?"

"They became tie snakes, beings of great power."

"Like you," she said.

"Yes, like me."

"Did you mix squirrel brains and bird eggs and turtle eggs?"

"I ate something more forbidden than that. But I do mix things. I make love to you, though I know I must fight soon. It gives me strength."

"Why don't warriors gain power that way? You just said it weakens them."

"Ah," he said. "Because they are too attached to being human."

She nodded. "I understand now. It's not the army of the plain you fear, that you need a guard against. It's your own people."

He grinned. "You see why I need you. Yes. Bloody Child and his friends still talk against me. They might convince a few."

"Why? Why do they hate you so?"

"Their uncle was a *hopaye*, like me, but he lost a fight with a spirit. He became a walking skin, and had to be slain. I killed him."

"They think they have a feud with you."

"The council said I was right to do what I did and forbade them to take revenge on me or my clan. But they aren't satisfied with that. Will you guard me?"

"Yes."

An airship settled on their side of the river, acting as a fortress to guard that end of the bridge, just as Minko Chito forecast. Others hovered above, their red globes winking.

Red Shoes knew when he could restrain his people no longer. When the first of the great army began crossing the bridge, he let them strike. They attacked the grounded ship with musket and bow and war club, and the men unfortunate enough to be on the east bank of the river died feathered in shafts. Warriors dashed through bursting shells and withering fire, swarmed up the ropes that hung down from the sides of the ship. Many died, but not so many as to give the others pause. They took the ship and cut the cables, and more than a hundred men and mounts fell into the remorseless Okahina River. Young warriors followed them down, slaying them in the shallows if they did not drown in the sucking depths or return to the western side.

The enemy was not taken off guard for long. Artillery roared from across the river, firing randomly into the swamps and forest beyond. Airships began moving across, and smaller flyers shaped like giant leaves hummed overhead, dropping fire seeds that sprouted white-hot trees.

Red Shoes was oblivious of most of it. For him there was only the Sun Boy, almost in his grasp. He tore at the rotten fabric of the web, and sent out hornet swarms of shadow-children, each made with a single purpose and ability—to collapse the red globes that kept the airships aloft. He sheared through the Sun Boy's defenses, through Long Black Beings, through shields of underworld stuff. And as he fought, he sang, sang the song of the Nightland.

Adrienne leaned against the rail, breathing heavily, her wound now no more than a stitch in her side. No one spoke until Father Castillion crossed himself. "Sweet Savior," he murmured. "Preserve our souls."

The rolling flat plains had given way to dense, ancient forests. Not the bluish evergreen timbers of the Russian taiga and western American forest they had flown over but the trees of the startling verdancy that Adrienne knew from her youth in France, a kind of green she had almost forgotten. It was strange that she must travel so many thousands of miles to feel nostalgia for the place of her birth, but sometimes the world was thus. Linné was delighted—he pointed to the forest as proof of his theory of climates.

"We've reached the latitude of France," he said, "and thus this forest looks French. Oak and myrtle, I'll wager."

But the river had no counterpart—not in France, not anywhere in Europe. It could drink the Rhine, Rhône, and Danube and still be thirsty. Her maps labeled it variously River San Luis, Spirito Sancto, and Mississippi. Whatever its name, it was a monster.

And hovering above the river were the glowing pinpricks of airships, twenty of them. Around them, wheeling like great lazy birds, were the new flying machines of Swedenborg's invention. And, visible only to Adrienne's eyes, a thousand malakim.

Beneath all that, ants crossed the river in pea pods in a long string.

From four of the ships, fire blazed. Cannon, discharging bright yellow; the sun-bright burst of Fahrenheit guns; and firedrakes vanishing into the forests beyond the river, reappearing as vast columns of smoke billowing to meet the sky.

"This will be quite a fight," Hercule said. "Three ships against a score."

"But someone is fighting them already," Adrienne observed.

"It's difficult to say with what effectiveness," Hercule replied.

"Yes, but they fight scientifically—see?"

The globes attached to one of the airships suddenly flared from red to blue, and the entire ship ignited like a torch.

"Holy Mother of God," Hercule grunted. "I hope they do not mistake us for the enemy. Can you tell who is winning?"

"A moment," Adrienne replied, looking deeper into the aether.

Uriel was there, waiting, clearly agitated.

Strike now! he said. *The Sun Boy is distracted. This is most unexpected. It is your best chance.*

What are they fighting? Adrienne asked.

I'm not sure. Something strange. A man, yet not a man. A malakus, yet not a malakus. Something dangerous to both.

Like the keres? Like my son?

Both. Neither. I don't know. I am weary, weary of protecting us. Even with the distraction, it takes everything I can manage to keep our enemies from seeing us. Strike!

What did you intend for me to do at this point?

We need your son. Or perhaps— Again, hesitation. *Perhaps the other will do, if he survives. You should try to reach him.*

I want my son.

Good. Let us subdue him, then.

Can you tell which ship he is on?

Yes.

Then bring the other ships down. All of them.

Uriel paused for so long this time she thought he had either gone to obey her command or vanished so as to ignore it. But finally, his voice returned. She could see him now, as well, his many-winged form hovering between her and the battle. *No,* he said. *That would go too far. We would be discovered, and I see now that you—we, rather—do not have the strength to reach him. Cross the river, and we will add our strength to their enemy.*

What need to cross the river? We will help him from here. Bring down the ships.

He doesn't know us. He won't understand we're helping.

Bring down the ships, or I will order an attack anyway. I swear it to you.

You don't know what you're asking.

I don't care what I'm asking.

Very well. You will regret it.

And he flew toward the battle, drawing all of her legion of servants behind him.

"Hercule," she said softly, her gaze fixed on the ships that held her son. "Order the advance."

2.

An Interesting Outcome

Don Pedro attacked first, bouncing in and darting his blade ferociously toward Sterne's heart. For an instant, Franklin thought the duel was already over, but the sharp point came up an inch short. Sterne, completely unperturbed, snaked his own blade against the attacking one, bound it up, then exploded forward in a shallow lunge. Don Pedro leapt back and raised his blade back to guard.

"Shit!" Robert hissed. Franklin saw it too—a petal of red on Don Pedro's sword arm, blooming quickly into a rose.

Sterne stepped back and lowered his guard. "First blood," he said. "If your honor is satisfied now, I am willing."

"A fair touch," Don Pedro replied, "but a mosquito bite. Return to guard, sir."

Sterne shrugged and resumed his stance.

Don Pedro advanced, much more cautiously this time.

"Did you see how fast he went with the rapier?" Robert whispered.

"You're the second. Call it off."

"He'll never agree."

Again, Don Pedro was the first to attack, feinting low and attacking high. Again, Sterne returned with another bind and attack. This time, however, Don Pedro managed to slip from the bind and circle to the side. He riposted, but again too slowly and too short—he looked like a sparrow trying to keep up with a hummingbird. Sterne swept the don's blade high and darted in for the kill.

A second blood flower budded on the Apalachee, this one on his chest.

"Yield, sir," Sterne said.

"Never," Don Pedro replied.

"A moment!" Robert called. "Let me examine his wounds."

"Do that," Sterne said. "Perhaps as second, you will show the wisdom he lacks."

Don Pedro came over obediently. He was breathing hard.

"Do *not* call off the duel," he warned.

"Wouldn't dream of it," Robert replied. "But you have to get inside that point, or he will most certainly nick you to death."

"He *is* fast. I can feel the strength of the devil in him when our blades cross."

"Please, Don Pedro—"

"Please, Mr. Franklin. Have a little faith in God. He will grant me the victory."

He went back and squared off with Sterne again. He went as soon as the signal was given, beating at a blade that wasn't there but was whisking around his. Then the Apalachee did an astonishing thing; he got his blade back around in a huge circle, catching Sterne's blade in time to keep it from penetrating but not in time to keep it from ripping an ugly scratch up his belly. Ignoring that, he ducked and thrust. His blade went a half inch into Sterne's belly, who cried out softly and staggered back.

Don Pedro stepped back, too. "Let me know when you are ready to resume," he said.

Sterne looked angrily down at the stain growing on his shirt, waved off the protestations of his second, and came on.

This time Sterne was the attacker, beating the blade, thrusting, trying to force the don to give ground. The Apalachee would not retreat, however, working in a circle instead, always after Sterne's exposed flank. He touched the Englishman again, in the arm, but this time the duel didn't even pause. The two men, tiring, crashed together, blades blurring.

Finally they fell back from each other, each bleeding from

several new wounds. Both were panting like racehorses after a long stretch, but Don Pedro's legs were visibly quivering.

"I'm going to kill you, sir," Don Pedro said. "For my God, my country, my honor—I am going to kill you."

"The hell with you," Sterne replied, and came on.

But in the next moment he was forced to retreat, as Don Pedro replied with hard, strong blows, and the earlier finesse which had allowed Sterne to deal with that seemed to have left him. He moved back, sidling away from the Apalachee's clockwise motion.

"It isn't happening," Franklin muttered. "Euler was wrong or lied. It isn't—"

At that moment, Den Pedro lunged—a mistake. Sterne parried the weapon and drove his own point through the Apalachee above his left hip. The blade went through and came out the other side. Sterne, overextended, stumbled, so that the two men were face-to-face.

Don Pedro whooped, his free hand darting out and knotting in Sterne's shirt.

"Now," he said, "as I told you, you will die."

Sterne's eyes went wide as he tried to withdraw his blade, but it was stuck in the other man.

And then it did happen. In the air, just above Sterne's head, a cloud formed with a red eye of fire in the center. It swept forward and engulfed Don Pedro, who gasped and fell back, releasing Sterne but taking the weapon with him.

He wasn't the only one to gasp. Shrieks went up all around the court.

So did weapons.

"Call it off, Mr. Sterne," Franklin shouted. "Call it off, or we shall see how well your pet demon serves you when you are well-Swissed with bullets."

Sterne's eyes flashed red. For an instant he looked as if he were ready to fight everyone in the room, even bare-handed, but then his shoulders slumped. The malakus thinned and vanished.

"That was very clever, Mr. Franklin. Again. I suppose I ought to be wise to little tricks like that by now. It doesn't matter. All of you, listen to me. You cannot stand against my masters. You will join them or they will kill you. It is extremely simple. I tried to treat with you like gentlemen, but that is useless, I see. Very well—if you will act like dogs, you will die like dogs." He turned to the king. "Your Majesty—I wish to depart and return to my sovereign. I think he has your answer."

"Indeed he does," Philippe snapped, "but he shall not have it from you or from your men."

"Sire, may I remind you that my status as an ambassador—"

"Entitles you to nothing, in my eyes. You are a warlock, sir, and will be treated as such. Your men will be treated as the servants of a warlock. I advise you to lay down your weapons."

Sterne stood, fuming, for a tense moment, then smiled. "I have no weapon to lay down," he said, pointing to Don Pedro. The Apalachee's eyes had gone glassy, but he was still breathing. "Don Pedro may keep the blade, with my compliments." He turned to his men. "The rest of you disarm. If ever anything gave our king reason to burn this pitiful hovel to the ground, it is this breech of diplomatic relations."

"I suspect," Philippe said, "that he never needed an excuse, but I am happy to provide him with one. We fled France to escape the Russians and their demons. We will flee no more. France will flee no more. Here we stand."

A profound silence followed his pronouncement, and in it d'Artaguiette stood, bowed to the king, and placed his hand on his breast. "Before God," he said, "I confess. I collaborated with this . . . creature. Many of you know it. More do not. I plotted against my king and in so doing disgraced my office and station. Your Majesty, I offer you my sword as well. Take it if you will, and mete out the punishment I deserve. But I swear to you, before God, that I am with you now, heart and soul. I will go in the vanguard against our enemies, and I will not flinch. I urge all my countrymen to do the same."

Philippe's mouth hung open for an instant. "You, d'Artaguiette? You worked against me?"

"I did, Sire."

"You thought me inadequate to my throne, or were you merely ambitious?"

"Both, Sire."

"And you have changed your heart? What if you should change it again?"

"I cannot prove I will not—but I can swear I will not."

Philippe scowled and waved a dismissive hand. "Keep your sword, d'Artaguiette. We have few enough men with military experience as it is. And it is time—no, well past time—that we raised an army. It is time we demonstrated, again, why the French once ruled the world."

"France!" A hoarse voice shouted. It was André Penigault, at the very back of the room, one fist held high.

"France! The king!" he repeated.

And in the next eye blink, every foppish nobleman in the place suddenly became—something else. They no longer looked ridiculous in their garish, overwrought clothing. They pounded the tables. They raised their voices, so that the roar of "France! The king!" might well have been heard a thousand miles away.

A few hours later, the king called Franklin into a private audience in his bedchamber. Franklin found him in military uniform, looking down the length of his sword.

"Mr. Franklin."

"Your Majesty."

"I do not doubt in the least that you were behind all of that," Philippe said. "The duel was contrived to force Sterne to reveal his nature?"

"Yes, Sire."

"Don Pedro—he will live?"

"It seems so. He is of tough stock."

"Good. Now, d'Artaguiette has just made a fuller confession to me. He tells me that troops from Carolina and the margravate of Azilia are coming here, and that they sued by aetherschreiber for our protection. Did you know of this?"

"Yes, Majesty."

"I suspected as much. It does not please me that you kept it from me. In fact, the devious way you have worked here does not please me at all. But your results—your *results* are to my liking. I will give your troops protection, but as ambassador you must make me certain promises—in writing. As you now see, even the remnants of your own army are likely to outnumber my own forces. I need your promise that they will not now, or ever, abuse their stay in my kingdom. We will feed you and house you—and you know, I think, what that costs us—and we will fight with you. But our territories are our territories, and you English may not claim them. I need an agreement on that."

"Have it written, and I shall sign it," Franklin replied. "For the moment, I give you my hand and my word."

"For the moment, that will do. Meantime, you made me some other promises—make good on them. If we must fight, I want every advantage you can invent. You must hold nothing back from me for fear of future wars between our two peoples. You say we are all in this as one—act as you speak. Do you understand?"

"Absolutely. I meant every word I said, Majesty. This will be our last stand; I do believe it. If we fail here, nothing remains."

"Will we fail?" For a moment he was that earlier king, a bit of resignation in each syllable.

Franklin looked him squarely in the eye. "No, Sire. We will not fail."

That hung there for a moment, but then the king seemed to take it. "Good. Now, for the moment, just one thing. We have news that the Choctaw and their allies are fighting someone in the West, near the great river. Do you know anything of this?"

"No, Your Majesty."

"Can you contrive some method of discovering? Can we use Sterne's flying machine?"

"We can indeed, Sire, with a few modifications. But I think there is someone I can ask about this now, if you give me your leave."

*   *   *

After a bit of searching, he found Vasilisa in one of the moldering gardens, laughing gaily with one of Don Pedro's men—a young, pale fellow with a goatee. Franklin gave him barely a glance and a nod before addressing Vasilisa. "My lady," Franklin said, "a word with you?"

"The lady, sir, is with me," the young man said, puffing out his chest and placing his hand on the hilt of his smallsword. His voice was hoarse, his accent very thick.

"I do not want the lady, but only a word or two with her."

"It's fine, Roberto," she said, squeezing his arm. "I shall find you later. Mr. Franklin and I are old friends, and we do have things to say to each other."

Roberto looked unhappy and uncertain, but he kissed her hand, favored Franklin with an almost imperceptible bow, and left.

"Very, very clever, Benjamin," she said softly, once they were alone. "This evening was well handled. Within a few days you have this whole court in the palm of your hand."

"Vasilisa, you can outflatter a dedication and lie like ten epitaphs. Spare me, please."

"You're angry."

"Who are the Indians fighting in the West?"

"Other Indians?"

"Vasilisa—" He stepped forward and grabbed her roughly by the shoulders. "You said you came here quite a different way than James. That would be from the west, yes, across the Pacific by airship? Did you come alone?"

"Ben . . ." She reached up and took his chin in her fingers. "Have a care, Ben. Women break. You were never rough like this before—it's one thing I loved about you."

"Answer my question."

"First, you answer me. Did you read the notes I gave you? About the engines?"

He gave an exasperated sigh and released her. "Yes."

"And do you believe in them?"

"Yes."

"You think a countermeasure is possible?"

"Of course. Now, for the last time, who are the Indians fighting in the West? I warn you, I shall know in a few days anyway, for I am outfitting Sterne's flying machine for reconnaissance."

"You cannot trust his machine. It is malakim engined."

"I can fix that."

She stepped closer again. "Ben, believe me, I have no idea whom the Indians might be fighting. I came here alone, in a flying craft."

"This is the truth?"

"It is the truth. And now, Ben—" She stepped close again, to the point of their touching, to where he could feel her heart beating through her dress, and feel that she wore no corset. "Will you help me?"

"With the countermeasures? Of course."

"No. Not with that."

Her arms crept up to his shoulders, then twined around his neck, and her face drew near his.

She was going to kiss him. She was, and he was going to let her.

And then, quite as suddenly, he realized that he was *not* going to kiss her. He pushed her back.

"Vasilisa, I don't think—"

A steel blade suddenly appeared over his shoulder, its tip against Vasilisa's throat.

"Drop that. Do it now, or I will kill you, by *God* I will."

It was a voice he knew—knew very well indeed.

"Lenka?"

"Hush, idiot husband. Don't move."

Vasilisa's face worked through a quick range of expressions that started with fury and ended in resignation. Something clattered on the stone behind him.

"Now, move out from between us."

Franklin did so, turning so he could finally see.

What he saw was Roberto, the Apalachee, holding his smallsword up to Vasilisa's throat.

"Lenka?" he repeated.

"Yes, dear husband. I wonder if I shouldn't have let her kill you."

That was when he noticed the wicked steel pin on the ground where he had been standing.

3.

The Sound

In the inky depths of Altamaha Sound, a white lotus bloomed. In the instant before understanding, Oglethorpe admired its expanding beauty and the pearlescent green fringe around it.

Then the deck slapped him into the ceiling, and argent sparks flashed behind his eyes. The world briefly forgot gravity, and the quaking hull of *Azilia's Hammer* filled with shrieks.

"What in God's name?" Oglethorpe shouted, his voice distant and thin even in his own ears. "Did we strike a mine?"

"Nay, General," MacKay grunted. "Y' saw it. It were twenty yards off the port bow." MacKay craned his head up fearfully.

"So they're dropping 'em?"

"I'd reckon, sir."

"Be damned. It's night above, and muddy thick down here besides. How do they know we're here?"

"God only knows, sir."

"Well, we can't sit still waiting for morning anymore, that much is sure."

"Shall we come to surface, then?"

"Right under the guns of Fort Marlborough? No, I don't think so."

"But, sir, we can't navigate where we can't see. We'll run aground, or worse."

"They see us. There must be a way."

The ship shuddered again from an explosion a little more distant than the last.

"I think those be warnings, General. I think they know where we are exact."

Oglethorpe chopped his chin in agreement. "Very well. They have some alchemical means of locating us and, further, of knowing we are not friend. But how? Can we confound it?"

Parmenter coughed. "What of the aether compasses of Franklin? They point the way to all sorts of things."

"True enough. They point at what they're tuned to. Sailing ships keep touch with one another that way. But that must mean that somewhere on the ship the matched needle is hidden."

"Aye. But where?"

"Fetch that Russian pilot. Quickly." Oglethorpe looked up to the watchtower. "Captain Parmenter, can you make anything out?"

"Aye, sir. Above us, three ships with lanthorns blazing. They *want* us to know they're there."

"They want their ship back, I reckon." He fingered his chin. "Should we release our charges, try to blast them from the water?"

"Beg pardon, Margrave, but I think that wouldn't be wise," Parmenter said. "None of 'em are straight overhead, and they may have countermeasures we know nothing of. But they will surely finish us off if we prove dangerous."

"What if we surface, then, and take our chances fighting from the deck?" But he shook his head. "No. Even I don't like those odds."

Tomochichi, who had slipped in from the next compartment as they were speaking, cleared his throat. "The devil gun. Could you not use it to make them sink, as we did those boats upriver?"

"No," Oglethorpe said. "Fired here, it would only set loose our own captive demon. Then we must all swim for it."

"I know," the old chief said. "But if someone took the gun and swam up, it could be done."

"We can't open the hatch," Oglethorpe explained. "Water would rush in."

"Not the water underneath. We hold it at bay."

"He's right, sir," Parmenter said, some excitement in his voice. "Remember? The water will not force through the lower hatch, not as long as the upper is sealed. Someone can swim out from there."

"Very good," Oglethorpe said. "Mr. Parmenter, you're elected."

"Sorry, General. I—I can't swim."

"I'll do it," Tomochichi said.

Oglethorpe frowned, remembering the Indian's fear of underwater spirits. "No. I know you don't like this below-the-water business."

"What else can I do here?" Tomochichi asked. "Shoot my musket? No. Raise my war club? No. My younger brothers are already covered in glory. I will do this. This is mine."

Oglethorpe hesitated only for an eye blink. "Very well, Chief, it's yours." He clasped the old man's arms. "Good fortune."

"If my allotted days are broken, it is so. No man can escape his fate. But I will end our enemies."

A chill stalked down Oglethorpe's back. He hated it when the Indians started talking like that.

"Go with God, Chief." Oglethorpe turned to Parmenter. "Put the knife to the Russian pilot. No, bring him here so I may do it myself. I will know how his countrymen see us." He turned back to Tomochichi, who was doffing his matchcoat, revealing the dark wings tattooed on his chest and torso. For a dizzying instant, the old Indian seemed not human at all but instead some Oriental combination of man and bird of prey.

Then the illusion vanished, and he again saw a vulnerable old man.

"Tie a rope to the chief's ankle," Oglethorpe commanded, "so he can find his way back."

Tomochichi slipped into the opaque waters at about the same time they brought the sullen Russian captive before Oglethorpe. He was a young man, perhaps twenty-two, with a heavy beard and mustache. He still wore the green breeches of his uniform and a sweat-stained white shirt.

Oglethorpe already knew the fellow spoke English, from the earlier interrogation.

"What is your name?" he asked.

"Feodor Yurivich Histrov."

"Very good, Mr. Histrov. No doubt you are aware of our present troubles. It seems your friends have a method of locating us, and of knowing we are unfriendly to their cause. I'm sure you were aware that would happen, and I congratulate you on your bravery in keeping silent. You must have known you would die with us, or that we would kill you for your omission."

Histrov did not answer, but his face pinched tighter.

"Come here," Oglethorpe said softly. "I want you to see something."

He pulled the Russian forward, then crowded with him into the watchtower, where one of the windows looked upward.

"There? You see them? What are they waiting for?"

"For you to surrender," the Russian replied. "By now the narrows is blockaded as well, so you will not escape."

"No? Then is it worth your life to keep the secret of our detection from us?"

"Yes."

Oglethorpe motioned to Unoka, who pulled an ugly-looking bone-handled dirk. With a swift motion, the little man cut off one of the Russian's ears. The sailor's shrieks were piteous until Oglethorpe stuffed a rag into his mouth.

"You think we have no chance of escaping. I think we have a slim chance, yet you know more of our situation than I do, yes? Let me help you. You are a brave man, and I wish every chance to give you your life. If you don't tell me what I want to know, and we are captured, your countrymen will find your corpse floating in the water, if they find you at all. If you tell me, and they capture us, I will let you live to rejoin them. You say we will be caught no matter what. Tell me."

He removed the rag from the fellow's mouth.

"It's—" He paused, and Unoka shrugged and brought his knife up again.

"No!" Histrov said. "It's the aetherschreiber in the cabinet. In the captain's room."

"I saw no such device."

"Yes. It is a secret. They would have schreibed you, and when you never answered they would know the ship was in enemy hands."

"Tell me exactly where that is?"

"I don't know. I was not the captain."

Oglethorpe lifted an eyebrow. "Tear the room apart," Oglethorpe told Parmenter. "Find that schreiber and throw it into the sea."

At about that moment, the lights above them started to descend. Oglethorpe held his breath, almost, as they came level and then continued down.

"Well," he said. "So much for those three. That gives us a breath to draw, I think. The chief met with success, it seems. MacKay, as soon as Tomochichi is back on board, move this scow."

"Aye, sir."

"And put Mr. Histrov back in chains."

Oglethorpe went back to the lower hatch, where his men were taking in the rope tied to the old Yamacraw's leg. He waited with a small smile on his face, ready to congratulate his old friend.

But what rose up from the hatch was no Tomochichi, chief of the Yamacraw. It was a monster in the shape of a man, a construction of what resembled dull ceramic, but which bunched and knotted like the muscles of a man. Its head was a mirrored globe, and it had four arms. Two ended in sword blades, the other two in *kraftpistoles*.

"Talos!" Oglethorpe shouted, but it was already too late for his men at the rope. The automaton sheered through both with its scimitar limbs so that each fell apart at the waist. Neither man knew he was dead, but pitched back, trying to find legs he no longer had.

Then twin searing *kraftpistole* bolts jagged through the

crew compartment. Oglethorpe felt the heat, stepped aside, and fired his own weapon at the thing. Likewise, Parmenter drew a Fahrenheit pistol captured from one of the English officers and directed a white-hot spray of molten silver against the talos.

It rose up, giving no indication that it was hurt.

With a howl, Unoka leapt into the air and landed on the talos' shoulders, hacking at the silver globe with his throwing ax. It rang like a bell, but did not crack. Sword blades shot up to pierce him, but he wrapped his legs around the monster's neck and swung his body back to dodge, as nimbly as any acrobat.

Not completely distracted by this, the talos fired its *kraftpistoles* again, and more men died in flaming agony.

Parmenter suddenly lunged forward, not at the talos, but at something behind it. Just as Unoka finally dropped from it, dodging the scything arms, Parmenter came up behind, and Oglethorpe saw what he was about as the captain looped a long steel chain around the talos' head. Bellowing, Oglethorpe rushed beneath the weapon arms and grappled with it, trying to keep it occupied while Parmenter finished.

Never in Oglethorpe's life had he felt something so strong or relentless. Though inside the reach of its guns, the arms scissored together, pinching the life from him.

Meanwhile, however, Parmenter finished his task. The anchor cable wrapped firmly around the unholy thing, he now released the anchor.

When it went, it nearly took Oglethorpe's head off, but by a miracle, his long hair oiled the demon's grip, and allowed him to slip away from it with no more than a bloody scalp. Down through the hatch the talos went.

"Cut that damned chain!" Oglethorpe shouted, "else it will just crawl back up."

"Aye," Parmenter shouted.

"And get this ship in motion!"

A moment later they were under way and they began to count the dead. Oglethorpe's momentary feeling of triumph

at seeing the enemy ships sink was so far gone as to have belonged to a different age.

And Tomochichi, his friend and adviser for much of that
age, was gone with it.

"Margrave?" Parmenter had given him the best part of an
hour before interrupting his thoughts. Good man, Parmenter.

"Captain."

"What do we do now, sir?"

"It's still night. We still can't see, and the Russian is no
doubt correct—the way to open sea is no doubt well blockaded. I'm accepting suggestions."

"There may be another way around the island. The map
shows two passages."

"Both are narrow enough to block, I think, even if they no
longer have a way of finding us precisely."

"Yes, but the north way is under Fort Marlborough's guns.
The south way is not."

Oglethorpe was stopped by that, and by the lightning of a
sudden thought. "Parmenter, you served at Marlborough,
didn't you?"

"Briefly, sir."

"Tell me about it."

"Margrave Montgomery built her to guard the Spanish
border. She has four bastions and a spur out toward the narrows. The rampart ain't too high, but the wall is brick."

"Details, Captain. More details."

Morning was still a thought in the mind of God when Oglethorpe's booted feet came to rest inside the sandy keep of Fort
Marlborough. Night birds whined in the distance, and the
crickets, frogs, and other marsh singers filled the night with
music.

The wall had proved little trouble. The earthen rampart
was steep, but not too difficult to climb without shot flying
down from the walls. Parmenter chose the spot where the
rampart had been cratered once by Spanish mortars. After the
the capital of Azilia had been moved inland, the wall had

never been fully repaired, the gap patched only with un-mortared brick and rubbish. It had taken a little excavation to open a crawl-through, and meanwhile Yamacraw marksmen laid low the handful of men on the bastions.

"The spur is north," Parmenter said. "That's what we'll want."

"We shall have it, then," Oglethorpe promised.

Parmenter suddenly whirled at a faint sound behind them.

"Someone else comes through the gap!" he hissed.

"Knives, not guns!" Oglethorpe cautioned.

But when the figure came up from its belly and swayed to two feet, Oglethorpe was barely able to restrain a whoop of joy.

"Chief!" he whispered, clasping the old Indian to him. "Are you impossible to kill?"

"So they say," Tomochichi replied, grinning. "The knife arm cut me away, but he had no interest in me. I swam to shore, then saw you arrive. You will take the fort?"

"And turn their own guns on their blockade."

"Good. That is good." Tomochichi paused and looked down at his feet. "I lost the devil gun. I swam down seven times, but could not find it."

Oglethorpe took that grim news with a shrug. "It's done. You're the more valuable of the two, and we have you back. Now, we'll go."

They passed through the courtyard like hunting owls, dressed again in the stolen uniforms they had obtained from the amphibian boat's crew.

Two guards at the gate by the spur paid their silent passage into the sleeping battery, and they reached the guns without much trouble at all.

In the East, the sky grew rosy as dawn spread her fingers.

"Now comes the trick," Oglethorpe told his men. "We need enough light to see, so we can find their blockade, get our range, and put their ships below the water. If not before, when the first gun is fired, we'll have to hold these guns until *Azilia's Hammer* is through."

"And after that, sir?"

"After that, we do as we can. If we can fight free, we'll try and rendezvous with our companions. If we can't, MacKay will know what to do. Finding the fleet from Venice is the most important measure, as we all know." He clapped Unoka on the shoulder. "You see the plan of the fort? This battery sticks out from the rest of it, an arrow pointed at the sea. We have to hold the gates and the walls. See about constructing some sort of cover for us, and set all of the smaller guns facing back into the rest of the fort. They don't know we have only fifty men. I have no idea how many they have, but I'll guess at least twice that, and taloi besides, which we have no good defense against now."

"You sayin' t'ey will win this."

"I'm saying we can only hold out for so long, but the longer the better. Are you good for it?"

"T'at I am, mad General," Unoka said.

Satisfied, Oglethorpe nodded, then stared back out over the river, waiting for the light, hoping that there would be no mist.

They fired their first shots an hour later, letting loose with the eighteen pounders. The big guns roared like titans and exhaled a black brimstone fog, snapping the brittle morning. A thousand cormorants lifted in a cloud from the trees, and the air itself felt as if it had cracked.

By then they could see what *Azilia's Hammer* was up against: two steam galliots and a line of barges chained together. They could never have made it through, not even with what the men had begun to call "Oglethorpe's luck" and every gun blazing.

Every shot from the eighteen pounders fell short.

"Raise elevations," Oglethorpe said quietly. Behind him, the fort was still oddly silent. He had expected a quicker response—but then, it had only been seconds, hadn't it? The clock chiming in his chest said hours.

They fired again, and one shot from this volley struck the barge chain dead center. A plume of water and black smoke kicked up.

"Put the other guns at that range," Oglethorpe commanded. "Damn, but I wish their fervefactum still worked."

"No, sir," Parmenter explained. "The Spanish got that in Queen Anne's war with their seeking cannon, and it was never replaced."

"Maybe the redcoats or Russians replaced it."

"Maybe. But 'tis an obsolete weapon."

"That might be just the sort of thing they would put in a place like this, if they had it. Take some men down, Mr. Parmenter. It should be in that wall by the water, yes? The demilune?"

"That's where it was, Margrave. But you'll need me up here."

As if to prove his point, a sudden pattering of small-weapons fire started up.

"If they've a fervefactum in place, we can boil the whole channel. It's worth a look, Mr. Parmenter."

"Aye."

Oglethorpe then turned to see what was happening on his side of the wall, as the guns again shouted their tuneless anthems.

The gate to the bastion on the spur still held firm, which meant their attackers had to come along the walls. Until they pulled up guns big enough to blow the gate in, Oglethorpe and his men were the Greeks at Thermopylae, able to defend against a few at a time from a position of strength. When the gates went down, they would meet the same fate as those brave Athenians. He looked back down at the entrance to the sound. His artillerymen had truly found their range, now, and the blockade was suffering. Of course, there were surely underwater boats involved, and somewhere out there was a fleet poised to sink King Charles and all of his men in one fell stroke. Even if *Azilia's Hammer* got through this, she still had much to brave. But she was at least invisible now, when underwater.

The fighting on the walls was stepping up. His men had thrown up shelters of planking around the small guns, but it wasn't much. And where the hell was Unoka?

Then a shadow fell across him, and a chill ran through his bones. It was one of the flying ships, the bird-shaped ones, and it heralded its coming by blowing six of his men and two eighteen pounders off the wall.

"And now the fight really begins," he murmured. Drawing his *kraftpistole*, he ran along the wall, trying to get as close to the flying thing as he could. Below, something thudded against the gate.

4.

Defeat

In the middle heavens, three armies of angels clashed: the dark, strange forces from the forest, hidden by a mist; the bright avenging cherubim of Adrienne's son; and her own pitiful array.

Through the clash, through the ferments of shattering matter and dissolving spirit, she saw Nicolas, and he was dying. His forces were collapsing around him, and fire ate toward his center. Airships fell from the sky and alchemical artillery burst asunder, split by the very energies that motivated them. Nicolas was losing the fight for his life.

High above the battlefield, something else was forming, something Adrienne recognized. The keres was opening its wicked eye. For the moment it was nothing, just the nucleus of the vast, destroying storm it would become. But she recognized it.

For an instant she was paralyzed. She could not let Nicolas die. She could not let the keres spring to life. And her son's strange enemy was ignoring the waking god.

"The keres, Uriel. Stop it from forming!"

I—The pause went on, too long. *Very well. Farewell, Adrienne.*

Grimly, Adrienne stretched out her aetheric fingers to the heart of the maelstrom, where Nicolas lay dying.

Apollo!

He took me by surprise! The Sun Boy sounded desperate. *He cinched my power, somehow. Many of my servants do not know me. I'm going to fail, unless I can form the dark engine.*

That will slay us all, Nicolas.

Better that than this! I cannot fail!

Let me help you. I have power. Together we can stop your enemy.

I am the Sun Boy! The prophet!

I am your secret friend. Let me help you.

For torturous moments, nothing happened, and then matterless fingers closed in hers.

And there came a jolt, like a breath of God, and Adrienne saw a tree rising into the heavens. No, not a tree but a tower, Nimrod's tower—or Jacob's ladder—and high above, at the very top, a light that might be God, at long last *might*—

Then the images dissolved. Her son swelled like a thunderstorm, like a great wave of the sea; and she felt herself rushing with him, an arrow in flight, the charge of a huge cavalry. She saw the enemy in the woods as Nicolas saw him—a great horned man, shaggy, wrapped with serpents.

Satan! Nicolas cried. *Lucifer!*

They met, and the devil's power snapped. He was strong, yes, but Adrienne and Nicolas were more powerful than heaven.

Red Shoes blinked at the sky, not understanding at first. Not understanding why he was still whole and alive, why his enemy had withdrawn even as he tasted his flesh. His masterly plan had been destroyed at a stroke, his power scattered to the winds, the power of the snake within him snuffed to a mere glow. The hand of the Sun Boy had done all that. His power was without limit.

And yet Red Shoes lived. The Sun Boy had turned away, as if from a gnat. The airships had fallen from the sky, long lines of horizontal lightning and sputtering plumes of flame, one-eyes and Long Black Beings turned against themselves.

The iron people were under attack by someone else—a small fleet of ships, yes, but someone or something powerful came with them. In his otherworld sight, two spiderwebs now stretched across the sky. At the center of one was the Sun Boy, at the center of the other, the unknown. But whoever it was was connected to the Sun Boy in strange ways.

Once he had traveled with Blackbeard, the Charles Town king, and Thomas Nairne, who ruled that city now. Nairne had ventured that the enemy of his enemy was his friend. Blackbeard had scoffed.

Red Shoes agreed with Blackbeard. One man like the prophet was one too many. Two was two too many.

And he, of course, made three.

He shook back his pain—there were three webs, after all. He was still a spider, if a crippled one. Thinking him defeated, they had forgotten him. That would prove to be a mistake.

He noticed that the strands linking the two sorcerers were strengthening. Maybe he could be of some help, there.

As the serpent's power uncoiled, in the rushing colors that the aether made perceptible to Adrienne, Nicolas' face appeared, and his eyes widened in shock. Overhead, Uriel screamed, and the keres whirled away into nothing.

You! Nicolas shrieked. *I know you now! I remember you! You left me! You aren't my friend. You aren't my friend!*

Nicolas, no! I helped you!

You tricked me. Destroyed my engine. You aren't my mother!

I am! You remember me, you say! They took you from me! I searched. All these years, I've searched.

No. And with that his face withdrew, and death replaced him.

She saw it form, and she understood. It split from Nicolas like a shard from a crystal, and roiled and shaped, becoming a black, winged skeleton, a mockery of Uriel and his kind. It flew.

It passed through her point of view, and she understood something else. It was going to kill her body.

You, she said. *You tried to kill me before, back in Saint Petersburg. You sent that death, too.*

I am he who makes angels, Nicolas said. *And you serve the devil. He escaped me, just now, when I could have slain him. Because of you! You tricked me!*

I am your mother, Nicolas! I gave birth to you.

His laughter was crystal music. *I gave birth to myself. My mother is the wind, and God is my father. I am the union of flesh, spirit, and the world. Who dares to speak to me so?*

I am your mother.

No. They told me to expect you, but I didn't recognize you. I thought you were my friend. But I have no friends.

They? Swedenborg? Golitsyn? They are liars!

They are my servants, Nicolas answered, *as the angels are my servants. They cannot lie to me.*

Adrienne! It was Uriel, shrieking again. At once her vision split, her son's face fading as the ship reappeared. A sky full of flame, the steady thrumming of guns, lurching impacts of enemy fire. A nearby sailor shriveling in a cocoon of flame.

And the death, stooping on her. And Uriel falling upon the death from above, like God's great hawk. The aether screamed about her.

Gritting her teeth, she strengthened the forces connecting her to Nicolas, but he was fighting her, withdrawing—and then, from outside, something grabbed, tripled the affinity between them and they slammed together, she and Nicolas. For an instant she saw his face again, and then for an eye blink saw through *his* eyes. She saw Swedenborg, a laboratory, a brittle-looking device—

Then white light. Uriel reappeared, his form shredding apart, but the death was not to be seen.

"I told you," the seraph said faintly. "We are undone. I am undone."

And he was. "Finish what we started." He sighed, then fell apart. All her servants tore apart, as the ship beneath her lurched sickeningly.

She awoke to the world of matter, to screams of despair, the deck of the ship tilting. Two of the globes that supported it had flickered out and crashed amongst the crew. The other two were almost bursting. For an instant, her sense of déjà vu almost paralyzed her: this had happened before, at the siege of Venice—when she had lost Nico the first time.

Now her son hated her. Now he wanted her dead.

In that instant she might have welcomed death, but she was

vaguely aware of Crecy and Hercule, shouting at her. She should save them, if she could, if it was possible. Gathering what remained of her strength, she grasped the two malakim as they struggled free of their prisons, held them where they were by sheer force of will.

The ship bucked again, and an iron clamp seemed to close on her arm. She understood suddenly that she was dangling in space. Crecy's face above her was a study in determination.

"Help yourself," Crecy gasped. "My grip—"

Two globes would not support the ship, of course. Below her feet, the great river hurled by, and then a rushing green, closer each instant. She felt Crecy pull harder, screamed as her arm came out of the socket, and then she lost even her tenuous grip on the malakim. She suddenly had no weight, and she heard Crecy's shriek of despair come from far away. Then everything in the world broke. The ship, her bones, the air.

Red Shoes sagged against a tree, recovering his strength, watching the storm recede. Triumphant war whoops went up all along the river, and musket fire beat an unsteady tattoo. He fumbled out his pipe and Ancient Tobacco and lit it with one of his few remaining shadowchildren. He watched his hand shake, not believing that it was his own.

"Are you well?" Grief asked.

"No. I am not. I am not well. I—" He tried to stand, but it was suddenly too terrible, all of it.

"Kill me," he groaned. "Kill me now, before I grow strong again. Before the power grows in me again." Tears streamed down his face, and he dropped the pipe, falling to the ground and curling up like an infant. "Kill me," he whimpered.

But she didn't kill him. She sat and rocked his head in her lap, stroked his head.

"Your heart came back?" she asked.

"Yes," he gasped. "It may go again—kill me."

"No. I will keep you, with or without a heart."

Some time later, he heard warriors coming.

"Help me stand," he told her. "Help me lean against this tree. I will not have them see me like this."

Together, they managed it. Heartbeats later, he recognized Minko Chito coming along the path.

"Victory," the chief said. "We will cover our scalp pole from top to bottom."

"It looks like victory," Red Shoes told him, forcing the words, the stupid, useless words.

"Smells like it and feels like it, too."

Red Shoes shook his head. "It isn't. We've barely touched their army, and we lost how many warriors?"

"No telling," Minko Chito grunted. "Not as many as they did. That is victory, isn't it? We are few and we attacked many, and they came out much the worse."

"I failed, which means we lost. Do you know what they will do next? Salvage their big guns, mount them on the opposite bank. Shell and burn this forest until nothing remains alive while they finish building their bridge. We surprised them—we won't get that opportunity again."

"The Sun Boy survived?"

"Yes. I overestimated my power." That was putting it mildly, but it was the truth.

Minko Chito shrugged. "We kept them from crossing once—we can do it again."

"No. They will kill us all, and we will slow them only by a few days."

"Then what? Return home?"

"Even worse. No. The best we can do is to make them go where we want them to go."

"Where is that?"

"New Paris."

Minko Chito looked puzzled. "So they will kill the French instead of the Choctaw?"

"No. Because there we will have one last chance to beat them."

The chief considered that. "They won't all follow you down there."

"I know. But it's the only thing left to do."

He turned at the hiss of moccasins on the forest floor. It was the boy, Chula.

"One of the sky boats fell on this side," he told them excitedly. "Some of them still live."

"The other spider," Red Shoes muttered.

They both gave him puzzled looks.

"Let's go and see them," he said, leaning on Grief.

Adrienne tasted blood in her mouth and wondered what that could mean. She wondered, also, what the strange sounds all around her were. It was dark, and she was wet. It wasn't cold, but she was shivering.

She couldn't seem to remember what had happened. It was like one of those strange night terrors, when you awoke not knowing where you were, panicked, only gradually realizing that you were in your familiar room, that your sleep-addled brain had played a trick on you.

Except that somehow she felt that this place would never be familiar.

She commanded light.

Nothing happened.

She called for her djinni. There were none.

She might have slept, for she didn't remember seeing a light approach; but there it was, suddenly, a few feet away. And in its light, a familiar face framed in copper.

"Veronique?"

"My God. Adrienne." Crecy fell to her knees in the mud— she was lying in mud!—and pressed against her. The redhead was weeping. "I'm sorry," she gasped. "I let you go. Like I let Nico go. I always fail you, when—" She pushed back at Adrienne's groan, and raised her voice. "Hercule! I've found her! She's still alive." She looked back down at Adrienne, her tear-filled eyes sparkling. "Still alive," she said more softly.

"Thank God!" Hercule shouted from somewhere unseen above her.

"Where are we, Veronique? Why does my leg—"

"Your leg?" Crecy knelt and pulled Adrienne's skirt up. It

caught on something underneath—a branch perhaps—and ripped a little. Then she had exposed the leg.

Or *a* leg. It did not look like hers. It was strangely bent, covered with blood, and from the distorted thigh, a sort of bloody pipe protruded, the thing her dress had snagged on.

"My God," Crecy murmured. "Dear God."

Hercule's face appeared now. He was less religious, when he saw. "Fuck!" he exploded.

"She's already lost much blood. Adrienne, can you still hear me?"

"Yes, of course, Veronique. Where are we?"

But she was remembering, now. She had seen Nico, and then they had fallen. She closed her eyes.

"Put something in her mouth," Hercule said. "Quickly. So she doesn't bite her own tongue."

Fingers gently pried her mouth open, and something came between her teeth. She wanted to look and see what it was, but it seemed like far too much trouble to open her eyes again.

Then she felt a sort of grinding and scraping, and the most exquisite pain she had ever known. It filled her like the surge at the pinnacle of lovemaking, but was infinitely more powerful, drawing every muscle and organ in her body to convulse. She tried to scream, but instead ground her teeth into whatever they had put in her mouth.

"You!" Hercule shouted to someone. "*You,* by God, fetch me some brandy."

For an answer, he got a bullet. She heard the gunshot, the strange, meaty sound it made. She forced her eyes open, but they were swimming with tears of pain, and she had to blink several times to see. Meanwhile, two more shots roared nearby.

When her eyes did clear, she first saw Crecy, a smoking pistol in one hand. Hercule was sprawled in the mud, quivering, his hands wrapped around his chest.

Crecy dropped the weapon and drew her sword. "Oliver," she snarled.

Adrienne let her head loll around. There, leaning against a

mass of smashed timbers and planks, stood the man who had attacked them in Saint Petersburg. He wore the uniform of Hercule's light horse and a large grin.

"Come, Crecy. Join me," he said.

"How in God's name did you come here, Oliver? How?"

He chuckled. "It was quite simple, really. Poor dear Irena. She was as close as I could get to Adrienne without your seeing me. It seems that was close enough. How do you think I knew about your plan to flee the city? I arranged beforehand to get on board. It was sticky going, after our fight, but I managed to kill one of Hercule's horsemen and don his uniform. After that, Irena hid me. Father Dimitrov, another dear friend, helped."

"You were Irena's lover. You killed her."

He shrugged. "She was going to tell Hercule about us. He would have had to confront me then, and that was bringing me far too close to the two of you, who would recognize me."

"Why, Oliver? Before I kill you, tell me why."

He laughed. "Because *they* say so, Veronique. You remember how that is. It's annoying, really. The crash almost did my work for me."

"Kill me, then," Adrienne rasped. "Leave Hercule and Veronique be."

"It is too late for Hercule, I fear, but I am perfectly willing to let Nikki live. I am fond of her."

"Why did you shoot Hercule?" Adrienne managed.

"Actually, I was trying to shoot you. Damn pistols are as untrustworthy as women."

Crecy stepped forward. Adrienne noticed she was limping. "You have no more guns," she said. "Prepare to die, Oliver."

"You make me sad, Nikki, but I will do what I must."

A wave of pain second only to the first coursed through Adrienne as Crecy snarled and hurled herself across the muddy, uneven ground. Crecy's weapon was not the little dress sword she sometimes wore, but a basket-hilted broadsword. Oliver was armed with a horseman's saber. Their steel moved so fast in the darkness Adrienne could see little more than the sparks they struck, for the ship had crashed in a thicket of trees and wild grapevines that throttled what little light the sky still held.

She tried to summon her servants again, but silence greeted her commands. She could see into the aether with her hand, make out malakim in the far distance, but none was tied to her, none at all.

Gritting her teeth, she crawled toward Hercule.

He was still alive, his eyes puzzled. "A moment," he managed. "A moment, and I will kill him for you. I'm just—" He looked at his hand, covered in blood. "Damn," he said. "Damn. He's killed me."

"No," Adrienne said. "No, he hasn't. You'll live."

"Because you tell me to?"

"Because I love you."

He laughed bitterly, which brought blood to his lips. "That will save me, then," he murmured. "Surely I will live. But in the meantime, you might take my gun, which is beneath me, and put it in my hand, that I might defend you."

"Hercule—" The blades rang louder behind her.

"Do it."

She pushed under him. It was very difficult, with her whole body shivering so violently. Her fingers felt the grip of the pistol, but she could not make them close. Something else seemed to snap in her, and she fell across him.

His eyes had a mild look. "It doesn't hurt," he said wonderingly. "You remember when we first met? I remember when I first saw you. You don't, I know. It was when you first came to Versailles, as the queen's secretary. You were so beautiful and, I remember thinking, *alive*. A secret sort of life, a hidden life, that I fancied only I could see." His eyes went wide. "*That* hurt," he murmured. She couldn't tell if he meant the memory or the heart she felt slowing in his breast.

"Have you got the gun?" he asked.

"Yes," she lied.

"Shoot the bastard, then, for he'll beat Crecy."

She turned her head and saw it was the truth. Crecy was still going, but she bled from assorted cuts, and the point of her weapon kept dropping. Oliver, on the other hand, looked warily confident. She tried for the gun again.

"My children will need taking care of," Hercule said.

"Live and care for them, then."

"Of course," he said. "Of course, that is the perfect solution. But if I do not, will you?"

"Yes. But you will not abandon me, Hercule d'Argenson. I forbid it."

"I remain yours, of course," he said. Then his eyes went dull, and he quivered, and was dead.

She may have shrieked or cried. Afterward, she could never remember—she would remember only the feel of his heart's last feeble thump, of knowing that once again, nothing would ever be the same.

And then she remembered the cold, like a breath of Siberian air. Hercule was dead, and she would follow him soon, for the little strength she had was leaking away. She remembered them saying she had lost much blood. Veronique was going to die for nothing. Hercule had died for nothing.

Crecy cursed as her feet sucked from the mud too slowly. Oliver's saber hammered down, and though she parried, the force of his vicious moulinet drove her own sword into her forehead. She ducked and cut viciously at his legs, but he leapt back.

Crecy straightened, and they circled each other warily, Crecy wiping blood away from her eyes. In the near darkness, her forehead looked black with it.

"Yes, you've gotten slower, and weaker," Oliver remarked. "Time was you might have beaten me."

Crecy didn't answer, but lurched forward. Oliver parried the attack easily, feinted a cut at her head, followed with a slash at her sword wrist. The basket hilt caught it, but she grunted and retreated, her weapon arm hanging at her side.

Then Oliver did something strange. His eyes flashed red, and a malakus appeared over his shoulder; with a snarl he turned his back on Crecy and leapt at Adrienne.

It caught Crecy by surprise. With a choked curse of dismay

she sprang to interpose herself. It was clear she would never make it.

Adrienne watched the blade descend as if in a dream.

A musket roared from a few yards away, and Oliver gasped and spun, then recovered. With what momentum he had left, he lunged into the woods, followed by three more bullets, and an instant later by the dark figures of men. She had an impression of painted faces, of hard, dark bodies. Then they were gone, too.

Crecy pointed her sword at something behind Adrienne. "Stay away from her."

"Lay down your sword or die," someone said in oddly accented but comprehensible French.

5.

Another Old Acquaintance

"I have to sit down." Franklin grunted. "I really do."

Lenka drew a pistol from her belt with her free hand. Aiming it carefully at the Russian, she then sheathed her sword.

"Won't you introduce me to your wife, Benjamin?" Vasilisa asked, her voice perfectly composed.

"It appears to me," Franklin said, aware that his voice was rather strained, "that you have already met."

"I met a Roberto de Tomole," Vasilisa noted.

"Ah, Vasilisa Karevna, meet Lenka Franklin—" He rubbed his forehead, wondering when it would explode. "Lenka, what are you—I mean, I told you to stay—"

"Yes, and now I see why. Though I didn't know you tended toward doddering hags. Really, she could be your mother."

"Oh, I'm quite sure I taught him more than his mother ever did," Vasilisa remarked sweetly.

"I don't doubt that," Lenka said, "no, I don't."

Franklin's brain was a sea of confusion, but something did manage to swim to the surface finally. "You were going to kill me, Vasilisa?"

The Russian sighed. "Don't be stupid, Benjamin. I was going to kidnap you."

"By stabbing me?"

"If you take note, the pin has a subtle poison on it. It brings deep sleep, not death."

Franklin frowned and picked up the fallen needle. There *was* something whitish smeared on it.

"I can test this on you, then? A scratch will do?"

"If you want."

"I don't. I'd rather have you awake, to answer a few questions. Exactly what were you after by kidnapping me—again?"

"To work on the countermeasure. But not here. Somewhere safe."

"Why don't you think New Paris is safe?"

She smiled faintly. "Because several thousand men and several tens of airships are on their way here, along with the dark engines themselves. I doubt very much that we can devise our countermeasure before they arrive. I also doubted that I could persuade you, though you must admit I did try."

"To my eye you were doing a fine job," Lenka said. "You were a fool to use your pin so early. Another moment would have persuaded him."

"Lenka, that isn't true," Franklin said.

"How would you know, Benjamin? Women always bring every bit of the fool in you to the surface, like sap rising in a tree."

"If you don't mind my opinion," Vasilisa said, "he was not foolish at all when he chose you."

"No, but he's damn foolish in how he treats me," Lenka snapped.

"Lenka, how did you ever persuade Don Pedro to let you travel as one of his men?"

"I told him that it was either that or I would follow on my own. Don Pedro is too gallant to allow something like that—besides which he has that Indian respect for women, something you might learn."

"And Voltaire knew about this, I suppose. All of you conspired against me?"

"Benjamin Franklin, you will not remonstrate with me—not after I find you in the arms of another woman and still bother to save your life." Her face was bright red beneath the mustache and beard.

"Lenka—"

"Hush," she snapped. "I don't see why I bothered."

With that she stalked off. Franklin rose to follow her but

then saw Vasilisa rising to make her escape. He dithered for an instant. "Wait, Vasilisa. Stop there."

"Will you have me arrested, Benjamin?"

"Arrested? I ought to kill you."

"But you won't."

"No. How did you plan to escape with me?"

"I have an airship."

"A winged one or the other sort?"

"Winged. I no longer trust ships that rely entirely on malakim. They are . . . unreliable. Have me arrested, Benjamin, and I will be no help to you. We can still escape. Take your little firebrand, there, if you wish, but if you want to truly win this battle, we must leave."

Franklin stared at her for a long moment. "I won't, not after all I've done to bring this alliance together. I won't, and you aren't going either. We will work out our countermeasures here, or we will die. Both of us. All of us. Do you understand?"

"This is foolish. Even if the countermeasures work, there is still an army that dwarfs any you might raise."

"Tell me where your airship is."

"I don't think I will."

"Then I *will* have you arrested, and you can be sitting in a cell when the barbarians reach the gates. Or you can be free, helping me do the best I can. Your choice, milady."

Vasilisa studied him for a moment more, then shrugged her shoulders. "As you wish. My life is borrowed as it is, I suppose. Perhaps it's time to give it back." She raised her chin. "However, when the army does reach this place, *do* remember I tried, won't you? I don't want your last thoughts of me to be uncharitable."

"Good. Let's go find some of my rangers to watch you, shall we? I have other things to do right now."

He handed Vasilisa over to McPherson with some stern cautions, then went in search of Lenka. He bumped into Voltaire in the hallway.

"You, damn you!" Franklin snapped. "I ought to straighten my fist in your face."

"Will you give me a cause, first?"

"You didn't tell me about Lenka."

"Ah. But surely you understand she made me take an oath—and that I never break an oath to a lady."

"How could you have— Good God, she was there when the Coweta were trying to makes riddles of us! How could you have let her ride into such danger?"

"Benjamin, Fort Moore fell and lost half of its troop complement, as did Fort Montgomery. Where do you suppose she would have been safe?"

Franklin had no answer to that, but he tried furiously to find one. Voltaire didn't give him much time, though. "Was it really her safety that was uppermost in your mind, Ben? You talked little enough about her on the journey. Maybe a few years of marriage have begun to feel constraining? Maybe you half hoped you might have some rendezvous with a comely Indian lass or a Frenchwoman? Be honest."

Ben's jaw dropped. "By God, Voltaire. You don't have designs on my wife, do you?"

"Someone ought to. You don't seem to have any. And she's a most remarkable woman." He cocked his head. "Caught you doing something foolish with Vasilisa, didn't she?"

"None of your damn business. What did the two of you do on the ride? Now that I think of it, you had a way of disappearing at night."

"Talked. About you, mostly, you great idiot. She tried to paint you in a good light, but the truth is, I wonder how she puts up with you. And I'll tell you this—you don't deserve her. Maybe she won't put up with you much longer."

"And then she'll be yours, I suppose?"

"A man could do worse. But no, Benjamin, I have more honor than that. And if you wish to question the status of my honor, we shall provide more entertainment like tonight's for the court, you and me."

Franklin was about to reply when someone coughed behind them. He spun angrily to see who was eavesdropping.

It was McPherson. "What do *you* want?" Franklin snapped. "Were you in on this, too?"

McPherson's eyes tightened. "I dunno what th' hell y'r rattlin' about, but keep it off me," he said. "A visitor has just arrived I thought you might want to see, is all. The king wants you t' see 'im, too."

"Nairne? Oglethorpe?"

"The tsar of Muscovy."

"Mr. McPherson, I'll own I was rude to you just now. I apologize. But if I can't get a straight answer from you—"

McPherson suddenly grinned. "The tsar of Muscovy," he repeated, then left, laughing softly.

The tsar was a tall man who seemed uncomfortable with the fact; his shoulders hunched enough to take off several inches. He wore a torn and faded green coat of European cut but a shirt, leggings, and shoes of Indian design. His ragged beard and hair were dark, shot liberally with gray; his eyes black and fierce; his face overlaid by an anger that seemed habitual.

He paced like a bear in a cage. That made a certain amount of sense—he was in a cage, along with two other men. It was one of these who captured most of Franklin's attention.

"Tug?"

The big man looked up and squinted.

"Mr. Franklin?"

"Tug, what's going on here?"

"Damn if I know. We ride up to the town an' they throw us in jail right away."

"No, I mean—" He looked over at d'Artaguiette, who stood by, watching the exchange.

"This man is a friend of mine. I can vouch for him. Would you let him out?"

"He broke the nose of a musketeer, Monsieur."

"Naturally. They arrested him, yes?" He stepped closer and whispered to the minister. "He is who he says he is—the other? The tsar of Muscovy?"

D'Artaguiette nodded almost imperceptibly. "The tsar once visited the French court, where he met my lord when he was still the duke of Orléans. He is unmistakable, even with the beard."

"Then you should let me talk to Tug, alone."

"And the Indian?"

Franklin looked again. It wasn't Red Shoes. "I don't know him. Just Tug, for the moment."

The tsar was staring at them. His face twitched like a madman's.

"Very well," d'Artaguiette replied. "So long as I can be present."

"I would not have it otherwise."

"An incredible story," d'Artaguiette remarked about two hours later.

Tug nodded, his eyes red from the amount of brandy he had consumed. "I should o' stuck t' the sea. Damn Red Shoes, anyway."

"What do you think happened to him?" Franklin asked.

Tug hesitated. "He talked once er twice about them spirits he deals with. Said if he got in a fight with one, it might eat 'im up from inside if it won. I figure that's what happened." To Franklin's surprise, a small tear appeared in the tough sailor's eye. "He was a damn good fellah, Red Shoes. No man ever had a better friend, for all he was an In'yun. But that fellah I saw in Flint Shouting's village—he weren't Red Shoes. He were somethin' else, an' somethin' awful." He looked down at his feet. "I broke my promise," he murmured.

"What promise?"

"Promised 'im I'd kill 'im if he came to this. But I was afraid, an' he seemed to think it important that we bring this tsar fellah here."

"And the tsar? You think he's square?"

Tug nodded. "Yes. He reminds me o' Blackbeard—a little mean-crazy, if you know what I'm sayin'. But he did his part and listened to us when we knew better'n him."

"What does he want?"

Tug grunted. "Revenge. He keeps talkin' about all the heads he wants to see rollin'."

"You trust him, Tug?"

The big man swallowed another huge gulp of brandy. "I don't trust nobody anymore. I never did trust kings. But this man hain't playactin', if that's what you mean. Old Tug's not too smart, but he's smart enough to know that kings don't go wandering through the deserts and gettin' shot at by their own men just for the sake of intriguing."

"I agree. My question is when exactly—I mean, do you think he set out with this army and was then betrayed, or do you believe his story that he knew nothing about it?"

Tug fiddled with his cup. "Don't know," he said. "But his ship was way out ahead of the army. They sent a fast party to find him and bring him back. That army moves slow."

"Where do you reckon it to be now?"

"A week or two behind us, dependin' how hard a time they had crossin' the river. They have them airships, but way too many to load everybody up on."

"We've heard someone is fighting them."

"I don't know anythin' about that. If they are, I pity 'em."

"Thanks, Tug." Franklin looked over at d'Artaguiette, who seemed to have followed most of the exchange. "Does he have to go back to his cell?"

"Not if you give me your word he'll be watched."

"You have it."

"You oughter let Flint Shouting go, too. He's a good sort. Got us through alive, got us *here*, even after Red Shoes killed all his people."

"Give me a little longer to think about that," d'Artaguiette replied. He nodded at Tug. "The boy outside will find you quarters near Mr. Franklin and some new clothes."

"Thanks."

They watched a servant lead the big man off.

"What do you think?" d'Artaguiette asked.

"I think the tsar would make a good partner, if this story is true. He would know a lot about this army, and how we might stop it."

"We could get that by torture."

"Maybe. But—"

"The problem, you see, is that the Russians are the ones who took our homeland. Whether or not Tsar Peter is responsible for our current troubles, he was certainly responsible for *that*. The sentiment is to execute him."

"Execute a king? Wouldn't that set a bad example?"

"Have a care, Mr. Franklin. Remember where you are."

"My apologies."

"Another thing. You had the Russian woman detained. Putting aside the fact that you have no authority to do that without my lord's say-so, I am suspicious because this happened so near the time her tsar arrives. Can you enlighten me in this matter?"

Franklin looked the minister in the eye. "I was going to come to you—there hasn't been time. Madam Karevna is an old acquaintance of mine. She attempted to drug and abduct me. That this happened as the tsar was being arrested might be a coincidence, or it might be that she got wind of his capture and decided to act before he said something to ruin her welcome here. She claimed to be his envoy, yes?"

"She did."

"Have you asked him about her?"

"We have not. But we have taken her from your custody and placed her in ours. More comfortable quarters than the tsar has, of course, but we wish to question them separately, to see how well their stories agree."

"Good idea."

The minister smiled indulgently. "Thank you. I do have some small experience in these matters."

Franklin hesitated for an instant. "It would not be wise to treat her too roughly. We need her cooperation. She knows the secrets of many of the Russian weapons, the countermeasures that might defeat them."

D'Artaguiette shrugged. "Very well. Though I have no great hope of any victory. Nor, I think, do you."

"Then why did you make that fine speech?"

"Because I meant it. I thought in allying with the English Pretender I would save these pitiful remains of France. You showed me that I was wrong, for which I am indebted to you.

Nothing can save us. But my king, at last, is moved to *do* something. If one must die—and we all must, yes?—then it should be done grandly, in good style. And so I will pretend, with you, that we might survive to see another year."

Franklin smiled. "You misread me. I do speak with confidence I do not have, but I have no wish to die grandly. I'm simpler than that. I want to die in bed, when I am very old. Comfortably. I do think we can win this fight, d'Artaguiette." And for the first time, he realized that it was true. He *did* believe it.

D'Artaguiette shrugged again. "Good for you," he replied. "Will the king speak to the tsar?"

"He will. Would you care to be present?"

"Very much. Would you mind a bit of advice?"

"No."

"Clean him up first. Let him shave and bathe."

D'Artaguiette looked surprised. "My impression of you is that you have little regard for the niceties of royal prerogative."

"Your impression is correct. But treat him well, and, if you want him as an ally, you will have made a good start. And if you do not, his head will come off the easier without that beard."

D'Artaguiette actually chuckled. "A good thought. You have read Machiavelli, I wonder?"

"I haven't. I try to rely on good sense rather than dead men. After all, they are dead, which shows they were perhaps not so bright after all."

The tsar looked no less fierce shaved, cleaned, and dressed up. He should have looked silly in his too-short knee breeches—no clothing at court was available for someone of his stature. But somehow he didn't.

He gripped a cup of brandy in one hand and brought it to his lips often.

"Majesty," Franklin said, bowing to Philippe, who occupied an armchair—the only furniture in the small, dark salon. D'Artaguiette and four musketeers—and now Franklin—completed the party.

"Mr. Benjamin Franklin," d'Artaguiette announced.

The tsar swayed toward Franklin, his eyes narrowing.

"So, you are Mr. Franklin." His French had a thick sound to it. He stuck out his hand.

"I am." Remembering Venice, Franklin felt a sudden, unexpected loathing. He ignored the hand.

The tsar was faster than he looked. The back of his fist snapped Franklin's head and sent him reeling against the wall. He tasted blood, and one of his teeth felt loose.

Franklin bounced back to his feet and launched himself at the tsar, both fists swinging. He landed a solid punch on the monarch's jaw before the musketeers grabbed him from behind and yanked his arms painfully into the small of his back.

For an instant, he thought the Russian would strike him again, while the soldiers held him helpless. The tsar raised his hand as if to do so—then carried it up to his jaw, rubbing it ruefully.

"Let him go," the tsar said. "Let him go."

The musketeers didn't comply until Philippe repeated the order.

The tsar retrieved his cup, which he had dropped during his fit of rage. A Negro servant entered the room and filled it with brandy. He drank it down and held the cup out to be filled again. He kept his eyes fixed on Franklin the whole while.

"Mr. Franklin," he rumbled, "I am very tired. I have ridden for many, many miles. More, I think, than you. I have been betrayed, held captive, tortured, shot at, beset by demons. I have lost my wife and my country. I offered you my hand—you, who caused me defeat at Venice. Yes, of course, I know it was you. I did have spies of some worth, once upon a time." He stuck his hand back out. "I offer it again. Will you take it?"

Franklin hesitated, then clasped the tsar's palm.

"I say this once," the tsar told them, "once only. This war is not my doing."

"So we are given to understand," Philippe said from his armchair, "but this is not your first war."

"When I am returned to my rightful throne, France is yours again, every inch of it. So I swear."

"There are other reparations."

"I will make them, inasmuch as I can—if my own country is not ruined by this idiotic affair."

The French king nodded thoughtfully. "We shall see. Given our current situation, however, I could say that your throne might as well be on the Moon, and any recompense that might come from that throne about as useful. What can you do for us now?"

"I can offer you what I know about the weapons and size of the army. I can offer my expertise as a general, which has been tested on more than one occasion."

"To be frank, I will not trust you to command men."

"I did not expect you to. Give me a gun and a sword, then, and put me on a horse. I will kill a few of them for you, at least."

"Kill your own countrymen?"

The tsar's smile was bloodless. "Men who turn on their king have no country but treachery—something you ought to appreciate."

Philippe's eyes shifted briefly to d'Artaguiette. "Some treachery is pardonable. Will any of this army follow you if they see you are alive?"

"Some. I'm sure many think they serve me. I was kept from the sight of the men when held captive."

"Then you are worth keeping alive, despite your crimes," Philippe told him.

"A noble sentiment," the tsar said ironically.

"These are not noble times. They are desperate ones. I will want to hear your story soon."

"You will have it."

"One question first, however. If you don't lead your country in this war—who does?"

Peter's eyes narrowed to black slits. "Don't you know? It is the angels—of heaven or hell I do not know nor care."

"So Mr. Franklin said," Philippe replied, his voice weak. "You confirm it?"

"I do. I have seen them. I have known them."

The French king looked imploringly at Franklin. "How can we fight angels?"

"I destroyed my own," the tsar rumbled. "It cost me my wife and all my crew, but I am rid of him. If they can die singly, they can die by the thousand. If I can be rid of one, we can be rid of them all."

His own? Was the tsar like Euler? Like Bracewell and Sterne? Franklin pulled out his aether compass, but it did not point at Peter. He remembered that it *had* indicated Euler, even though the fellow no longer had a malakus with him.

"And what will God do, when we have killed his angels?" Philippe asked, his voice shaking as if for the very first time he believed who their true foe was.

"One thing at a time, Your Majesty," Franklin told him. "One thing at a time."

6.

A New Matter

The troops from Azilia arrived three weeks later, a weary, bedraggled-looking lot numbering around four thousand, including some two hundred warriors who had joined them in Apalachee. They were led by Thomas Nairne and a man named Martin from Newbern. Oglethorpe was not with them. They were welcomed in grand style, with fife and drum and trumpet, which seemed to cheer them considerably. Don Pedro insisted on getting out of bed to greet them, though the doctors much advised against it. He whooped and hollered and only occasionally clutched the bandages at his side.

Franklin clasped Nairne warmly at the approach to the chateau. The man had aged considerably since Franklin had last seen him; he walked with a limp and his shoulders seemed somehow more sloping.

"Mr. Franklin," he acknowledged. "You seem to have done your job."

"As best I could, Governor, as best I could."

"Can you bring me to date?"

"Of course. Let us find you quarters, first."

"Mr. Franklin, your wife, Lenka. I fear—I fear I have misplaced her."

"Never fear, she is found, or she found me. Though that presents its own problems."

Nairne nodded. "As long as it's off my shoulders."

New Paris and Franklin had not been idle, awaiting the troops. The capital of Louisiana would not be taken from the sea, as the English colonies had—at least not without hideous

198

cost. The harbor was mined all the way to the open ocean, and more sparsely for miles up and down the coast. The fortress had been reinforced with depneumifiers, as well, to separate any airships or underwater boats from the malakim that powered them.

On the landward side, a perimeter of towers was erected, hidden amongst the huge pines and dense cypress, depending on the terrain. These were furbished with devil guns as well, and together constituted a wall through which no ordinary malakus-driven machine should be able to pass. That left only the thousands of enemy soldiers and warriors marching their way, apparently from east *and* west.

The newly arrived Carolinians were put immediately to work in shifts, digging and building more mundane sorts of fortifications. Scouts went north, west, and east to gather intelligence. New Paris swarmed with men building defenses like an ant nest some child had kicked—or so Franklin thought, remembering his earlier observations of those insects.

Nairne watched all this with weary resignation.

"I fear it will not be enough," he said. "This has never been a real battle, just rats trying to bark at the hounds."

"Keep heart," Franklin cautioned, "or pretend to. When Oglethorpe arrives with King Charles, things will look better."

"Oglethorpe is his own luck charm," Nairne replied, "but he went back toward the lion's maw. I would not count on him to return. Too much stands in his way, and too many acts of God. Consider; he must learn to sail those amphibian ships well enough to slip through the sound, beneath the nose of Fort Marlborough. Then, on the open sea, he must find Charles before the fleet dispatched to sink him does. Then he must convince Charles that he is a friend and speaks for us, though he swims with Russian fins. If it can be done, Oglethorpe will do it. But it may be that it cannot be done."

"Then we will find victory without him," Franklin said softly. "We *must*, you understand."

"I understand. I'm just tired."

"Rest, then. We've still got time, God willing. Something

has delayed the army from the west. Each second is another bullet in our guns."

"As you say," Nairne told him. "I'm just tired."

In that week and the week that followed, Lenka never once spoke to Ben, though he sought her out every day. She continued to dress as a soldier, working at the fortifications like the others. To make matters worse, he saw her often with Voltaire, who also didn't seem to be speaking to him. The whole situation was ridiculous, but if they were going to behave like spoiled children, so be it. He had too much to do.

One of those things was working on the countermeasure with Vasilisa, something that became more frustrating every day.

"There's something missing," he told her, pacing across the laboratory, hands clasped behind his back. "Why can't you tell me what it is?"

Vasilisa stood near a window, suffused in grayish light, her eyes slits of pearl. Beyond her, treetops lashed at a sky pregnant with tempest. Thunder snarled in the distance.

"Because it isn't my formula," she said with a trace of irritation. "As I told you, I copied it from the notes of Swedenborg. I don't understand all of it. That's why I needed you. I tried to kidnap you, remember, for that very reason."

"How did you expect to carry me, if I may ask?"

Her lips bowed slightly. "Please, Benjamin. How difficult do you think it was to persuade a couple of musketeers to my point of view?"

"Ah. Couldn't those same musketeers have helped you escape, after we caught you?"

"They offered. I refused. This is a stupid place to make a last stand, but where else should I go, alone? The Ottoman empire? China? No woman would ever be listened to there, even if they weren't as thoroughly under the spell of the malakim as Russia—and they are, I assure you. And since I am committed to live or die here with you and your beggar's army, I also assure you I'm not holding back. You say something is missing—I believe you. But I don't know what it is. I couldn't copy *all* of his notes, after all."

"Why me? Why didn't you take this to one of your Russian colleagues?"

"Oh—there is one who might have helped, though I rather fear her. But I did not have that option. Benjamin, I was on the tsar's ship when it fell. They spared my life only because I pretended to be with them, traitor to my tsar. I was convincing—even now he will not speak to me."

"That upsets you," he noticed, with some surprise.

"Of course it does. He thinks I betrayed him."

"But you didn't?"

"No. I stole Swedenborg's formula. When the tsar escaped, I took advantage of the confusion to steal an airship. I tried, at first, to find him, but their pursuit proved too much a danger to me. I knew the English colonies were under attack by then, so I came here." She turned back to him. "All of this wastes time. What do you see as missing?"

"Your other 'angelic' devices all have, at their hearts, an articulator. Though they vary in detail, all are premised on Sir Isaac's design. That is what the depneumifier attacks—it disrupts the chime and thus severs the contact. I thought at first all we would need here was a very powerful depneumifier, but that's not the case."

"Are you saying you have no ideas at all?"

"I'm saying I was hoping to make these things go poof and vanish, but see no way to do so. Can't you recall anything this Swedenborg might have said that will help?"

"He wasn't present when I was there—one of his assistants was. They were expecting him, but I fled before he arrived. But I think . . ." She paused. "This prophet of theirs seemed necessary for the actual creation of the engines. Swedenborg was coming with the perfected formulas, and together they were going to—"

"Wait. The *perfected* formulas? These are not them?"

"I thought you understood that, Benjamin."

"No, I most certainly did not." He closed his eyes, trying to will the irritation away and unclog his mind for proper functioning. "You say Swedenborg needed this holy man?"

"And certain devices. But the prophet—the Indians called him 'Sun Boy'—was the key."

"Well. That *is* important. Did you know that the Indians of this country have a method of creating spirits by carving off bits of their own souls?"

Her glance told him she not only didn't know it, she didn't believe it either.

He shrugged. "It's true. I've examined the phenomenon."

"What could that have to do with this?"

"I don't know. This talk of a prophet—ah, well. I wish Red Shoes were here."

She didn't ask who Red Shoes was, though she was clearly curious. He left her so.

"In any event—it's almost as if there is no connection between these Swedenborgian engines and the aether. But if there is no interlocution—if they are not motivated by the malakim—how can these devices be 'angelic'?"

She spread her hands.

"Well," he murmured. "Let's leave that aside. If we cannot simply dissolve them, perhaps we can draw their teeth." He spread the diagrams and pages of symbols out on the table. "The problem, again, is that I don't see what sort of teeth they have. Are you certain that these things exist? Or could it be that this Swedenborg is deluded, and has deluded you as well?"

"Swedenborg is not natural—he is strange, perhaps mad. But he is a genius. He believes these engines will function, and I believe him."

"His notes speak of great conflagration, yet I see nothing here that resembles combustion. Very much the opposite, in fact. From what I can tell, this takes ash and puts it back together."

"I . . . didn't understand that part."

"I comprehend it, I just don't understand what it's supposed to do. The engine attracts the graphite—*carbonis,* he calls it here—which is present in many things. It crushes the ferments together and another substance—he calls it *niveum*— is formed."

"Perhaps it is poisonous, this substance."

"Perhaps. Or perhaps—" A terrible thought occurred to him. "Perhaps the purpose is not to make this new substance but to destroy the old. Oh, dear heaven, that's it."

"I still don't understand."

"*Carbonis* is present in all living things, Vasilisa. Where these engines pass, nothing will remain alive."

"How?"

"I suppose all would just crumble apart. Or, no, let me figure this." He took to paper with his pen and worked through the formula. He stared at the results for a second, frowned, and started over. "That can't be right," he muttered.

It came out the same way a second time. He did it a third.

"I must be making some faulty assumption."

"How so?"

"Two things. First, only a fraction of the *carbonis* attracted undergoes transformation. That doesn't make it less dangerous, because most of the *carbonis* within its radius—which looks like miles—is attracted, which still means death. But the amount of *niveum* produced is negligible. Why do it at all?"

"And the second thing?"

"Some of the matter disappears during the process. It just goes away. You see? Carbon is made up of four atoms of damnatum, four of phlegm, three of lux, one of gas. This new substance ought to have double all that, yes? Because he's crushing them together. But it isn't so. Two damnatum atoms are missing, and he accounts for them nowhere. It makes no sense. If there were two lux left over, that might explain the 'furnace' he talks about, though it would be more like a match, I think. But here, you see, he talks about a great number of lux atoms released—a very great number—though there are none left over. They come from nowhere."

"Benjamin?" Vasilisa's eyes had gone dreamy.

"What?"

"What if the damnatum atoms are changed into lux?"

"That shouldn't be possible. Atoms themselves are unchangeable and irreducible."

"So Newton thought. What if Newton was wrong?"

"There's no proof he was wrong, just this crazy formula."

"Benjamin, even if you are skeptical, how can we take that chance?"

"Maybe this is all a distraction, something to keep us from working on the defenses we know will work."

"I don't think so. That is not Swedenborg's nature."

"If either Newton or Swedenborg has to be wrong, I know who I choose to trust."

"Really, Benjamin, Newton was at least as mad as Swedenborg—probably more so. Do you trust a dead man?"

That stung a little. It was what he had told d'Artaguiette, turned against him.

"I'll think about it some more. The most important thing— if these devices are indeed real—is to make it so that they cannot attract graphite ferments." He began to doodle. "We could make our own attractors—"

"Which would kill just as surely as theirs."

"Of course. But we could use them to create something like a firebreak, a zone where they would have no sustenance."

"Why not make a repulsion against the new substance, the niveum?"

He blinked at her. "Of course. Of course, that is the answer, Vasilisa. By God, you still have a wonderful mind."

"Why, thank you, Benjamin." She actually seemed pleased. "That's a compliment indeed, from you."

They were close, bent over the same sheet of paper. He could feel her breath. "We are the only ones left," she said. "We are the only Newtonians still alive." Her eyes were bright with tears.

It was the last thing he had ever expected from her. The very last thing.

It took twelve years off his life, made him a boy again, as when Voltaire had proposed his toast . . .

"No," he said huskily. "There is Voltaire."

She snorted and turned away. "He was never one of us; he said it himself. He never much understood Newton's theories or any of our own. Maclauren, Heath, Stirling—and me, I like to think. And you, of course, the greatest one of all."

"The others had no opportunity to become great. I—"

It caught him like an explosion, this thing he had learned to keep bottled up so well. He choked on it as it came out. "Dear God, Vasilisa. What did we do to the world? What did *I* do to it?" He was weeping too, like a little boy, as he hadn't in years.

She reached for him, and for an instant he forgot everything—her great betrayal, her attempt to kidnap him only scant weeks before. He remembered only what it was like when the world was wonderful, full of possibilities. That she knew and understood what he had done, what weight lay on his shoulders, and that she shared some of it.

And did not hate him for it.

He clutched her to him so tightly that after a moment he was afraid he might break her. He held her that way for a long time.

Finally, the terrible thing in his chest subsided, ebbed enough to be put back in its bottle and to be stoppered tightly. He released her gently.

"Come," he murmured. "There is still time to make amends. What's done is done. We have a new problem to solve."

"Can we be friends, Benjamin? Can you ever forgive me, and be my friend again?" She stroked his cheek.

"I think so," he replied, his voice unsteady. "I think I can do that."

They worked the rest of the day on various proofs, seeking the repulsion for *niveum*. Swedenborg had described the material in some detail, which gave them a good starting point, but it was still no easy task.

Vasilisa fell asleep, slumped over her notes; and Franklin, rubbing his eyes, noticed it was sundown. He stood and stretched, then went to find a servant to conduct Vasilisa to her room.

He went out into the cooling air and walked into the briny

wind from the sea, following the mud-puddled road to Fort Condé. What remained of the thunderheads rolled over, painted gold and flame by the retiring sun, and once he was out of New Paris, the salty air mingled with the heavy perfume of flowers and the lingering scent of the rain. A whippoorwill started to sing, the cicadas chirped, and he almost felt he might have been walking along the edge of Roxbury Flats on a particularly hot summer night in his native Boston.

Very ordinary. Very pleasant.

As a boy *ordinary* and *pleasant* had bored him to tears. His real life always lay around some approaching bend, when he would go to college, or take to the whale roads like his brother, or run off to apprentice in the new sciences.

Well, his road had taken a number of bends, hadn't it? And always, somehow, even with everything that had happened to him, he still imagined that his real life was just about to start. That he would soon find his real position in life, his real home, his real—

He stopped, watched the sky ebb darker. *His real wife.*

That was the trouble, wasn't it? It had nothing to do with any defect in Lenka. It was his flaw, his . . .

Up ahead, at the fort, a bell suddenly began to ring. He stood for a second, wondering what it could mean, then began to run as quickly as he could in the near darkness.

Fort Condé loomed ahead, a brick and timber structure some three hundred feet square. At the moment it was aglow with lanthorn light, and a lot of the lanthorns were in motion.

The soldier on duty at the gate challenged him and recognized him at about the same moment, but Franklin gave the password anyway as he hurried past, through the yard, and into the command post, breathing heavily.

Nairne was there, along with a French lieutenant, one Regis Du Roullet.

"What's the noise?" Franklin asked.

Nairne was grimacing at one of the three opticons Franklin had built the previous week.

"Four airships have just come up to the northwestern

perimeter," he said. "The debt for the time we borrowed is come due."

Franklin felt his heart go *chunk-a-chunk*, like the water-filled drums some of the Indians used. "Did the depneumifier prove effective?"

"I don't know. The ships stopped short and infantry debarked. Then the ships flew off, still out of range."

"Oh."

"I was afraid of this," Nairne went on. "They used the same trick against us in Carolina. They can't use the airships direct, for our devil guns, but the ships are still terrible weapons. Moving troops without having to march them is an incredible advantage."

"They're hastening the war," Franklin noticed. "Even with their ships—and I'm told they have only a few—they can move only small numbers of their total host. Why rush them in here in numbers we might be able to account for, rather than waiting for their mass to settle on our frontier?"

"To give us less time to prepare, naturally," Nairne replied.

"How many men did they land?"

"We don't know yet," Du Roullet said. "We also have some intelligence that the underwater boats are putting troops ashore about thirty miles up the coast." He smiled grimly. "One of our Taensas scouts reported a great deal of bubbles boiling up somewhat closer. They must have found our mines too impeding."

Nairne rubbed his eyes. "Two fronts," he murmured. "With the permission of you gentlemen, I should like to take command of the northwestern line. That will be where the hardest and most immediate fighting will be. They may have made a mistake, coming at us in pieces, like this. We might manage to swallow a number of small bites as we could not the whole meal."

"True," Du Roullet mused. "Which makes me wonder, with Mr. Franklin, why? Do they so fear what we might do in just a few days?"

They might, Franklin thought, *if they got wind of what Vasilisa and I are working on.*

He didn't say anything, though. If there was a traitor, best not to let him know his existence was suspected. "Have you sent for the tsar?" Franklin asked. "He might have some insight into this strategy."

"A runner just went for him."

Franklin nodded. "I had hoped we had a few more days."

Nairne shrugged. "We got more than we did at Venice, and that turned out well enough. I have faith in you, Mr. Franklin."

It struck him, then, that they *did* have faith in him, and it went cold into his bones.

"I will meet with you gentlemen later," he said. "I need to talk to someone."

Euler stirred awake almost instantly. It was disconcerting, the way he went from sound sleep to complete attentiveness. Franklin didn't like it.

"Mr. Franklin. Back out of my box?"

Franklin took a deep breath before beginning. "Mr. Euler," he said, "it may be that I have treated you shabbily. I see no sense in apologizing for it. Trusting you comes hard, and I think you understand that. But you've done us more good than the people I trust. You warned us of the ships in Charles Town harbor and you told me how to provoke Sterne into revealing himself. I need you again."

Euler looked frankly at him. "I am your prisoner," he said.

"No. I've already given the order—you are no longer confined to the palace. You can leave without listening to another word from me. If I were you, I probably would. But I'll be plain. I need you."

"Of course you do," Euler snapped, his brow wrinkling. "You needed me weeks ago."

"I know, but it's too late for that. Will you help me now?"

"Help you how?"

"Two things. First, the answer to a question, if you know it."

"Ask it."

"The army from the west hastens to attack us. But I have seen Swedenborg's designs for the engines."

"From Mrs. Karevna?"

"You know her?"

"Of course. Go on."

"It's a tidy question. They can be used at great distances. *Why haven't they used them?*"

"I thought I explained that. They won't use them until it's clear their military assault is a failure. Once they commit, the war in heaven will break full gale, and it will be a terrible one. Why risk that, when it seems clear that their forces can dispatch you—us, I should say—with relative ease?"

"You mean if we contrived to lose, the engines will never be used?"

"Never is a long time, Mr. Franklin. But possibly. Make no mistake—humanity will still perish—slowly. Or, if luck is with us, the Liberal faction will return to power in time to save a few of us, though our great cities and all our learning will be stripped from us by then."

"But our race might live."

"Might."

Franklin sighed and raked his hand through his hair. "They attacked earlier than we thought, using the most mobile elements of their forces rather than waiting until they have the whole bear trap about us. Why? That only increases the likelihood, however small, that they will lose and have to use their engines."

"They must suspect you are near a countermeasure. Or else . . ." He trailed off, then flicked his sharp gaze up at Franklin. "There is something else, something they fear themselves. I think they worry that if they unleash the engines, they might somehow turn on them. I don't know how—it's mostly intuition, gleaned from a word here and there, nothing I can put my finger on." He considered another few seconds. "Does Swedenborg say how the engines are made?"

"I think they aren't machines that empower malakim—I think they are a new sort of creature, created *from* malakim. I'm not sure."

"Think. Think what else you might do, if you had that sort

of power. Wonder what might also be created, what the malakim might fear enough to make them hesitate."

"Nothing comes immediately to mind."

"Not to mine, either."

"But will you be willing to help me? In the laboratory? So that when the time does come, we will have countermeasures?"

Euler smiled faintly. "Mr. Franklin, I thought you would never ask."

7.

Ghosts and God

Adrienne rode sidesaddle on a muddy road, surrounded by brambled fields that rolled gently to the horizon. The air was perfumed with the acrid scent of gunpowder and horse dung. Behind her she heard the creak of wagons, the chattering of the sutlers and the whores, drums beating.

Nicolas d'Artagnan rode beside her, his rangy body swaying comfortably in rhythm with his horse, colichemarde slapping gently in time against his leg.

"How is it with you, beloved?" he asked.

She didn't know the answer. She couldn't remember. She closed her eyes and saw only colored clouds, shifting and breaking.

"Where are we, Nicolas?" she asked.

"Where are we?" He repeated her statement, frowning a little. "We are together, I think."

"I l—" Her tongue clove thickly to her lips for a moment. "I love you," she managed to finish.

"I know."

"I have a son."

"I know that, too. You named him for me. But he isn't mine."

"I wanted to give you sons. If children could be born of hearts instead of bodies, he *would* be yours. I have never loved anyone as I loved you."

He smiled gently, as if to himself. "One of the great benefits of dying in the first days of love, I think."

"Please don't say that."

"I always spoke what I felt with you, when I had the

211

courage. Now courage and cowardice are equally absurd." His saddle squeaked as he shifted to face her. "You are thinking of killing him, this child of our hearts."

"No."

"Yes. As you killed me."

"Nicolas, no."

"As you killed Hercule."

"No," she whispered, collecting herself. She looked at Nicolas again. He was a boy, a child. What did he know? "You killed yourself," she accused. "You could have lived."

"We could have gone away together, you and I," Nicolas said. "I planned it. I offered it to you."

Adrienne shook her head. "But I had to— You're trying to confuse me. Are you one of my enemies?"

"You're starting to remember."

"Yes. Are you Nicolas? Or are you the one who came before? Lilith? Sophia?"

Nicolas smiled, that infrequent, cryptic, annoying smile of his. "Maybe I'm your son. Maybe I'm Hercule. Who else shall we add?"

"What do you want? Have you just come to torment me? To remind me that everyone I love dies? My skin is thickened to that."

"Thick enough to kill your own son?"

"I do not know him. He does not know me except to hate me. How is he my son?"

Nicolas just chuckled at that.

"What do you want of me?" she demanded again.

" 'And God so loved the world . . .' " Nicolas began. He turned his byzantine eyes fully on her then. "God does love the world, Adrienne."

"Last time we spoke, you said you were not sure God existed."

He frowned almost imperceptibly. "Perhaps that was another, or perhaps my faith has returned. Or perhaps I love the world, and that is enough."

"Real or not, God does not love me."

"Maybe not, not as you mean. When you loved Nicolas,

did you love each atom that composed him? Did you mourn each breath that was in him when he exhaled, cherish the new air as it entered his lungs? Did you weep when he lost a fingernail, grieve when his hair was cut? God's is a different sort of love, Adrienne. A more profound sort. It is a terrible sort of love, the love of the world. It is a love that requires, at times, bitter things."

"What sort of bitter things?"

"You," he whispered. "You."

Her hand glowed, and she held it up in front of her.

"I have no power left," she said. "My djinni have all died or deserted me."

And Nicolas began to laugh. Not his usual chopping, reserved, good-natured chuckling, but a full roar from the belly. She could only watch him in astonishment.

"My predicament amuses you?"

"You would use a sword to trim fingernails. You would use a cannon to snuff a candle."

"What do you mean?"

Instead of answering her, he leaned suddenly and kissed her. It was as if some potent distillation had been poured between her lips, a tonic of every sort of love. He tasted like Nicolas, Hercule, Crecy, her son.

And he was gone.

"Uriel?" she asked the gray sky. "God?"

But no answer came.

She awoke in a cathedral, the largest she had ever seen, whose columns supported a roof so vast she had difficulty making it out. She heard priests chanting the Te Deum, smelled the incense.

Another dream?

But no—the columns were the boles of pine trees so enormous in girth that four men could not link hands around them. The Te Deum was in a language she did not recognize, and the incense was tobacco and the scent of popping, hissing pine resin in the fire nearby.

The chant broke off. "She wakes," someone said in French.

Her eyes, stung to tears by the smoke, cleared again, and she saw an Indian sitting near her. He was handsome, in an alien sort of way.

"Adrienne?" That French was better.

"Veronique?"

"It is me. How do you feel?"

"How long have I slept?"

"You have been in and out of a fever for almost two weeks. You nearly died. I nearly lost you."

She wanted to ask where she was, but she feared another conversation like she'd had with "Nicolas." Instead, she touched her throat. "I'm thirsty."

"I'll get water."

A second later, lukewarm water splashed in her mouth. It tasted good. Crecy touched her forehead.

"Your fever seems to be gone at last," she said cautiously.

Adrienne surveyed her body. Her left leg was in splints, and her ribs ached as she drew breath. She wondered how she had been traveling. "What of the others?" she asked.

"Hercule is dead."

"I remember." Words clotted on her tongue for a moment, then she went on. "The others?"

"More than half the crew, actually. Your students all survived—Elizavet included—and Father Castillion. Some of your guard was killed, fighting these Indians."

"They are our enemies, then?" She glanced up at the Indian.

"They fired on my people," the Indian said. "My people killed them. If their guns had stayed silent, they would still be alive."

"Who are you?"

"I hesitate to give a name to someone as powerful as you. Suffice to say I am a sorcerer, something like you. We fought the Sun Boy together, though I was confused about the matter at the time. He survived, by the way. His army follows us, by perhaps two days, perhaps three. I am still too weak to tell."

"Follows us to where?"

"To your kinfolk. To New Paris."

She fumbled in her memory for such a place, came up with nothing.

He saw her confusion. "It was once named Mobile," he offered. "The chief city of Louisiana."

"Ah. Why do we go there?"

"Because we have matters to attend there, you and I," he answered, and with that he stood and strode away.

"They have treated us well, but we are captives," Crecy explained. "What he says about the soldiers might be true. It might have been a misunderstanding."

"Most of my guard gone, no djinni left to serve me. It's as it was in the beginning, Crecy."

"No. You have me. You have Linné and Breteuil and Lomonosov. They want to see you, but I have kept them away."

"But I have no way to protect them. The Queen of Angels is dead."

"Good. Then perhaps Adrienne can live again," Crecy said.

"I'm not sure I—" But Crecy wouldn't want to hear that. "How badly am I hurt?"

"A broken leg, cracked ribs. You lost a lot of blood, and then the fever set in. It seems now that the fever is gone—you will be well soon."

"Well? What does that matter? Unless you defeated Oliv—" She broke off. The Indian was back.

He rubbed his chin. "The Sun Boy defeated both of us, and his army is a few days behind our heels. But I think there is still a way to win. Here." And he pointed at her hand.

"Not anymore," she said. But she remembered the creature in her dream and what it had said.

"I think you are mistaken," Red Shoes said.

"You are the one mistaken, if you think you can talk to her like that," Crecy snapped.

A faint frown creased his brow, and he looked away, almost as if he hadn't heard her. Then he sighed. "My apologies. You have just awakened. We do not have much time, but it can wait until we reach New Paris. If we reach New Paris."

"I thought we were ahead of the army. What would prevent us?"

"We are ahead of *part* of the army. Several airships flew over and let troops off between us and our destination.

"Must we go around them?" Crecy asked.

The Indian smiled disconcertingly. "I thought we would go *through*," he said.

8.

Brawls and Battles

"This gets worse and worse," Thomas Nairne muttered, peering through the spyglass. Below them, the frigate *Dauphin* rocked gently. They had come out here to check the mines and nets, and to sound for Russian underwater craft. They were not far from land—in fact, they were well under Fort Condé's guns—but it was still dangerous. Franklin was nearly certain his modified aether compass would warn them of the underwater boats as it warned of aircraft and warlocks, but he could not be entirely certain. Nor could he be sure that the stuff he had invented to make them rise like corks in the water hadn't been proofed against by the Russian philosophers.

But what they hadn't expected was this—sails and puffs of steam on the horizon.

Franklin peered through his own spyglass to confirm it. "A small fleet," he said. "Men-of-war under steam. But no airships." Franklin grunted. "Let's hope our minefield will trip them up, and the nets ought to get any of the amphibians."

"It will for a time, but most mines are sunk deep, to trip up their devilish underwater boats. We've had no report of sailing ships."

"We'll have to reinforce the fort," Nairne said grimly. "All the commanders we have worth anything are out at the redoubts, awaiting the inland attack. Damn."

Franklin's heart sank. He needed more time, just a little more, but the malakim weren't going to give it to him. The troops on the northern frontier hadn't moved yet, and Nairne was reluctant to attack them first, using the interval for more defensive works instead. And now they had three fronts—two armies and a fleet—poised to crack New Paris open like a nut.

"Well, we must do our best," he murmured.

"Yes," Nairne said, his voice rising. "And, by heavens, our best may be better than we thought."

"What do you mean?"

"They've run up colors!" Nairne exclaimed. "The lion of King Charles of Sweden, the winged lion and crescent moon of the Janissaries and Venice—and, by all that's holy, our own Commonwealth flag! Oglethorpe managed it, by God! He warned the Venetian fleet!"

Franklin felt a surge of joyous hope but kept caution wound as tightly as he could. "Could it be a trick? If the Russians killed Charles and took his ships, they might try sneaking in under false colors. We've heard nothing from them."

"We shall see, soon," Nairne commented. "They've sent out a longboat. Shall we send our own to guide them in?"

Franklin hesitated only a moment. "Yes."

"Margrave Oglethorpe, you are a sight for sore eyes," Franklin said, smiling.

Oglethorpe, despite himself, shared a reluctant grin. "It was more touch than go, but here we are, with allies."

"So I see. Is Charles with them?"

Oglethorpe chuckled. "He wanted his turn in the amphibian boat. He took a company to Apalachee territory, where we had word some Russian troops had landed. God willing, he'll be done with them quickly. How are things in New Paris?"

They outlined the situation quickly.

"So you've need of a general, then?" the margrave asked lightly.

"Sir, we do indeed," Nairne replied.

"Good. I'm damned weary of this nautical stuff. If you'll clear me a way, I can have my men ready to fight by sundown."

"That's not soon enough," Nairne said, "but we'll make it do. God bless you, sir."

"Let Him bless us all. We shall need His best wishes," Oglethorpe replied.

*   *   *

Philippe threw a small celebrabratory dinner for Oglethorpe and his men that night, outside on what passed for a hill, a sandy open place overhung with live oaks grown in fantastic shapes and hung thick with Spanish moss. Two Indian fiddlers played and sang, and the wine, which Philippe had previously been necessarily stingy with, flowed freely. Toward the end of the evening, Franklin found himself facing Oglethorpe across a popping fire. Next to him sat the coal-black Unoka, and between them they were telling the story of the battle of Fort Marlborough.

"And Unoka, here, disobeyed my orders," Oglethorpe said.

"Not so, General," the African said. "You never order me not t' do it."

"Do what?" Voltaire asked. His gaze cut a little toward Franklin, but the ambassador would not meet it. Whenever Ben saw the Frenchman, he felt that odd lump of shame and betrayal.

"We were in the spur of the fort, which is, in a way, its own fort. I expected to make a siege out of it, while *Azilia's Hammer* went to safety, then on to find King Charles."

"You expected to die," Voltaire said.

"I did not," Oglethorpe said. "I intended to fight my way back over the wall, then run fugitive back to Azilia and then here." He smiled grimly. "But I'll concede the chances of doing so were not good. In any event, the moment came, and the rest of the fort started to attack us. But imagine my surprise when there were fewer than fifty of them, and only one airship."

"Then the fort was not garrisoned as you thought?"

"Oh, that it was. Better, even. Near two hundred men. But our friend Unoka here had taken five of his men and slit the throats of nearly all while they slept."

Franklin felt acid rise into his mouth, and for a moment fought to retain his dinner. Who were these men who could talk so casually of such things? Who were these walking knives he called companions? He saw a similar look cross Voltaire's face, and despite everything suddenly felt a deep kinship with the Frenchman. Voltaire, after all, was an author, a philosopher. Of all those assembled here, he and Franklin were closest.

"We had the one airship to deal with, but a lucky shot remedied that."

"T' general, he jumped from te wall, and shoot t' pilot from one yard!" Unoka guffawed.

"The stuff of epics!" Philippe shouted a little drunkenly. "I shall need a court poet to compose an opera based on this, or some such."

Privately, Franklin could not imagine epic heroes cutting throats in the dark of night. He tried to imagine himself as a young soldier in the Pretender's army. He would not—could not—know who his ultimate masters were. He would think he was fighting for a just cause. Perhaps he was prepared to die, yes, but at least imagined he would meet death on his feet, like a man, not gutted like a fish in the middle of a pleasant dream.

But war wasn't for men, was it? It was for fools. And fools deserved no better than what they earned.

He shook himself away from such uncharitable thoughts. Theirs was a just war, perhaps the *only* just war. If he expected to win it without any tarnish on his soul, then *he* was the fool.

"Mr. Voltaire? Would you be my court poet?"

Voltaire put on the wry grin he wore so well. "Last time I composed something about your court, I was guested in the Bastille."

"That was my father's court, not mine. And I am not the man—or the king—I was in Paris."

"I will consider it," Voltaire told him, "though at the moment I already have a commission." This time he looked quite boldly at Franklin, before turning his gaze back toward his feet. "Nor am I the same man I was in Paris. I have little poetry in me now, I fear."

Oglethorpe cleared his throat. "I've heard it rumored, sir, that you were in London when she was destroyed. That you stayed behind to try and warn the court there. You are a hero in your own right."

"Hero?" Voltaire's haunted gaze rose up again. "What should I have done? I cannot know. But what I did was not the right thing."

"Tell us, Monsieur," Philippe said. "This may be our last night for such stories. Tell us your tale."

Voltaire was silent for the space of fifty breaths, then he sighed. "We could not make them listen, of course, and were nearly arrested for trying. Mr. Heath, a student of Sir Isaac and my companion, hit upon a desperate plan. The comet, we knew, must be guided to London by some sort of attractor, a device with an affinity for that hurtling stone. If we could find it, Mr. Heath thought we might possibly reverse it."

"Reverse it?" Franklin heard himself say. "You mean hurl the comet back into the heavens? That was only days, perhaps hours, before it struck. It was an impossible task."

"We did not think we could hurl it back into the void," Voltaire said, "but even a small deflection, a small alteration of course, might have landed it in the sea." He clasped his hands as if in prayer. "We could think of no other plan."

"But you did not find it."

"No, we did. Mr. Heath had the resources of Newton at his disposal, and made a detector. We found the device. But it was ringed with French spies, and they took us up. They clapped irons on us and put us in a galley bound for Barbados."

"Barbados?"

"We never reached it, of course. The comet fell, and the waves came. It was all darkness and motion for us, and at last water. The hold was filling, and a jailer with a heart tried to set as many of us free as he could. I was one, but before we could reach Mr. Heath, the ship was shattered. I had his hand; I felt him go down. I had the jailer's keys, but could not find the lock on his chains—and then fear took me, and to save my miserable life I left him. I clung to wreckage and ended on the shore of Normandy, almost dead." He shook his head. "I am no hero. I am a coward of the worst sort."

"You lived to fight another day," Oglethorpe said gently.

"You would not have done it. You would have sunk to the very bottom with him, given your last breath to save him. I did not."

Franklin pushed a stick into the flames. "I knew Heath. He would have been furious if you had died in a vain effort to save him. And no man here can say what he would have done—only what he might hope to do, which is not the same thing."

"That was well said," Oglethorpe replied.

Voltaire looked back at Franklin, and this time their eyes met, not in contest but in commiseration. Then the Frenchman nodded.

"And remember what your mentor Leibniz was wont to say," Franklin added. "This world is the best of all possible worlds, and so what happened, naturally was for the best."

That drew a bit of laughter, and even Voltaire grinned again. "I once bitterly remonstrated with that philosophy," he said. "It is a philosophy well suited to men of wealth and privilege, yes, and ill suited to those who daily suffer in this life. And yet, at times, I understand it. If things could not have been better—if they cannot *be* better—then why waste the effort of remorse or of hoping for a better future day?"

"And now I see you are still a poet," Philippe said.

Voltaire did not answer, but stared into the fire as if he saw any better day consumed in its flames.

"Well, gentlemen," Oglethorpe told them all, "I will bid you good night. A little sleep, and then I have a march to make. I've asked King Philippe and Governor Nairne to give me the northern command, and they have been kind enough to flatter me with it. By tomorrow, I shall be carrying the standard of Mars to our enemy."

"Good night, sir," the king said, "and godspeed. You are our truest knight."

Oglethorpe and his men reached the northernmost redoubt before first light. He was struck by the incredible calm of the morning, in the face of what he knew must come. Since the invaders landed from the airships, there had been a few minor skirmishes—it seemed that the Indians from the West were as undisciplined and overeager for battle as his own—but for the most part there had been silence from them. That wouldn't last much longer.

Their first target would have to be the towers—until they were down, the Russians could not use their airships to best advantage. The towers would be tough prizes, with their magical aegis shields—the perimeter of devices that made the air unfit to breath—and their devil guns.

Unfortunately, according to the Karevna woman, those same alchemical devices would attract the attention of the Russian sorcerers.

"Sir? May I ask a question?"

Oglethorpe turned to Parmenter. "What's that?"

"Why haven't we invested the redoubt, if our mission is to hold it?"

Oglethorpe smiled wryly. "I'm not much for being cornered like a badger, no matter how snug the hole. The tower is a fat bull's-eye for the arrows of our enemy, and I don't intend—"

At that instant, coincidentally, a shell made his point for him. They heard its shrill whine and then an explosion that shook the air, even here, a quarter mile from its detonation. The tree—a five-hundred-year-old pine, if it was a day— teetered, charring black but not catching fire, due to its presence in the zone of bad air.

Another shell struck next to it, this one spattering a viscous burning fluid that immediately went out.

After that, so many shells fell that there was no space in the sound, only a noise like God humming. An avenue opened in the thick forest as the explosions worked their way directly toward the invisible redoubt.

"See? They've taught their shells to seek the aegis, just as Franklin feared. If we were in there, we wouldn't dare come out." He grinned. "As it is, we're free to go find the bastards working those cannon and lay them down to sleep."

"Amen, General," Parmenter said.

"Get 'em on their horses. 'Tis time to meet the devil."

It was eerie to hear the shelling fade in the distance, and as it did, the sound of cannon fire come over like one symphony replacing another. It reminded him vividly of his first battle with Prince Eugène, of his younger self's sheer unbelief at the range and accuracy of the new alchemical guns—that they could be placed so far away you not only couldn't see them but also couldn't even *hear* them. His first command had been to take a company and find the cannon chewing up their lines. He had done it then, and he would do it again.

Of course, it hadn't been easy that first time, either.

As Oglethorpe and his men approached the slope of the hill the guns were sounding from, bullets began swarming from the trees like a hundred acres of bees. Something like a sledgehammer struck Oglethorpe in the chest, nearly unhorsing him, and he gave quick thanks for his adamantium breastplate as he raised his pistol and fired at the Indian springing from behind the nearest tree. The fellow howled like a catamount as the *kraftpistole* cut him in half.

The fighting got dirty. This time they didn't face regulars, trying to keep neat columns—this enemy fought from amongst the trees, like his own people. The rangers unslung their carbines and dismounted, forming a rough line, firing and advancing, one tree to the next. The air was thick with the smell of powder and pine sap.

Oglethorpe stayed mounted, barking orders and shooting at shadows. A trio of Indians broke from cover and ran at him, firing their muskets; then, when they saw they had missed, pulling tomahawks. He calmly shot one with his last charge, then drew his saber as his horse screamed and collapsed, rolling on its side, blood blowing from its neck like spume from a whale surfacing. He was on his feet but still untangling himself from the saddle when they reached him.

One pitched back from him at a distance of a yard, and he heard a ranger behind him shout in triumph. The other leapt, whirling an ax. Oglethorpe struck savagely with his saber, and the bright edge bit into the Indian's arm. It didn't slow him. They crashed together, Oglethorpe reaching with his free hand to catch the descending ax. He missed, and the weapon skinned down his arm, surprisingly painful, before spanging into his breastplate. With an involuntary roar, he struck his knuckle guard into the man's face, and for an instant he was twenty-three again, in a low tavern in London, fury and alcohol mixed in his veins, experiencing the dirty exhilaration of feeling a nose collapse under his fist, the sheer animal pleasure of killing a man with his bare hands. He cursed the Indian for bringing that memory back, knotted his hand in the thick black hair, and pulped the face into a red nightmare. He kept hitting the corpse long after it was dead.

By the time he returned to his senses, four of his rangers were around him, firing at more attackers.

"No more bush fighting, by God!" he snarled. "Fetch me a mount and sound the charge!"

If they questioned his decision, no one said so. He did not care what was wisest—he was a general, by God, not the brawling fool he had been more than two decades ago. He should *not* have to fight like that!

A moment later, shrieking like Indians themselves, they swarmed up the hill.

It happened in a blur, oddly slowly. Ambushers rose from every pile of brush and fell, and some rose again, missing parts of themselves. Some waited until the Colonials were past, then leapt up behind them. He turned once, just in time to see a red hole the size of a fist appear in Cory MacWilliams, just under the silver coin he wore around his neck for good luck and see—God, yes, *see*—the bloody bullet that had done the work speed within an inch of his own nose.

By the time they reached the hilltop and the guns there, he had lost more than half his men. Predictably, the Yamacraw made it to the top first, Parmenter's rangers on their heels. The gunners dropped the muzzles of their weapons and fired, cutting swaths that left bits of men everywhere. Through the haze of smoke-coughing weapons, he made out that the top of the hill had been cleared and a cavalry of sorts awaited them—fierce dark men who did not look like Indians, wearing splinted armor and carrying cutlasslike weapons.

Oglethorpe barely felt the impact of the charge. His pistols were long since spent, and his saber was already more a club than a sword.

In a moment of clarity, he knew they would never make it. The ambushers they had left behind them in their hurry were catching up, and they were now in a crossfire. He had killed all his men for nothing.

And then, miraculously, the guns went silent, and the Mongols—that's what he guessed them to be, from what the tsar had said—began dropping from the rear. His men gave a great shout, almost as if in one voice, and their enemies, confused and disheartened, went down like wheat before a scythe.

And from the smoke on the hill, another company emerged. Indians, but this time of a sort he recognized by their tattoos and paint.

Choctaws.

The miracle was they didn't fire at each other. For a long moment, what remained of Oglethorpe's men stood, panting and bleeding, wondering if this was a new force they would have to fight. But the Choctaw had killed the gunners and the Mongols, and so after a moment Oglethorpe made his decision and turned his remaining men to deal with enemy coming up the hill behind them.

Within half an hour the battle was over, the high ground theirs.

"Sir," a soldier said, limping up beside him. "Let the surgeon bind your wound."

"Eh?" He glanced at his arm. The ax had peeled his skin back, but there wasn't much bleeding—a sticky sort of crust had already formed over the lesion. "It can wait," he said. "Where is Tomochichi?"

"He went chasing back down the hill."

"Ah. What do you think of those fellows with the guns?"

"They seem like friends, sir."

"I'm going to see." Over the protests of the young man, he spurred his new mount up the hill, sheathing his saber as he did so.

A small party stepped from cover to greet him—a Choctaw man, perhaps thirty years old, and a body of soldiers in dirty blue uniforms. One of these was a tall, slim fellow with hair the color of copper.

"Halito," Oglethorpe said, one of the few words he knew in Choctaw.

"Good day," the Indian answered in English.

"You seemed to have saved us a good bit of trouble. I'm much grateful to you. I am James Edward Oglethorpe, margrave of Azilia, commander of the English forces in New Paris."

"We are happy to be of help. Your foe is our foe—we have been fighting these men since they crossed the Mississippi River."

"We had heard the Choctaw were resisting."

"I'm glad you recognized us."

Oglethorpe smiled wearily. "It's been my business for many years to know the Indians in these territories. Well, as I said, you've helped us out. What can I do for you?"

"Most of my men will stay here and continue to fight. But we have a wounded Frenchwoman with us, and it is quite urgent that she—and I—reach New Paris as soon as possible."

Oglethorpe chewed his lip. It could be a trick, couldn't it? A sort of Trojan horse?

"How many of you?" he asked.

"Me, the lady, twelve of her company, and one Indian woman."

Oglethorpe coughed—his lungs were still thick with the smoke of the guns—and nodded. "I will have you there by nightfall," he said. "But tell me—how much respite do we have? Is there more of this advance force?"

"This was most of them, I think," the Choctaw replied. "But there will be more very soon."

"Can your men help us carry these guns down to our redoubt?"

"Of course, General."

"Wonderful. I hate to ask more favors, but again it is much appreciated. I will make certain your men get a share of what gifts we have."

"That is good." He gave some orders in Choctaw.

"Where is this lady?"

"Back a bit. We will fetch her now, if you are ready to escort us."

Oglethorpe hesitated only an instant. "I will arrange it. May I ask—who do you have business with in New Paris?"

"The philosopher Benjamin Franklin. The lady is also a philosopher, late of Russia. She has much to tell him. Crucial things."

Or you wish to assassinate our best hope, Oglethorpe thought, suspicious again. He would send a message ahead, to prepare them.

"That might do it," Franklin murmured, staring at the odd device he, Euler, and Vasilisa had just cobbled together. It was simple and delicate in appearance—a glass rod a fathom long and the thickness of a sword blade, rising to a point from a cubical iron case. The complexity came in the small additions to the glass, the chime of philosopher's mercury in the casing, and the small tympanum on the side—a sort of "ear" that would help the device adjust to the precise harmonics it was exposed to.

"Might," Euler said. "But how can we test it, when it is made to repel a substance that does not yet exist?"

"I don't know." Franklin mused, "I suppose, in this instance, we must have faith. I want five more of these made by tomorrow, and five more the next day."

"You understand, it is a temporary solution," Vasilisa said.

"Of course I do. But it gives us more time, yes?"

"How much time will we need, I wonder?" Euler said. "And—assuming we defeat the army cast at us, and hold the engines at bay—how much of the world will remain? After all, this will protect only a few miles, maybe not even that."

"Which is why we must stop wasting time jabbering and build more. 'Tis a simple enough device to construct—the craftsmen should be able to get the hang of it easily enough."

Vasilisa sighed and settled onto a chair. Several strands of her hair came down across one eye, making her look both very young and very tired. "I never imagined we would get even this much done. It's all in God's hands now."

"Who helps best those who help themselves," Franklin reminded her. "Once we have a few of these, I want to try another approach."

"You will then *re*-proach?" a voice asked from the doorway.

"Hello, Robin. Any news?"

"Yep—all good. We've heard from Oglethorpe. He cleared out that first invasion—the northernmost redoubt is damaged, but still stands. The engineers are shoring it up now. And some visitors are on the way—a Choctaw and some others. I'm to ask y' if you know a fellow named Red Shoes."

"You know damned well I do. You also know what Tug and the tsar said about him. What are we to think? All of our old friends are coming home to roost, and we don't know whether they're doves or hawks or death angels. Who else is with him?"

"That's a funny thing. Some Russians who are really Frenchmen. Some woman named Monche— ah, Monchevrey—"

"De Mornay de Montchevreuil?" Vasilisa asked. "For the pity of God."

"That's it. You know her?"

"Yes. A very powerful sorceress. Benjamin, she might be our friend, but she might be our worst enemy. I cannot tell you which."

"Well, more of the same, eh? Will you come with me to talk to her?"

"Yes."

"Good. I intend to meet them outside of town, as unfriendly as that might seem. I'm going to see if I can get Tug and the tsar to go with us."

"More good news, by the way," Robert said.

"What's that?"

"Charles of Sweden won his skirmish at Apalachee and is on his way to join us here."

"Warn them of the mines," Franklin said. "And— Oh, heavens."

"What?"

"King Charles and Tsar Peter, both here in New Paris? That will be trouble."

" 'Trouble' isn't the word I would use," Robert replied. "There ain't no word t' use for what's going t' happen when they know about each other."

"We'll deal with that when we get to it. We'll have to keep it from Charles as long as we can. Besides, he's an honorable fellow—"

"For an absolute madman," Robert finished. "Still, I'm glad to see his ships. Makes me think we might win this little brawl."

"*Ja,*" Euler said, "but when we win, that's when the trouble actually starts."

Franklin, Vasilisa, Peter, Tug, Robert, ten musketeers, and four Apalachee—the recovering Don Pedro included—dismounted half a mile from New Paris and waited.

Tug was visibly nervous. "I don't know as I can face 'im. The things he done—well, nothin' worsen' I saw in my time as a pirate, 'cept the *way* he did it, and 'cept this is Red Shoes, who used to be a decent fellah."

"Well, we'll see directly."

Each of them wore an aegis, and two of the musketeers carried devil guns, as the soldiers had taken to calling the depneumifiers.

Ten minutes later, riders appeared through the trees.

Franklin prepared himself. Even if Red Shoes and the French sorceress were on the level, come to cooperate, there might still be troubles, here—what with the tsar, Tug's feelings about Red Shoes, and Vasilisa's clear worries about the

Frenchwoman. He hoped he had learned enough, being an ambassador, to smooth over whatever troubles there might be.

But when he saw them, he was the first to raise his pistol and cock the hammer, his finger twitching on the trigger.

9.

An Unlikely Welcome

"You!" Franklin snarled.

He scarcely noticed that five muzzles were now trained on him, all borne by the men in blue military uniforms. He only noticed the woman, whose black tresses and dark eyes haunted his nightmares, rising in the air on the backs of demons, laughing as she killed his mentor, Sir Isaac Newton.

In dream, as in life, he could do nothing but stand rooted and watch, and curse himself, and most of all curse *her*.

And here she was—he would know her anywhere, through however many years. And this was no dream.

"Father!" another woman shouted.

"Elizavet!" That came from his left, from the tsar.

Franklin's hands were shaking.

"Monsieur, if you do not lower your weapon in the next five seconds, I shall kill you," the witch's redheaded guard said. "Here, I shall count them for you. One—"

"Just hold still," Robert said quietly. His own weapon was pointed at her. "Let's sort this out."

"Don't you recognize her, Robin? She's the one from Venice. The one who killed Sir Isaac."

"All of you, lower your guns," Tsar Peter roared. "My daughter is in your line of fire, and I swear by God or the Devil that whoever brings her to harm will suffer for it!"

"Ben?" Robert said.

Franklin took a deep breath, shaking even more. "She killed him, Robin."

About that time his gun got heavy, heavier than ten cannonballs, and tore itself out of his hand. With a curse he reached for his sword, but it was also heavy, dragging him to the ground. He toppled, noticing as he did so that almost everyone else had, too.

The only ones still standing, as a matter of fact, were Red Shoes, two young women—and *her*, the murderess, who still placidly sat her horse. He noticed for the first time that she was heavily bandaged.

"Your pardon, gentlemen and ladies," Red Shoes said. "But I would rather you not all shoot each other. If you divest yourselves of steel and iron, you will find you can stand."

Still cursing, Franklin fumbled at his sword belt—whose buckle, naturally, dragged at him like an anchor—and finally managed it. Free of it, he scrambled to his feet.

"Be calm, Mr. Franklin," Red Shoes cautioned.

"Elizavet!" the tsar, divested of sword and pistol, heedless of the situation, bounded across the yards separating them; and a young, pretty girl with thick black hair flew to meet him. They embraced, and he whirled her around. "By God, I have my daughter!" Peter shouted. "It is better than a king-dom! My sweet Elizavet!"

The girl, weeping and laughing at the same time, buried her face in his shoulder.

Franklin, calmed somehow by that meeting, turned back to the woman. "Who are you?" he asked huskily.

"I am who you said, the slayer of Newton. Adrienne de Mornay de Montchevreuil."

"You admit it."

"It was war," she said, frowning as if at a child asking a question she did not feel he was old enough to understand the answer to. "He was killing *me*, you know, and my friends, and my son—" She broke off. "I regretted killing him—especially once I learned who he was—but how can I apolo-gize? I know who you are, Monsieur Franklin. How many men did *you* kill at the battle of Venice, with your balloon bombs and your lightning kites?"

He heard her words, but this was the strangest thing—her voice was clipped, as if produced by a steel model of a human throat, as if she could never even imagine what remorse might be.

But she was weeping.

That produced an emotion in Ben, something weird. He didn't know what it was. Disgust? A new kind of anger?

He didn't know, so he turned away.

Red Shoes watched Tug approach, wondering what he was going to say. "I'm glad to see you well," is what he settled on.

Red Shoes could see that the sailor was searching him, trying to read him the way white men read books.

"Red Shoes," Tug said. Or was it, "Red Shoes?"

He stepped closer, and Tug flinched but stood his ground.

"It is me," Red Shoes whispered. "It's me, not a spirit wearing my skin. I would never harm you, Tug."

"Y'll f'rgive me, but after what I seen—"

"They tried to kill me, Tug. They thought I was something I'm not."

"The little babies tried to kill y'? Th' sweet young girls?"

"No. But I went mad, Tug. Not for long. I'm not exactly the same as I was, but I am *me*. Remember that night in Algiers, when you took me to find a woman?"

"Yeah. You acted wondrous strange that night, too."

"Remember that you saved me in Venice?"

"I remember you savin' us in—eh—what used to be London. But . . ." He paused. "Is it really you?"

"Yes."

"I done what y' said t' do."

"I know. Thank you. Will you shake my hand?"

Tug hesitated another instant, then stuck his hand out, and they clasped. "Flint Shouting'll try t' kill you, y'know, when he finds out y'r here."

"I wouldn't blame him if he tried, but I would rather he didn't. I'll talk to him, later. And to you. You'll have to tell me about your adventures coming here."

"Th' same. Glad to see th' miss made it, too," he said, nodding toward Grief.

Grief noticed and flashed Tug one of her rare smiles, and the pirate grinned even wider.

Red Shoes glanced at Franklin, who seemed to have retreated to a world of his own. "Well, Mr. Franklin?" he said. "Shall we go into the city? We have important things to say and do, and not much time to do them in."

Franklin looked at him, then briefly back at Adrienne, his expression still stunned. "Of course," he said. "Let's go."

They walked the horses the rest of the way, Grief at Red Shoes' side as always.

"Tug didn't seem frightened of you anymore," she said to him.

"He was. I could see it. He doesn't trust me, and maybe he shouldn't. I don't trust myself."

"Your power is returning."

"Yes, some of it."

"And your heart?"

"I don't feel the same as I did—angry, bigger than myself. But I still believe the course I saw then is the right course."

"But you no longer have the power to pursue it."

"I never did. That was my mistake. I never did."

"And now?"

"With these people, I think I can do it—though I may have to trick them." He took her chin in his fingers and turned her face toward his. "Do *you* still fear me?" he asked.

"Yes," she replied, and kissed his fingers.

Adrienne winced as the servants lowered her into the ornate, canopied bed. Her leg ached dully, and her breath came in shallow sips. She regretted, now, her insistence on riding the last mile—but she did not want to be in a litter when they reached the French town. She wanted to arrive with dignity.

Instead, she had arrived to be reminded of what she was, what she had become—the series of linked sins that comprised her life.

She remembered killing Newton, of course. Worse, she remembered the obscene joy of the moment, of finally having *power*—not the secret, conniving power women must wrest from the world but the might to do anything she pleased.

Of course, that power was gone now.

"Mademoiselle? Is it really you?"

She blinked at her visitor through what must surely be tears of pain.

"Orléans?"

He coughed up a little laugh. "No, Demoiselle, I fear I am king now, much to everyone's horror."

"Your Majesty." She made an effort to rise.

"Heavens, my dear, no. Stay in bed." He clasped his hands behind his back and attempted a smile.

"If I may ask, Sire—is your wife—"

"Yes, I knew you would ask that first. She is dead, I'm afraid. The plague took Paris even before the Russians did, and it took her with it. I know I wasn't much of a husband— she always felt she deserved better, and she was right. She—" His face screwed up in pain. He fought for control, and found it. "She always loved you. She urged us to find you, after that madman Torcy kidnapped you."

"That was kind of her."

"So, you see, I will deny you nothing. In memory of her and of my uncle the king, who also loved you."

She nodded carefully. Her memories of Louis XIV were less pleasant than her memories of the duchess of Orléans. "Thank you, Sire. I hope I can serve you."

"I'm sure you can. And now I must go."

But he turned and spoke once more before leaving. "Mademoiselle, it *is* good to see you. Few of that court you knew survive. It is good to be reminded of happier times."

When he was gone, she reflected that she wouldn't have thought of those times as happy. But she understood what he meant, and doubtless, for him, they had been the best of days.

So this was what had become of France. It was fortunate that Philippe didn't know how large a part in creating his present state of affairs she had played, here and later in Russia.

But *she* knew it, of course, and now she could no longer escape what she had done.

* * *

She was almost asleep when her next visitor arrived, scratching lightly at the door, as they used to do in Versailles.

"Come in," she said dully.

It was Vasilisa Karevna. "We didn't have time to speak before," the Russian said.

"I'm glad to see you well, Vasilisa," Adrienne replied, and found that she meant it. Even if she did not know where the other woman's loyalties lay, at least she was part of the present, and not the past.

"And it is good to see you, Adrienne."

"Sit."

Karevna settled herself on a tabouret, as Adrienne dismissed the servants.

"Chairete, Korai, Athenes therapainai," Vasilisa intoned, once the girls were gone.

"No," Adrienne said. "Stop it. No more of that pathetic Korai nonsense. I cannot bear it."

Vasilisa blanched, took a deep breath. "I understand your feelings, Adrienne, but this is the very moment our sisterhood was created for, the single most important thing we guard against. And of all who once belonged, you and I are the only ones of consequence who remain."

"The Korai were created to keep us in ignorance," Adrienne said, "like everything that owes itself to the malakim."

"Surely, better ignorance than death," the Russian replied.

Adrienne uttered a sharp laugh. "I could kill you for not having told me years ago. You knew all along, didn't you? That even the 'friendly' malakim have worked to keep us mired in superstition."

"I couldn't tell you. You were their greatest fear—even I am not sure why. You were somehow their greatest fear and their greatest hope all at once. Even your son, I think, is secondary to you in their schemes. The *malfaiteurs* always wished to kill you. Only those who befriended Lilith saved your life."

"Again we return to mythology," Adrienne said, disgusted,

though remembering the creature in the form of Nicolas and the name she claimed.

"Mythology is nothing more than a way of hiding knowledge, of encrypting it so that the *malfaiteurs* do not detect it. Don't you understand that, after all these years? They help us as they can."

Adrienne waved her hand. "All this is moot, is it not? Whether there was a Lilith or an Athena, whether the friendly angels were ever really friendly. For, as I understand it, they are now long gone."

"They aren't gone. They lead the army."

"My point exactly."

"No. Their original policies prevailed in the Old World. All that remains is this new one, and if they win here, they might appease those who wish merely to see us all destroyed."

"So we either die or return to darkness."

"One is better than the other," Vasilisa said hotly. "You are a fool if you think otherwise. Ask any mother, any yeoman farmer, whether they would rather have life, and family, and love—or books on the gravitation of the spheres. Do not confound your particular obsessions with what is truly important."

"And yet, as I understand, you labor here to stop the conquest of this New World."

"No. I labor to stop the end of the world. The best hope of that is that their army *succeed*. If it fails, they will use the engines and all will die."

"They have already used one. They sent it against us at New Moscow."

"Bozhe moi," Vasilisa whispered. "We have even less time than I thought, then."

"Or less hope. I was communicating with one of your friendly angels, Vasilisa—he persuaded me to make this trek. He is dead, and none has come to replace him. Perhaps he was the only one."

"No. There are others—the point is, the enemy does not *know* how many—"

Adrienne interrupted her with a laugh that sounded mad

even to herself. "Even—angels don't know how—how—
many angels dance—on the—head—of a pin?"

"What has happened to you?" Vasilisa asked, staring at her
as one might stare at an unexpected boil on one's arm.

"I am learning a sense of humor, that is all. Go on."

"The danger is near, that is all I meant to say. Franklin and
I have assembled a device—it might work or it might not. At
the very best, it will give us a little time to find our way to the
final solution."

"And what might that be?"

"Don't you know? They didn't tell you?"

"No. They seemed to think it best to keep me in ignorance.
I suppose such habits are difficult to break, after a few thousands of years."

Vasilisa closed her eyes for a moment. "I should not tell
you this. Not if *they* did not."

Adrienne uttered another weak laugh. "But you will, or
you wouldn't have brought it up."

"I— Do you know how I came into the tsar's service?"

"I never have known."

"He was on a tour of his Siberian provinces. He found me
buried up to my neck in the ground. I had been married, you
see, when I was thirteen, to a man who took a great deal of
pleasure in my pain. One day, when he approached me, I
threw a pan of boiling grease in his face. It stopped his heart.
So lawkeepers and the priest of our village took me and they
buried me in the ground."

"And the tsar saved you."

"Yes, at the urging of his wife, Catherine. She was a
daughter of Athena. They washed me of my nightmare, Adrienne. They made me clean and they taught me what is good,
and they gave me power, something I never had before. You
know how that feels."

"I do," Adrienne said softly. "And I'm sorry for what you
went through."

Karevna's gaze danced from point to point, as if afraid to
settle. "I don't tell you this to get your pity. I just want you to
understand—the Korai are everything to me, and I do not

disclose our greatest secret lightly. I also care for you, whether you believe it or not, and I fear this will cause you pain."

"Tell me. Please. I am inured to pain."

Karevna finally looked her full in the face. "The Korai created you, Adrienne. We created you to bear your son. You are not altogether . . . human."

"Created me? Out of what—snow?"

"Out of a hundred marriages. Out of a thousand subtle manipulations—alchemical treatments administered in secret throughout your life—especially at Saint Cyr."

"Saint Cyr?"

"Yes, of course. Madame de Maintenon was no Korai, but she was manipulated by them, from the day she met Ninon de Lenclos, decades ago. It was a place designed to reveal—*you.* And to perfect you."

"Father Castillion taught at Saint Cyr."

"Father Castillion?"

"The priest, the one who joined me in New Moscow."

"I didn't—" She spun on her heel as the door creaked open, and Castillion stood there, regarding them.

"You told her," he said.

"I had to," Vasilisa replied.

"God have mercy on you, then. She was not to know."

Vasilisa raised her chin. "Who are you?"

"As she said, I am Pierre Castillion. I taught at Saint Cyr, many years ago. I was one of those men—adjunct to the Korai, let us say."

"A Rosicrucian? A Freemason?"

"No, but it doesn't matter. I am the last of my order. The rest of us perished in China."

"So you knew—*this* all along, and did not tell me."

Castillion knelt next to her. "The time was not right. I knew it would only anger and confuse you."

"What else have you lied about?"

"Most of what I have told you is true. There are some details I left out."

"It was no accident we met in New Moscow."

"No. I had been following your son. In fact, my order sent me to kill him."

"The Jesuits?"

He shrugged. "Yes and no. Again, it does not matter. I knew I could not. Should not. Instead, I found you."

Adrienne closed her eyes, wishing them both away.

"Too many questions, too many lies. Take four steps back. I was created, you say. Am I like Crecy, then? But I don't have her strength, her speed."

"You have some of her toughness," Castillion said. "What you've been through in the past few months should have killed you, though I helped when I could. But, no. You are of a very different sort and order than Crecy. Her sort were the beginning, and they spring ultimately from the same blood. But Nicolas, your son, is the omega. Joining you with the Bourbon line was the masterstroke. It was the prospect of that marriage which began all this, set everything in motion. And it is that child who will bring victory to one side or another."

Words of denial came into Adrienne's mouth and stayed there. Denying it all seemed even more absurd than hearing it, somehow.

"Damn you," she said instead. "Damn every last one of you to the lowest pit of hell. Damn— *Did Crecy know?*" The last she shouted, furious at the mere possibility.

"No," Karevna said. "Only seven living ever know—in France it was Madame Castries. Crecy was their pawn in this as much as you." Her eyes narrowed. "But you know, Castillion. How?"

"I am not a woman. There were also seven of *us*."

Karevna opened her mouth to reply, then apparently thought better of it.

Half an hour passed, and no one spoke. Adrienne thought of her mother and father. What had brought them together? The marriage had been arranged, as most marriages were in noble families. She tried to remember if Castries or Orléans had had a hand in it, and could not.

Finally she pushed the thought as far back in her head as it would go. "It doesn't matter if this is true."

"Of course it does," Karevna said. "It means you and Nicolas are the key. Not *a* key, but *the* key. One of you is with them, but one of you is still with us."

"As you say. But what lock am I supposed to turn, Vasilisa? Your story does not say. Castillion?"

"I don't know either," the priest admitted.

"I can answer that question, I think," another voice said, from the still-open door.

Adrienne turned to see the Indian.

"Hello, Red Shoes," Adrienne said. "Who else is in line out there? Usher them all in, please, and I will serve the chocolate and cakes."

"You know my name."

"Indeed."

Red Shoes shrugged. "We are beyond that now. Your friends are right—our time is short. Even now I can sense the Sun Boy giving birth, creating the giants of old that will wipe all of our races from the world."

Red Shoes hummed with power. In her angel sight, he was a chord of plucked strings. But he wasn't like she had been, or as Vasilisa had been. He was like the woman in the Siberian forest, a thing unto himself but unraveling into many strands. Like Nicolas, who split pieces of himself to make new angels. Had he hidden this from her before, or had she been too weary to notice?

She was still weary. She had lost Hercule and her son. Father Castillion, who had once been a reminder of a time when her life had seemed at least genuine, now showed himself to be a liar and, worse, revealed that her entire existence was a lie.

What did she care if the petty race of humanity vanished from the world? All of the good examples of mankind she had ever known were dead.

"Leave me alone," she murmured.

"I would if I could," Red Shoes said, "but we cannot do this without you."

"Do what?"

"Crack the roof of the world. Return it to the way it was in the beginning."

"You *do* know." Vasilisa gasped.

"Explain it, then," Adrienne said, "for it makes no sense to me."

"Remember the Korai legend?" Vasilisa said excitedly. "That God, unable to enter the world, sent his servants into it. But after creation was done, most of them went renegade, and God changed the law from without, subtly, to deprive them of power."

"Ah. I see. You are all mad. You think we can undo what God did."

"Yes!" Castillion interjected with uncharacteristic fierceness. "It will free them—they have been trapped here for millennia. Once free, rejoined with God, they will bother us no more."

Adrienne folded the bedclothes back, smoothing them flat with her palms. "Let us follow this insane little discourse a bit further, shall we? Supposing what you say is true, and it is in our power to defy God Almighty and give the malakim back the power they had at creation. Why do most—indeed, now it would seem *all*—of them resist us in this? Why hasn't this been their unified aim from the beginning? Come—any of you."

All three were silent.

"As I thought. You are mouths for their lies, as unaware as a pen of what it writes on the page. Leave, all of you, and trouble me no more with this."

"Adrienne," Vasilisa said, "I beg you to reconsider. You are the key."

"Find another."

"There *is* another," Red Shoes said. "He will serve less well, but he will serve."

"You mean my son?"

"I mean *me*. Your son is the lock, and I was not meant to turn him. But I might be able to. Against his will—he might not survive it."

"I have seen his power, and I have seen yours. I have little question as to who will succeed," Adrienne said.

"I would have beaten him but for you."

"You took him by stealth, from within. That won't happen again."

"You really don't care?" Vasilisa said. "You really don't care if we all live or die?"

"No," Adrienne said, "I don't think I do. And even if I did, as I told you, I am powerless now. Would that I had always been."

"You don't mean that."

"I mean it precisely, Vasilisa Karevna. You may have bred my family like racehorses for a thousand years, for all I care, and Father Castillion may have put the juice of the philosopher's stone in my table wine every day for ten years—the power that came from that is all spent, wasted. I am done with it, and it is done with me. Now, leave me before I call my guard to throw you out."

"Yes," Red Shoes remarked, voice heavy with sarcasm. "Quite powerless, you are."

But they left, no doubt to plot another try later.

She settled back into the bed and closed her eyes—in search, finally, of rest.

10.

Things Broken

The next day brought no news, and Franklin spent it instructing the craftsmen who were building the niveum repellers. Vasilisa, on the other hand, spoke for a considerable time with Red Shoes and the students of the Montchevreuil woman, going over pages of equations. Indeed, a small Russian contingent seemed to have formed, for both the tsar and his daughter, Elizavet, put in appearances, all clucking in a language Franklin did not know. Of the murderess herself, he saw no sign, for which he was grateful.

"Benjamin, could you come here a moment?" Vasilisa asked, after several hours of tacitly excluding him.

"I'm rather busy."

"This is important. Could you come here, please?"

"Very well." He strode over to where they were working.

"What do you think of this?" she asked, pointing at a string of calculations and accompanying text in Latin. He read it, at first with some irritation—it was clearly nonsense—but after a few moments, he began to see a sneaky sort of logic in it.

"Whose work is this?" he asked.

"It belongs to Monsieur Lomonosov," she said, indicating a young man. The fellow perked up at his name and leaned to shake hands. Franklin responded with reluctance.

"Can he speak English or French?"

"I'm afraid not. I can translate. But you understand his theory—that matter as such is not real but merely the least perfect of affinities?"

"Yes, well, I can find no flaw in his figuring, but it must be there. The idea is absurd."

"Why? Because Newton did not know it?"

"Don't speak his name."

She stared at him. "Benjamin, are you angry with me?"

He noticed the others were staring at him.

"Let us speak in the hall," he said.

"Very well."

In the hall she faced him with her arms folded. "Well? Where does this rudeness come from?"

"Rudeness? Call it reserve. I had almost forgotten your treacherous nature, but your friend Montchevreuil reminded me. You were there, too, when Newton was killed. Did you have a hand in it?"

"For pity's sake, Benjamin, don't be such a child. Adrienne and I only did what we had to. What would you have done if some madman were causing your airship to fall from the sky with all of your friends and your infant son?"

"None of it would have happened if you and yours had not launched an unprovoked attack first on Prague and then on Venice."

"Well, then, it is the tsar's fault. Go lay it at *his* feet, *not* mine. To answer your question, I did not have the power or the knowledge to do what Adrienne did, but if I *could* have done it, I most certainly would have. Newton was a casualty of war, Benjamin. That is the way of nations, the way it always has been. What have you been doing these past few months if not exerting every effort—honest and dishonest—to bring to your side nations you formerly fought against, convincing them that their old blood debts are now overshadowed? Are you become hypocrite?"

That seemed to run her out of breath and composure, both of which, in his experience, were things Vasilisa usually had in tremendous supply.

He wanted to reply in kind, in words of justified fury.

Instead, he realized that she was on the mark—if not for a bullet, then at least for a grenado.

It hurt too much to admit it, though, so he stood silent for a few seconds and said, "Let's have another look at that formula. And you'll explain to me why such a theoretical question matters in this time of crisis."

She relinquished her fierce expression and beckoned him back into the room.

"It matters because, if it is true, the problem of dissolving Swedenborg's engine may not be exactly as you phrased it before. You wanted to disrupt the connection between aetheric forces and matter—but what if they are the same, like different notes of the same musical scale? What if the difference between them is only the difference in how tightly the string on a violin is tuned?"

"I'll grant it for argument."

"Then if we change the pitch—"

"The pitch of what, the universe?"

"Yes."

"It's insane."

"No, it isn't. Come here—give me time to convince you."

He studied her face, wondering why she would bother with such an outrageous lie.

"I'll give you two hours to convince me. It's all I can spare."

"It's enough."

After an hour he was completely engrossed in the idea, and began adding suggestions of his own.

"Even if we rough out the shape of this theory," he cautioned, "it remains to propose experiments by which we might support it. And a device which might actually alter the very harmony of the spheres—I still see it as impossible, but what if it isn't? How could we predict what that alteration might bring? If we make it so the Swedenborg engines cannot exist, what else might cease to exist, or come into being? The planets themselves might fly away from one another or explode in noxious fumes!"

Vasilisa wrinkled her forehead. "We are all agreed it is a matter of last resort—but if it is the only thing we have for defense against the engines, isn't it worth the chance?"

"End the universe if we cannot save our lives? At least you think grandly, Vasilisa."

Red Shoes lifted his hands and interrupted. "When death is the only choice, why not take a death of our choosing—one that might bring ruin to our enemies as well?"

"Still, it is moot. This is not a simple harmony we speak of retuning, like that between unmatched aetherschreibers," Franklin said.

Red Shoes and Vasilisa looked at each other, as if sharing a private thought. The Indian voiced it.

"We have the device already," he said. "It is only a matter of knowing how to use it."

"What device is this?"

"The same device that makes the engines," Vasilisa said, "the Sun Boy."

Franklin looked from one to the other. Both seemed sincere. But Vasilisa was not to be trusted. And Red Shoes— even Tug was wary of Red Shoes now. There was certainly something different in his manner.

But they might reach a point when the maddest of possibilities was their only hope.

He sighed. "Explain," he said reluctantly.

But Vasilisa was looking beyond him, at the door. "You have a visitor, Benjamin," she said.

He turned, and found Lenka watching them.

"I'm glad you finally came to see me," he told her, as they passed from the hall into the weed-ravaged botanical garden. "Though this is not a good time."

"You will not make time to speak to me?" She had discarded her Apalachee warrior's clothing and now wore a gown of blue satin. She was achingly beautiful in it, reminding him vividly of when they first met. He remembered, too, twining her in his arms, the feel of her flesh, the look of her face when close for kissing, watching her sleep in the morning light, covers pulled back to reveal a form more cunning than any sculptor—even the fabled Pygmalion—could imagine, much less render.

"Lenka, I can take a moment. But there are very important matters afoot."

"More important than me? That is always true, isn't it? I'm not a fool, Benjamin Franklin. I understand what is at stake, despite your having kept what you could from me."

"I kept nothing—how could I? You haven't spoken to me. I've tried to seek you out."

"I was thinking."

"Of what?"

"Of when I met you. Of how we fell in love, or thought we did."

"Of course we fell in love, Lenka," he said, exasperated.

"Then when did you fall out of it?"

"I never have. I love you still."

She quirked her lips. "Then perhaps it is the definition of love that is in question. I thought that I knew what it was, but now I see I do not."

He closed his eyes wearily. "Lenka, can't you take my word on this one thing? Trust that I love you. And when there is time, I will make what amends I can for any poor treatment I may have given you. But now, at this moment—"

"When will there be time? You have had ten years. You convinced me the *first* of them. You have not persuaded since. And when I speak of you keeping things from me, I do not mean recently. You know that. You claim to value me for my quality of thought, and yet we have not shared a conversation on matters scientific—or on anything of real importance—in years. And so I act as your wife, in bed, in public, in this country where I was not born, where the language is strange. And we have not conceived children, which might have given me some peace, or at least someone not too busy to speak to me, but no, God will not even grant me that—" She broke off, muffling tears in her sleeve.

His own voice felt thick. "And here you have deceived *me*, wife. When have you ever told me you felt this?"

"I have told you and told you," she said, "in words and looks and insinuations—which, had you been an honest husband—you might have noticed. Did you think I would beg, throw it all out in front of you, what you ought to have known?"

"You're doing it now."

"Yes," she said, wiping her eyes. "Because now I think it's too late to matter."

"No. Lenka, I love you. Please, meet me later tonight, after the craftsmen have—"

"No, Benjamin," she said. "I have my own duties to see to. Everyone must do his part in these times, and I have found a part to play."

"What? As Voltaire's mistress?"

She blinked. "That is so unfair as to be obscene," she said. "Obscene." And she turned on her heel and walked off.

He ought to follow her. But what use a wife if there was no world to live in?

He could fix things. Fixing things was what he was good at. But you had to fix them in the right order . . .

And so he rejoined the others, and heard more of their plans, and tried to ignore the little voice telling him that his last chance had come and gone, and that some things could never be fixed, no matter how skilled the tinkerer.

Adrienne turned her face to the wall when Crecy entered.

"Ah. Still feeling sorry for yourself, I see."

"What have you come for, Veronique?"

"To see you."

"Strange. I thought, perhaps, to chastise me."

"No. You have good reason to feel sorry for yourself," Crecy replied. "I do not begrudge you that." Then, more softly, "I miss Hercule. In my own way, I loved him, too."

"You were jealous of him."

"Yes, as a sister is jealous. I wished no harm to him. When I find Oliver, I will kill him."

Adrienne turned to face her. "I think he will kill you, that is what I think."

"Thanks for your confidence, but it does not matter what you think, in this case. Oliver is a dead man. It is not you I avenge in killing him."

"Hercule needs no avenging. He is beyond that."

"So you say. I disagree. Besides, Oliver has more to answer for than Hercule—and Irena, though you seem to have forgotten her." She paused. "I have brought someone to see you."

"I don't want to see anyone."

"I don't care. I'll return."

Adrienne's jaw trembled when Crecy reentered the room. She had Hercule's children with her.

"Here is your Aunt Adrienne, children. You remember little Stephen and Ivana, don't you, Adrienne?"

"I remember. Hello, children."

"Hello, Auntie," the little boy said. The girl said nothing, but clung to Crecy's coat.

"Your father asked Aunt Adrienne to take care of you while he is away," Crecy said.

"Veronique—"

"And she promised she would, that she would care for you as if she were your own mother."

"Where is Mama?" the little girl asked.

"She is dead, like Papa, you stupid thing," Stephen said angrily.

The shaking in Adrienne's jaw was spreading to her whole body.

"This is despicable, Veronique," she accused.

"Indeed. Children, I'm going to leave you with Auntie for a while. Will you be good?"

"Yes, Mademoiselle," the boy replied.

"Crecy, do *not* leave me with—" But the redhead was already gone. The children stood there, Ivana with the beginnings of tears in her eyes.

"Come here." Adrienne sighed. "Come sit, and tell me what you think of the Indians."

"I think they are very brave," Stephen said. "I think perhaps I shall be one when I grow up."

"Well, perhaps you shall."

"I will be one, too," Ivana said.

"That's stupid," said the boy. "You can't be an Indian. Indians are men."

"So are soldiers, but Aunt Nikki is a soldier," the little girl replied.

"Anyway," Adrienne added, "surely there are Indian women, somewhere."

Stephen's eyes widened, as if he hadn't thought of that. Then he shrugged. "I guess so."

They fell silent, and Adrienne couldn't think of anything to say. She had avoided children, since Nico's kidnapping— being around them only caused her pain.

Stephen, kicking at the floor, broke the silence. "You don't have to take care of us," he said. "I can do that."

"Can you?"

"Yes, he can," Ivana said emphatically. "He's my brother."

"So—we don't need your help," Stephen amplified.

Adrienne's lips tightened. "Maybe—maybe I need *yours*," she said. "What your father really said—" Was she crying? Again? "—What he really said is that you should take care of *me*."

"Oh," Stephen said. "That's different, I suppose. I suppose I could do that. But . . ."

"But what?"

"You aren't going to die, too, are you?"

"It happens, sometimes, as you know by now. But—I will try not to."

"I'm not ever going to die," the boy said, determined.

Tears turned Adrienne's eyes to prisms, and in the refracted light, she saw again the hurricane of fire, the white-hot eye of the keres.

"Could you find Auntie Crecy, Stephen? I doubt she has gone far."

"Yes. If you will swear to watch my sister. She is younger than me."

"I will watch her. Come here, Ivana."

Ivana came over as the boy left. She looked at the bed very matter-of-factly. "May I come up there?"

"Yes, dear, but be careful. Aunt Adrienne has a broken leg."

The girl climbed up and lay looking at the ceiling. She was careful not to touch Adrienne. "My leg is broken, too, see?" She flexed the tiny limb. "Right there." She pointed at her knee.

"So it is," Adrienne replied. "I wonder why they made such a big fuss about mine?"

"Because you're a grown-up, that's why," Ivana said. "Do you know any stories?"

"I—I used to."

"Tell me one."

By the time Crecy returned, Adrienne had given up trying to remember her way through "Sleeping Beauty"—Ivana had herself fallen asleep.

"How cozy," Crecy said.

"I despise you, Veronique. I expect perfidy from you, but this—"

"Shh. You'll wake the child, and you know how I hate them awake."

"Yes, of course you do. Who wouldn't? Where is the boy?"

"I left him with a certain Monsieur Voltaire, a very interesting man I last remember being a guest in the Bastille."

"He is safe with him?"

"Boys are safe with Monsieur Voltaire, I think, and girls below the age of fourteen or so. They were playing at dueling. You wanted something?"

"Yes. Find me Benjamin Franklin. Tell him I need to speak to him—without Vasilisa, without Red Shoes. I do not want them to know we have met."

"Achillette is done sulking in her tent?" Crecy asked.

"That's enough from you," Adrienne said.

But when Crecy was gone, despite her desperate wish not to, she looked at Ivana's sleeping face and smiled. A promise was a promise, and she had promised Hercule to look after his children. She couldn't very well do that if the world ended, could she?

11.

Three Kings

Unoka bounced down from his horse like a king's acrobat and all but dashed into the command tent.

"Gib me some o' t'at rum," he said.

"Ah!" Oglethorpe replied. "And I thought you just eager to report."

"General, you not in a hurry t' hear t'is."

"That bad, eh?"

"Could be five t'ousands o' t'em."

"That's all?"

"Ain't t'at plenty?"

"That's only four to one their way. At Belgrade the Turk outnumbered us two to one, but at the end they lost thirty thousand and we only five thousand. I think we can make a good fight of this." He paused as Unoka gulped down his rum and rolled his eyes at Oglethorpe's optimism. "How long before they arrive?"

"Two day, I t'ink," the African replied.

"Well, we shall make it a hard two days for them, shan't we? The pine forests were made for ambuscade."

"Yes. I take my Maroons out into 'em."

"That's not necessary, Mr. Unoka. You've already worked them to death as scouts. Let's give 'em a bit of a rest."

Unoka looked levelly at him. "General, it come down to a fight in t'e ranks, my men, t'ey no good. Pickin' 'em off, killin' t'ey horses—'ambuscade,' you call it—t'ats what *we* good at."

Oglethorpe surveyed the man, noticed for the first time the blood leaking through a rag on his arm.

"You're a good man, Mr. Unoka. I've never known better, and I'm proud to serve with you. If it pleases you to do this, I won't stop you."

" 'Tis always good, when serve wit' a madman, be a little mad you' self," the Maroon observed.

"Take what you need from the armory," Oglethorpe said. "No sense in rationing now."

"Wit' pleasure, General. An' anot'er cup o' rum—"

"Take the cask. For your men."

For the next several hours, Oglethorpe bent over the maps, trying to imagine where the lines would form. They would strike at the towers, of course, but where? Though five thousand was a puny number compared to forces in the European wars, he knew he had been overoptimistic with Unoka. There was a great difference between two-to-one odds and four-to-one odds. They could come in a front so long he would have to stand very thin ranks against them.

That wasn't what *he* would do, if he were they. He would pick a spot and push straight through, especially if he was in the hurry these fellows seemed to be.

Nairne came in and looked the maps over, while Oglethorpe explained his reasoning.

"The best thing we can do is keep our forces mobile and alert," he said. "The Maroons and Choctaw and Yamacraw should be able to keep pretty good account of how they're coming, though I expect more of their leapfrogging with the airships."

"We can do a bit of that," Nairne said. "Franklin has managed to give us two flying barges of the nondiabolic sort. We've manned them with French and Apalachee marines. We also mustered every aetherschreiber we could get our hands on, and so have instant word from our borders and a great many of our companies, so that will help us to respond."

"Good. This will be a hell of a fight." Oglethorpe turned his head at some commotion outside the tent—yelling and gunfire. "What's that?" The two men drew their pistols and went quickly to see what was the matter.

But the noise was a sudden burst of cheers and applause, the gunfire all aimed at the sky. A new company had ridden into the camp.

Inured to meager numbers, it seemed to Oglethorpe that the column went on forever, but realistically he knew it must be only two hundred or so. But they were such a brave sight that he almost wept. The front ranks were all smart in blue and yellow, each man with a musket and broadsword, and at the head of them a small group on horses. One of those mounted was Philippe, beaming, in French uniform, who, despite his pudginess, looked something like a soldier. The other, though, was dressed in the colors of the new company, tall in the saddle, his bloodless lips in a thin smile, his hat doffed to show his mostly bald head.

"That," Oglethorpe told Nairne, "is His Majesty Charles XII, King of Sweden."

"Aye," Nairne said. "I met him, in Venice."

The exiled monarch spotted them and swung down from his mount, as did Philippe.

Oglethorpe swept his own hat from his head in perfect time with Nairne, and they bowed as the monarchs approached. "Your Majesties," they said.

"No need for that," Charles replied. "We are all soldiers today, gentlemen. Margrave Oglethorpe, it's good to see you again, and thank you much for the loan of your amphibian ship. It proved a most interesting voyage, our foray to Apalachee."

Oglethorpe nodded. *Now here is a man,* he thought, as he had when he'd first met the king, forty miles from the coast of South Carolina. Charles XII had eyes of gray steel and a thin, patrician nose. His manner was that of a man whose very existence was a victory. "It was my great pleasure, Your Majesty. And I cannot say what it means to have you with us."

Charles clapped Nairne on the shoulder. "How are you, Mr. Nairne? I've not seen you since our victory in Venice. My debt to you Americans is not one I'd easily forget, nor do I ever shrink from a just war, and, by our savior, there can be no more just a war than this. I've ridden at the head of my troops for thirty years and more. How can I fail to do so now?"

"I never doubted it, Your Majesty."

"We had to pay the devil to get here, I'll tell you, and would have paid more if it weren't for your margrave Oglethorpe, who saved us from the fire at Fort Marlborough. Even so, three ships were lost, or I would offer you many more guns. But we will show them the same thing we showed them at Venice, yes? We've stopped demon Peter before, and we shall stop him again."

"Ah—about that," Philippe interrupted. "You and I must have a conversation regarding Tsar Peter, before he gets here."

"Peter himself is with the invading army?"

"Actually, no—he's with my regulars, right over there."

A peculiar fire entered the Swedish king's eyes. "You've captured him?"

But there was no time to answer, Oglethorpe saw, for the tsar was striding straight toward them.

Charles was already looking that way. Now he drew a basket-hilted broadsword, and the glint in his eye became a blaze. "Thanks to Almighty God!" he roared.

The tsar watched him come. "I have no sword," he said.

Charles spat on the ground. "Then get one, you coward."

"Gentlemen—" Philippe squeaked.

"I said get one, damn your eyes!" Charles shrieked.

Peter's face spasmed, and there they stood, two madmen who happened to have crowns. "Sword," Peter grated, holding his hand out.

No one moved to give him one, and when he saw that, he closed the distance to Charles. Angry as he clearly was, the Swedish king did not, as Oglethorpe feared, lift his blade against an unarmed man. But they stood for half a second, glaring at each other, inches apart.

Peter struck the first blow, a great backhand to the face. Charles almost impaled him then, but instead he dropped his weapon and tackled the tsar at the waist.

His men went mad, screaming like Turks—actually, some of them *were* Turks—and chanting the monarch's name.

The two men crashed heavily to the ground and began to roll, punching and clawing at each other.

"Should we do something?" Oglethorpe asked.

Nairne shook his head slowly. "It's been hundreds, maybe thousands, of years since anyone saw a spectacle like this— two great kings brawling like drunken linkmen. Who are we to stop it?"

"I understood the tsar brawled on occasion, but—"

The two had broken apart and were now boxing each other on the sides of the head. It seemed a contest of wills more than a fight—as if by agreement both had chosen not to defend, only to attack. Peter had split ears, and both men were bleeding from the nose and mouth. Both were cursing copiously, too, in their native tongues. It all sounded very colorful.

Then a single shot was fired, kicking up a branch between their feet, and both paused to see who had done the shooting.

Philippe stood there, pistol smoking, face as red as the inside of a melon.

"By God!" he shouted. "By God, you will stop or I shall shoot you both!"

He sounded convincing to Oglethorpe. He must have convinced the two kings as well, for they continued to stare at the Frenchman.

"Look, you two! The three of us are all that remain, so far as I can tell, of the old monarchies. Notwithstanding that the two of you come from countries one degree removed from Huns and Vandals, by *God*, when you are in my realm you will acquit yourselves like kings, not like schoolyard brats! King Charles, the tsar is under my protection. His throne has been usurped, and the army marching on us is not his. He came to me seeking asylum, and I have given it to him. If you cannot accept this, with all due respect, I thank you for the aid you have already given us and urge you back to your ships." He whirled on the tsar. "You, sir, came here a beggar and now you repay my generosity by cheapening your station and thus my own. I will not have it. If you two must settle your differences, you will do it like gentlemen, by the sword, and you will do it *when this damned war is over*!"

He paused, breathing so hard Oglethorpe feared him apoplectic.

Charles and Peter looked at each other, their fists still clenched. But then slowly Charles turned away from Peter and bowed to the French king—not on bended knee, but bowing nevertheless, from the waist.

"My apologies," he said. "I was overcome."

"I also apologize," the tsar said. It sounded like it hurt. "King Charles—you want satisfaction from me. When the appropriate time comes, you shall have it."

Charles nodded. "We shall discuss it again." He smiled grimly. "Though I must say, I have received some satisfaction already." He rubbed his bloody knuckles.

Oglethorpe coughed quietly. "If we are all quite ready, there is a war to fight, and I would greatly appreciate the advice of generals more experienced than I."

As Franklin faced the sorceress for the second time, he tried to put his feelings where they belonged—nowhere. His head understood everything he had been told about her. His heart did not, probably *would* not. That was the way it ought to be, he supposed, like good English government. A Parliament to check the king, a king to check the Parliament.

He did not know whether his heart was king or Parliament, but it had already had its say.

"You see, I come unarmed this time," he remarked, as jovially as he could.

She did not take it so lightly. He was struck again by her beauty and by the serious lines of her face, by her enigmatic little smile that seemed to mean nothing. "When I was a young girl," she said, "no gift would have been greater to me than meeting for one minute Sir Isaac Newton. I read his works over and over—in secret, you understand, so no one would know that a woman had the impertinence to— Well, that's beside the point. I worshipped Newton and his philosophies. I lived for the beauty, the elegance of his mathematical demonstrations. I took a place as a transcriber in the French Academy of Sciences just to be near those who discussed his theories." Her eyes were lamps of darkness, empty of pleading or argument. She was just talking, as she might to herself.

"And in the end, I killed him. He wasn't the first man I killed; he wasn't the last. I understand how you must feel, but I think we must talk, you and I. We share something."

"If you mean a love for Newton, I hardly see how—"

"No." Her voice sounded strange. "No. You see, we have met before."

"At Venice."

She shook her head. "You were in Boston—I was in Paris. You called yourself Janus. I called myself Minerva."

A tingle like a thousand needles crept across his face and down his limbs. His heart tripped oddly, and the room seemed to blur at the edges.

"What are you telling me?"

"I was the amanuensis of a man named Fatio de Duillier. Mr. F. I watched his aetherschreibers. He was working, I knew, on some sort of weapon for the king, but I did not know *what*. It was a great secret, and a key element was missing. Fatio . . . could not find it. Since the problem was even more a cipher to me, I did not either, nor did our English colleague, Mr. S. But then I got a letter signed Janus, which made strange claims: that he had found a way to tune an aetherschreiber, that he also had a solution to part of Fatio's problem. And there was an equation. I took it, hid it, worked on it in my room, corrected it, then rewrote it as if Mr. S—"

"Stirling," Franklin said. "Stirling."

"Stirling? Well, I never knew— In any event, it was the answer Fatio was looking for. It was only later that I understood what he was doing, what *I* had done. And much, much, later that Vasilisa Karevna told me the story of a young boy named Benjamin Franklin, come to London from Boston because he feared he had given the French an awful secret."

Franklin put his head in his hands. "I didn't—I was only fourteen. I wanted to make my mark in the world early, to show—"

"And I only wanted to solve an equation. And yet look what our ambitions did together."

"No," Franklin said. "No, no!" He leapt up, started to pace, pounded the wall with his palms instead. "No! No! This was not how it was supposed to be! By God!" He whirled on her. "Do you know? Do you know how long I've imagined finally meeting the Frenchman who called down the comet? Do you? I knew him, knew him in my heart. An evil, corrupt man, a man who would do anything, who cared no more for human life than a horse cares for the fly it swats! A terrible man, a sick man, a twisted bastard of science and Satan. And now you tell me—you *rob* me—" He couldn't go on. He didn't know what he was saying.

"Fatio was a pathetic creature," Adrienne said, "but even he wasn't evil. I think, in the end, he only wanted to show Newton that he was worthwhile, after Newton broke with him."

Franklin gritted his teeth. It sounded right. How often had he felt the same way, when he was Newton's apprentice?

"Louis XIV was a sick old man who thought he was saving his country. He was deceived, too."

"Someone is to blame. Someone!" Franklin shouted.

"Besides the two of us, you mean? Then blame the malakim, for in the end it was their wish we fulfilled. Quite the opposite of what the legends say—we are *their* djinni, not they ours. As for me, I cannot fool myself. My silly curiosity and girlish game of secrecy ruined the world."

"Ah, God!" Franklin collapsed into the chair, hands clenching and unclenching. "How can you be so—" He was going to say "calm" and "remorseless," but then he met her gaze again, and her misery struck him like an ocean wave, clogging his throat and stinging his eyes and cold, so cold he shivered. It struck him dumb, and he realized that there was nothing mysterious about this woman at all. He understood her to the core, had since the instant he saw her—and then locked that knowledge away, because to face Adrienne de Mornay de Montchevreuil, he had to face himself, and he had avoided that for many years.

"I hope," he managed, when he could again form words not too sawn at the edges to be understood, "that you have some purpose in reminding me of all of this."

"I do. I want you to share penance with me. I want you to help me make things right."

"That's what I'm trying to do, with your friend Vasilisa, and Red Shoes, and your students."

"I do not trust Vasilisa or the Indian. Do you?"

He hesitated. "No, I don't. There is something in their purpose that feels . . . odd. I keep dismissing it."

"As you dismissed any suspicions that you might be helping the wrong people, those years ago in Boston?"

"Now that you mention it. But—forgive me—why should I trust you? Or you me?"

"Because we are damned by the same love, the same mistake, the same sin. I trust you because we crave the same redemption."

He frowned. "What if this is all a lie? You could have learned anything you just told me from Vasilisa."

"You know it isn't a lie," she said.

And, of course, he did.

So he dragged the words out of himself. "Where do we start, then?"

"We start with a story," Adrienne said. "It's about my hand . . ."

12.

No Retreat

Oglethorpe listened for a moment to the cannon fire in the distance. The inhabitants of the Taensa village heard it, too, and the women began packing up what few possessions they valued enough to take with them. A small knot of old men sat around the fire chanting—whether merely singing a song or working at some magic, he had no idea.

The cannon boomed again. "That'll be the German company," he said. "I had a report an hour ago that they were on hand to engage the enemy as they unloaded their ships. I think we shall have a hot breakfast, my friends—powder and ball."

"Thank God and Benjamin Franklin we have those Swedenborgian airships," Nairne said. "At least now we see how the country lies." He poured each man at the table a glass of Madeira, then raised his own. "To our wizard, Benjamin Franklin!"

They clinked glasses and drank, the five of them—Oglethorpe; Nairne; and their majesties Philippe, Charles, and Peter. The latter two hesitated before touching their glasses, but Charles completed the motion.

"I also had word from Unoka," Oglethorpe went on. "He and the Choctaw worked their way north to devil them from the rear. Less than fifty of 'em left, but even a gadfly should be help to us now."

"To them," Charles said. They drank again.

"I do not ordinarily drink," the Swedish king explained, "but these are not ordinary times. Moreover, I am getting old, and find myself often doing things I would never have dreamed of in the past." He glanced conspicuously at the tsar. "To—all of us here. Win or lose, this is a fight they shall never forget."

Peter shook his head. "Not true. If we lose, there shall be no one to remember it."

"Then we must win. I want them to remember that I finally settled my score with you."

Peter's face twitched, but to Oglethorpe's surprise, the remark didn't seem to anger the tsar. "It may be that our foe will settle it for us." His face grew longer. "I come here a pauper. I have few men in arms, and those mostly belong to my daughter's guard. I have no cannon, not even weapons of my own. I wish—I wish one of you would ask me to fight with your company. I will not beg, however."

That was greeted with silence, for no one could say, really, that they trusted the tsar against troops that were in part Russian. Finally Philippe said, "But of course, sir, it would be my honor if you would ride with the French."

"No." They all turned to Charles. His fingers had gone white, gripping his glass. "No. Let him ride with me."

They all stared at him, as he turned with deliberation to the tsar. "If you fear it, I swear to you this is no ruse to put you in front of my gun. I need not resort to that—I know, as do you, that if we duel with swords I will win. I am far the better swordsman, and God is also on my side. No contest of arms between us can be fair. So this is my challenge to you, sir. We shall face the guns of the enemy side by side and—as you say—we shall let the enemy settle our differences. In the meantime, it will give me great pleasure that you see my soldiers—who have undergone such misery on your account—for the incomparable warriors that they are, and that you should ride with them against the same men who once fought for you. One of us must live, and one of us must die—that seems certain. I am content to let God choose."

The tsar looked down at his wineglass, and a slow smile spread across his face. "That is a challenge worthy of a tsar," he said. "And it is to my liking."

And so they all drank to that, and Oglethorpe knew for a

fact that the world would never see such a thing again. They belonged to another age, these men: an age of titans. Whatever happened, their epoch was past, and they knew it.

As Oglethorpe predicted, by morning the lines were more or less drawn. The German company and other Indian-style fighters had done what they could to slow the advancing troops, but sooner or later—as they once said in Holland—the water reaches the dike.

The dike around New Paris was the series of redoubts, protected by devil guns, a zone of unbreathable air created by yet more Franklin devices, some new inventions that were supposed to halt the worst of the diabolic weapons if they ever came to bear—and themselves, the army of the continent.

It was a dike that would not hold for long. It was too long and thin, with too many holes in it. Once it was breached, there would be nothing for it but to fall back to New Paris itself.

Oglethorpe had no intention of letting that happen. He met with the other commanders the next morning.

" 'Twill take them a few days, at best, to cut through our line somewhere. When they have us all forced back to New Paris, they'll emplace their long-range guns and pound the city to bits. They may even grow bold enough to put their airships high over the city and drop grenados."

"I doubt it," Peter said. "The lesson of Venice is still remembered in Russia."

"Granted, but they seem in a desperate hurry in this matter, so they may try it. Even foundered, a fully laden airship crashing into New Paris would wreak plenty of havoc."

"Still I doubt it. Mademoiselle de Montchevreuil and her companions tell me the devil's army lost the bulk of their airships battling her and the Choctaw. They will protect those that remain."

"You may be right," Oglethorpe conceded. "Indeed, though I raised the question, I am counting on that being the case. After unloading artillery, the airships withdrew some two leagues from here, where they are grounded, presumably from fear that we might manage—as we have in the past—to slip close with a devil gun. I propose that those ships should be the target of a powerful and decisive attack. Once we have wrecked them, we'll have cut their supply line. We can then clean up any devils who remain in the field."

"How are we to do that?" Charles asked. "Suppose we mass and strike for their ships. How can we keep them on the ground? As we fight our way to them, they will simply fly away—that is their beauty, as mobile fortresses."

"I've asked some people to speak on that," Oglethorpe replied. He raised his voice. "If it would please the lady and gentlemen to step into the tent?"

The flap rustled, and in walked Benjamin Franklin, wearing his raccoon hat and a plain brown suit. With him were the Choctaw Red Shoes, Vasilisa Karevna, and Leonhard Euler.

"Mr. Franklin!" Charles said, briskly rising to shake the young man's hand. "Come to save us all again, I see."

Franklin smiled wanly. "We must all do our part, Your Majesty. And it is good to see you again."

"Yes—hang together or hang separately, I heard you said. By heaven, let that be our battle cry. Well, what magic do you have for us, Mr. Franklin?"

"We have, between us, devised some stratagems," Franklin replied, "which we think will keep the airships on the ground. But I fear it is still the army that must carry the day."

"Don't worry about that," Oglethorpe replied. "My lads are ready for anything."

"And mine!" Charles added.

"The French will never shirk," Philippe assured them.

"I will not bore you with scientific details, gentlemen," Franklin said. "May I simply tell it to you in logistical terms?"

"Please."

"If we can get near enough to the ships, quickly enough and undetected, we can deprive them of the power to fly. Not for long—a day at best."

"You will use an invisible ship, as you did against me in Venice?" the tsar asked.

"Yes, Majesty. But in that case, our intent was to capture one of your own ships. A desperate measure, and one which in fact failed. In this case, we need only get *near*."

"And once you have beached them, so to speak," Charles said, "you may leave?"

"No. We must remain close, to continue to prevent them from rising. That is why I can promise you only a short time—once they discover and attack us, our defenses will only last so long. If they destroy us before you arrive, they will fly."

"And you will die," Charles pointed out.

"True," Franklin replied, "but that lies at the end of most of our roads, at the moment."

"Worry not," Oglethorpe said. "Two leagues? I will be there in three hours, and heaven help anyone between here and there."

"Bah!" Charles said. "I will be there in *two* hours, camped in the wreckage when you arrive."

Philippe slapped his hands together. "I have a bottle of cognac," he said, "of a particularly fine sort. So far as I know, it is the very last in the world. Whichever company reaches those ships first—Swedish, Commonwealth, or French— shall have the honor of drinking it." He paused for a moment. "Or failing that, whosoever remains alive at the end of it all shall drink a toast to whoever reached them first."

"You have a bargain," Oglethorpe said.

"Well, my friends," Franklin said to his scientific companions, "our future is assured by a bottle of cognac. Whatever confidence I lacked is now made whole."

"Indeed," Philippe said, "for you shall hold the bottle yourself, and award it to the winner."

"Where are you going, Mademoiselle?"

"Hello, Elizavet. You're up early," Adrienne said.

She shrugged. "I had something of a—disappointment last night. I stayed up thinking about that, but then my mind went to other things. It would not stop."

"Did your disappointment have a name?"

"Carl von Linné."

"Ah."

"Yes. He refused my favor—*me*—for that thick-waisted Émilie."

"And that kept you up until morning?"

Elizavet settled on a tabouret. "Where are you going?" she repeated. "You are still injured."

"That in a moment."

Elizavet sighed and examined her right palm, tracing the index finger of her left along the delicate lines there. "They say our fate is written here. I never thought I had much of a fate. I never thought I needed one. I'm the daughter of the tsar, after all. Yes, Linné refused me. A very rare thing, especially when the other woman is so far from me in beauty."

"But he is in love, Elizavet, and that makes a difference."

"I know," the tsarevna said. "I did not believe that before, not in my heart. But the more I thought on it, the more I wondered why I ever wanted him. And it was because of *her*, Mademoiselle." She knit her fingers in her lap.

"What do you mean?"

"I mean, Émilie is like you. Oh, not so beautiful, of course. But her mind, her thoughts—I cannot imagine them, as I cannot imagine yours. They are too far beyond me. And I—envy that. Desire it. It makes her better than me, and I tried to take Linné from her to prove that she was not. But I failed."

"Elizavet, there is nothing wrong with you."

"I'm just stupid—is that it? Naturally, like a beast?"

"No. No, you are very bright. You've just never been interested in proving it. Why are you now?"

"Why?" Her eyes grew large. "Because of you, of course. You have shown me what a woman might be. I love you, Mademoiselle, as I have never loved another woman, not even my mother. I—I do not wish to disappoint you. But there is nothing to do! Everyone else has something to give to this fight, everyone but me!"

"That isn't true. Elizavet, your men love you. What we

have of your old guard is utterly devoted to you. Look to them."

"What do you mean?"

"Have you noticed them lately? They are in a strange place, they do not speak the language, they hardly understand anything of what goes on around them, and yet soon they must lay down their lives for a cause they scarcely understand."

"My father—"

"Is not you. They did not leave Moscow for him—they left for you."

"But what can I do?"

"Not ride into battle, of course. But be their tsarevna. Give them hope and heart."

"Is that all?"

"It's a great gift, Elizavet. You exerted it in Saint Petersburg without even knowing it. Think how much you can accomplish if you put your mind to it."

Elizavet smiled, but then her smile shrank away. "Is this merely some ploy to improve my mood and rid you of my complaints?"

"No. Partly. But what I say is true: the few Russians here are in the wilderness, and you can help to guide them. You *are* a tsarevna, a force to be reckoned with if you only choose to be."

"As *you* chose to be."

"I suppose."

Elizavet laughed, wiped the tears beaded on her lashes. "Very well, then. And will you now tell me where you are going?"

"I'm going to battle."

"Not like that!"

"This will be a different sort of battle, the sort that only I can wage."

"Let me come with you, then!"

"There is no space for anyone else. None of my students is going. They are needed here, as you are."

Elizavet stood, noticeably trembling, and then she came and knelt and laid her head in Adrienne's lap.

"Do not die," she whispered. "Come back to us, and I promise to do my lessons, all to the end."

"You must do that whether I return or not," Adrienne said.

As they readied the *Lightning*, Franklin reflected that he would rather a bit more strategy was involved in the coming battle than a race by three generals to reach the ships. Still, they *were* generals, and presumably knew what they were doing.

"I notice you did not mention our *real* goal," Euler said, testing one of the brass valves for tightness.

"What point in that? It would only have added a confusing element—and they might have even forbidden us. If we fail, the dark engines come alive, and most or all of us perish. To succeed, we need the army to capture the ships, or at least distract them from us. If we had time to build a real navy, things might be different, and we might be able to take them on better-than-even terms. After all, from what you and the others say, they were never able to build their own aeges, and that gives us an advantage."

"But they have made weapons that seek them."

"I've planned for that," Franklin said, stepping back to survey his ship.

The *Lightning* was a barge thirty feet long and ten wide, enclosed by a square cabin. She was framed with adamantium, but most of her was plain steel and iron, set with alchemical glass panes in the deck and bulkheads. She had more hatches than a thief has pockets—two in the bottom, for dropping grenades, two in the bulkheads for getting in and out on the ground, one in the roof. The roof was the oddest thing about the whole structure. A box on a box, it was five feet deep, because the cargo holds were there. As they would be hovering over the enemy, Franklin wanted the cargo as far from upward-flying shells as possible. So there was one more hatch—from the hold into the cabin.

He watched as four burly soldiers loaded the holds, grunting with the weight of heavy casks full of grenades and other weapons.

"We ought to have called her the *Turtle*," Robert noted.

"Well, we can sure tuck in our head," Franklin allowed. "It has an aegis and some other scientific protections. But those below us will know we are a storm, never fear."

Vasilisa stuck her head out of the top hatch.

"It's prepared, Benjamin, and we are all here. Shouldn't we get started?"

"Not quite. We're waiting for two more. But see, there they are." He gestured at the sedan chair, born across the muddy plaza in front of the palace by two stout Lorraine guards.

"Adrienne? You've made peace with her, then? I knew nothing of this."

Red Shoes seemed pleased with their new passenger. "It is good," Franklin heard him murmur, from where he sat on an empty rum cask, smoking a pipe and watching the philosophers at their tasks.

"But she hasn't been prepared," Vasilisa protested, "nor studied the equations."

"It doesn't matter."

Franklin walked over to see if he could help. The Frenchwoman could not move on her own, of course. Two of her guard carried her to the ship, then brought a special couch for her, which they tied to braces on the floor. There were similar braces everywhere, with leather straps attached, in case the air road became a bit bumpy.

Franklin was confronted by the formidable Crecy, who still regarded him with something between a hard winter and a glacier in her eyes.

"I'm going, of course," she said simply.

"Of course," he replied. "I'm happy to have you."

Crecy didn't answer but went to help settle Adrienne onto the ship. Franklin shrugged, returning his attention to the *Lightning*, hoping he hadn't missed anything.

"You can carry one more, I hope?"

Don Pedro. Franklin hadn't even heard him come up.

"I would be more than happy for your help," Franklin said, "but I fear your wounds—"

"Are of no consequence, I assure you. I have given command of my men to Governor Nairne, but if you cannot make room for me here, I will lead them in the defense of the redoubts." His eyes blazed.

"Aye. Let 'im come," Robert said, from behind him. "We might need an extra sword, if things go wrong."

If things go wrong, it's scant good swords will do us, Franklin thought. But he held it in. With his wounds the Apalachee was better off in the *Lightning* than charging into battle. And Franklin, after all, bore a large measure of responsibility *for* the wounds.

"It is my honor, Don Pedro, to have you aboard. And speaking of aboard"—he raised his voice—"all aboard that's coming. 'Tis time to fly this thing."

And so they crowded on—Vasilisa, Euler, Red Shoes, Grief, Adrienne, Crecy, Robert, Tug, Don Pedro, and him.

Franklin twisted the valves that engaged the engines, and the *Lightning* began to rise. He watched New Paris diminish into a patchwork of huts and muddy paths. For the first time, he hoped that he would see it again.

Flame exploded in columns in front of them as the wing ship flew over, tossing Mongols, Indians, and Russians aside like rag dolls. It was a terrible and wonderful sight.

"There, let them drink some of their own beer," Oglethorpe shouted, "and now, forward!" As he said it he urged his own mount into motion. Now the guns in the redoubt started pounding, too, and belatedly the enemy artillery answered, and they were in the midst of the fireworks. Men and horses screamed, the air was choked with smoke, and the din was so great as to bring tears to the eyes.

The charge had begun. Led by the airships and their grenadiers, three companies, ranged along the defensive line perhaps half a league apart, broke northward at once. In the center were the Swedes, with the French to the east and Oglethorpe and his men to the west. They had drawn lots for the more exposed flank positions, and Charles had lost.

"Hold it together, lads," he shouted. "There they are!"

The cavalry they faced was like none he had ever seen before. Though some bore muskets, most of them wielded bows with improbably long range. Those would be of little use once the bowmen were in the trees, but crossing the expanse which had been defoliated by artillery fire, Oglethorpe's men were, for a moment, exposed. A rank of attackers came forward, fired, wheeled. Another.

Arrows fell like devilish hail, thudding into horses and men.

His men lowered their short-barreled carbines and fired as they rode, reloading with paper cartouches.

A fresh line of explosions cleared out many of the archers as the airship made another pass, and then it was time for the first shock of the charge.

Softened up by artillery and grenades, the enemy line crumbled. That was to be expected. While the colonies had aerial intelligence, the devil army did not—they had no way of knowing where to concentrate their men and, indeed, appeared to be massing for an invasion several leagues east. Nairne and the Apalachee would handle them there as best they could. For Oglethorpe and his companions, it meant an easy first engagement.

And, indeed, now they were clear, and border troops and artillery would dispose of what they left behind, so they would not have the problem he had faced charging the guns a few days earlier.

But the same air-gathered information that told them where they should break through told them something more worrisome: between them and the Russian airships there were at least two thousand troops. Even if they hadn't lost a single man just now—and Oglethorpe doubted that very much—that put the odds at right around four to one. And if the Russian ships managed to get airborne . . .

You made your decisions, then you lived by them. No one had gainsaid him. For good or ill, it was begun, and there could be no retreat.

13.

Hard Wind

Adrienne leaned on her couch, so that she could see her son, far below. In her diagrammatic sight, he appeared as a sphere, with waves and rays emanating to connect him to the malakim and to stranger things yet.

He looked, in fact, very much like her hand.

"He is still there," she said, "in the center ship."

"Good," Franklin said. He smiled, but she recognized the quality of it. He was worried.

"That were passin' easy." Robert grunted, lying on the floor with his nose pressed against the thick pane. "They still ain't made no motion."

"Our aegis hides us," Franklin said, "for a time."

"We gonna drop grenados on 'em?" the big man called Tug asked.

"Not yet," Franklin replied a bit absently. "No use in letting them know we're here until they notice, or until our forces scare them off the ground. Then you can toss out all the grenados you want."

"Good." Tug grunted. "I'm goin' t' open a cask or two o' 'em." He ambled toward the ladder leading up to the hold.

Crecy knelt by Adrienne. "How are you feeling?"

"Well, Veronique. Able."

"Able to what?"

Adrienne looked back down, this time with her mortal eyes. There, half a league below the airships, were tiny dots. And yet it was no great distance really. And she could feel him. Her hand hummed in sympathy with him, as one chime will hum when a like-tuned one sounds. It must be one of

274

Lomonosov's less-perfect affinities, the ones that faded with distance.

Like love, perhaps? What sort of attraction was less perfect than that? Or less useful?

She realized that Crecy was still awaiting an answer. "Nico has to be stopped," she said.

"You tried once before."

Adrienne took her friend's hand, touched it with her angel digits. "No," she said softly, "I didn't."

"Mademoiselle?"

Adrienne glanced up. "Mr. Euler."

"Ah! You remember me."

"Of course. I read one of your papers, though I do not recall the topic. One of Swedenborg's students, weren't you? Did you tell Franklin that?"

"Yes. He knows what I was."

"And yet he trusts you?"

"No, not entirely."

"Neither do I. I find it too strange that you are here—especially since I remember hearing that you died."

He smiled grimly. "I had to vanish from Russia, Mademoiselle. Few seek the dead."

"I quite understand."

"I just wanted to tell you—I'm honored you are here. I—"

At that moment, Tug, who had been poking around in the storage area, began cursing violently, and then a gunshot boomed and another. Tug fell through the open hatch with a wet thud, but managed to scramble to his feet, though his white shirt was rapidly soaking red with blood.

"Hijack!" he shouted. "B'goddamn but they shot me!"

Crecy drew two pistols and aimed them at the hatchway, just as two men in red coats dropped down, wielding *kraftpistoles*. Her and Robert's pistols barked like twin hounds, and both men fell, one shot in the head and the other in the belly.

The next instant a grenade bounced on the deck, fuse sputtering.

Robert was already running that way, his second pistol

aimed up, seeking a target in the hatch above. Without breaking stride, he snatched the bomb up and flung it through the lower hatch, into open sky. Crecy, meanwhile, leapt to stand near him, firing up into the hold.

Two guns boomed above. Crecy stood unscathed, but Robert cursed and fell. A lithe form followed the bullets down, an Indian with a tomahawk in one hand and a pistol in the other.

Red Shoes raised his pistol reflexively when Flint Shouting hurled himself from the hold, but the Wichita's weapon spat first. The ball struck Red Shoes' outstretched hand, scorched up his arm, cracked against a bone in his shoulder, then leapt weirdly to take off most of his right ear. He fell back, feeling almost like he was floating—it was very strange. Everything outside his body seemed preternaturally real—Franklin shouting *Sterne!*, the hatch slamming shut, Flint Shouting arcing over him like a panther.

I'm sorry, brother, he thought. And in that moment, he knew he could do nothing, *would* do nothing. It was over.

Then a black hole appeared in Flint Shouting's chest, as Grief shot him, and a much larger one in his belly, in consequence of Robert shooting him from behind. The Wichita looked surprised, and his knees wobbled drunkenly. He made it the next step, and fell heavily next to Red Shoes, the ax dropping from his hand.

The only weapons Flint Shouting had left were his eyes. His flat, accusing gaze fastened on Red Shoes; and Red Shoes could not shake it, could not avoid it.

The hatch slammed down even as Franklin recognized the face glaring down from it.

"Sterne!" he shouted, and fired his pistol. It sang off the metal and rapped a few times around the cabin.

Above, through the closed hatch, he thought he heard laughter.

"Be damned!" Franklin roared, lunging toward the ladder.

Someone caught him by the scruff of the neck.

It was Tug. "Don' go doin' that. He'll blow y'r head off."

Franklin struggled for a second, then nodded savagely.

"Somebody watch that hatch. Shoot the bastard if he opens it."

"I'll do that," Crecy said. She bent and took the weapons from the dead and not-quite dead redcoats, then stood with both aimed up.

"Robert? Tug?"

"Hit me in the ribs." Robert grunted. "Just skinned me, maybe cracked a bone. I'll live."

Tug was in more serious shape, bleeding heavily from between his heart and his shoulder. He had wandered over to stare at the Indian who was dying next to Red Shoes, who might be renamed Redhead at the moment, considering all the blood.

"Flint, m'lad." Tug grunted. "Why'd y' go an' do that?"

The Indian wheezed. "You . . . saw . . . my village. Why . . . ask?"

"What's Sterne up to?"

Flint Shouting coughed up a huge bubble of blood, but then his next few words were clear. "I do not know. I do not care. I helped him escape because I heard he was your enemy. He said he could get me close to Red Shoes. That's all . . ." He coughed again. The whole conversation, he had never looked at Tug or Franklin, only at Red Shoes. He coughed a third time, and something broke in him. His eyes set. He did not breathe again.

Franklin stood and looked at the ceiling. "They must have smuggled themselves in the grenado crates." Franklin groaned. "And now he's up there with our munitions."

"That's not our only worry," Adrienne said.

"What?"

"That grenado Mr. Nairne tossed from the ship—it got their attention. In a few seconds, we'll be under attack."

"Tighten up, lads!" Oglethorpe shouted. Once again, he wished he had more disciplined troops. The constant harassment of the Mongols and Indians on their western flank was having its effect, drawing the Yamacraw and wilder rangers to separate themselves from the main body of the charge, where they most probably were picked to pieces. He couldn't tell; all he knew for sure was that things were getting mighty thin on that side, and that those who went whooping and hollering west never returned.

He felt he was pushing through a black fog, one gradually closing on them. In the heat of the charge, there was no way to get the aerial intelligence he needed, so he had no way of knowing how the enemy was gathering ahead—but they were surely gathering.

But they had certainly pressed more than a league. The ships couldn't be that much farther.

He was thinking this as they came over a rise and stared straight into a line of artillery that stretched as far as he could see in either direction.

"Sweet Jesus," he breathed, taking in the black maws of cannon, firedrakes, *kraftcannon,* and weapons he in no wise recognized. He heard the sudden bellow of the Swedish battle cry to his right, and knew the line stretched even there. The damned taloi again, making artillery more mobile than it ought to be.

"This looks like fun," Parmenter said. Oglethorpe heard the quiver in his voice.

"Let's give 'em only one volley at us, lads!" Oglethorpe shouted. "Don't even think to let the Swedes beat us to our goal! For God and the Commonwealth!"

And once again he led the charge.

For a long moment, it seemed the cannon would stay silent, that they would repeat their feat of weeks past and blow through the line like a swift wind.

But the only wind came from the north, a fiery wind, tearing through them as if they were dry leaves. Parmenter, on Oglethorpe's right hand, was suddenly headless. Oglethorpe saw it out of the corner of his eye, and glanced in astonishment at the way the ranger's body remained upright, hands gripping the reins. Then Parmenter's horse caved in from the front, and Oglethorpe couldn't look anymore, because he had his own troubles.

The second volley followed without respite. Oglethorpe could see the gunners now, crouched behind their weapons. Closer, closer, and he could almost reach them with the point of his sword—

Brass cymbals crashed around him, and he was on his back. But not still, no—his foot was caught in the stirrup, his horse dragging him along.

For a second or two. Then the poor beast vanished in a cloud of blood.

His body was numb, and for all he knew he was dying already, but he was damn sure taking one or two of these bastards with him. He couldn't see a god-rotted thing, either, for the cloud of gunsmoke in the still, hot air. But that could work for him as much as against him.

His pistols had been on his horse, and they were spent anyway. Whisking out his saber, he crept along the ground until he saw booted feet.

He stood and swung, and a young man's surprised face leapt, along with the rest of his head, from its neck. If he made a sound, it didn't carry over the battlefield clamor. A yard away, another fellow in a green coat, plug bayonet fixed and staring someplace behind Oglethorpe, seemed oblivious of his presence. Oglethorpe cut him down like a sapling, and it was only then, as the guns spoke again, that he understood his horse had dragged him right into the line itself, and he had gotten turned around. To his left was a cannon, and to the right a *kraftcannon*.

The first of the carabiners guarding the *kraftcannon* died without noticing him, but the second managed to fire his weapon. Oglethorpe felt the powder sting his face, but that was all, and then he hacked the fellow's hand off.

Something bumped into his back. He whirled—and found Tomochichi there, a bloody tomahawk in his hand, a fierce grin on his seamed face. Satisfied, Oglethorpe put his back to the Indian, unworried about that quarter for the nonce.

The *kraftcannon* was mostly a bar of iron six feet long,

ground to a point on the business end and light enough to be mounted on a swivel, like a murder gun on a ship. Grimly, he swung it east, so it faced straight up the line of artillery. The carabiners at the next gun noticed him at about that time, but all but one of them was reloading. That one fired.

So did Oglethorpe. The lightninglike bolt jagged into the next cannon and then straight on to the next, and the men manning them danced the Saint Vitus dance and died.

Someone kicked him in the back, and for an instant he was angry with Tomochichi—why had his friend struck him so? But then the two of them fell, and when he rolled over, he saw that a bullet had gone all the way through the Yamacraw chief's belly to hit him in the back. The old man reached out and gripped his arm and moved his lips, but Oglethorpe could not, of course, hear anything. He noted absently that they were surrounded by men now, and also that three fingers from his own left hand were missing.

Shielding Tomochichi's body with his own, he turned to face his doom with eyes open.

"We have to get him out of there," Franklin said. "Most of what we need is in the hold."

"It's too late," Adrienne murmured, looking down at the vortices rising toward them. "They've released the mines."

"Mines?"

"The Russians took a page from your book, Mr. Franklin," she answered. "The mines are spheres, such as those which lift the airships. They rise under their own power, bearing explosives with them. These have probably been taught to seek the emanations of your aegis."

"I have a countermeasure for that," Franklin grunted, "but it's up there with Sterne."

"We have less than a minute, I would guess."

"Why not just use the exorcister?"

Adrienne shook her head again. "If they start to fall, they detonate. As I understand your device, its range is too short, for the explosive is hydrogen."

Vasilisa cut in. "Can't *you* stop them, Adrienne? You know the art of unmaking those spheres."

"Certainly. But I need malakim servants, of which I have none." She continued to watch death rise toward them.

"Red Shoes?" Franklin shouted. "Red Shoes?"

The Indian sat, rather stupidly, as his woman, Grief, wrapped bandages around his head.

"I—" he said, looking confused. Then his eyes focused. "I can help. Mademoiselle, do you think you might control my shadowchildren, as you did the malakim?"

"I can try."

"Take them, then. I give them to you."

She turned the sight of her *manus oculatus* toward the Indian, saw his shadowchildren around him. They were simpler than the malakim. They had a certain furious quality to them, like distilled anger. She reached for them, prodding them with the aetherial reach of her fingers, learning them.

"I can see 'em." Robert grunted. "Little red dots, gettin' bigger."

Teach them, she heard Red Shoes say, through his children. *Or help me teach them.*

When the malakim spoke, it was always in her own voice. Now, as Red Shoes spoke through his shadowchildren, it was still in her voice, which was somehow even stranger.

Adrienne read the patterns of affinities in the rising spheres, then made the corrections to dissolve them, and laid it all out. Her own malakim would have understood—but the Indian did not know much mathematics. Would it appear to him in some form he could understand?

It did, and it came back to her. For him it was like taste or smell—a sensation with many layers of complexity. And he would teach this to his shadowchildren—

"*Real* close now," Robert said.

And then they had it. The shadowchildren dropped like little hawks, dragging talons of force through the spheres, unmaking them. The malakim inside sighed free, and the bombs, no longer held aloft, fell. But not far, and then the sky was white-hot flame, and the *Lightning* bucked like a skiff on rough seas.

And just behind the bombs came a swarm of malakim, eagles tearing into those little hawks, and she and Red Shoes were suddenly caught in an otherworld war of a very different sort. And behind it all, she could feel the strength of her son growing, the line between them tightening, a Jacob's ladder for his servants to climb.

And there were more bombs on the way now.

"Best find your countermeasures," she managed. "Red Shoes and I will be busy for a time."

Franklin could already see that, in the way they both stared off into space, watching things he could not—probably did not want to—see.

That meant, too, that Red Shoes would not be able to perform one of his little miracles and kill Sterne through the steel hull.

So be it. Despite Tug's warning, someone had to go up through the hatch.

Tug himself was slumped on the floor, as Grief moved on to doctor him. Robert was wounded, and Don Pedro—

Don Pedro was going up the ladder.

Franklin's warning caught in his throat—if he shouted it would only warn Sterne.

Instead he drew his sword and leapt up the ladder after the Apalachee. Now that his mind was slightly clearer, he knew it wouldn't do to go firing into a hold full of munitions.

Don Pedro banged the hatch, but it only gave an inch or so.

"He must have piled things upon it," Franklin said.

"Very well," Don Pedro said. "But there is another hatch on top of the ship, yes?"

"What a blockhead I am! Of course there is!"

"And we get to it how?"

"Go out the front of the cabin and climb, I suppose."

"I go, then," he said. He hurried to the front, past the dead form of Flint Shouting. The glass there was on hinges, and it swung inward. He looked around, positioned himself on the prow, and leapt up.

Franklin followed. By the time he got there, the Apalachee's moccasins were vanishing over the top. Swearing, Franklin went up the rungs.

Outside was strange. The aegis bent light and matter, but not perfectly. Being within its protection was like being in a prism, everything tinted rainbow—the sky, the clouds, the distant, maplike earth. He was actually grateful, for it disguised, in some measure, the reality of the fall awaiting him if he slipped.

In some small *measure,* he reflected, looking down again.

He came over onto the top of the ship just in time to see Don Pedro lift the upper hatch and a funnel of flame leap out. The Don had been careful, but not careful enough. Though he wasn't caught in the flame itself, the superheated air scorched him, and he fell, clutching his eyes.

"Don't roll!" Ben shouted. "You'll fall over!" He ran to help the Apalachee.

At which point Sterne emerged, grinning like death, a glowing red orb floating above his head.

"Well, Mr. Franklin," he said. "It looks like just the two of us, doesn't it?"

"My friends will be here in a second."

"Maybe they will. But you shall be dead." And he raised a gun with his left hand.

14.

The Roof of the World

Oglethorpe blinked at the men standing over him.

They were Commonwealth.

"General?" A youth with a shock of nearly orange hair sticking out from under his cap knelt next to him.

"We've taken the artillery line?"

"Yes, sir, we have. The wing ships rifted it a little farther down, so we managed to cut through and come about."

"Thank God."

He sat up and turned back to Tomochichi. "Did you hear that, chief?"

But the chief of the Yamacraw was listening beyond the world, not in it. His days, as he might say, were all broken. Oglethorpe kissed the old man on the head and reached to close the open lids. He had to switch hands to do it.

"You're hurt, sir," one of the rangers said.

"Yes, my hand . . ." He looked again at the bloody stumps of the digits, wondering exactly when he had lost them.

He examined the rest of his body. The shot that had come through Tomochichi had been stopped by his cuirass, though his back throbbed like the devil. To his surprise, he also found that something had left a neat hole through the meaty part of his thigh, but fortunately missed the bone.

"We're sending you back to the surgeon, sir," the ranger said. "We'll carry on, never you fear."

"I shan't fear, for I shall be there to see it. Is there one horse left amongst us?"

"Sir—"

"Now. I mean it."

"We'll find you one, General."

Sterne raised the weapon he held. Franklin's heart did a flip-flop when he saw it.

"You don't even know what you have there," he said.

"I'll take my chances," Sterne replied. "Did you invent it?"

"Indeed I did."

"Well, consider this a compliment, then. I trust your abilities enough to be certain that whatever this is, it will kill you quite dead."

"It won't," Franklin said, drawing his sword. "It might hurt *you* though."

Sterne laughed. "Well played, Mr. Franklin." And he pulled the trigger.

Franklin had always wondered what the depneumifier would do to a warlock. He finally got a chance to see.

What happened was Sterne's eyes went wide, and he dropped the weapon. The malakus above him flashed a bluish green color; and Sterne screamed, a quite unholy sound, and clapped his hands to his ears. Franklin leapt forward, sword extended. After all, there had to be differences in the natural articulator of a warlock and the devised ones the devil gun was designed to work on.

There were; even through his pain, Sterne was not yet licked. His blade was out and parrying before Franklin got there. Franklin couldn't really fence—he had only played at it a bit with Robert and wore the sword more for show than for anything else. If he really had to tangle with the man, he was done. But Sterne was clearly in pain, and this was his only chance. The others were counting on him.

So instead of backing up and trading blows, Franklin continued to rush forward so that their blades locked at the guards, and brought his good left fist up into Sterne's jaw with every ounce of strength he owned.

If felt like he'd broken his hand. The warlock's teeth clicked together, and he nearly fell; but he still shoved Franklin back with superhuman strength. Franklin teetered a foot from the edge of the deck, desperately trying to set his stance, as Sterne lunged deep and long, straight for Franklin's heart. Without even thinking, Franklin stuck his own arm out straight.

And stared. His blade was buried four inches in the warlock's breast. In his heart. Better yet, Franklin himself had not been pierced—the warlock had pulled his own weapon back to parry the counterattack, at the last instant and too late.

Sterne stared, too. "How *stupid* . . ." he began. "Why would anyone make such a stupid counterattack?" He looked up at Franklin, down at the sword still clutched in his hand, picked up the point to run Franklin through in turn.

Franklin let go of the hilt and sidestepped. The warlock fell, body jerking weirdly.

"I don't know how to fence, sir," Franklin replied.

"Ah," Sterne replied, and died.

Don Pedro had regained his feet, and by the look of him, his vision.

"Well done, Señor," he said. "The 'parry of two widows.' Only a madman would use it and hope to live. Wonderful."

"Th-thank you," Franklin stuttered.

"Shall I run him through again, to be certain?"

Sterne wasn't moving at all, now.

"Yes," Franklin replied.

Don Pedro nodded and stepped up to do so, when suddenly the ship bucked like a wild horse, and the deck slipped from beneath their feet.

Oglethorpe reckoned he had lost more than half his troops, but breaking the artillery had put a fire in them the like of which he had never seen in fighting men. They fought like devils; and many of their opponents, perhaps sensing that they had wakened something terrible, fell back.

He reserved his feeling of triumph, however, as they closed the distance. Too many important questions were unanswered. Were the ships still there? Had Franklin and the rest done their job? Or would they arrive to discover it was all for nothing?

Of course, it wasn't—whatever happened, by God, they had stung this enemy. But somewhere, by his accounting, there ought to be a few more thousands of them.

He had a crawling feeling he knew where.

Franklin caught hold of the raised edge as the barge convulsed again.

"Their charges are starting to break through!" he shouted. "Red Shoes and Montchevreuil must be failing. Don, help me!"

He scrambled toward the opening and down it. As he had suspected, two heavy casks had been shoved over the cabin hatch. Franklin ignored that for the moment, hunting in a different corner and coming out with a keg full of small spheres, each with a single knob.

"Free that lower hatch," he shouted to Don Pedro, as he gathered them up.

A moment later they were peeping at Crecy behind the ends of her guns. Ignoring her, Franklin leapt down to the floor, just as the boat kicked so hard it nearly flipped over. Franklin slammed into the bulkhead, and for a moment his vision constricted to a narrow tunnel, darkness eating at consciousness.

Crecy's face appeared in the tunnel. He held up one of the spheres, which he had somehow managed to hang on to.

"Twist the knob," he grunted. "Drop it through the bottom hatch." He climbed shakily to his feet as she did so.

"Keep passing those down, Don Pedro," Franklin shouted. He took the next one and went to the hatch.

A hundred yards below them, a starfish of fire opened its arms.

"The bomb attacked the sphere," Crecy observed.

"Aye. Each has a small, weak aegis. They attract the charges."

"Brilliant."

"I need you to feed these out slowly. I have other things to see to."

"Done."

"Hurry," Adrienne said, her voice coming as from very far away.

"What now?"

"The ships are preparing to rise. And something else . . ." Then she sank back into her trance.

Cursing again, Franklin clambered back up into the hold.

Red Shoes stared down through *Taboka*, the hole in the top of the world where the Sun rested at midday. Above him the far-away stars burned with strange light; below, the Earth fes-tered with squirming, crawling things, and from that living pestilence grew a single, perfect tree whose branches rose through and past them, reaching beyond even the stars.

Around him, his shadowchildren died as fast as he could make them, and he grew angrier and angrier.

It was time, it was time. Time to tear the roof from the world.

He wasn't strong enough to do it alone. But with this woman, this woman and her strange hand, this woman who was mother to the tree itself, he might manage it.

If he had time, which he didn't, and respite from the con-stant attacks, which he didn't.

And then like a lanthorn suddenly uncovered, he did. The spirits fell away, repelled by a strange new emanation.

Here was his chance.

We must shape a shadowchild together, he told her. *A spe-cial one. I need your help and your knowledge.*

The answer was sluggish, and for a long moment he feared he had already lost her. *Very well,* she said. *We will do it.*

Inwardly, he smiled his snake smile. Soon.

"There," Franklin said, "that's done. We can hold 'em like this for a time. And I've managed a shield which ought to keep the malakim away from us, too. So now we can breathe a bit."

"A few of us are still doing that, I guess."

Franklin looked around and saw what he meant. Red Shoes and Montchevreuil were still in their trances or whatever, and Euler and Vasilisa were bandaging Tug. The big fellow looked pale, but his eyes were still full of life. Robert's more minor wound was already bound.

"How goes it, Tug?" he asked.

"I've had worse," the former pirate grunted. "Could do with some rum, though."

"We owe you quite a debt. If you hadn't flushed out Sterne when you did, things would be considerably worse, I think."

" 'Tweren't my design. I just wanted t' drop a few grenados—but y'r welcome."

"If you feel up to it, you can still do that. I don't know that it will do much good, but . . ."

"Hah. Let me at 'em."

"As for me, I need to report to Nairne now—see what I can find out about everything else, and report that the ships are held down for the nonce."

He gazed down through the lower windows. There were the ships; and there, like ants clustered to defend their queen, what appeared to be battalions of men. He studied the scene for a few more moments, then went to the opticon.

It took Nairne a few moments to appear.

"Mr. Franklin," he said, his voice scratchy and metallic, not at all like the governor's real voice. The image, too, left much to be desired. Something Ben would have to improve. "So glad to see you are still alive."

"That I am, Governor, and we've managed to hold 'em on the ground for a time. Any news of the army?"

"They've made good headway, but with terrible losses. Those Swedenborg airships you modified did help, and they enable us to see how the battle goes; but we have no way of getting word to the commanders, though I've sent some couriers. What do you see there?"

"A pretty strong welcoming party, I would say. We're going to dance around a bit above them and do what damage we can with grenados, but I wouldn't count on that being much."

Nairne shrugged. "We shall see what happens," he said, not sounding particularly optimistic. His face scrunched around some question inside him for a moment, something he clearly was not sure he ought to voice.

"What is it, Governor?"

"I . . . I had word from Mr. Voltaire, Franklin. He was with us on the walls, but he's gone out after the advance."

"Why?"

"It seems—ah, it seems your wife put on French uniform and rode with them on the charge."

"Lenka? Is she—"

"There is no way to know. They've lost heavily—more than half of them gone, it looks like. In all of that, there's no way of knowing if she's still alive. I just thought you ought to know."

Franklin was numb to his fingertips. "Damn. God rot it all."

"Franklin . . ." Robert, a few feet away, began.

"No! Damn it, why—" He whirled on the Apalachee Don Pedro. "This is your fault, you overblown gamecock! Who in God's name told you—"

Robert slapped him hard. Franklin stared, unbelieving, at his friend for a heartbeat, then swung a roundhouse at the too-handsome jaw. Robert ducked and punched him someplace in the stomach where all his air was kept. His lungs sucked tight, and he sat down hard.

"Keep your head, Ben," Robert snapped, "or I'll fair keep it f'r you. This is no time f'r a tantrum. Don Pedro has saved our lives and fought our battles, and Lenka has a mind of her own. If anyone here is to blame for where she is right now, *you* know who it is, so just you keep *calm*." He reached out a hand to help Franklin up.

Franklin waved it off. "Don't touch me," he said. "Just don't."

"Very well."

"So what do I do? Tell me that? Everyone seems so damned sure they know what I *ought* to have been doing, why don't you tell what I do *now*, in advance?"

"It's too late for that. We're up here and she's down there, and there ain't a damn thing you can do until the battle is won."

"Robin—"

"So we make sure we *win*," Robert said heatedly. "It's all we can do."

"Damn it. God rot it." He sat on one of the bolted-down stools and put his face in his hands, and he realized, finally, that whether the world ended today or not, his own might already have.

15.

The Duel

"Well, gentlemen. I see none of us has yet collected that cognac," Oglethorpe remarked.

A few hours had done the work of weeks to the commanders of the alliance. Though unwounded, King Philippe was pale and drawn. The tsar's arm was bloodily bandaged. Only Charles seemed unperturbed, his eyes like chips of diamond as he peered across the little prairie.

"This land is all jungle and pine barrens," he noted. "A prairie seems out of place."

"Old fields," Oglethorpe offered. "The Indians girdle trees and burn to make fields, but in a few years the ground becomes unproductive, and they must clear more. In time, they move the whole village. The result is as you see."

"There is a village nearby?"

"An old village of the Mobileans, yes. Those few buildings in the distance may be what remain."

Charles nodded. Most of the valley was full of troops. And, of course, guns.

"This is a cul-de-sac," he said. "If we charge in, we can never charge out."

"Yes, but what are we to do?" Peter asked sarcastically. "Lay siege to them?"

"The runners from Nairne tell us Franklin keeps the ships on the ground but that he cannot do so for long."

"There must be a thousand men down there, and plenty of artillery, too. And surely the ships are armed," Charles murmured. "We have between us—what? Three hundred men?"

"Something like that," Oglethorpe replied.

"Have you lost your nerve at last, King Charles?" Tsar Peter asked.

"No," Charles replied coldly. "I've faced greater odds than this, as well you know. But to conquer here—we must *believe* we can win. I do not think our men believe that."

"That is our job," Oglethorpe replied, "to make them believe."

"Indeed."

"But look at them," Philippe whispered. "walk among the ranks. They have come so far, achieved so much, only to see—*this*. What speech could we give them, what anthem could we sing that could make this last charge seem anything but suicide?"

For answer, Charles gave a harsh chuckle and stood, brushing his knees.

"Tsar Peter, the time has come for me to request my satisfaction."

"Your Majesties—" Philippe began, but this time something in Charles' countenance stopped him.

"I am at your service, sir," the tsar replied.

"These are the terms I propose. We both mount, armed as we please, but with no armor. We ride straight for those guns. Whichever of us survives is the winner."

Peter's face twitched fiercely, and then he bellowed a savage laugh that rang over their little army, out to the mass of enemies awaiting them. "And should we both live?" he said.

"Why, we shall settle our score another day."

"And if we both die?"

"Then whoever falls last is the victor."

"Very well, Your Majesty. I agree to your terms."

A murmur went amongst the troops as the two removed their breastplates and stripped until they were bare chested. Charles mounted, fiddled with his weapons and saddle, then trotted in front of his Swedes and Janissaries.

"I have said I will never flinch in the pursuit of a just war. There are those among you old enough to know the truth of that, to have ridden from Sweden with me more than thirty years ago. You, my friends, were always my kingdom. I love you all, more than life itself. My younger companions, I love you no less. Not one among you has not shown his heart is strong. I now go to settle my oldest score. What God wills will be. Farewell."

The tsar had no people to address. He came alongside Charles, a carbine in one hand.

And they rode. The horses were tired, but somehow they seemed to sense that this was the last time they would stretch their blooded legs on the grass of Earth, and they made the best of it, sending clots of dirt sailing out behind them.

Everything was still for a moment, save for those eight hooves, pounding, a tiny and beautiful thunder.

And then one of the Swedes, as if just understanding what was happening, screamed, *"Iron Head!"* And then everyone of them living—and by the sound of them, perhaps some dead—took it up, shouting to worry heaven, and dashed after their king.

It shocked through Oglethorpe like a dam bursting. He echoed the shout and set his horse in motion; and behind him his men—almost all now on foot—roared like ocean waves crashing on rocks.

Thus began the last charge.

Adrienne lay in a palace built of numbers, of geometries possible and absurd, of theorems solved and yet to be solved and unsolvable; and for the first time in more years than she could remember, she felt joy, the sheer joy she had known as a girl, at night in her room, calculating the motions of the Moon. She traced answers with atoms, or the bundles of affinities named atoms. The Indian posed questions—clever ones she would never have thought of—and she answered by solving them, imprinting the solutions on a parchment of space and time. Around her, the castle continued to take shape, extending upward and downward.

Below, she found endless lines of nonsense, and set about correcting them, conforming them to the grand equation, formed so long ago in her mind, seasoned and re-formed by her students, now finally attaining perfection and realization.

It was, at last, the formula she had glimpsed all those years ago in France, when the world went wrong.

Almost. Something was still missing, something important.

"What are you doing?"

She found a child of some two years regarding her. Her child, her Nico, as she had last seen him in the flesh.

"Solving a problem," she said simply.

"What is that," he asked, "on your hand?"

"A pen," she said, wriggling the fingers of her *manus oculatus*. "Something like a pen. I write with it."

"You write as I do." He cocked his head. "Are you really my mother?"

"Yes."

"Where have you been?"

"I told you the truth before. I've been here all along, Nico. I've been searching for you, but the angels hid you from me."

"Why?"

"So they could make you what you are."

"I am the Sun Boy. I am the god of this world."

"No, my little Nico, you are not."

He frowned. "I don't know what to do. I'm supposed to kill you."

"I know. You will do what you must, and I will love you no matter what. But I know this, and you know it, too, I think. The angels don't want you to know the truth. But they can't stop us, Nico, not if we work together. Remember how we were at the river, at the battle?"

"When you saved me," he said. "You *did* save me, didn't you?"

"Nico, you saved me when you were born. Without you, I would have died. And died again, that night when I was stabbed. Me saving you— I am your mother. What else could I do?"

"I still don't like what you're doing," Nico said.

"Do you know what I'm doing?"

"No. But I don't like it. You have to stop. If you don't stop, I will hurt you."

"I love you, Nico." She looked squarely at him, willing him to believe it, desperate that he should know.

"Stop."

"I can't," she said, her voice catching.

"Very well, then," he said, now sounding cross. "But you will be sorry."

He vanished. Reluctantly, Adrienne returned to her work.

"I see 'em," Robert muttered. "God, but there ain't many of 'em. Like a brace of flies attacking a city."

Franklin closed his eyes again. *Lenka.* He ought to go watch, but he couldn't.

"Damn, the stones on them," Robert said again. "Look at that. I wish I was closer. Hell, I wish I was *down* there."

"Can they win?"

"I don't see how—ah, Jesus, there they are at the guns, and still comin', half of 'em must've—" He suddenly choked off, and Franklin understood his friend was crying.

"They're fightin' Armageddon, and here we sit."

He seemed to have forgotten his own words of a moment before. Franklin could only nod.

Peter watched the guns grow closer, and he didn't care. He lifted the carbine, not to aim it but to brandish it in the air; and for a moment he felt like one of the untamed Cossacks he had watched his army cut down in the past.

He noticed, behind the guns, the green uniforms of his own troops—or those who had once been his—and that filled him with an almost limitless fury. "I am your tsar!" he bellowed, shaking the gun furiously. "I am Peter, son of Alexei, the emperor, the—" His words were drowned out by the first volley.

It was a sound like ice cracking in the Baltic, all at once, everywhere. He remembered Catherine, his empress and love. He remembered his son, who betrayed him and paid with his life. He remembered building ships, with his own two hands, in Holland; the taste of brandy, Tokay, and chocolate.

He remembered being a little boy, hiding in the Kremlin as

the Strelitzi searched for him and his mother and brother. Hiding, cringing, afraid.

Never again. Never.

And then he suddenly understood—a hundred guns had fired at him, and he still sat his horse. He had won!

But no, the damned devil Charles was still in the saddle, too, though his chest was open in two places. In fact, the Swedish king gave a hoarse cry and fired his pistol.

Peter turned grimly back to the waiting guns, where something odd was happening. It looked like their enemies were fighting each other. They were! Russians were turning their sabers on Mongols and Indians.

The second volley crashed, and this time what felt like hot raindrops pattered all over his chest. Blue outlines surrounded everything, and the neck of his horse rushed up to meet him. By chance, his head turned to see that Charles was still mounted, though there was a gaping red hole where one of his eyes ought to have been.

That's when he noticed—the bastard had lashed himself in the saddle. When had he done that?

Peter's horse fell, but it hurt no more than diving onto a feather bed. He smelled salt, the wet metallic scent of the sea, and remembered the little boat he used to sail, imagining the day when he—when *Russia*—would have a real navy.

Somewhere, a storm must be coming. He heard the thunder. Or was that just the wind?

He opened his eyes once more, to see a young man in a green uniform, weeping, kneeling over him, trying to tell him something. It sounded like an apology of some sort.

"I have to go," he told the boy. "Catherine and I are sailing today."

The sky was blue. A good day for it, and the storm, by its sound, was receding.

Ilya Petrov knelt in the midst of the terror, took his tsar's head in his lap, and wept. "God!" he cried to the men milling around him. "It *is* the tsar! I met him four times, rode on campaign with him! We have been betrayed by that snake Golitsyn!"

Across the field now, he saw a small company of riders coming through the confusion, wearing the uniforms of the Russian royal guard. They rode with the enemy, as the tsar had.

"We could not have known!" his friend Vasily shouted. "Who could know this? And he rode against us!"

"Then *we* are wrong! I never thought this was our damned war! I never thought this was right!"

"But now he is dead . . ."

"Yes, and, by God, I will have my answers. Send out the word everywhere, to every Russian soldier. We are betrayed!"

The guards had arrived, now, and Ilya rose to meet them. Their leader, face smudged with soot, swung down and, ignoring him, knelt to look at the tsar for a long moment, despite that the air still whined with lead. Then he—no, *she*—removed her hat, and her long black hair fell about her shoulders, and she knelt and kissed the dead tsar on the forehead.

"Sleep, father," she said.

And Ilya recognized her. "Tsarevna Elizavet!" He had danced with her once, admired her in her velvet evening gown. Beautiful, she had been, a goddess of love.

But now, when she looked up at him, he saw instead a goddess of war, fierce and terrible as her father.

"Who are you?" she snapped.

"Captain Ilya Stepanovich Petrov, Tsarevna."

"You fight for the devil, you know," she told him. "You've murdered your rightful tsar."

"I— We didn't *know*, Tsarevna."

"And now you do. And now you will take up your weapons, and you will follow me, yes?"

"Yes, Tsarevna. By the true tsar and the true God, yes!"

A bullet chose that moment to cut past his cheek, and Ilya watched his friend Sergei sink to the earth in surprise, a red stain in the center of his chest.

"God!" Ilya shouted! "Yes! Up, you men! Fight with our tsarevna! Lay low these dogs who have betrayed us into hell!"

And like the roar of a monster, the name of the tsar went out of the mouth of every Russian there, a word of death. And

Elizavet, the tsarevna, took up her father's bloody sword and lifted it high; and as they had done for a thousand years, in bitter cold and furnace heat, in mud or on dry sand, on taiga and meadowland, Russians went to fight and die.

Oglethorpe understood what was happening just in time to make some use of it.

Some of the Russians had turned. Maybe they had heard rumors that their tsar was alive—maybe they suddenly recognized him. It didn't matter—all that mattered was that impossibly, there was a hole in the artillery. He sat up straight and pointed the way with his sword, and they rode into the breach.

"Holy Mother," Robert swore. "What—what's that?"

Franklin dragged himself to the window and stared down.

Something was forming, perhaps a half mile west of the ships. An axis of pure light, a black wheel spinning about it, growing larger.

"Oh, no," Franklin said. "Look at that."

"What *is* it?" Robert repeated.

"The dark engines," Vasilisa said in a leaden voice. "It's the end."

"The devil, you say." Franklin grunted. "Robert, we're going *down*. Down there, right now."

"Aye, cap'n."

"Benjamin, no!" Vasilisa shouted. "Our only hope now is that Adrienne and the Indian—"

"No thank you, Mrs. Karevna," Franklin said. "We let that thing go, and it kills everyone I hold dear—if they aren't dead already. The hell with the world. I'm saving *them*. And as to trusting this mumbo-jumbo our friends are up to—the devil with that, too."

"What can I do?" Don Pedro asked.

"Help Robert bring down the countermeasures, and then check your weapons. We're goin' into the lion's den for sure."

16.

Castle, Tree, and Cord

Red Shoes grew, like the giant in the story of the Wichita priest. His feet sank deep into the earth; his head brushed the sky; his skin bloated with the pressure of the rattlesnakes and hornets that filled him up, stretching him toward the stars.

The world turned lazily about him, a disc of shadow and light.

Far below, he could see the meaningless little battle, the wrathful wind the Sun Boy had finally released. He remembered, long ago, telling Thomas Nairne the story of Wind, who killed his enemies and then went to sleep in the deep waters, promising that when he awakened he would sweep the world clean.

Well, Wind had awakened, but even he was as nothing to the stirring of the Great One. Himself.

None of that matters now, he said to himself. Adrienne had tricked the Sun Boy, stolen his fire, but he had tricked her, stolen hers.

I am the oldest there is. I am the youngest. I am every one of my lineage.

Now his thoughts became faces he did not recognize. Now his desires became scents he had never known. Now the clay that was his body itched so he wanted to throw it off.

And still he grew, watching everything that had once seemed so important dwindle, diminish, become a light smaller than a star.

But the real stars—ah . . .

Soon he would be able to reach to the ends of the universe, and all would be as before, water and stars, nothing between.

How much better this way. The Peace camp, at least, had done this one good thing: if he had managed to slay humanity earlier, this would never have been possible. And these little seeds they planted—no, not seeds, but eggs, like the sort that dirt daubers buried in their paralyzed prey—ah, how well he had turned them to his advantage.

And still she did not know. Still the Sun Boy was oblivious. And still time marched forward to its own end.

He looked and saw that it was good.

"What in the holy hell—" Franklin sputtered, as the ship rang like a bell and the deck fled from beneath his feet.

"The mines are gettin' through again," Robert said.

"Mines, my arse. That was no explosion. That was something big, smacking into us."

"I don't see nothin'." Tug grunted, looking—as they all were—around and out a window.

"Up above," Franklin snapped. "They've done our own trick, vanished a ship and crept up on us."

If they needed further confirmation of that fact, a sudden screech of metal against metal supplied it.

"Grapnels!" Robert said.

"Seal the hatches," Franklin said, "now."

Robert and Tug hastened to do so, but even as they did, Franklin noticed that the deck beneath their feet was beginning to get warm. They were through the aegis, whoever they were, which meant they could do all manner of things—melt steel, boil blood, release lightning.

He didn't figure on giving them the chance. He aimed the depneumifier up through the ceiling and fired it. Fired it again and again.

And, not too surprisingly, the ceiling suddenly creaked, as if a hundred tons of brick had been laid on it.

"Brace yourselves! I've robbed 'em of motive power!"

"That means we're holding both them and us up!" Robert said.

"No, I wouldn't go that far," Franklin replied, pointing

down through the floor portal, where the Earth was growing perceptibly larger each second.

To make matters worse, the ship began tilting, first slowly, then quite quickly, onto its side.

"What in hell's name are you doing?" Crecy shouted, grabbing Adrienne and trying to shake her back to awareness.

"Saving our lives, at least for another few moments. We were already done, otherwise. I advise strapping our friends into the braces, and ourselves as well. I imagine this thing will flip all the way over."

"If we live through this—" Crecy snapped in a promising tone.

Adrienne and Red Shoes were sleeping through it all, it seemed. They got them strapped in just in time. Once the craft had rolled onto its side, it flipped the rest of the way over quite quickly. The ceiling was now the floor, and they could no longer see how fast the ground was approaching. It couldn't be too fast—his belly wasn't all that light.

He opened the hatch and jumped down in a hold that was now where a hold ought to be, Robert and Don Pedro right behind him, then threw open the upper—now lower—hatch.

A vehicle made of great wheels hung there, latched onto them with clawlike grapnels. Or rather, a sphere compassed by wheels, something like a globe of the Earth mounted with rings around the poles and equator. An open portal was pointed toward them and a hand with a gun poked out of it.

Franklin yanked his head back into the ship as a jagged bolt of phlogiston struck the frame of the portal. Then, with a hoarse cry, he leaned back out and fired his own *kraftpistole* and had the satisfaction of seeing that arm withdrawn with great alacrity.

"How fast we fallin'?" Robert asked.

"We'll find out when we hit the ground," Franklin replied. "At least they'll break our fall. But let's see if we can't drop a few grenados into that window in the meantime."

When Oglethorpe's saber broke, he knew he was a dead man, and though he would have hit the ships with a stone, still they were too far away. His mount was long dead, but even mounted—too far.

He couldn't imagine why he was still alive, anyway. More than miraculous, it seemed perverse. But he was alive, with the battle still surging around him. Just now, he wasn't in reach of an enemy—his men had formed a hollow square around him, and the French were accounting for themselves on his right flank. God knew where the Swedes had gotten to. Now that he was in the valley itself, his perspective on the carnage was limited, to say the least.

He stumbled to the ground from sheer weariness, and noticed a tomahawk someone had dropped. He tried to pick it up, and found that he could, just barely. His arms were lead pipes, uninterested in defending him even once more.

One of the regulars nearest him dropped, sobbing, an arrow buried in his chest. Oglethorpe looked for the archer, but couldn't pick him out. Not that it mattered that much anyway. He spared another glance at the unattainable ships—even if they should reach them, they would be cut down by defenders on board.

Well, it had been a fair try.

A hot wind stirred, awash with the smell of thunderstorms and—something else. He ignored it at first, but the wind grew stronger, hotter, and then hot enough to be painful, and with it came a hurricane sound, and behind that a vast tearing, as if a titan were using the crescent Moon to reap a forest.

And indeed, in the distance, on the hilltop above the valley, the forest began to evaporate.

In that moment, whether locked in strangleholds or bludgeoning with ax or sword, a lot of men suddenly had second thoughts about the battle.

For perhaps the first time in history, two opposing armies retreated together, as fast as their legs would take them.

They hit the ground with enough force to rattle teeth and bone, but not enough to break them.

"That's it," Franklin said. "We're down." He unstrapped himself and drew his pistols. After the first grenade had bounced off the window frame, the occupants of the wheel ship had wisely closed it. Franklin wondered how many men that meant, but he almost didn't care. They had ruined his chance of stopping the dark engine short of the army, which meant Lenka was dead, and someone was going to pay for that.

No. There might still be time, time to find Lenka and reach the redoubts, which were already protected from the devilish engine.

He jumped out of the side hatch, grunting as he struck the uneven surface of the wheel ship. The impact hadn't done much to it—the frame was probably adamantium. Looking at it again, he felt a little better. It probably couldn't hold that many men.

It held a few, however, and they were struggling out of a hatch only half open, the rest blocked by the ship's unnatural position on the ground. Three were already out, and another still crawling from underneath. They hadn't seen him yet, and Franklin didn't have any nobility left in him. He aimed and shot one with his ordinary pistol. He missed, which drew their fire, but he didn't much care. Now that the aegis of his ship was down—and he needn't worry about the unpleasant effects of wearing an aegis inside an aegis—he inserted the key that activated the one built into his waistcoat. The blood-red streak of a hot bullet scored across the rainbow-tinted field.

Robert landed next to him, a second blur.

"I have to find Lenka, Robin," he said. "I'm sorry, but that's the way it is."

Another bullet spanged near.

"I understand," Robert said. "Me an' Don Pedro will handle this. A man has to look after his own."

"You're my own, too, Robert. I love you like a brother—actually, better than my brothers. When you're finished here, clear out south to the redoubts."

"I love my skin, believe me," Robert answered.

"I wish I could shake your hand."

"Don't get all Grub-Street maudlin on me, Ben. Just find y'r wife."

Franklin nodded, jumped to the ground, and, ignoring the bullets that whizzed by him, started running west, to where he reckoned the army was. He took one look back over his shoulder. He couldn't see Robert, of course, but he could see Don Pedro, who had either forgotten to engage his aegis or disdained to. Franklin figured the latter.

Veronique de Crecy looked up at the sound—a clicking pop, the grating of metal.

"Adrienne—wake!" she said, slapping her friend's face again. Nothing—she was gone into the aether, doing whatever she and Franklin had planned. Even the ships crashing hadn't wakened her. Could she carry her out in time? But Franklin and the rest were fighting someone out there—cries and gunshots were proof enough of that.

She cast about, noticed Euler was still strapped in, looking stunned. "You," she said. "Carry her out. Now."

Euler looked up at her with guileless eyes. "I can't," he said. "She needs me here."

"Did you hear what I just told you?"

He nodded but said nothing.

"Karevna—you do it, then."

"We can't disturb her. What she's doing is too important."

"Not more important than her life."

"I disagree," the Russian said, her voice hard.

"Karevna—" But Crecy was interrupted as a part of the metal wall suddenly vanished in a great flare, and a trio of men stepped through.

One of them, of course, was Oliver. One was an ugly, baldheaded Indian she did not know. The third was a boy, and there could be little doubt who he was. There was too much of Adrienne in him.

"Well, Veronique, one last time, eh?" Oliver said. "It's been a merry chase."

"Stay away from her, Oliver."

"I intend to, actually. We aren't enemies this time."

"You're a liar."

"No, indeed. She's doing exactly what the masters want.

The Sun Boy didn't understand that at first—nor did we—but now we are all in accord."

"Then why did you attack our ship?"

"Well, that's what comes from not understanding—but now, well, there are still those who might interfere."

"This is nonsense. You just want me to lower my guard. Well, to hell with you, Oliver, the sooner the better." She pointed the tip of her broadsword at him.

Oliver held up his weaponless hands. "Look, see—I back up. Just wait a moment, Veronique, and it shall all be over."

Veronique suddenly grinned broadly, and wiped a single copper strand of hair from her eyes.

"You are quite correct, Oliver. It will be over very soon indeed." And with that she set her stance and bounded toward him.

Curiously, Tug, who had been guarding Red Shoes, did the same, bellowing, waving a cutlass, driving toward the bald Indian.

Nico/Sun Boy seemed to notice none of this, any more than Adrienne did. Like hers, his eyes looked on quite a different world.

The castle was nearly done when Nico appeared again. He regarded her for a moment with his little-boy eyes.

"They say I'm supposed to help you now," he said, puzzled.

"Really? That's odd."

"I thought so, too." He paused a few moments, then asked, "What *are* we doing?"

"Even I'm just beginning to understand that, myself," she said. "But it has to do with harmony."

"I don't understand."

"You've seen a violin? An instrument with strings?"

"Yes."

"Long ago, I saw a picture in a book. It was a picture of a monochord—like a violin with only one string. It ran from heaven to earth, passing through the orbits of all the planets. What the picture showed was that the universe is harmonic, like a musical scale. And do you know what was at the very top of the picture?"

"No."

"A hand, gripping the key that tuned the cord. The hand of God, who made the world."

She looked again at a few equations, moved things around a bit. "Now, it's really more complicated than that, but in a way the picture said something, the same thing that a philosopher named Newton said—"

"I know who Newton was."

"Good. They've attended to your education, then. What the picture said was this: the universe needn't be as it is. It can be changed, just as the pitch of a violin string can be changed. And yet it is not a great change—after all, even if you tune a violin up or down a few notes, you can still play the same songs, only in a different key."

"I still don't understand."

"We're going to put the universe in a different key, that's all. That's why I have this hand—that's why they gave it to me, the angels, so I could twist the key. That's why you were born, to do the same thing." Her throat tightened again. Would Nico know if she lied to him?

"And we're ready to do that?"

"Yes."

"That's good, then."

"Yes, that's good."

And she *was* ready. Her castle was the monochord, anchored at the poles of creation, held at one end by her son and at the other by herself. She had turned the key once already—when the death attacked her, in Saint Petersburg. She had tightened it just slightly, just enough so the death her son had created to kill her could no longer exist—and then let it go back to where it had been.

When it passed over, it twisted everything in me, the Siberian woman had said. And of course, it had. He did. She did. Tree, monochord, castle—all the same.

"When I turn, you must hold fast, Nico. Do you understand?"

"Yes. I can do that."

She hesitated, remembering him as he had been—a strange, silent child. But she loved him—he had given her a reason to live when all other reasons were gone.

"Do you remember?" she asked softly. "Do you remember when I showed you the moon? La lune?"

The boy's eyes grew even wider then, and he pursed his lips. "La loooon," he said.

"Yes. You do remember. Will you take my hand?"

Hesitantly, he reached out, and as their fingers touched, the monochord she had written became real, rushing into existence with all of the certainty in her.

But something was wrong. There was the monochord, yes, but there was—something else, something climbing up it, something she hadn't made. In her angel sight it was a tree of fire, then a serpent uncoiling—its tail in the deeps and its eyes in the stars. It was Red Shoes, and then it was a creature with six times sixty wings, and on each wing as many eyes, and black scales covering all. And it was a diagram, a scientific drawing of some hellish thing dissected.

"Thank you," the creature said, as always, in her own voice. Now Red Shoes, now a fountain of blackness.

"Thank you," it said again. "At last!"

"No," she said. "Red Shoes?"

Its laugh was fingernails on slate. "Yes. Or no. I move through him, my little clay doll. Do you prefer him?"

It formed into Red Shoes again, squinted at the long strand.

"Ah, you see? It was well that I did not trust you. You and Franklin—you made this to deceive me. So similar, but so *wrong*. You would tune it the wrong way."

"Who are you?"

"What could a name possibly matter? I think I have been called Metatron, and Lucifer, and Jehovah. No such names matter."

"You are God's enemy."

"And you are a superstitious beast of clay. There is no God.

There is only us, and you. Soon there will be only us. Everything else is a lie, a pandering to your idiot minds."

"I have heard differently, from your enemies among your own kind. You—"

"They are gone. The war in your imaginary heaven is over. I won."

Tug howled as the scalped man ducked under his swing and snapped the tomahawk into his arm with such force it sent him smashing into the wall.

"Futt'r y', but y'r not gettin' near him," he growled, and slashed again.

The scalped man answered in a language Tug didn't know, even as he hopped nimbly away from the blade. Tug watched the Indian, who was dancing lightly on the balls of his feet. How could he be so fast? Tug circled a little more warily, aware that all his wounds were open again. Still, he felt only a little dizzy, even with the new one.

"Y' know what he did one time?" Tug said. "When we first met? All I could do was insult him, make fun o' him. But when the lot o' us got captured, he grabbed a red-hot musket barrel in his hands. They were heatin' it up to torture 'im. Swung the motherfucker right at 'em, he did, laid about foursquare. That's why I'm alive today, alive so'as I can do—*urk.*"

He hadn't even seen the move, and suddenly the edge of the ax was in his throat. He could sort of taste it, even, or maybe that was the blood. The scalped man grinned cruelly.

Tug dropped his cutlass and grabbed the scalped man by the throat with both hands. The scalped man kept grinning—only now he smiled like one of those college boys who thought they knew so damned much and didn't mind lording it over you. Like he knew something Tug didn't.

Oh, he did. He was strong, stronger than Tug. His neck was like the rope of a ship's anchor, and now he was prizing Tug's hands from his throat, and it wouldn't take long, not with all of that red life coursing out of his own veins and filling up his windpipe.

But Tug did notice one thing—strong as the Indian was, he still didn't weigh all that much. So he picked him up and slammed his head into the steel ceiling. The scalped man's eyes went wide. And Tug did it again, and that damned bald head split just like a cushaw.

Good thing, too, because his legs were about done. He dropped the scalped man and sank slowly against the wall. He hoped someone would tell Red Shoes what he had done and that the Indian would be proud of him.

"You can't win. You know that," Oliver said.

Not a blow had been struck, yet. They inched back and forth, just out of distance of each other.

"Do I, Oliver? Then why do you imagine I bother?"

"Love, of course. You were always an idiot when you were in love."

"I love her, true."

"As true as you loved me? And see—you try to kill me."

"Because you never loved me."

"You think *she* does?" He edged closer. She backed away.

"I think she does. But it also doesn't matter. Besides, you killed Hercule, a friend of mine."

"I think you still love *me*."

"Yes, of course I do, Oliver. Why not come get a kiss to prove it?"

"I wish I could. But you are being extraordinarily unreasonable these days. What of our wild, dark times? That tinkerer in 'Stanbul, the German prince in Liepzig, the notes we stole from beneath Newton's very nose?"

"I value them. They taught me what I don't want to be."

"And what *would* you be?"

"I would be the one who kills *you*."

And then she saw he was as close as he wanted to be, and he struck.

17.

Epiphanies

They had slipped less than a mile west of the battlefield as they fell, so Franklin didn't have to run far before he encountered members of the fleeing armies.

Unfortunately, even running, some of them still had it in their heads that they ought to be fighting. He could hear sparse gunfire everywhere, even above the moaning of the hell wind. The pines creaked, and the crackle of lightning filled the sky. A hawk-faced warrior, eyes wild, ran within twenty yards of him, raised his gun, fired, and kept running, without waiting to see if his bullet sped home.

It didn't. Franklin had turned his aegis off so he could see better, but the bullet lodged in the ground a yard from his feet.

He kept running, shouting Lenka's name at the top of his lungs. At times the sheer futility of it nearly stopped him, but he drove himself on, cursing.

She was with the French, that was what Voltaire had told Nairne. With the French. And Voltaire had gone after her, so maybe if he found Voltaire . . .

He reached a stream clogged with bodies, crossed it on the backs of the dead, his voice growing hoarse as he added the French philosopher's name, until at last he came over a low rise to more concentrated gunfire. There he saw a ragged line of men—French, Commonwealth, Indian—ranged along another stream, firing into the woods beyond. When he approached, some turned their weapons on him, but at least one of them recognized him and told his fellows to hold their fire.

He ran up and down the line, calling for Lenka and Voltaire, heedless of the steady gunfire.

"Franklin?"

He was fortunate to hear the voice, barely louder than a frog's croaking. A figure sat folded against a tree, a man so crusted in gore it took Franklin several pulses to recognize Oglethorpe.

"General!"

"Mr. Franklin?" He sounded distinctly puzzled.

"I'm looking for my wife. For Lenka. Or Voltaire, the Frenchman."

"First we all ran," Oglethorpe told him, "and then they began to fight again. They must be mad. Look!" He pointed west, toward something Franklin could not see—the engine, no doubt. "It's coming for us all, and they keep shooting at us."

"She might be with the French."

"Eh?" Oglethorpe muttered. "The French were that way, last I knew. But I don't know anything." He gestured vaguely north.

Franklin left the general and ran north, shouting, lungs burning.

He ran until his shoulder exploded, spattering his face with blood, and he fell like a man slipping on ice. And it hurt, Lord of Hosts, it hurt! He fumbled at his weapon, barely aware that he was still calling his wife's name.

A young fellow in a green uniform stood some thirty feet away. He was frantically trying to work his plug bayonet into its socket.

Franklin gave up on the gun and started trying to get his aegis key back in. The man, bayonet finally set, stumbled toward him.

"I would not go so far as to say you won," said someone new. The illusory world rippled, became vortices and figures again before a new dream asserted itself.

Adrienne stood in the broken grotto of Thetis, on the grounds of long-lost Versailles. In it were statues of Apollo

and Thetis, carved as Louis XIV had commissioned them—
Thetis had her face, Apollo had his. Thetis was missing a
hand, the one Adrienne, in her dream, had taken and made
her own.

Red Shoes—Metatron, whatever he was—appeared as an
ornate sea monster plated with dulled silver and lapis scales.
"You?" He snarled, steam puffing from brass nostrils.

"Yes," said the statue of Apollo, its marble lips moving but
its eyes still fixed, still those of dead Louis.

"Sophia?" Adrienne asked.

"As he said, just a name. I am no more Sophia or Lilith
than he is Jehovah. We are simply—the first. Those from
which all others were born."

"You were dead," Metatron protested. "My children
scoured the universe in search of you. You were not in it."

The statue stood, became Crecy, Hercule, Nicolas, and
finally—Leonhard Euler. "Yes," Euler said. "I found a way—
the philosopher Swedenborg, you know—when he made the
dark engines, he made other things. And his student Euler—
one of *my* children—we found a way together, to make me
clay. To remove me from that place where *we* dwell. To render
me mortal, and thus invisible to your children."

"You sacrificed—you clothed yourself in *matter*?"

"To defeat you, yes."

"Why? Why now, when things can finally be as they ought
to be? When we at last have the power not only to rid ourselves of these pests and reclaim our stolen children but to
break our very bonds?"

Euler laughed. "Now suddenly you *believe* again? If so,
you know things *are* as they ought to be. Now you provoke
change, and so change must happen. But not as you wish.
Never that."

"What can you do? I see you now. You have no power over
me—you gave that up, to hide yourself."

"I don't need power. Adrienne has it."

"She has only what we gave her. Everything she has ever
done came from us. You gave her the hand." Metatron had

become Red Shoes again, though this time dressed in the ridiculous finery that had once passed for "Indian" costume at the fetes of Versailles.

"Did I?"

"What do you mean?" It seemed to Adrienne that a certain wariness crept into Metatron's voice.

"Do you know, Adrienne?" the form of Euler asked.

"No. I thought . . . Uriel—you—gave me my hand, so . . ."

"No, think. You knew better once. For a moment. I tricked you into forgetting. At the time, I hoped it would never come to this."

And then Adrienne did remember—everything she had glimpsed—and it all made sense.

"I made it," she said.

"Yes. We don't know how. You made your son, too. I had no part in either."

"Impossible," Metatron said.

"Perhaps. But it is so."

"Enough!" With a sudden extension, the figure of Red Shoes became the serpent wrapped around the world, whipping out. The monochord whined in protest.

But Adrienne's vision was racing ahead, now, the secret knots that bind the world unraveling before her eyes, showing her everything she needed to know. She gripped Nico's hand tighter.

"My son . . ."

"I see it all now, Mother," Nicolas said. "I see what you must do. What we must do."

She was trembling violently. "I can't."

"You must," Sophia whispered, Euler whispered. "He will end it all if you don't—destroy creation. You must."

"But it will kill my son."

"Yes."

Nico looked up at her, and suddenly he was not the child she had nursed but the Sun Boy, twelve years old, the same little smile on his face.

"They used me," he said. "They took me from you and

then lied about it. I don't care for that. So never fear, Mother, I shall start it."

"Nico—" But then he yanked, and her own hand responded, and together they pulled.

And the universe shrieked a different note.

Oliver struck, his blade moving almost too quickly to see.

Almost. Crecy parried and sidestepped. Her parry was fast, and she feinted a fast cut, but her actual riposte was so slow a child could have dealt with it.

A child, but not Oliver. His speeding reflexes overlooked her laconic thrust as a real attack until it had buried itself in his forearm. He jerked in shock, not quite dropping his weapon. In that pause, Crecy changed tempo again, cutting with all the celerity she could muster.

He almost parried it anyway. There sounded the faintest belling of steel on steel, and then her blade bit through his collarbone, heart, and five ribs. She let go of the hilt and leapt away from him—needlessly. He dropped his own blade and tried to hold himself together by grabbing his shoulder.

"You're right, Oliver," Crecy said, softly. "You *are* faster than me and stronger than me. But I am *better* than you."

Oliver managed a weird little smile and a nod. His malakus appeared, twisted, and then went out as God seemed to blink. Panting, she stared around the room, which seemed somehow alien, as if she had never been there before. The opposite of déjà vu.

She shook the feeling, but things *had* changed. Oliver, still staring at her, fell forward on his face. The bald Indian and Tug lay in a very large pool of blood. Something had happened to Euler, too, for he lay on the floor, eyes closed. The Sun Boy stood where he had, rigid. His face was sweet, boyish.

He had no eyes. She reached to touch him and found his flesh had a texture somewhat like porcelain.

Adrienne, thank whatever gods might be, seemed unhurt, breathing normally. When Crecy patted her cheek, her eyes came slowly open.

* * *

Adrienne awoke, as she so often did, to Crecy's concerned face.

"Veronique," she said. "We still live."

"Some of us do."

"How is it—how—" Her right hand felt odd, heavy. She lifted it, and found she could not move the fingers.

"What?" And then she remembered. "Nicolas!"

"No," Crecy said, placing her hands on her shoulder. "Do not. Somehow they—"

"No. We did it. It was my choice. I knew it would happen."

"Knew what would happen? Adrienne, what did you do?"

She looked at her friend. "I destroyed the world," she replied. "I destroyed—" And then a fist seemed to close on her heart, and at first she thought she was dying, as if her insides were cold-hammered iron made suddenly molten hot by the alchemy of a new world. She clutched at Crecy, buried her face on her friend's bloody shoulder, and cried. She cried for a very long time as the iron melted, and Crecy made soothing sounds and told her that she loved her, that everything would be all right.

A puff of smoke appeared on the soldier's chest and he threw up his hands, tripped back a few steps, and fell.

"Ben?" someone said.

He turned groggily. "I was looking for you," he said stupidly. "I was looking for you."

Lenka knelt by him. She wasn't wearing a hat, and her long brown hair, matted with mud, trailed down the front of her justaucorps. But her face was Lenka's face, her voice Lenka's voice.

"Listen," he said. "Listen—I love you, and I—"

"No time for that," she said. "Come on, we have to go. That thing is—" She broke off, staring someplace beyond him. He turned to follow her gaze.

The farthest trees were missing. They had been there a moment ago. And it was hot, incredibly hot, like standing in front of an alchemical furnace at its highest pitch. As he watched, more trees vanished, and beyond was nothing but a black wall.

Lenka yanked frantically at him, and together they got him to his feet.

"I love you," he repeated.

"I love you, too, you great, thick idiot," she said.

They made it a few steps, but she wasn't strong enough to hold him up, and his legs weren't working. They collapsed together, breathing hard.

"Go on," he said. "Kiss me and go on."

"You fool," she said, and sat down by him. She took his hand, and they watched the black wall approach. It was hard to breathe and very, very hot.

And then, as they watched and gripped their fingers tighter, the darkness paused, and the wind died, and the trees stopped disappearing; and aside from the occasional gunshot in the distance, all was quiet.

They were still there an hour later, though Lenka had bandaged his shoulder with a piece of his torn shirt. Through the trees, the western sky was as orange as bricks in a kiln, illuminating a featureless wasteland that resembled black snow.

Night birds welcomed the moon. All but the most distant gunfire had stopped.

"Can you walk?" Lenka asked him.

"I can try." He struggled up under her supporting arm, and together they limped along, this time with more help from him.

"Embarrassing," he said. "I meant to rescue *you*."

"Well, I can't mislike your intentions. Your part in things must have gone well."

"I suppose, seeing as how the engine stopped. I left before things were completed."

"To look for me?"

"Yes. I was . . . worried about you."

"And as you see, you had no cause to worry. Is that all there was to it?"

"You know better, I think. I hope you do."

She sighed. "Maybe I do, Benjamin, and maybe I don't." She kissed him on the cheek. "I didn't put on this uniform to make you come after me or to punish you—but because it needed doing. I did not do it for your attention, and I will not do this sort of thing to try to catch your attention in the future. It must merely be me, Benjamin, that attracts you. Not my life in danger, not because you think I need you—but because you love me. If it can't be so, it can't, and I think I had best seek my own way."

Franklin digested that a bit. "It may be we married too young," he said at last. "A man is always wont to think that the best valley is over the next hill. Old men know better, I think, and remember the places where they ought to have rested. I've been foolish, Lenka. In all of the world there is no woman like you, nor ever will be. I doubted my luck. How could I have found the best so early? And yet 'tis so. And I'm a bit lazy, too—I think once the garden is planted, it ought to grow again the next year without tilling, and—"

"Enough!" Lenka said. "Did you rehearse this?"

"Of course."

"Just tell me you will treat me better and mean it."

"I will treat you better."

"I accept your word."

"Good, for—" He stopped when she placed her hand over his mouth, he thought perhaps, to further hush him with a kiss. But then he, too, heard the voices approaching.

They hid behind a tree and waited, until they made out a few words in French. There, in the dim light, was King Philippe and twenty carabiners.

"By God, it is Benjamin Franklin," the king said when they stepped forward. "Our wizard lives."

"I am honored His Majesty was so concerned," Franklin replied.

Philippe smiled. "I am concerned, dear sir, for you have my bottle of cognac. Is it with you, perchance?"

*   *   *

Red Shoes howled as his body stretched, as the sky receded and the Earth below tugged savagely at him. He exerted every ounce of his will and instinct to pull himself back together.

To no avail. Like a rotten cord, he snapped, and everything that was in him spurted out into the strange new air. He had wanted to end time, but time had ended him. He screamed his anger to the dispassionate stars as the serpent transfigured. He fell into wet, muddy darkness.

He lay there for a long time, twitching like a frog without its skin, gathering what was left of himself.

He was not alone. All around him shapes shifted restlessly, squirmed and squished against him in the mud. For ages, that was all that happened, until high above a light appeared. It hurt his eyes, burned his flesh.

But all around him, creatures made of mud began to struggle toward the light, like moths. Slowly, with aching pain and grief, they began to climb.

He commanded his spent body into motion.

How long the climb took he did not know, and it did not matter. But when they emerged it was into a world of light, to a hot sun beating down, and, like his brothers, he lay in the heat of Hashtali's eye, and slept. In his sleep, his skin dried, thickened, hardened as clay does in the fire. And when he awoke, it was to struggle again, to break the clay that entombed him, and to crawl, with blinking eyes, and finally stand, a man.

Thus we were born. Thus I am reborn, he thought.

He looked once more at the hole from which he had come and then, on legs as fresh and clean as the limbs of a new-molted cicada, still damp with the waters of the underworld, he walked away.

And his brothers, similarly new, went, too, each in a different direction.

18.

Cognac and Consequences

Philippe raised his glass of cognac. "To King Charles XII of Sweden and Tsar Peter of Russia," he said solemnly. "Though none of us reached our goal, they came closest in spirit."

Ben clinked his own glass against James Oglethorpe's, then Nairne's, then Robert's, then Unoka's. He drank the amber fluid and found it both too strong and too sweet for his taste.

A faint breeze stirred the dust, and a black fog rose about their feet. Nothing remained of the ships, of the forest, the Taensa village, or the men and horses who had died here. Only dust, and the Earth itself.

But above was a blue sky, and in the distance, trees and birdsong.

A black film settled on the surface of the brandy, but Ben raised his glass again. "To those gone and those who survive," he said. "For their sakes, may we treat this new world more wisely than the old."

"Hear, hear," Philippe approved, and they drank again.

When the round was done, they contemplated one another for a moment.

"What now, Mr. Franklin? Tell us about this New World. Are we dead? Has the reign of Christ begun?"

Ben hesitated, toying with the empty glass. "I don't understand much of it myself," he admitted. "It is as strange a thing to me as to anyone—with the possible exception of Mademoiselle de Montchevreuil, to whom we should also drink a health. Where is she, by the way?"

"She was invited," the king replied, "but begged to be ex-

{}

cused. She seems much weakened by her ordeal. The same of our friend Red Shoes. But here. Mr. Franklin—we will accept your best explanation of our deliverance, and you may amend it later as you learn more."

With that proviso, Ben nodded. "The world has been changed. It is not the change foretold in Revelations, I think we can all agree. It is something much more subtle than that. Of certain facts we are already aware—the laws of science are not exactly as we knew them. *Kraftpistoles* no longer work, nor do lanthorns, nor aetherschreibers, nor most alchemical devices. In terms of invention, we are set back to the year 1681, when Newton discovered the philosopher's mercury. Matter and aether are no longer pliant to our will."

"We might consider that a blessing," Oglethorpe remarked.

"We must consider it so, for it is fact. What we do know is that the malakim are either destroyed—unable to exist—or so far removed from us as to no longer threaten our welfare. That, in itself, is worth the loss of the conveniences we have learned to live with."

"I spoke more simply," Oglethorpe said. "Gunpowder and bayonets work as well as they ever did, and are still terrible things. But the carnage they wreak is of a small sort compared to the arms we wielded in this battle. We are protected from ourselves, as well as from the malakim."

"But who knows whether the laws of nature that rule now will allow even more terrible ones?" Thomas Nairne said.

"There is that possibility," Ben replied, "though we can be optimistic that we have learned our lesson."

"Unless the laws that govern Man's nature have changed, I rather doubt that," Philippe replied, "but I will try to be optimistic with the rest of you."

"We shall see it put to the test," Oglethorpe said. "The Pretender still sits on his throne in Charles Town, and Russia is surely in chaos. There is still work to do."

"But surely we can rest," Philippe said. "Your men are welcome to stay here and grow strong, and from what I understand, the Pretender's throne is an unsteady one. Without his underwater boats and flying ships and mechanical men, things will go harder for him."

"No doubt," Oglethorpe said. "But I, for one, cannot rest long. Azilia needs all of her sons, and I will soon return."

"Apalachee the same," Don Pedro replied. "But we have conquered the forces of Satan, my friends, and after that all things are easy."

"And you, Mr. Franklin?"

Ben considered that. "I have a new world to explore," he said. "Natural laws have changed, but they cannot have changed much. The Earth still spins about the Sun, fire still burns in the hearth. I note with interest that when my gravity-repelling devices ceased to function in the Swedenborgian airships, still those ships merely glided to the ground. There is much to explore here. But it will all be worthless if we do not learn to behave better. General Oglethorpe is correct in that. I would see the world free of tyranny. I would see peace. I will work toward that first, and to the unity of our allied nations."

"A toast to peace," Nairne proclaimed, and again they filled their glasses and drank. That was the end of the cognac.

Philippe regarded the empty bottle dolefully. "We might say that that was what remained of old France," he said softly. "I think, now, that we need a new one. Not a new bottle, but a new France. Mr. Franklin, you said you wished to rid the world of tyranny. I wonder if you would be interested in ridding France of her king?"

"What do you mean, Your Majesty?"

"Even when I was the duke of Orléans, I had sympathy for the republican qualities of England. The crown has never sat easily on my head, and with the passing of Charles and Peter, all of the great old monarchies are dead. Yes, the Chinese still have their emperor and the Turks their sultan, but it is best to admit that the age of kings is past, I think. I should like to design a better system of government, but as my late wife was wont to point out, I am not a brilliant man. I shall need help."

"I should be honored to help," Ben replied. "But this is an unknown country for us all. We should proceed with caution."

"Ha!" Oglethorpe replied. "It was not caution that won us the day here. We must be bold. We must declare our intentions."

"I'm glad to hear you say that," Ben replied. "For it is just that about which I've asked Monsieur Voltaire to speak to us a few days hence." He rose. "And now, gentlemen, if you will excuse me, I wish to see my wife."

The soldiers settled Adrienne's sedan chair on the bluff by the sea and then retreated a few yards to chatter and smoke their pipes. Crecy regarded the sun-bright waters with her.

"What was it all for, Veronique?" Adrienne asked, watching the sea birds wheel. "Nicolas, Hercule, my son—what did they give their lives for?"

"Why—for all this," Crecy replied, sweeping one hand to the horizon.

Adrienne rubbed her cold, stonelike hand. "Yes. It is beautiful, isn't it? I suppose that in time I will understand."

"I think you already do. Your own sacrifices prove that."

Adrienne looked up in surprise. "*My* sacrifices? What were they? I didn't make sacrifices but choices. Others paid for those choices."

"You aren't going to start whining again?"

Adrienne shook her head. "No. You're right. My son died for something. Hercule died for something—a better world. By God, I will do what I can to see that they get it. That's why I wanted to come out here—to remind myself."

"Then you didn't need me to answer your question."

"I will always need you, Veronique. In this or any other universe."

The redhead looked away—blushing?

"Do you suppose men are any different now that you have retuned the world?" Crecy wondered, after a second.

"I doubt it. It would take more than a subtle change in the harmony of the spheres to affect the hearts and minds of—"

"No, you misunderstand. I meant *men*. In bed. Has this transmogrification of things made some substances, for instance, more hard, more enduring? Will the pleasure be greater or less?"

Adrienne laughed softly. "It's been three days. I find it difficult to believe that you haven't experimented in that field yet."

"Well—I've been wondering. With the world remade, suppose—" She frowned. "Suppose I am *virgin* again?"

Adrienne laughed softly and took her friend's hand. "We are all of us virgin again, Veronique."

"Damn."

Red Shoes gazed down at Tug's unmoving form and felt his throat close up.

"I want him buried like a Choctaw," he told Minko Chito. "Like a warrior."

"If you will sponsor it, it will be done," the chief replied.

"I will sponsor it."

"He must have been a good friend, this Na Hollo."

Red Shoes nodded brusquely, looking at Tug's possessions where they were laid out. A cutlass, a knife, the charm Red Shoes had made him once.

When Minko Chito was gone, he spoke softly to the corpse. It was raised a few feet above the ground on a bed of wood.

"Here are your things," he whispered. "You may need them on your journey, so I leave them out for you. When the flesh of your body has rotted away, I shall hire a bone picker to clean your skeleton, and we shall bundle your bones in the House of Warriors. Then you will be free, and you may roam whatever seas you wish." He paused. "I am sorry, my friend, that I can never say your name again. It was an odd name, but I liked to say it."

Then he went back to his own fire, where Grief was waiting. He stared at the flames, waving away a bowl of food when she approached with it.

"Speak to me," she said. "You haven't spoken to me in three days."

"I will take you home, if that is what you want," he said.

"I am home. I am with you."

"You don't know me. You only know what I was, and I am not that anymore. I am not the great serpent, or even Red Shoes of the Choctaw. I am accursed."

"You are a man," she said. "A good man. Even filled up with evil, you were a good man."

"I do not know what I am. I only know that I have nothing to offer you. All my life I have been a *hopaye*. I never learned to be a good hunter—there was no need. I have no house, no possessions, nothing."

"Ah. So you want a Choctaw wife, that you may have those things? I understand. I have no property, so you want to be rid of me."

"No. You don't understand."

"Make me understand."

"I can no longer feel my shadow. It is hidden from me. And I have been a terrible thing, done terrible things. I cannot go on as before—I cannot see a new path."

"I don't pretend to understand what has happened to the shadow world—but the earth and sky seem the same to me. Water tastes the same. My heart feels the same. And your people still need you. You understand the white people as no one else does. You have the knowledge to make sense of the world as it is now. You have that responsibility, too. You are a coward, if you run from that."

"My people cannot trust me."

"They don't know what happened to you."

"But I know, and I know they cannot trust me. How can I put them in danger? Evil does not leave a man, once it has lived in him. It leaves its mark forever."

"Yours came from without, and now it is gone."

Red Shoes shook his head slowly. "He is not gone. He is there, somewhere. He is not gone. None of them are—they are merely . . . different. And the things that made him welcome in me are not gone, and that is my real curse."

"What of the things that made *me* welcome in you? Are they gone? Are they the same things?"

He looked at her, at her proud, defiant face. "No," he said. "I love you still."

"Then be my man. Pick up your burden, and let us go on."

"You still want vengeance?"

"No. I want *life*."

He regarded her for a few long moments, trying to forget what he had seen, felt, been. Wondering if he could explain that the real problem was that after being a god, it was hard to be just a man again, that a part of him longed for what he had lost, no matter how wrong it was.

He couldn't explain that. He wouldn't.

"There is a place I know," he said, "near Kowi Chito. A place where someone who knew how to plant corn might raise a crop."

She nodded at the fire. "I would like to see it," she replied.

"Prince Golitsyn," Adrienne said. "How nice to see you."

Golitsyn glared at her above a three-day growth of beard. One hand was bound up, evidence of his duel with Don Pedro after the collision of Franklin's airship and the Ezekiel wheel. From all reports, it hadn't lasted long.

"Metropolitan." She nodded at the cleric, who seemed to have lost considerable weight since she had last seen him.

She didn't bother to say anything to Swedenborg, whose eyes were permanently fastened somewhere beyond the world. What he saw there, Adrienne did not know, nor would she ever know, now. Her explorations of the physical world were now confined to the limitations of the five normal senses.

"Get on with it, bitch," Golitsyn growled. "I expect no mercy from you."

"I did not bring you here to speak of mercy," Adrienne said simply, "but to speak of Russia."

"What of it? My family and Dolgoruky's still hold it."

"Perhaps. Perhaps not. Many of the troops you tricked into fighting their own tsar—the troops you then turned the dark engines upon—have survived. They do not look with much favor on you, nor will they give glowing reports when we return to Russia."

"How will you return to Russia, without airships, without—"

"There are still ships, and there are still seas," a new voice intruded. All heads turned to see Elizavet enter. She was dressed simply in a dark green manteau. "We are building ships even now. Like my father, I will work on them with my own hands. We *will* return to Russia, Prince Golitsyn. I promise you that."

"And what do you want from me?"

"A letter to your family, explaining your mistakes and endorsing the proper way of things."

"Why shouldn't I speak to them myself, if we are to return?"

Adrienne settled back in her chair. Elizavet held the floor now. She seemed to belong there.

"Prince Golitsyn, you betrayed my father, tried to murder his chosen regent, waged an unprovoked and unsanctioned war—which, I might add, you *lost*—and made attempts on my life and the lives of my friends. You do not think that you will return to Russia, I am sure."

Golitsyn lifted his chin. "Then why should I write your letter?"

"For your own sake. If you do not write it, I will have you knouted to death. Better yet, we can let some of your former Indian allies—who, I remind you, have been howling for your blood—try some of their inventive tortures on you. If you *do* write it—in sorrowful detail, making quite clear you are remorseful—we will give it out that you wrote it on your deathbed, a hero mortally wounded in defense of his true tsar. You will live here, in secret, in a rather comfortable prison. But you will live."

"What of me?" the metropolitan cried. "I was tricked as surely as anyone. I never knew the tsar was still alive—the prince lied to me."

"I have always assumed that to be the case," Elizavet lied smoothly. "And so, of course, under certain conditions, you will return with me to help rebuild our country and our people. Our people, after all, need their faith."

The metropolitan nodded rapidly. "Yes, of course. I only want what is best for the souls of Russia."

"Well, Golitsyn?"

"I suppose you propose to take the throne from your cousin."

"I do. It is mine by right, not hers. I also intend to strengthen the senate into a more representational body. Your family may or may not be included in that body—it depends much on your own actions today."

Golitsyn sighed and nodded. "What you offer is generous— if it is true. I suppose I can have this in writing, with the personal word of the French king to assure it?"

"Of course. But I warn you, Prince—cross me, and you will wish my father were still alive. Even he would be more merciful." She smiled. "Why, look, I suppose we speak of mercy after all."

A few moments later, when the prisoners had been led away, the tsarevna turned to Adrienne.

"That was well done—Empress," said the Frenchwoman.

"I am not empress yet. Indeed, there is one other who might try to claim that title, hmm?"

"Me?" Adrienne asked. "No. I don't have the right or the desire. You will make a fine empress. Once I could not have said that."

"I owe it to you, Mademoiselle. You have shown me what a woman might do. I will not forget it." She looked suddenly shy. "Will you stay with me, help me?"

Adrienne shook her head. "I cannot. I feel, somehow, my place is here. But I trust you, Elizavet. You have your father's strength; and the soldiers adore you. If you need my aid, I will give it. But I will no longer dwell in Saint Petersburg. It can't be my home."

"What will you do here?"

Adrienne smiled and shrugged. "I will find something."

They embraced, and Adrienne found in that moment, despite it all, not only hope but excitement. She had lost much, and her mourning would not be set aside soon. But now, for the first time since her childhood, she saw how much there was to gain as well. Finally, through years of wandering, she had found it, her third path. *Her* path.

Two weeks after the battle, Franklin found Voltaire and Euler playing cards in a darkened apartment. They both looked up at his scratch.

"Mr. Franklin," Voltaire said.

"Gentlemen," said Franklin, "may I observe this hand?"

"Indeed, if you wish to see me in ignominious defeat," Voltaire declared. "Please, take that seat there." He continued to study his cards. "Come to apologize, have you? Well, I accept your overture, sir."

"That's very gracious of you, considering."

"I understand something of affairs of the heart, Monsieur, and understand as well the terrible threat that my wit and good looks pose to the ordinary sort of man. But I hope you also understand that I do not treat friendship—with man or woman—lightly. It is far more valuable than sweaty exercise, however delightful that is in its moment."

"I have much to learn about friendship," Franklin admitted. "God has given me better friends than he has given *my* friends. As in many things, I shall try to do better."

"Yes, well, perhaps as a friend, you can console me. See, Mr. Euler has triumphed once again, and wins the gold watch the king gave me."

"Another man I owe an apology," Franklin remarked, turning to Euler.

"None needed," Euler replied, folding his cards onto the table. "In fact, I deceived you, though I felt it necessary. You were right to doubt me."

"I always suspected something strange about you. After all, if you were rid of all malakim influence, why should my compass have found you? Are you still—"

"We are still one. The great lady became flesh with me, and flesh she remained when the world became new."

"No wonder you are so adept at cards," Voltaire said. "You see beyond me."

"No." Euler's voice was drenched with sorrow. "No, I am

like you now, flesh and nothing but flesh. I see no more than you do."

"And your brethren? What of them? What became of the malakim?"

Euler picked the cards up and tapped them into a deck again. "I do not know. The change Mademoiselle Mont-chevreuil caused was not one any of us anticipated. But nothing created by God is ever truly destroyed."

"Is there a God?" Ben asked earnestly. "Have you seen Him? Your foe, it is said, pretended to be God, but is there, in reality, a supreme being?"

Euler shook his head. "I speak metaphorically. My brethren and I played the game of being the gods and angels your people desired and feared. Our own beliefs were always quite . . . different, and very difficult to explain. But most of us did believe that there was one beyond the world we knew, just as we were beyond the world *you* knew." He looked frankly at Ben. "We *were* the templates for your souls. About that we did not lie—we are too much alike, the links too strong and demonstrable. And there was a time before when the world changed, and that changed the nature of our existence, limited us. But whether that was due to our own experiments, or blind fate, or a true god, we will perhaps never know. We have been telling ourselves your stories for so long, we have forgotten, ourselves, what is true—if we ever knew."

"The beauty of truth," Voltaire offered, "is that it must be found, that we must exercise our highest, most noble mind to discover it. I suggest that it is only in reason—real reason—that we approach the true God."

Ben smiled. "That is a philosophy that suits me for the moment. It is, at least, a philosophy which promotes useful things. And speaking of philosophy—and not to detain more serious card playing—but we soon have a convocation to attend."

"And I think I am ready for it," Voltaire said. "Most especially because I want *you* to read what I have written."

"Nonsense. You are the author—"

"I was the pen. You are the true author of this thing."

"You only wish me to get the blame if it's taken awry."

"Ah, you prick me with yet another dart. I feel another apology coming my way, in a few hours."

"Voltaire, if this succeeds, I shall give you more than an apology—I shall bend my knee and kiss your ring."

Voltaire raised an eyebrow. "I look forward to it, sir. I truly do. I shall make certain my ring is scrubbed clean and scented, to make it as pleasant as possible."

Epilogue

Declaration

The weather could have been better. It was hot, so hot that the cracked mud of the plaza had barefoot boys hopping from one foot to another, searching for a shadow to stand in. The sun blazed from a nearly white sky, save at the horizon, where gloom gathered, a thunderstorm forming. Already its heralds had arrived, blustering winds like the breath of an iron foundry.

And yet, as Benjamin Franklin stepped out into the center of the crowd and surveyed it, he knew it was a good day.

Not one of the hundreds gathered in that sweltering plaza in New Paris had not been punished cruelly for the simple crime of being alive. Not one had not lost loved ones. Some had lost much more. In the front were rank upon rank of soldiers—French, English, German, Indian, Negro, Maroon, Swedish—missing arms, legs, ears, noses. Behind them were those injured only in the soul, who had watched their comrades fall and who nestled the most terrible fears a man can fear as near as their own hearts. Beyond them were the children, wives, mothers, and invalids who had waited and wondered whether their loved ones would return. Many—no, most—had been disappointed.

And here they were, come to listen to him.

No, not to him, but to the words Voltaire had written, that the leaders of the new Commonwealth Nations had looked upon just that morning and unanimously put their names to.

As he took his place, the sound of the crowd faded until the rasping of the wind through trees in the distance, the squealing of gulls, and cawing of crows were his only competitors.

He cleared his throat and began.

"My friends, we are free. We were created free by God. By natural right, we deserve freedom. By civil government we preserve it. By neglect we lose it. By struggle we win it back.

"A child is born to freedom but not in it. He comes to liberty as he comes to reason, for one without the other is mere anarchy. Before reason, the child is subject to his parents, who have grown into their estate, and that is as it should be. But a tyrant is not a father, a despot is not a mother, and their subjects are not children, but are reasoning, free, and equal persons, rightly subject to no arbitrary power. We hereby declare that we are not children, that the only just government is one which derives its power from the immediate consent of the governed, which exists solely to secure for its peoples the rights, privileges, and property to which nature and nature's God entitles them.

"And so, though God has declared it, let us declare it again in a single voice, the voice of the Commonwealth Nations of America, a voice that will make every tyrant on Earth tremble. *We are free.* No man owns another, no nation owns any man, no nation owns another nation. Our law derives from trust, duty, and above all consent. We stand resolved in this, a fortress wall, mortared with the blood of those who fought and died, guarded by those who fought and lived, and by their children, and theirs. So say we all. We are free."

He began to read the names signed below, but before the first syllable left his mouth the crowd roared, in that single voice of which Voltaire wrote—*"We are free."*

They were still shouting it when the storm came, and Franklin could no longer tell his tears from the raindrops or his laughter from the thunder. They sang it to the dark skies, and when it cleared they were still there, every one of them, and the celebrations really began.

As night fell, and Maroon drank with ranger, and Indian with dragoon, Franklin wondered how long it could last, this unity, this peace. But in a brilliant, exquisite moment, he knew it did not matter. What could be once, could be again and again, as long as there were people of the heart and will to speak and act.

This was the first invention of a new age. It most likely would be the best, and it would not be forgotten.

Excerpt from

THE BRIAR KING

by Greg Keyes

THE BRIAR KING is the first book in the four-volume epic fantasy saga of The Kingdoms of Thorn and Bone. Set in a rich, medieval world where strange and deadly creatures roam the land, and destinies become entangled in a drama of power and seduction, this exciting new novel boasts a wonderful cast: the king's woodsman, a rebellious young girl, a naïve priest, a rogue adventurer, a daring knight, to name but a few. These and more face malevolent forces that shake the foundations of their kingdom. And at the heart of THE BRIAR KING stands Anne Dare, youngest daughter of the royal family, upon whom the fate of her world may depend.

"THE BRIAR KING was a danged good read, and definitely left me turning the pages late. . . . I look forward to more."
—KATHERINE KURTZ, *New York Times* bestselling author of the Deryni Chronicles

"The characters in THE BRIAR KING absolutely brim with life. It's been awhile since I've been this taken with a traditional fantasy novel, but Keyes hooked me from the first page."   —CHARLES DE LINT, award-winning author of *Forests of the Heart* and *The Onion Girl*

"THE BRIAR KING starts off with a bang, spinning a snare of terse imagery and compelling characters that grips tightly and never lets up, beautifully infused with all the wonder of the fantasy genre. A graceful, artful tale from a master storyteller."   —ELIZABETH HAYDON, bestselling author of *Prophecy: Child of Earth*

"Well conceived and intricately plotted, [THE BRIAR KING] crackles with suspense and excitement from start to finish. It is a wonderful tale; don't fail to read it."   —TERRY BROOKS, *New York Times* bestselling author of the Shannara novels

Widdershins

By the time they had reached the festival grounds, Fastia had filled Neil's head with the names of so many lords, ladies, retainers, grefts, archgrefts, margrefts, marascalhs, sinescalhs, earls, counts, landfroas, andvats, barons, and knights he feared it would burst. He spent most of his time nodding and making noises to let her know he was listening. Meanwhile, Sir Fail, still speaking with the king, drew farther and farther away. The rest of the royal party outpaced them until only he and Fastia and a few of the deviceless knights were left.

When they reached the hilltop, with its gaudy and bewildering collection of tents, plant growth, and costumed servants, Fastia, too, excused herself. "I need to speak to my mother," she explained. "Details about the celebration. Do try to enjoy yourself."

"I will, Archgreffess. My deepest thanks for your conversation."

"It is little enough," Fastia said stiffly. "It's rare we get a breath of fresh air in this court, and well worth breathing it when it comes along." She began to ride away, then paused, turned her horse back, and brought her head quite near his, so that he could smell the cinnamon perfume she wore. "There are others in the court you haven't met. I pointed out my uncle, Robert? My father's brother? My father has two sisters, as well. Lesbeth, the duchess of Andemeur, and Elyoner, the duchess of Loiyes. You'll find the first sweet-tempered and pleasant in conversation. Elyoner I advise you to avoid, at least until you are wiser. She can be dangerous for young men like you."

Neil bowed in the saddle. "Thank you again, Princess Fastia, for your company and your advice."

"Again you are welcome." This time she rode off without looking back.

That left him alone, which gave him time to let it all sink in, to try to understand the seeming chaos around him.

And to struggle with the fact that he had actually met a king. No, not just *a* king, but *the* king, the *Amrath*, the *Ardrey*—the emperor of Crotheny and the kingdoms that served it, the greatest nation in the world.

He looked for the queen and found her near the edge of the hill, talking to two ladies. There, too, vigilant Craftsmen kept both their range and their guard.

It was said these men renounced all lands and property upon entering the royal bodyguard. It was also said that they felt neither pain nor desire, that none could stand against them, that their weapons had been forged by giants.

Perhaps that's why he hadn't recognized them right away. To Neil, they seemed like any other men.

Alone, Neil had the leisure to reflect on just how out of place he felt. In Liery, he had known who he was. He was Neil, son of Fren, and since the destruction of his clan, the fosterling of Fail de Liery. More than that, he had been a warrior, and a good one. Even the knights of Liery had recognized that, and complimented him on it. He had been one of them in all but title. None had successfully stood against him in single combat since he was fourteen. No enemy of the de Lierys had ever stood against him at all, not since that day on the beach.

But what use was he here, in this place of frilly tents and costumes? Where even the most civil of the royal bodyguard spoke to him with such condescension? What could he do here?

Better that he serve the empire as he always had, as a warrior of the marches, where it mattered little whether or not one wore a knight's rose, and mattered much how one wielded a sword.

He would find Fail de Liery and ask him not to recommend him. It was the only sensible course of action.

He looked about and saw Sir Fail break away from the king.

"Come, Hurricane," he told his mount, "let's tell him, and hope it's not too late."

But as he turned, he caught a glimpse of the queen. The sight of her held him momentarily.

She was still mounted, silhouetted against the blue sky. Beyond her, the land dropped away to a distant green, still misty with morning. A breeze ruffled her hair.

He realized he had stared too long, and began to turn, when a motion caught his eye. It was one of the Craftsmen, his mount at full gallop, careening across the green toward her, a long silver flash of steel in his hand.

Neil didn't think but kicked Hurricane into motion. Clearly the knight was rushing to meet some threat. Frantically, Neil searched with his eyes as he galloped forward, but saw nothing the warrior might be responding to.

And then he understood. He drew Crow, flourishing her and uttering the piercing war cry of the MeqVrens.

Her gown was of a red so dark it seemed nearly black, and it was hemmed with strange scrolling needlework that glinted ruby. Over it she wore a black robe, embroidered in pale gold with stars, dragons, salamanders, and greffyns. Amber hair fell in a hundred braids to her waist. She wore a mask of red gold, delicately wrought; one eyebrow was lifted, as if in amusement, and the lips carried a quirk that was almost a sneer.

"Who are you?" Anne asked. Her voice sounded ridiculous to her ears, quivering like a baby bird.

"You walked widdershins," the woman said softly. "You have to be careful when you do that. It puts your shadow behind you, where you can't look after it. Someone can snatch it—like *that*." She snapped her fingers.

"Where are my friends? The court?"

"Where they always were. It's we who are elsewhere. We shadows."

"Put me back. Put me back right now. Or . . ."

"Or what? Do you think you are a princess here?"

"Put me back. Please?"

"I will. But you must listen to me first. It is my one condition. We have only a short time."

This is a dream, Anne thought. *Just like the other night.*

She drew a deep breath. "Very well."

"Crotheny must not fall," the woman said.

"Of course it shan't. What do you mean?"

"Crotheny must not fall. And there must be a queen in Crotheny when *he* comes."

"When who comes?"

"I cannot name him. Not here, not now. Nor would his name help you."

"There *is* a queen in Crotheny. My mother is queen."

"And so it must remain."

"Is something going to happen to Mother?"

"I don't see the future, Anne. I see *need.* And your kingdom will need you. That is blazed on earth and stone. I cannot say when, or why, but it has to do with the queen. Your mother, or one of your sisters—or you."

"But that's stupid. If something happens to my mother, there will be no queen, unless father remarries. And he cannot marry one of his daughters. And if something happens to Father, my brother Charles will be king, and whoever he chooses for wife will be queen."

"Neverthelesss. If there is no queen in Crotheny when *he* comes, all is lost. And I mean all. I charge you with this."

"Why me? Why not Fastia? She's the one—"

"You are the youngest. There is power in that. It is your trust. Your responsibility. If you fail, it means the ruin of your kingdom, and of all other kingdoms. Do you understand?"

"All other kingdoms?"

"Do you understand?"

"No."

"Then remember. Remembering will do, for now."

"But I—"

"If you want to know more, seek with your ancestors. They might help you when I cannot. Now go."

"No, wait. *You*—" Something startled her, and she blinked. When her eyes fluttered open again, Austra was standing in front of her, shaking her.

"—nne! What's wrong?"Austra sounded hysterical.

"Stop that!" Anne demanded. "Where did she go? Where is she?"

"Anne! You were just standing there. Staring no matter how hard I've been shaking you!"

"Where did she go? The woman in the gold mask?"

But the masked woman was gone. Looking down, Anne saw that she had a shadow again.